KILLING IT

About the Author

Asia lives in London with her husband, four children and two dogs. She can't remember the last time she had a full night's sleep.

Asia Mackay

KILLING IT

ZAFFRE

First published in Great Britain in 2018 by
ZAFFRE PUBLISHING
80–81 Wimpole St, London W1G 9RE
www.zaffrebooks.co.uk

A CIP catalogue record for this book is
available from the British Library.

Paperback ISBN: 978–1–78576–453–0
Export Paperback ISBN: 978–1–78576–454–7

also available as an ebook

1 3 5 7 9 10 8 6 4 2

Typeset by IDSUK (Data Connection) Ltd
Printed and bound in Australia by Griffin Press

The paper in this book is FSC® certified.
FSC® promotes environmentally responsible,
socially beneficial and economically viable
management of the world's forests.

Zaffre Publishing is an imprint of Bonnier Zaffre,
a Bonnier Publishing company
www.bonnierzaffre.co.uk
www.bonnierpublishing.co.uk

For my parents
for everything
I get it now

I PULL MY PISTOL OUT of my striped Cath Kidston nappy bag. A half-eaten rice cake is stuck to the barrel. Fabulous. Keeping my gun clean used to be not only a matter of pride but one of professionalism. And now here is my beautiful custom-made snub-nosed .38 suffering the indignity of having small snacks crushed on to it. Looking closer, I see that the formula container has leaked and powder is caught between the ridges on the handgrip. Nightmare to clean. At least if anyone looks too closely they'll just assume it's cocaine.

I stare at myself in the mirror and take a deep breath. I always knew this was going to be tough. This was the life I chose when I came back to work. Plan a hit, stalk a target, pull the trigger and still make it home for bath time.

When you become the elite of the elite, you really do believe you can do anything. But now here I am. Admiring my injuries in a Starbucks toilet, officially under investigation at work and very aware of the fact that someone wants me dead.

'I'm sorry little one, I'm doing my best.' I look down at the perfect, chubby-cheeked baby lying on the hard, plastic changing table. I still can't believe she's mine. Blissfully unaware of the morning's drama, she is safe, and that's all that matters. If I can survive the week, I have a chance. That is all I need. A few more days to work out who wants my name in the mud and my body in the ground.

'Let's get you all nice and clean.' I reach into the bag and take out a nappy and wipes.

I try to make sense of it all as I change her. The men today were nobodies. Toy soldiers blindly following the orders of an unknown general, doing his dirty work while he stays hidden in the shadows. To defeat him I have to unmask him.

I stare down at my baby daughter and stroke her cheek. I'm grateful I got away with my life but I can't help feeling a little insulted such low-calibre professionals were sent to do the job. Underestimated to the bitter end.

The nappy changed, I pull her little tights back on and adjust her corduroy dress. She looks up at me, chewing on her fist. Big blue eyes watch as I check my gun again, load it and lock it back into place. I need to work fast. My need to stay alive is more than just a selfish desire to continue enjoying life. I have someone relying on me now. Someone whose life will be inextricably changed if I'm taken out of it.

I lift up my shirt and look at the large purple bruise forming across my midriff. My enemies have got it wrong if they think that becoming a mother has made me weaker. I stare down at her as she holds my little finger. There is nothing I wouldn't do for her. Climb mountains. Fight tigers. Track down and kill every single fucker trying to tear us apart. I will show them all.

I look at my watch. Shit. But first I have to get to Monkey Music.

Two months previously

Part One

Weaning

wean[1], *v.*

Gerund or present participle: **weaning**.

1. Accustom (an infant or other young animal) to food other than its mother's milk.
2. Accustom (someone) to managing without something which they have become dependent on.

Chapter One

'KILLER MAMA. MUMMY BOND.'
I tried the words out loud. Today was my first day back at work after six months of maternity leave and while searching through the depths of my wardrobe I was trying to think of a name for my new dual status.

'Assassa-Mum. Slayer Mother. Breastfeeding Bullet Bitch.'

It was an attempt to distract myself from worries that undoubtedly struck every mother taking that first step back into the workplace. Is it too soon? How much am I going to miss her? Will she forgive me for leaving her? Is this the right thing to do?

There were also a few, perhaps a little less usual, other concerns. Is baby brain going to affect my aim? How am I going to fare in combat when my boobs are so damn sore? Is the extra baby weight going to be an operational issue?

Could 'having it all' really extend to mothers who were also highly trained assassins in covert branches of Her Majesty's Secret Service?

I had been looking forward to leaving babyville and heading back to the cold hard grind of my underground office. But now last-minute doubts were creeping in. Not helped by a call a few minutes ago from my boss, Sandy, telling me not to come to our headquarters but to go straight to Legoland, our name for MI6's

HQ, as we had an urgent meeting. Such a meeting would require a suit, which had languished at the back of my wardrobe for so long I was having trouble finding it.

I flicked back through the hangers again. I caught a flash of white amid a sea of black. There it was. I pulled the shirt and suit out. Trousers with a waistband. My new nemesis.

I squeezed into them and hurried into the kitchen. Beata, the nanny I selected so carefully, was busying herself at the sink. Gigi, my beautiful baby with round cheeks and soft brown hair that always seemed to naturally spike into a Mohawk, was sitting in her highchair at the head of the table, examining the food laid out in front of her. Blissfully oblivious that today would be the first day of her short young life where I wouldn't be there for her every waking moment. I took a deep breath, kissed the top of her head, shouted a goodbye to the hulk of Beata's back as she was loading the dishwasher and rushed out the door for the tube station.

Packed into a full eastbound commuter train, I deeply missed the VIP status of Transport for London's tacky 'Baby on Board' badge. I stood rammed up against the doors and looked around the carriage. It was all dark clothes and solemn faces. The only splash of bright colour came from a woman in a party dress with panda eyes and bed hair. She kept tugging down at the short frayed hem as suited men watched her over the top of their newspapers.

I had forgotten how miserable the morning commute was. I pulled out my phone and clicked on my 'GigiCam' app. Up popped a live feed of Gigi, now indulging in a strawberry yoghurt facial. I stroked the screen. I missed her already. But having access to an arsenal of government-issue surveillance equipment was definitely helping.

Thanks to motion-activated cameras hidden all over the house and the GPS tracker in the pram I could not only keep an eye on what Beata was pureeing for Gigi's lunch, but track their movements all over Chiswick. I had also tasked Bryan in R & D to work on a prototype tiny camera that could be hidden inside Gigi's amber teething necklace. He had been making good progress although he had warned it was unlikely the image quality would be the requested HD. To make up for this disappointment he had added a sound sensor notification to the app – if Gigi's crying reached a certain decibel I would immediately get an alert to my phone allowing me to check the cause of her tears and assess Beata's reaction to them. Hands-free parenting made easy.

Gigi was currently staring transfixed at Beata, who was balancing a bright pink plastic cup on her head and wobbling around the kitchen with more grace than I expected from someone of her build. Gigi had thankfully taken to the no-nonsense mother-of-four immediately. My own confidence in Beata was undoubtedly helped by the office undertaking several exhaustive background checks, a month of surveillance and even arranging for a local agent to visit her small home town in Eastern Poland.

The cup fell from Beata's head and Gigi squealed with laughter.

The worries I had quietened, the tight knot in my chest loosened. Gigi was being well looked after, I was getting back to work, this is what I always wanted. To have it all. And, one day, it would prove to my daughter that she could, too.

But hopefully with a job that didn't involve quite so much bloodshed.

I looked around the carriage and saw nothing but glazed eyes and stifled yawns. Not me. I felt more awake than I had been since I entered the baby haze of sleep-deprivation. I felt ready. Fully prepared for my first day back. Excited, even. I could do this. I was an Assassa-Mum.

I definitely needed to work more on the name.

The tube rattled on past graffitied walls, the morning sun brightening an otherwise grey streetscape, and I turned my mind to the meeting. Everyone who had heard the MI6 building at Vauxhall Cross referred to as 'Legoland' assumed it was down to its unusual art deco exterior. An easy mistake to make. But my colleagues and I called it Legoland because, to us, Six was a toytown. Little figurines were lined up and placed wherever they were wanted. They copied each other's homework and called each other names. Building blocks of intelligence were painstakingly built up and then swiftly demolished. Legoland was a playground compared to the real world *we* lived in. They were still children, with clean hands and full deniability. We were the grown-ups who sullied our souls with the dirty work that was necessary to keep them safe. Yet parenting was a thankless task. They threw tantrums when we asked them to share, and would sit rocking with their hands over their ears when told Father Christmas *did* exist – just not anymore because we had put a bullet in his head.

The train jerked to a stop. Then a crackle and the voice of the driver entered the carriage.

'Apologies, ladies and gents. Signal failure up ahead. We're being held here for a few minutes. We'll be on our way shortly.'

A few people sighed loudly and looked at their watches. The rest didn't even look up from their reading material. I was the only one smiling.

I wondered who my colleagues were interrogating.

In a fitting nod to the underground nature of our work, our offices were located in a disused network of rooms and tunnels coming off Platform Eight at Holborn tube station. It was a set-up that worked well for us as we could roam all over London, under the streets, away from the all-seeing CCTV and the inconvenience of traffic. The sound of the trains also helped disguise any troubling noises from our less cooperative interviewees. 'Signal failure' was often caused by over-enthusiastic interrogating shorting the electricity supply and affecting the whole underground grid. Whereas what would be reported as a 'person on the tracks' was actually a highly effective way of disposing of those who would rather die than answer our questions. This tactic worked well for us because 'splatters' were near impossible to do autopsies on.

Not everyone appreciated the benefits of our location. Many years ago a disgruntled unit leader, fed up with the lack of natural light and the constant background rumbling of the trains, had complained that being stuck in such conditions made him feel no better than a sewer rat. He had not lasted long, but the name had and Rats were how we were referred to by those in the know.

As the train started up again I wondered which Rat had been leading the interview that caused our delay and whether they had got all the answers they wanted. Those who entered our underground interrogation room rarely left without relinquishing their secrets. Information on an impending terrorist attack, tips on which container needed to be intercepted at customs; everything spilled out before their guts did. Afterwards a Black-outtini, a Platform Eight special cocktail, ensured subjects woke up in hospital with memory blanks and injuries concurrent with whatever a helpful bystander was reported to have witnessed. '*It was terrible – the car rammed him, reversed and then drove over his hand as it sped off . . . Yes, that would exactly explain why all the bones are crushed.*' Or in a particularly reticent subject's case, '*He fell from a second-storey balcony and landed in a puddle that must have been electrified.*' That one really should have ended up a splatter. Reportedly, interviewees never did regain their memory, although after-effects included an inability to ride the tube without sweating profusely and a screaming, hyperventilating need to be back above ground. But, then, didn't most Londoners using public transport on a hot summer's day exhibit those symptoms?

At the next stop a new flood of people entered the carriage, pushing us all further into each other. While squashed up against some bearded man's armpit, I looked down and noticed how much my shirt was straining to contain my chest. Great. In all the joy of managing to just about fit into my trousers, I had overlooked how my cheap polyester shirt was going to be no match for my breastfeeding-sized boobs.

Legoland. It was fitting that MI6's home was a huge shiny building out in the open, pinned on Google Maps for all to find, while us Rats scurried around underground in offices with peeling walls and dank, crumbling corridors. A division that didn't exist in a headquarters that didn't exist.

12

I headed through security and after pulling out my ID card signed myself in as an employee of GCDSB, which stood for Government Communication and Data Specialisation Branch. On paper we were a data consultancy firm whose services could be called upon by both MI5 and MI6, yet our longwinded official name was routinely ignored by those in the know in favour of the catchier Platform Eight, or just the Platform.

We were one of our country's essential security services. There was Five, Six and then us – Eight. The numbers that kept our country safe.

I got into the thankfully empty lift and pressed the button for the third floor; we always used the same meeting room for our visits to Legoland – the corridor cameras were angled so that anyone entering and leaving #0341 were never recorded. I had a look in the lift's large mirror and tried to pull the shirt further across, which made things slightly better, as long as I didn't try to breathe too much. I straightened up and reached to pull my ponytail out – at least my hair could help divert attention. Ping. Just moving my arm had been more strain than the shirt could take and off flew the top button. A seriously distracting amount of bra and cleavage was now visible to anyone looking my way. That combined with my ruffled hair gave me the look of a sexy secretary out of a clichéd porn film. All I needed to complete the look were the fake glasses.

I was busy worrying about my reflection when the lift doors opened at the third floor.

'Why, hello, Mummy.' It was Jake. There he was in all his six-foot-four glory, wearing a dark suit, bright red tie and with his eyes firmly on my chest. 'I've been waiting for you.' He studied me closely. 'You look just the same. Except with bigger breasts.'

He smiled. 'Isn't this the longest we've been apart?' He was clean-shaven and his dark hair effortlessly styled.

I stepped out of the lift and pushed past him, catching the all-too-familiar smell of stale cigarettes, coffee and Hugo Boss.

'Come on Jake. We're going to be late.' I put my hair back up and unfolded my jacket lapels to limit the exposure from my missing button. He followed behind me.

'So we're saving the tearful hug and how much you've missed me for after the meeting?'

I ignored him as I opened the door to our meeting room.

My boss, Sandy White, stood alone next to the large conference table fiddling with his garish multicoloured tie. In all the years I had worked for him, each time I saw him in a suit I marvelled at how uncomfortable he made it look. He turned as we walked in.

'Welcome back, Lex.' He paused. 'Now, please let's all sit the fuck down.' He clutched his right leg as he eased himself into his chair. A bad gunshot injury that had never healed properly had meant desk-work for the last decade. You could tell from his frame and the way he carried himself he used to be a hardened ball of muscle, but the forced sedentary lifestyle had taken its toll. He was losing the battle against middle-aged spread. The leg gave him a lot of pain and at first I'd tried to be a little more understanding about his moods and general dark demeanour until one of the other Rats told me he'd been just as miserable before he'd been shot.

'Russia.' Sandy swung his leg up on to the chair next to him. 'That's why we're here. They're about to gain control of a new weapon to use in the silent war they've been raging against the West. This meeting is to get you two up to speed and to discuss our plan of action with Six. Let's all be at our most agreeable and we can get the hell out of here and I can get this hangman's noose off.' He motioned to the accessory knotted around his thickset neck. Sandy had always insisted that the poor sods who had to wear ties every day to a dreary nine-to-five were just 'dead men walking'. If you couldn't sit around all day in a T-shirt and battered combat trousers planning how to kill people, life was, to him, quite clearly not worth living.

The meeting room door was flung open and two men walked in. Handshakes and nods were exchanged. The shorter of the two, with broad shoulders and auburn hair, cut off Sandy as he was introducing us.

'Alexis and I know each other. University.'

'Yes. Right. Exactly.' I had no idea who he was. He obviously saw through my super spy poker face as his face darkened. Just what I needed, some guy from Six having it in for me because I didn't remember sitting next to him in a lecture.

It was only while he was droning on about Russia's current political climate that his name came to me. Dugdale. Harry Dugdale. Duggers. He played a lot of rugby. Back then his hair was thicker, more foppish, his face a little less full. His gold signet ring tapped against the table as he used his hands to emphasise a point he was making. He still had that cocky self-assurance of someone to whom life had always come easily.

I recalled something else.

I had slept with him. No wonder he was pissed off I hadn't remembered him. I tried to keep a straight face. It had only happened once, after some college event that involved black tie and a lot of vodka. I now remembered how he had had some weird obsession with sticking his tongue in my ears. I touched my ear, cringing at the unpleasantness of the memory. Maybe that was his thing. Some guys love the ear. Obviously now I kept thinking about it, I kept wanting to touch my ear. Maybe he would pick up on that and think I was mocking him. Or trying to seduce him. Shit, I touched it again. What was wrong with me? I sat on my hands as he continued his long-winded diatribe.

'. . . make no mistake, this is a new cold war, waged through information campaigns, where knowledge is power. It's a digital battlefield and right now Russia is winning. We already know our main ally has been compromised. I ask what more—'

Sandy cut in. 'Look, we get it. We can't count on America. The special relationship is over. Big Daddy's dumped us for a Russian mistress. We need to kick the bitch out the marital bed and get our man back.'

'Yes. Quite.' Dugdale looked round at us all. 'And things are about to get a hell of a lot worse. Rok-Tech is Russia's largest privately owned technology corporation and our sources tell us they've just created software that could change the world as we know it. Richard, take us through it.'

Dugdale's spectacled colleague leaned forward on to the table with his hands clasped.

'Rok-Tech has created an app called VirtuWorld. They are at the final stages of testing and plan to launch it early next year. VirtuWorld has taken Google Street View to the next level. Users can put on a headset and walk virtually down any mapped street in the world. The possibilities are endless. You could "walk" from your house to a shop on the other side of town, ask the sales-person questions and even purchase an item to be delivered to your home. Your real address, obviously, not your virtual one.' Richard sniggered as we all remained silent. 'As you can interact with other users on VirtuWorld you could even arrange to meet a prospective luuuurrveee' (I winced at Richard's pronunciation of 'love') 'interest in VirtuParis and go for a romantic walk along the Seine together. Eventually you would be able to VirtuHoliday in any destination you want. It's really quite amazing.'

I could totally see the appeal of exploring new places without ever having to worry about the traumas of a flight with a baby.

Dugdale broke in to Richard's delight. 'Get to the point.'

Richard straightened up. 'Just like with Google, Rok-Tech has its own fleet of cars with inbuilt scanners for mapping the streets. The difference is the software in the Rok-Tech scanners is able to spoof a building's wireless network and record the Media Access Control address of every electronic device inside and store it on a central database. If any of those devices then download the hot new VirtuWorld app the database links their name and registration details to their MAC address, remote access is activated and . . . kaboom! Life as we know it will explode.'

He looked round at our blank faces.

'Okay let's say there's a girl out there called Melissa . . . Melissa . . . Melissa X. If I'm in control of the VirtuWorld software I can search the VirtuWorld database for a "Melissa X". If her name and details pop up, with one click I could go through her texts, emails, her photos, contacts, everything as if her phone was in my hand. I could even access her camera and start recording. And because I can also see every wireless network and mobile phone tower that has ever logged Melissa's MAC address, I will know every place she's ever been and now be able to track her movements in real-time.' Richard let that sink in. 'I can even do a search for what other MAC addresses were on the same network as her on the same date and time. I would know everyone she's ever met with and when and where. She couldn't lie. I would know.' He tapped the side of his head.

I made a mental note to check in on the real Melissa in Richard's life and warn her to stay the hell away from him.

Richard continued, 'The very existence of the VirtuWorld software is a worrying sign of how things could escalate. Within ten years, our sources predict the majority of the whole world could be mapped and the software advanced to the point the app doesn't need to have been downloaded to take control.' Richard pushed his glasses back up his nose. 'We could be looking at a future whereby we have to give up mobiles, iPads, in fact all digital hardware, to protect data and try to keep any semblance of privacy.'

Turning our phones against us.

I tried to imagine life without my mobile. What the hell would I stare at during those boring midnight feeds? And how on earth would I distract Gigi on a long car journey without the bright flashing images of YouTube? And no Google to answer my panicked 'what kind of rash is a bad rash' questions?

Dugdale cut into the silence, 'As you can understand we can't go public with this information – there would be wide-spread panic over the fact this technology even exists.'

'I understand the need for discretion but couldn't we at least come up with a story to discourage people from downloading the app?' Even as I asked the question I knew what the answer would be.

'We could,' said Sandy slowly. 'But as terrifying as it is to think of the damage it could do *against* us, it is exciting to think of how much it could do *for* us. Imagine if we had concerns about an upcoming terrorist attack – at the click of a button we could be monitoring the movements and conversations of a hundred different persons of interest and everyone in their immediate circle.'

'That's all very well, but what's to stop our enemies doing the same to us?' asked Jake.

'Once we understand exactly how the VirtuWorld software operates our engineers could set up protection protocols to stop foreign powers using it against us,' said Dugdale. 'The current owner and chairman of Rok-Tech is eighty-five-year-old Viktor Tupolev. Upon his instruction Rok-Tech were in the process of setting up a black-market sale of the software to all interested international agencies. Being an astute businessman he recognised just how much everyone in the security services would be willing to pay for this technology. However a few days ago Tupolev had a massive stroke. He's still alive but it looks as though there could be brain damage. Doctors are running tests.'

'As if that stroke was really from natural causes,' Sandy guffawed. 'Dimitri Tupolev, his eldest son, will be the one taking over from his father as chairman of Rok-Tech. Dimitri has been living in London for seven years now, running Rok-Tech's UK subsidiaries. Five months ago, as soon as we first heard rumours of the VirtuWorld software, we put Dimitri under surveillance and started gaining intelligence on him. It looks like even though his old man is a die-hard capitalist always wanting to add to his fortune, Dimitri is a die-hard supporter of The President. He subscribes to the regime's belief that companies should advance the interests of the dear motherland.'

'And that means not selling the software so only Russia can use it to her advantage.'

I shook my head. This was going to be one hell of a first mission back.

'This spells disaster for the rest of the world,' said Dugdale. 'If Russia remains the only country with this technology, this weapon of mass intrusion, we might as well surrender. If you think The President can crush opponents and influence elections now, imagine what he can do with that kind of power.'

Sandy took his leg off the chair and pulled himself up. 'Dimitri's younger brother Sergei shares his father's greed and he's the man we need to ensure will take over Rok-Tech. He wants to sell the software to as many buyers as possible and get himself a nice big payday. Right now the Rok-Tech leadership is in limbo. Old man Tupolev needs to be declared incompetent before Dimitri can take over. The incompetency hearing has been set for three months' time – in December. It's the official process a billion-dollar company has to go through, but it will undoubtedly declare the old man unfit.' Sandy paused to take a long gulp from his water glass while he gave his tie another yank. 'Before Dimitri can be officially granted full control of Rok-Tech he must be covertly eliminated.'

'So something a bit more subtle than radiation poisoning in a Knightsbridge hotel, then?' Jake smirked. 'This will be fun. A nice welcome back for you, Lex.' We grinned at each other. The band was back together.

Dugdale cleared his throat. Perhaps being reminded that someone he once slept with was a trained killer made him feel uneasy.

'I speak for Six when I confirm that we're fully behind whatever action Eight deems fit to take. The Committee have instructed that we help as and when you need it.'

All of us within the Security Services answered only to the Committee. They were the ones who really ran this country. The prime minister and government were about as effective as a close-the-door button on a lift. There merely to give the appearance of control. The Committee believed in democracy. They just considered themselves a helping hand to make sure it went the right way. The best way for the country. We were part of the tiny percentage who knew that what was played out in the public eye very rarely reflected what was happening behind closed, reinforced doors.

Sandy stood up. 'We'll get things moving and keep you updated.'

The meeting was over. We had played nicely and they had let us know they were all too happy for the grown-ups to handle everything for them. With formal handshakes all round, I managed to avoid any more ear touching and made a fast exit.

Every time we visited Legoland I thought about how this world, away from the slime and grime of the sewers, could have been my life – if I didn't have this part of me that could kill on command, for Queen and for country, while still having a good night's sleep. Seeing Duggers reminded me how different the paths we had taken had been. Oxford University was nearly twelve years ago. Like me, he would have been recruited just before graduation. Both of us would have faced the same rigorous testing, the extreme psychological profiling and at the end been assigned a number. Five, Six or Eight. Just like in Harry Potter when the students of Hogwarts put their faith in the Sorting Hat, we had to trust the Committee had called it right. Got us right.

I thought back to Duggers' discomfort at the mention of the planned hit. He had grimaced while I had smiled. They had got it right, all right.

Chapter Two

SANDY'S PLATFORM EIGHT-ISSUE black BMW was parked right outside Legoland, ready and waiting to whisk us back to Holborn and our underground world. I looked out of the tinted window as we weaved in and out of traffic, the siren on the roof making drivers freeze and get out of our way like startled rabbits. There was no emergency, but the logic had always been our time was better spent out of the car than in it.

I saw a woman up ahead waiting at the traffic lights with a pram. Before Gigi I had never noticed mothers and their babies. When I assessed a street, looking for threats, I glossed over the women pushing prams. Harmless. Irrelevant. Invisible. Now I saw them everywhere I looked. They stood out like beacons. I noticed the model of pram they were using. How old the baby was. How sweet the baby was. How old the mother was. How tired she looked. How flat her stomach was.

The woman looked up from fussing over the baby's blanket as we came to a halt at the lights, waiting for a large coach to pass by, and stared straight at me. Her brow furrowed and she tilted her head slightly. I leant back from the window and looked away before remembering the car's blackout glass and that it was her own reflection she was looking at so intently.

The coach moved and off we sped.

I tried not to think of my baby, in her pram, being pushed by someone other than me. In the front Jake and Sandy talked about the meeting over the noise of the siren, their ties already removed and stuffed in their pockets. It felt good to be back. Eliminating Dimitri Tupolev was not going to be easy. Working out how to kill someone covertly, to make it look like an accident or natural causes, was the crème de la crème of the assassinating game. It was like being given an incredibly difficult puzzle at school. Except more fun and involving poisons, guns and knives. It was Sudoku for the sadistic.

And I realised now how much I had missed it.

I don't know when being a Rat became such an intrinsic part of me; at what point exactly it stopped being a job and became a calling, a way of life. I didn't grow up wanting to kill people. I wasn't one of those troubled children who had a propensity to pull the wings off flies or torture little puppies. Life was simple and unremarkable and nothing in my textbook childhood could have predicted my violent adulthood. I had no innate desire to take a life. What I did have was a need for something more than the nice, normal existence I was headed for. By the time I was a teenager I looked around at the sleepy town in Berkshire I was growing up in, and at my caring, middle-class parents and rather than being grateful for what I had it made me want to scream. It felt so predictable. Life was beige and I wanted fire-engine red. With a small sprinkling of leopard skin. I didn't want to live on auto pilot, be just another nobody on life's long treadmill. I wanted to have a strut in my walk, a flash in my eyes, a knowing secret to my smile. I wanted to be goddamn special.

I watched as the cars continued to part for us. This definitely made me feel special. Forget having the power to take a life; having the power to beat traffic is what really gave all us Rats a bit of a God complex.

Sandy turned off the siren as we pulled into the NCP car park in Covent Garden. He leaned round and looked at me.

'Good to be back home, away from the Pigeons? Or are you rethinking things now you're a mummy?'

In Eight we called those from Five and Six 'Pigeons' as they were scattered all round London and had the tendency to shit all over everything.

I was transferred to Five for the majority of my pregnancy to stay out of harm's way and live my cover story of being 'just a GCDSB data analyst'. The hours may have been nine to five and the work completely sedentary but the days had dragged by and felt much more tiring. I still wasn't sure if that was down to pregnancy or the boredom of no deadly action.

I shrugged. 'I'm still a Rat. This is where I belong.'

'Thank fuck for that. Because we need you.'

We drove down and down until we reached what appeared to be the bottom level. We screeched past the rows of parked cars towards a large booth at the far end. A sign advertising a hand car washing service hung above it. Once parked inside, Sandy inputted an eight-digit code into the keypad by his window and a metal roller door rattled down behind us. He then typed in a second, longer code and with a lurch the floor started lowering and we descended another level further underground. This was us. The lowest of the low. There was a high-pitched shriek as the lift mechanism came to a halt and the doors opened into Platform Eight's very own private car park.

The expansive space, the size of two football fields, was lit by rows of overhead strip lighting. Ten identical white vans, a series of black cars like the one we had arrived in, as well as a few private cars were all parked neatly in a line. A number of Rats drove to work; free parking in central London was considered a real perk of the job. The other side of the car park had been commandeered by R & D as a space to build and test their latest inventions.

We got out of the car and headed for the tunnel that led to Platform Eight's network of offices. On the streets above us people were deciding what sandwich to buy from Pret a Manger, browsing the rails at New Look, stocking up on condoms at Superdrug. Down here we had meetings discussing how someone was going to die. Life above ground was the bright, bustling place where everyone shared everything. Trending hashtags, viral videos, hysterical front pages; always in glossy-coloured, high-definition, full-megapixel glory. But it was all pretend. The real truth was quiet. Plotted out in grey faceless rooms, by grey faceless people. Us Rats were a part of this world. The gritty, dirty one where no one talked and no one tagged. But it was where everything was decided, and it was how everything got done.

As we passed a group of men in white lab coats surrounding a Toyota Prius, its passenger doors open, Sandy called, 'Don't forget we need it for next week, boys.' The windows had been darkened and the interior-door handles had been removed. 'One of our little Uber adaptations,' he explained to me. 'Our drivers will definitely be getting one-star ratings.' He chuckled to himself as he typed a code into the keypad next to the tunnel opening. The door slid back and we walked through, blinking slightly as we adjusted to the darkness. Naked bulbs hung sporadically from the ceiling in a line running through the tunnel. Enough light to see your way but not enough to see anyone coming. Our very own little hallway to hell.

'Meeting room in ten minutes,' announced Sandy over his shoulder as he reached the end of the tunnel and opened the door into the main corridor of Platform Eight. He limped off in the direction of his office.

'I'll tell the others.' Jake followed him. 'You might want to sort your tits out.' He nodded down at my chest where once again my bra was on show. 'Unless this is a new look you're going for. In which case I'm all for it.' He disappeared off round the corner before I could come back with a line that was just the right combination of witty and disparaging.

I stood alone in the empty corridor. I had not set foot down here for nearly a year. The fluorescent strip lighting gave a whitish glow to the grey chipped concrete walls and floors. The low drone of the air vents and the soft buzz of electricity powering the high-wattage lights were punctuated with the noise of the tube trains rattling past. I took a deep breath. Everything was the same. Yet everything was different.

I ran my hand along the rough wall as I headed towards the locker room. People had been plotting and planning down here for decades. It was one of these custom-built underground offices the War Cabinet used to meet in before the War Rooms were created. We were carrying on the tradition, except we fought wars most people didn't even know about.

When the Services approached me in my final year at Oxford, I knew it was because I had been getting various bearded professors very excited by the first-class Economics papers I had been writing. They no doubt envisaged using me as an analyst or in some other important desk job where I would pour over reams of data to help keep the country safe. Yet my rather interesting psych test results evidently made them think perhaps there was another calling for a highly intelligent (scored 9.6), moderately attractive (scored 7.2) female with seriously questionable morals (scored 2.1).

I entered the locker room and looked at myself in the mirror hanging on the wall. I wondered how much of a battering my attractiveness rating would have taken since Gigi was born. I tilted my head from left to right. A few extra kilos and permanent bags under the eyes could definitely knock a couple of points off. The official name for this superficial round of testing was 'Individual Appearance Assessment'. Although much maligned and referred to by the catchier 'Hot or Not', it was considered essential in fully assessing an individual's viability as an active agent. Reportedly, a score of 2.2 and under or 8.7 and over meant you were too memorably attractive or unattractive, ruling you out of certain missions.

We all often wondered exactly how those on the judging panel assessed our looks. Scientifically? By measuring the symmetry of our features? Instinctively? By how much they wanted to see us naked? Or had some award-winning mathematician come up with a special algorithm taking both into account? I was just grateful I had a score that ensured eligibility for all missions and the somewhat smug satisfaction of being officially, as judged by my country, more Hot than Not. I flashed my reflection a grin.

I walked towards my unit's corner of the locker room. Since I became a fully-fledged Rat I had only ever worked within the same team. There were around sixty of us within Eight, all rattling around in our underground lair, with the added bonus of a canteen and gym. Half of us were Rats. The rest were Tech Support or working in departments like Surveillance, R & D or Special Projects. Despite the sinister nature of our business, we weren't that dissimilar from the companies in Holborn working directly above us.

Rats and Tech Support were divided into units, each headed up by a unit leader, and assigned specific missions which could be on home soil or anywhere in the world. Each unit was named by its leader; a power that was routinely abused as a chance to try to show off their wit or lack thereof.

I looked up at the 'Unicorn' scrawled in paint across our line of six metal lockers and shook my head. Sandy had named our unit this, saying, 'What else would you call a group of dickheads who don't officially exist?'

Other unit name highlights included 'Megatron' (big *Transformers* fan), 'Watermelon' (a reference to the ball size required to do this job) and 'Jagger' as that leader genuinely believed he had 'moves like Jagger'. I would often think how our American counterparts probably had unit names like 'Freedom', 'Independence', 'Patriot' or other such worthy, inspiring monikers whereas we were proudly British in our schoolboy humour.

I entered the code for my locker's padlock. In a defiant nod to the extreme security measures and the complicated passcodes that filled my working life, for this padlock I used 0000. I was not sure exactly who this was a middle finger to, but it was a small act of rebellion in my otherwise cautiously secure existence. I also figured if anyone really wanted to steal a bag of gym kit, spare underwear and a little black dress, they were welcome to it. I took off my suit jacket and stuffed it into the locker and pulled my hoodie out my gym bag. I put it on, zipping it up to my neck.

I passed Sandy's office on my way to the meeting room. I saw a flash of him sitting at his desk.

'Lex, come in here, will you?' He had obviously spotted me, too.

I walked into his small office. The concrete walls were empty except for a poster that had been blu-tacked up behind his desk. It was a photo of a rat with its back to the camera. Underneath was the slogan 'I'm all out of fucks to give . . . but here's a rat's ass'.

'Yes, boss?'

'Take a seat.'

He waited until I was sitting bolt upright in the plastic chair on the other side of his scuffed desk before he spoke. 'Don't get me wrong, Tyler, I'm delighted you're back.' His face remained deadpan. 'But I need to know you're going to be all right. That your head is back in the game?'

'Sandy, I took a few months off and had a baby, not a psychotic break. Of course I'm fine.'

'Good. I just had to check. As you know. Hormones.' He twirled a finger round next to his head. 'You're taking the lead on this mission. Not Jake. Everything's riding on you being on top form.' He leaned forward in his chair. 'If the Russians get even the slightest hint of what we're up to, retaliation will be brutal.'

'Sandy, all of us in Eight know exactly how unforgiving the Russians can be.' A couple of years ago a Rat had been caught inside the home of a general from The President's personal guard. He had been tortured for a week before he was executed and his body left in pieces on the steps of the British Embassy in Moscow. 'It sounds like you don't fully believe I'm up to the job.'

'You're the first female agent in our history to have had a kid and come back, which is making a lot of people very nervous. This is one hell of an important mission. It doesn't get much bigger than this. Knowledge is power and with VirtuWorld behind him The President becomes god. We mess this up and Russia will be in charge of us all.' He pointed his right index finger at me. 'Everyone is going to be watching you very closely.'

'I have *never* failed you. Do you really think having a baby has suddenly made me a liability?' I may have had my own doubts, but he didn't get to judge me from his supposed high horse of male superiority.

'I'm just warning you, Lex. You've always gone on about being treated the same as everyone else and that's exactly what we're going to do.' He lifted his bad leg up on the table. 'So no trying to pull a sickie if the kid has a sniffle. No coming in late because your babysitter was stuck in traffic. If you want to work somewhere that has to be legally understanding about you being a mother you can head back over to Five and fucking stay there.' He stared at me unsmiling. 'What we do is too important to have someone trying to slack off because they feel their vagina gives them special rights.'

'Understood.' I clenched my jaw so tight my teeth started to ache. I left his office, letting the door slam behind me. First day back on the job and already they were watching me from the sidelines, doubting I could do it. And after everything we had been through together.

It had been a busy and bloody ten years since my first day as a Rat when I had entered the joint-briefing room to report to Sandy that I was his latest recruit.

'You're Alexis Tyler? I thought you'd be a bloody man.'

'Well it looks like you have enough of those.' I had gestured at the all-male faces around me. 'And you can call me Lex. But not Lexi. Unless you want me to shoot you and blame it on PMT.'

'I think we're going to get on just fine, Lex.'

He was right, we had. He had been a good unit leader; he was blunt and to the point but his mission planning and tactical support had been faultless. I had always done everything he had asked of me, and more. I liked to think I had shown you didn't need actual balls to do this job; just hard-assed grit, determination, and the ability to always succeed in getting the shot, pushing the button, plunging the needle.

But, then, that was old Lex. New Lex and her baby were a whole different commodity. It looked as though I was going to have to prove myself all over again. Some welcome back.

Chapter Three

I GOT TO THE MEETING room to find Jake was already there. Although most of the Platform's furniture was Formica, this room, for reasons no one seemed to know, was furnished with an enormous antique oak dining table. It looked somewhat ridiculous surrounded by tacky orange chairs, with the opulent wood reflecting the yellow glow from the unflattering fluorescent lighting, but I liked it. It made me feel like we were in *Downton Abbey*, about to be served a seven-course meal, rather than meeting to discuss how best to kill someone over cups of tea and digestive biscuits.

Jake stared at me. 'I'm devastated. You've changed.'

For a moment I thought he too was having a dig at my new mother status. That I was a different person.

And then I realised he was referring to the hoodie.

'Come on, unzip it just a little. This briefing will need some livening up.' He leaned forward on to the table, cupping his face with his hands.

Jake Drummond may have been a prick but I had missed him. As my partner in Unicorn he had been a constant presence in my life for ten years. Always there, always impossible to ignore. Blessed with conventional good looks that hid the unconventional nature of his work, he was smug, irritating, bordering on psychotic, and someone I had started sleeping with within a few months of our unit first being formed. In my defence, studies have shown that nearly forty per cent of the working population will at some point indulge in a workplace romance, thanks to factors like the daily close proximity to each other and the thrill of the illicit. And that was before you added in the adrenaline surge of escaping a life-threatening situation or the high after taking out men twice your size.

Post-mission, with blood-splattered clothes in an alleyway, in the store cupboard of a five-star hotel while waiting for security to stop sweeping the building, in the back of a Land Rover Pickup while on a two-day stakeout in the middle of some godforsaken desert . . . We had done it all. Killing and fucking went terrifyingly well hand in hand. I once read somewhere that funerals could get people going as they were reminders of the fragility of life. Well, our work was a daily reminder of how quickly life could be over. What an aphrodisiac.

I should've known better.

I should've been better.

Jake was hard to resist, but it didn't take long to see past the good looks and the easy charm. His smile never quite reached his eyes; his laughter was a little hollow. He knew what was expected of him and he played the part. For Jake, being a Rat was a way to give meaning to what he really enjoyed. He was a tamed lion. There were flickers, in the heat of a mission, interrogating a par-ticularly reticent suspect, and his mask would drop, I would see it. I would see him. It should've scared me but it didn't.

I would focus on how, by working at the Platform, he had at least chosen to use his dark talents for good. I knew I was making excuses for a bad man, just like I'd heard friends make excuses for bad boyfriends. 'My lover is a cheating bastard who doesn't want to settle down – but he really does love me,' was every bit as deluded as, 'My lover is a sadistic killer who enjoys inflicting pain – but he's a nice guy really.'

But it was never my place to try and fix Jake. He was just a sideshow for me, simple workplace entertainment, and like all spectators of caged animals I wasn't going to be so stupid as to put my hand through the bars.

Over the years we had stopped and started, stopped and started.

And then one day we finally stopped for good. All it took was nearly dying together. It changed us. Since the day we were choppered out of China, ashen-faced at the close call and the bodies left behind, he'd never tried and I'd never been tempted. We'd been strictly business for over three years now. I couldn't remember if back when I was at least benefitting from Jake's body I'd found him less annoying than I did now.

I looked at him leaning back in his chair with hands behind his head, smirking at me.

'You're a dick.' The sleep deprivation was clearly affecting my usual razor-sharp wit.

We were interrupted by the arrival of the rest of Unicorn.

'Good to see you, Lex!' Geraint Callewaert, a sweet IT whiz with a name no one really knew how to pronounce, was in charge of Unicorn's technical support. He was short and slight with trendy, thick-framed glasses that were an attempt to make him look more hipster than hacker.

'You too, G-Man. And hello, Nicola.' I nodded at the petite woman with long black hair next to him. Nicola Adams worked alongside Geraint. She was ridiculously trendy. The fact I called her trendy was a giveaway as to how uncool I was. There was probably a better word for it. Fly? No, that was definitely only used back in the 1990s. Nicola looked as though she might be half or a quarter Indian, although political correctness and her unfriendly nature had prevented me ever asking. She wore a diamond stud in an upper ear piercing and would slouch around the office in harem pants, tight bandeau tops and leopard-print metallic edged trainers. I wasn't sure I'd ever seen her smile. She seemed to work hard and without complaining yet had a permanent air of being bored. Quite an achievement in our line of work.

'Hiya.' She flicked her hair and gave me a nod.

I looked over at the grinning Chinese man standing by the door. 'And good to see you're still with us, Robin.'

'Come here.' He walked towards me, opening his arms. 'Everyone knows Mummy cuddles are the best.' Robin Goh was an agent-in-training, a baby Rat. Having grown up in Glasgow he spoke with a strong Scottish accent. The majority of us in the industry presumed, when we met him, that his Asian heritage meant he would be some kind of martial arts expert. Sadly no. He couldn't karate chop his way out of a paper bag. That disappointment aside, he was a fast learner and a good addition to the team, despite his insistence on being the class joker.

Sandy entered the room and I was thankful that Robin lowered his arms.

'Good, you're all here. Let's begin.'

The five of us took seats round the grand dining table while Sandy stood at the front of the room next to a large whiteboard.

'An hour ago you received the briefing email.'

Our mobiles and laptops were set up so that all Platform Eight's encrypted emails looked like junk mail. What would appear to be something like another offer of 'PeNi$ extension!!!' was actually a secure email we could decrypt by typing in our unique authorisation code. We had five minutes to read it before it reverted back to being just another email telling us how to improve our sex lives with the help of little blue pills.

'The target is Dimitri Tupolev. The action is covert elimination. I repeat: *covert*. This has to look like an accident. If The President gets one hint of UK involvement in Dimitri's premature death it's all-out war. Timeframe is as soon as bloody possible. We have three months and the clock is ticking. The incompetency hearing is set for December but Dimitri's lawyers are battling for it to be sooner. There is also the risk his old man could be finished off by another stroke at any given time. Our objective is to make sure Dimitri beats his father to the fiery gates of hell. I say "hell" as if you're familiar with the Tupolevs, you know it's where they belong.'

The Tupolevs' reputation was one of brutality; business associates who crossed them disappeared and were rarely found, and certainly never in one piece. None of us would be having any sleepless nights over Dimitri's untimely demise. Sandy looked round the table at us. 'This is not going to be an easy job. The Russians we are making a strike against are an unforgiving enemy. If we get caught it's not a question of whether we live but how painfully we die. We can't afford any mistakes.'

Jake shook his head. 'I don't like the timeframe pressure. Have the Committee requested any additional action or can we go straight to devising a kill plan?'

Eight offered a full elimination service, from conception through to finish with all the time-consuming admin in between. This was so no one at Five or Six could ever be traced

37

back to a mission that ended in an ordered assassination. We did everything in-house, from initial surveillance, required reconnaissance, through to the final kill and clean up. A nice package deal.

'The Committee have decreed that we can make the hit as soon as we've confirmed that Dimitri's death will lead to his younger brother, Sergei, taking over the company. To succeed in this, we're going to need some Russian help.'

Jake frowned. He hated having to work with anyone outside the Platform. 'Why? It's a family business, and with Dimitri gone Sergei is the only option.'

'Sergei is a cokehead whose only skills seem to be partying and pissing people off. Rok-Tech currently has five people on its executive board. Intelligence confirms that three of them are fiercely loyal to both Dimitri and The President. If they stay on the board they will undoubtedly vote against the black market sale of the VirtuWorld software. We therefore need to recruit three Russian businessmen who can hand-hold Sergei through his takeover of Rok-Tech and replace Dimitri's three allies on the board. We get this sorted and then' – he grinned – 'the Weasel gets popped.'

'Weasels' were what we called targets. No one had ever determined which came first, the codename or the bastardised version of the nursery rhyme that you would now and again hear echoing down the corridor.

Half a pound of C4 and knives,
a 30-calibre rifle.
That's the way a Rat plays.
Pop! goes the Weasel.

'Any questions?'

'We're all good,' said Geraint. 'We have a few new gadgets for Lex and Jake to try out. Isn't that right, Nicola? Some great stuff.'

'Yep. Great,' was all he got back from Nicola. She was twirling a long strand of glossy hair round a perfectly manicured navy-blue fingernail. I tried not to think of how my own beauty rituals had declined to such a degree that I used a two-in-one shampoo and conditioner as I didn't have time for a second rinse.

'We're going to need more than new gadgets,' said Jake. 'Trying to take out Dimitri is near-suicide – he's a violent billionaire paranoid about security with a twenty-four-hour heavily armed security team. And on top of this we have to make it look like an accident? We can't do this without an inside man.'

'Or woman,' I added.

'Yeah, yeah, Lex. Do you always have to be so bloody politically correct?'

I ignored him and looked at Sandy.

'You have the wife, don't you?'

The briefing email had included a helpful summary of the key players. I had noticed the profile on Dimitri's wife, Dasha, had included the words 'political activist'.

Sandy broke into a broad grin.

'Listen up everyone, Lex will be the lead agent on this mission. And she is absolutely correct. We have the very glamorous Dasha Tupolev, wife of Dimitri, mother of his three children, on our side. G-Force, get up the file on Dasha please.'

Geraint clicked a button and a society magazine photo of Dasha and Dimitri at a black-tie event was projected on to the whiteboard. She was wearing a strapless full-length black fishtail dress and was giving the camera her best megawatt smile. Diamonds sparkled round her neck and on her ears, her long blonde hair was styled poker straight. Dimitri was mid-conversation with someone out of frame. He was a big man, broad-shouldered, with heavyset features and thick black hair. A hulk in a tuxedo. Beauty and the Beast.

Sandy motioned towards the photo. 'Dasha and Dimitri Tupolev have been married eight years. Dasha is thirty-one, Dimitri is forty-five. They have three children; Viktor aged seven, Natalya aged four and Irina aged one.'

Another photo flashed up – Dasha and Dimitri next to an impressively huge Christmas tree, Irina in Dasha's arms. Their two elder children in front of them. No one was smiling.

'Dasha grew up on a farm in Siberia and at eighteen moved to Moscow after being scouted by a model agent.'

A photo collage of Dasha's modelling shoots replaced the family Christmas card.

Sandy continued, 'Looks like the move to the big city led to the start of a heavy interest in Russian politics. Here she is at a demonstration protesting The President's regime, just before she met Dimitri.'

The grainy photo showed Dasha in a woollen hat surrounded by other protestors. Anti-President signs were held aloft by those around her. The photographer had captured them mid-shout; their mouths were open and brows furrowed. In a sea of people, Dasha and her cheekbones stood out.

'Dasha's irritation at Dimitri's serial adultery and horror at his plans to empower The President further meant she was always a prime candidate for turning. And as luck would have it, a couple of months ago Dasha was coming out of her favourite London hair salon when a violent mugging took place right in front of her.' Sandy smirked. 'Over the course of the summer, I got to meet with Dasha several times at Kensington and Chelsea Police Station.'

A standard Eight technique was ensuring a person of interest witnessed a crime. It gave them a reason for spending time at a police station where they would be escorted to Eight's specially commandeered interview room to give their statement. Follow-up sessions all gave further excuses for private conversations away from prying eyes and overenthusiastic bodyguards.

'Last year, Dasha's cousin, a cousin she grew up with in Siberia and who was more like a brother, disappeared while working for Dimitri.' Sandy rubbed his leg and sat down next to Geraint. 'During one of our interviews I showed Dasha proof that Dimitri was behind his death, dismemberment and distribution into the Thames. He believed this cousin had been stealing from him. Knowing Dimitri approved the murder of a close family member was more than enough to guarantee her cooperation.'

'And she knows that what we have planned for Dimitri is elimination, not incarceration?' As far as I was aware, being angry at your other half was a little different to actually being complicit in their death.

Sandy turned to Geraint. 'Play tape number two.'

A video of Dasha sitting in an interview room was projected on to the whiteboard. The tell-tale thick black band of a lie-detector monitor was strapped across her dusty pink Chanel jacket.

'I've known for some time that I'm married to a monster.' I was surprised at how English Dasha sounded. Her years over here, and no doubt spending so much time with mothers at

her children's exclusive private schools, had helped hone her speaking voice and soften her accent. *'The things he has done . . .'* Her eyes dropped. *'It makes me sick. What he did to my cousin . . . I . . .'* Her voice broke. She paused and took a sip of water. *'My cousin was not the first and he won't be the last. That's how Dimitri works: violence first, questions later. I know he's a marked man. It's only a matter of time before one of his enemies finally succeeds in killing him.'* She looked back up towards the camera with a steely stare. *'I've already mourned him. And if I agree to help you, then at least I will be taking a stand against The President. Stopping him gain even more power. He—'*

Sandy pressed a button on Geraint's laptop, pausing Dasha mid- sentence and mid-frown. He looked round at us. 'Interrogation ran the stats on her vitals during this interview three times. She meant every word she said. Remember, it's not that big a jump to go from exchanging wedding vows with someone to wanting to see them dead.' His lip curled. He was a bitterly divorced father of two. 'Our problem is that two weeks ago, all communication stopped. Her protection detail has doubled; which either means hubby is worried for her life, or fearing for her loyalty. We can assume her emails and phone are now being closely monitored which makes re-establishing contact a severe ball-ache. Which is why, dear Lex, you' – he pointed at me – 'are such a special asset. They will always be on the lookout for someone like Jake, someone like me. So you, a woman, a fellow mother, are the only chance we have of making contact covertly. If we can't reopen a channel of communication with her the whole mission fails.' He leaned forward. 'So, Mummy, are you up for it?'

You had to admire the Platform. My first day back at the office and they had already found a way to take advantage of my new status as a mother.

I wasn't surprised. In this job you needed to use everything you had to get by. To make yourself worthy of being one of the elite. For me, being a woman has always been one of the unique skill sets I brought to my team. People trust women more. People want to hurt women less. Women don't need to be taken seriously. Women aren't a threat . . . *Pop!*

I understood now why Sandy had made a point of saying I would be taking the lead on this mission. I was the perfect undercover mum to get close to Dasha. And the success of the operation was reliant on the inside information she could provide about her husband.

Everyone round the table was staring at me.

'Of course I'm up for it, Sandy. The whole reason I had a baby was to advance my career.'

Sandy ignored the dig. 'Robin, call Surveillance. We want everything they have on Dasha brought here. Lex, you and Jake have the rest of the day to work out how to engineer a chance encounter. You need to make contact with Dasha tomorrow; we're on a tight schedule and we can't move forward without her intel.'

Eight's surveillance team had started following Dasha and Dimitri five months ago, as soon as rumours of VirtuWorld's software had started circulating. Dasha's life seemed to be a flurry of coffee mornings, charity committees and highly regimented beautification rituals that involved six different technicians at three different salons. No wonder she looked like she did, despite having three kids. Sandy's analysis was right. If I was going to make contact with Dasha without arousing the suspicions of her paranoid husband and constant entourage of minders, I would need to use my secret weapon.

My beloved six-month-old daughter.

Chapter Four

THE NEXT MORNING I was doing a good job of pretending it was just another normal day right up until the moment I had to squeeze my .38 revolver into my overflowing nappy bag. I picked up Gigi and held her close, breathing in her soft, sweet smell. Bringing her into this dark world of mine, even just for a cameo role, terrified me. Above all, my priority was to keep her safe. No matter how much I wanted to prove to myself and to the whole Platform I was still worthy of my job here, I was not going to let anything happen to her.

I laid Gigi into her pram, wishing there had been time for R & D to create a bulletproof onesie. I had reviewed the potential risks of this op over and over again. Each time I concluded that being hit by the bus we were about to catch was about as likely as Dimitri's bodyguards raining bullets down on us in broad daylight outside an exclusive London school. But that didn't stop my hands shaking a little and my heart hammering the whole way to Notting Hill.

As we got off the bus, I looked down at Gigi fast asleep with her hands next to her head as if she was in a state of surrender. We turned the corner and I could see Dasha on the other side of the road leaving her five-storey mansion. She got halfway down the steps and then turned back towards the open front door, where a dark figure filled the frame.

Dimitri.

He was dressed in a suit and his hair was slicked back.

I couldn't make out what they were saying. She was gesticulating as he glared down at her. He put a hand on his hip and pointed at her as he spoke before abruptly disappearing back into the house. The front door slammed behind him. Dasha stared at the closed door for a few seconds before turning round and continuing down the steps to where her four-year-old daughter was waiting with her scooter and two burly bodyguards. Dasha gave her daughter a kiss and they set off together along the pavement. The men followed ten paces behind. They both had earpieces and, from the bulge in their jackets, concealed weapons. I took a deep breath. I am normal. Normal, normal, normal. I sped up and crossed the road.

'Dasha! Dasha!' The statuesque blonde turned. She tilted her head and stared at me. She was dressed in skin-tight trousers, high-heeled boots, a clinging silk shirt and a soft leather caramel-coloured fitted jacket. I was deeply grateful that my long black River Island coat covered my porridge-stained top and hid the fact the top button of my jeans was undone.

'It's me, Alexis! How are you? Remember me? We met at Sandy's party. She was saying the other day she hadn't heard from you in ages. She'll be so excited that I've seen you. We must plan a play date.'

To me, my words came out too high-pitched and too fast. I needed her to play along and put the fast-approaching bodyguards at ease. From what I had read about her I had concluded she had to be bright. A farmer's daughter in Siberia could not rise to the palatial heights of Notting Hill without having some brains to match her beauty.

There was a silence that seemed to go on forever. Until finally, she replied, 'How is Sandy? That right leg still giving her trouble?' She cast a glance down at the pram, nearly looking surprised at seeing a real sleeping baby within it.

She was a clever one. No doubt.

'It's her left leg, actually. But yes, it still hurts to walk. Poor old Sandy.'

'You must send her my love and say sorry it's been so long. Things have been crazy.' She tilted her head back very slightly at the hovering bodyguards behind her.

'Mummy, hurry up! We're going to be late.' Her daughter had scooted back to her side and was staring up at her, brows furrowed.

'Hello, Natalya. What an adorable scooter you have, with its very own pony head.' I tapped the neon purple smiling horse head fixed to the middle of the scooter's handle bars with two fingers and stared at Dasha and returned my own subtle head tilt. 'He really is wonderful. I bet all the girls at school wish they had one too.'

'Who are you?' The little girl looked at me briefly before turning back to her mother. 'Come on, Mummy. Now!' She turned on her heel and scooted off.

'I must go, Alexis. So nice to see you. I'll be in touch to plan that play date.' She nodded. Hopefully a confirmation she had got the message. She stalked off, her bodyguards trailing behind her, no doubt pretending they were too professional to appreciate the impressive sashay the four-inch Christian Louboutin boots gave her walk.

I waited until they were out of sight and pushed Gigi down the road to a Caffè Nero I had spotted getting off the bus. She was still sleeping and barely stirred as I manoeuvred us in and bought a large cappuccino to go. I sipped it slowly as we walked up and down the street, the innocent picture of a mother soothing her baby to sleep. By the time the cup was empty it was time to make the drop-off.

I checked my watch as I approached Natalya's school. The bell would've rung over fifteen minutes ago and the main door was firmly closed. The street was empty. Adorning the outside of the imposing building, just inside the railings, were neatly lined-up children's scooters in all the colours of the rainbow. I slowed as I walked past them until I spotted Natalya's distinctive horse-head scooter, then leaned over and tucked the small flier I had in my pocket inside the horse's mouth. I looked around. I was just another mother looking at just another scooter.

The flier announced the launch of www.westlondonyum-mum.net and was covered in photos of smiling mothers and smartly dressed children doing an array of highbrow activities from mastering chess to playing the violin. 'Members Only Access to the Finest Tutors West London Has to Offer' it screamed across the top. I had written on it, 'Sandy thought you would like to join! Alexis.'

I had included a login name and password that would give Dasha access to a secure encrypted chatroom that Geraint had set up. Anyone monitoring her web browsing would just see a long list of chatroom topics with such gems as 'Can five-year-olds be bipolar?' and 'So gifted could be autistic?'

Mission accomplished, I stepped back from the scooter and headed towards the bus stop making faces at Gigi, who was now wide awake, gurgling appreciation at my efforts to make her laugh, and none the wiser at being witness to any international subterfuge.

Back home, after safely delivering Gigi to Beata and a waiting bowl of puree, I went upstairs. Shutting the bedroom door behind me, I leant up against it and slowly exhaled. It had all gone to plan. Contact was made, drop-off successful and apart from me ruining Gigi's appetite with an abundance of snacks, no harm was done. I unzipped the nappy bag on the bed and saw Gigi's colourful baby rattle, her small pink hat and the cold hard metal of my .38 nestled between Sophie the well-chewed giraffe and a half empty Tupperware box of mini breadsticks.

So this was my life now.

How the hell did I end up here?

I didn't expect to ever settle down. Even as an adult I still ate Kellogg's variety packs. When faced with so much choice down the breakfast aisle I found I couldn't commit to one whole box. And that was just cereal.

How could I give up my mix of men coming in all their different flavours, shapes and sizes? Not to mention the small issue of having to keep my day job a secret. I couldn't imagine changing and didn't have any desire to. Men were my sweet treat. Fun to snack on but nothing substantial. Just like in my working life now, my love life back then was all about getting to know the target, working out what made them tick and swooping in for the kill. I would then abandon the scene of the crime and move on without a backward glance.

But then Tianjin happened.

Three years ago Jake and I had flown out to China to eliminate a high-profile target. It should have been an easy job but we were double-crossed. What was meant to be a routine meeting at an empty restaurant with one of our informants ended in us being bundled into an unmarked van and taken to a remote building.

Even now, years later, on the other side of the world, in the safety of my bedroom, my heart started beating faster as I was taken right back to what I had thought were my final moments.

We were screamed at, blindfolded and marched outside. Thrown to the ground, then roughly pulled up to our knees as our perceived crimes against the state were read out.

Kneeling there in the dirt, the cold wind whipping my cheeks, I tried to prepare myself. Death was coming. But I wasn't going to let myself down. I could barely breathe. My heart beat so fast and strong I could feel it in my throat, hear it in my ears. Every part of me was throbbing with such force I was shaking. My body was screaming with life, one final standing ovation before the curtain fell.

I felt movement next to me. It was Jake, reaching for my hand. My first thought was hope. He had a plan. He was slipping me something, anything that could be used as a weapon.

But there was nothing there. Just his hand, holding mine. He squeezed it once. There was no code, no message about what we could do next. Simply an attempt to calm me down. A goodbye.

It was the most intimate moment we had ever had.

There was more shouting and we were pulled further apart as we were lined up for the firing squad. I kept holding on to Jake's hand and tried to focus everything on that, the feeling of warmth, the fact I wasn't alone.

There were a series of clicks as they readied their rifles. Then the '*Ready, aim, fire,*' in clipped Mandarin. I squeezed my eyes shut and held my breath. My body stiffened. Death was coming. And all I could do to prepare was brace myself for the onslaught of bullets. I could feel the tension through Jake's hand as he did the same. A burst of gunfire sounded. I hoped for a fast end.

But nothing hit. I dared to exhale. What the hell was happening? Footsteps came towards us and the black of my blindfold was replaced with the sweet familiar sight of armed SAS. Sandy had called in the cavalry. We were rushed past the bodies of the fallen firing squad and out to a waiting helicopter.

It was a lucky escape. It stayed with me for a long time afterwards. It was the closest I had ever come to facing death and in that moment when I was waiting for the bullets to hit, thoughts flew into my head. And one shouted the loudest.

I never got to have a baby.

You convince yourself you have everything you've ever wanted and right down to that last breath you realise you've been kidding yourself. Despite everything I had achieved, everything I had done to prove everyone's preconceptions of me wrong, I was sad I had never had a baby.

I hadn't even known I wanted one, but how could I deny the truth of what came into my mind as I knelt there preparing to die?

Down at the Platform all the veteran agents, having had more than their fair share of near-death experiences, spoke reverently of the 'absolute truth'. That moment when faced with the end, your mind empties and you are granted a moment of total clarity that can never be ignored.

But ignore it I did.

I had tried to get on with life as normal. Pretend it had never happened. Yet it was always there nagging in the back of my mind.

I never got to have a baby.

I looked back at the nappy bag. It had chased me down and got me in the end.

I went to the dresser and picked up the silver framed photo on it. In it, my head was down, my mouth curled up in a small smile. My hair was loose and I was wearing a simple white silk dress. My brand-new husband, Will, was whispering into my ear or kissing the side of my cheek. It was hard to tell from the angle, and I couldn't remember. It had been a day full of whispers and kisses. A few solitary red rose petals dotted the photo, one in my hair, two on his suit, confetti showered over us by merry friends and proud family.

Was he 'the one' or just 'the one at the right time'? The seed of a baby already planted in my mind and the need to have one nudging me forward into his arms. I looked down at the photo and the face I knew so well. His boy-next-door-all-grown-up good looks. Brown hair always that little bit too long and curling over the back of his white shirt. Slight stubble even though he'd only shaved that morning. His suit, only worn for a couple of hours, already rumpled. I could nearly hear his deep laugh that was more like a roar, the feel of his hands as he picked me up and spun me round.

No, it was real. That day I had smiled so much my cheeks ached. This new teeth-filled grin was in nearly all of the photos from our small wedding. Unguarded, face contorting joy. Honest, all-consuming happiness captured on film.

Those photos are hidden in a drawer somewhere.

The Doc down at the Platform would perhaps pounce on this as evidence I could not bear to look at my true self. That I must be ashamed of who I really was.

But it was purely vanity.

I look prettier with a small, contained smile. Like in this photo in the silver frame.

I put it back on the dresser. William Marshall had changed everything. We met in a packed bar in the City, me drunk on vodka and the adrenaline of a completed mission, him drunk on red wine and the high of winning a case. One lingering look across the room was all it took. He was the one-night stand that never went. He wouldn't leave me alone. Until one day he did. And to my surprise, I missed him. I told him. And that was it. I was a convert. Variety packs to bulk buys.

Within a year we were living together, within two we were engaged. I was on the fast track to normality seemingly no longer fearful of the monotony of coupledom. Because being with Will was fun. He was clever but not patronising. Ambitious but not aggressive. Sexy but not shallow. Kind but not a pushover. He never felt like a fling. He never even felt like a boyfriend. He felt like family.

I never took the time to think about what I was giving up. I got on with the present and forgot about my past life of long nights and no last names.

Just three years after meeting him, I was living in the suburbs, married to a lawyer and proud mother to a baby girl.

Thank God I still had a horribly violent job or I would start to bore myself.

I tried not to imagine exactly what Will, dear husband, father of my child, would do if he had any idea that I had undertaken my very own 'bring your daughter to work' day. That being if he had known what my actual 'work' was, rather than the safe data analysing he thought I was doing for 'Government Data Co.' – his easier-to-remember nickname for 'Government Communication and Data Specialisation Branch'.

The grit and grime of my working life felt a million miles away when I stood here, in the master bedroom of a nice three-storey terraced house in Chiswick; a place that was a beautiful warm bubble of wholesome family life. Here, if you sidestepped sick on the pavement, it would be good, middle-class, kale-speckled vomit, thrown up by a morning-sickness-suffering yummy mummy. None of that post-pub kebab-flecked puke you would get in lesser areas.

I took the gun to the bathroom and opened the cupboard under the sink. I moved several boxes of Tampax until I got to the hidden panel at the back and replaced the gun behind it. It was unlikely Will would ever venture under there, but I figured they were the best line of defence. Nothing could make a man recoil faster than the words 'heavy flow'.

Chapter Five

M Y FIRST DEBRIEF OF the mission was starting in three minutes, yet I was standing in Platform Eight's canteen trying to decide between an apple or a brownie. By the time I had arrived at Holborn and swiped through the steel reinforced doors of our grey office building adjoining the underground station my tummy was rumbling. Normally I loved the kick of walking into the waiting lift as an everyday commuter, pressing a combination of buttons that took me deep down to the hallowed halls of Platform Eight, and walking out an underground secret agent. But today I was just desperate to get to this happy place that was always kept well stocked with a wide array of food and energy drinks. Fully-fuelled agents were more effective weapons.

I was interrupted by an unfamiliar face approaching me. A very young unfamiliar face.

'You must be Lex. Easy to work that out.' He sounded as if he was speaking through a pinched nose – he either had a serious problem with his nasal cavity or it was an accent borne of a particularly exclusive private school. He grinned at me. 'Not many of you girlies here.'

'And you are?' I stared at him unsmiling. Trained killers do not get called 'girlies'.

'I'm Bennie McGinn.' He leant up against the counter. 'I was the one covering for you when you were off in babyland.'

I couldn't believe it. He looked like a twenty-year-old estate agent. And 'Bennie'? It sounded like a nickname a doting mother gave him as a toddler and he hadn't yet outgrown.

'I was hoping you'd like the kid enough to stay home. I enjoyed working with Jake and I know Sandy would love to have me back. He said I'd been a real asset.' He puffed out his chest like a schoolboy who'd just been praised by the headmaster.

'Sorry, little guy, I'm not going anywhere. I'm sure you'll get another chance to come back and play with the big boys.'

He laughed. It wasn't as high-pitched as I'd expected.

'I already am one of the big boys. I've spent the last few years at Six honing my superior skillset. The Committee transferred me to Eight for a little playtime to indulge my darker side.'

In case I couldn't hate him any more than I already did he made air quotes with his fingers when he said 'darker side'.

'I'm over in Jagger now. The Committee just gave us the green light for popping the Head of URDaBomb.com.' I cringed at the street accent he attempted while pronouncing the name of the Birmingham-based youth terrorist recruitment agency. 'It'll be fun but I'm sure it won't be long before I get back to Unicorn. This is no work for a woman. Let alone a mother.' He reached over and grabbed the apple I had been eyeing up. 'You'll see.' He stared at me as he took a large bite.

'Beat it, kid. Mummy needs some quiet time and you're late. The rest of Jagger left ten minutes ago and the last guy who held up departure got a watch stapled to his wrist.'

He threw the apple in the bin. 'You're full of it. But I'm bored. Goodbye, Lex, and fuck off back home soon, please.' He gave me a little wave as he left the room. I watched him all the way down the corridor alternating his speed of walk as he wrestled with which was worse: losing face or losing feeling in his wrist.

He was going to be a problem.

I looked on the bright side.

At least he had left the brownie.

One decadent intake of calories later I headed to the meeting room. Jake, Geraint, Nicola and Robin were already sitting round the table; Sandy hovered in front of the large whiteboard.

'There you are. Come on, then, Lex. Talk us through it.'

'All went to plan. I made contact with Dasha, her bodyguards didn't give me a second glance and the flier is now in the scooter.' I looked at my watch. 'Dasha would've picked up her daughter by now. We should check the chatroom.'

Sandy looked at Geraint. 'Are you sure this chatroom is secure?'

I could understand Sandy's paranoia. Even before the dawn of the VirtuWorld software the risk of electronic correspondence being compromised had driven us to rely on more simple forms of communication.

Sometimes the easiest way to hide is in plain sight. It was a mantra the Platform held very dear, which is how one of our analysts came up with the idea of using the Underground's buskers as our very own carrier pigeons. Anyone following one of our assets on their journey to work would be on the lookout for physical interactions, anything changing hands. Like most commuters they wouldn't notice what music the buskers were serenading everyone with that morning. It was just background noise. Yet every asset knew what song was a warning they had been compromised.

It was a tactic we employed all over London. From the homeless man always outside the station holding a different coloured sign to key words hidden within the tacky graffiti scrawled along the walls. Everything ignored and invisible we used to our advantage.

For day-to-day communications we had a team of analysts with fake profiles on social media who would befriend online our assets all over the UK. Those constant streams of innocuous Instagram and Facebook posts were not as mind-numbingly dull as they seemed. A toddler wearing a red jumper cuddling a doll meant an urgent face-to-face meeting was needed. A dog wearing sunglasses: going dark on all communications. Smashed avocado on toast: watch out, it's all gone to shit. Our analysts' comments on these photos told their own story. 'OMG I need to squidge those cheeks right now!' *Get to the rendezvous location immediately.* 'YUM. You can come round and cook for me anytime!' *Come into the Platform as soon as you can.* Eight had recently implemented a new rule banning analysts from having their own social-media accounts ever since one recent hire accidentally confused her work Facebook account with her personal one and a 'You okay, hun?' on the wrong photo led to an asset prematurely breaking cover from an organised crime syndicate.

Using so many different communication techniques meant that when we did revert back to simply talking online everyone was a little more nervous.

Geraint looked round at us all. 'You don't need to worry – I've followed protocol and it's one hundred per cent secure.'

'Okay G-Force.' Sandy drummed his fingers on the table. 'Let's give it a go.'

Geraint pressed a few buttons on his laptop and the chatroom was projected on to the whiteboard. There was a new chat topic titled, *Sharing is caring*. He clicked on it. There was one posting.

I.O. made a list of boys who DH doesn't like at their play date last Friday. His nanny records everything and the tapes are kept safe at home in the study.

Clearly Dasha shared our concerns about the chatroom's security and had decided it was safest to keep to a loose code just in case.

'I've run a keyword search and I.O. has to be Isaac Onegin. Surveillance have been following him for the last few months as he was flagged as a close confidante of Dimitri's. They grew up together and it's widely rumoured Dimitri will bring him on to the board of the company once he takes over.' Nicola's eyes did not leave the screen she was scanning. 'Lives in London. Maida Vale.'

'Okay, so Isaac and Dimitri had a meeting last Friday and they made a list of his enemies. Isaac's "nanny" – his PA? – records everything and the tapes are stored in a safe at Isaac's home office.' Jake paused. 'DH. That doesn't make sense. He's Dimitri Tupolev. Why didn't she write D.T.?'

I looked at the message again.

I knew this one.

'Dear husband,' I announced. 'DH is mums' chatroom slang for "husband".'

Just after Gigi was born, during the lonely 3 a.m. feeds, I found myself scouring the internet for all the questions I had that were too mundane to bore Will with or too stupid to ask the health visitor about. This was how I discovered Mumsnet, a popular website for mothers with a chat forum where everyone seemed very knowledgeable, incredibly forthright and talked in acronyms outsiders could not decipher.

My initial analysis: they were Parenting Terrorists.

Blowing up on anyone who went against their principles of how to raise well-balanced, over-achieving children. I would watch transfixed and wait for someone to drop an 'I can't be bothered to breastfeed' bomb and bear witness to the outrage that streamed in.

But in time I saw it wasn't all ferocious attempts to convert the non-believers to the best way to parent. There may have been the odd pocket cell of aggression but on the whole it was a place of support and camaraderie. A safe place for information to be shared, questions to be answered and mother-in-laws to be complained about. It was, however, not for the faint-hearted. The phrase egg-white cervical mucus was used enough that EWCM was in their acronym glossary.

Sandy frowned at me. 'DH means "Dear husband"? Seriously? Thank God we have our resident in-house translator. Right, let's get to it. We need that list.'

Anyone Dimitri considered an enemy could be a potential candidate for one of the three Russian allies we needed to join Rok-Tech's Board and help Sergei both take over the company and push through the sale of the VirtuWorld software.

The whiteboard screen updated to exterior shots of Isaac Onegin's five-storey house.

'I've got the architect's plans from their recent revamp. The study is on the ground floor.' Nicola's fingers were flying across her keyboard. 'Looking at the plans of the room's inbuilt joinery, there's one floor-to-ceiling cupboard that's reinforced and fire-proofed. That must be where the recordings are stored.' Like most of those paranoid about how anything that left a digital imprint could be hacked it wasn't surprising that Isaac relied on old-school tapes to record his meetings.

Sandy looked round the table. 'This type of intel is exactly why Dasha is essential to this mission. The break-in to Isaac's house needs to happen tomorrow night. The sooner we get the company takeover plan in place the sooner we can move to popping the Weasel.' He waved us away with a flourish. 'So get to it.' We all stood up, the plastic chairs scraping on the concrete floor.

I reached for my mobile and looked down at the screen. Three missed calls from Will. I tried to ignore the fact my heart was now beating twice as fast. Gigi would now be with Gillian, my mother-in-law. She looked after her three afternoons a week as Will and I had thought as a lonely widow she would relish quality time with her granddaughter. And then there was also the fact she was free childcare.

If something was wrong she surely would have rung me first.

Unless she hadn't been able to get through.

Even with the special signal boosters the reception down here could still sometimes be patchy.

I walked out of the meeting room into the corridor and rang him back. Five long rings before he answered.

'Hello, darling.' It sounded like he was eating. 'I was in Sainsbury's, just wanted to know if we needed anything and if you'll be in for dinner tonight?'

I exhaled a long breath. Why was my reflex reaction to panic? New-mother paranoia? Or because I knew too much about how bad things happened?

I thought back to the question my nice, normal husband was asking his nice, normal wife. I sighed. We had just over twenty-four hours to work out how to break into a fortified mansion.

'I'll probably be working late, so sadly not.' Now that I was back at work Will and I would undoubtedly see even less of each other. While my job was never going to be a normal nine-to-five, Will's involved just as many late nights. He was often dragged out to client dinners or stuck in the office until it was far past Gigi's bedtime and nearing mine.

'Well that's disappointing. I was going to whip up a little . . .' – a pause and a rustle – 'beef bourguignon and dauphinoise potatoes.' More rustling. 'Or a Thai red chicken curry with fragrant rice.'

'It will have to be another night, Masterchef.'

As much as I now cherished having Will to come home to, it had been a big adjustment at first. I had to think of answers to the inevitable awkward questions, like why did I keep getting called in to the 'office' in the middle of the night? The explanation that a lot of the data we received was from all over the world and time sensitive was greeted with grumbles that I should get a pay rise. And how was it I was so accident-prone, he had wanted to know, when in the space of one week I had bruised ribs (someone got a lucky kick in) and a sprained wrist (a bad fall from a moving car). He'd laughed as he'd gently suggested that I should perhaps stop cycling in to work as I clearly wasn't very good at it. Such concern was touching but also annoying. A few times after that I'd found myself wanting to shout at whoever I was fighting, 'Not the face! Not the face!' knowing that blows there were always the hardest to cover up.

'At least you got the morning off, right? What did you and Gigi get up to?' There was a crunch as he continued to eat his lunch.

Truth? I used her as a prop to help me covertly make contact with a woman who, just like the shadowy Secret Service branch I work for, wants her husband dead. You know, just usual mum stuff.

'We had a nice walk, stopped for a coffee, nothing too exciting.' I looked up and saw the rest of Unicorn making their way out of the meeting room. 'I'd better go.'

'Okay, sweetheart. See you later. Love you.'

'You too.' I could never say the word 'love' out loud down here. In a place where the sun never shone and people screamed more than they laughed, hearing heartfelt sentiments was as incongruous as seeing a bright shiny rainbow streaking across the mottled grey walls.

I never thought I would be one of the Rats to try to stand with a foot in both worlds. To juggle the dark with the light.

At first it had been easy. Will may have married me but he didn't change me. I still had my secrets. I was still me. From single to spouse was no great journey. Wife to mother was the leap that took me out into the unknown. I was dominated, exhausted and overwhelmed. I couldn't remember me anymore; it was now all about her.

On my first trip back home to introduce my parents to their granddaughter, we all ate dinner in the kitchen that I grew up in. A living snapshot from my childhood: Beatrix Potter coaster incongruously stuck halfway up the wall just right of the sink to hide a chipped tile; multicoloured dishcloths hanging over the leather armchair in the corner. Everything looked the same. Except there was Gigi perched on top of the worn wooden table, asleep in her bouncy chair. Mum couldn't sit still, she kept getting up and down, bringing condiments we didn't need, filling up drinks that were already full. Will talked to Dad about his latest case while I looked over at the red Aga. Beneath it a ratty old dog bed with a black pug snoring on his back. When I lived in this house I would spend hours sitting on the floor leaning against the warmth of the oven, one hand on the head of a different snoring black pug. Planning my escape from my gilded life of normality.

It was at this kitchen table, nearly twenty years ago, I had sat with a policeman, stirring a milky tea. At thirteen I didn't drink tea but I hadn't wanted to say no. It seemed tea was part of the whole ritual of making someone feel better.

'So you and your friends saw everything?'

'We heard shouting and saw a man being chased by two others. He ran straight past us, across the road and right into the car.'

'And you were the first to reach the body?'

I had understood, then. You die and you are just a body. An empty vessel. The body, when he was still a person, had gone flying up in the air upon impact, a strange mid-air dance, where arms flailed, and his bag's contents came rising out in a long arc, until they all landed with a loud thud and a crunch on the tarmac. There was a pause and then the high-pitched screaming started. I heard my friends over my shoulder as I walked towards the crumpled man on the road. His limbs at right angles to each other. Blood pooling round the back of his head. A couple of wallets, a broken pearl necklace and a few smashed CD cases circled him. His eyes were shut, beads of sweat were still slowly rolling down his forehead. There was a slow gurgling noise that seemed to be coming out of his mouth. I had tilted my head and listened as his lungs, already full of blood, expelled his last breath.

'I was the first there, along with the driver.' The elderly man who had come out of the driver's seat had taken one look and started retching by the side of the car.

'It must have been very upsetting for you.'

'Of course.' I knew then it was best not to share that all I had thought as I stared down at the broken body was, 'That's what you get for being on the rob.'

I had sat tracing the outline of the chipped corner of the kitchen table as the policeman continued to ask me questions. Inside I was buzzing. A dead man on the road was a different reality to the one I knew, where life was safe and all about schoolwork, fumbling boys and well-meaning adults.

I looked at my beautiful sleeping daughter as I ran a finger along the bumpy ridge of the table corner. For these last few years, before she arrived, I had had a life where everything may have been darker but brighter for it. It was a rip-roaring technicolour ride of danger, close calls and big guns.

But now here I was. Bouncing Gigi's chair with one hand as I toyed with a forkful of shepherd's pie with the other. Will and Dad had moved on to discussing the ups and downs of the stock exchange. Mum reached over and tapped my plate. 'You really must finish all that. Your milk supply will suffer if you don't eat.'

I was firmly back in the beige.

Stripped down of all that made me special, that made me different.

That was more frightening than the danger that waited for me at work.

After those three long days with my parents I'd sat in a play-ground listening to screeches of 'You give that back, Archie! Sharing is caring!' and 'Isla, if you keep pushing you're going in the naughty corner,' interspersed with the crescendo of toddlers laughing and screaming.

Real life. No colourful gloss or sheen to it. The paint on the climbing frame was chipped. The snot on the kids' noses was crusted. Maclaren buggies were parked by the swings, sprinkled with crushed biscuit crumbs and smoothie stains – remnants of bribery to keep their passengers content. This was the frontline of parenthood.

I checked my watch for the fourth time since I'd sat down and looked at my beautiful daughter. I would do anything in the world for her.

Anything except do this every day.

I needed the dark to appreciate the light.

I'd confirmed the start date for my return to the Platform as soon as I'd got home.

Chapter Six

MEN WERE IRRITATINGLY WEAK. Last night Jake had left the Platform complaining he had a sore throat coming on. This morning he had called in to report he couldn't get out of bed, let alone undertake a covert break-in.

'They would hear my hacking cough miles away,' was his pathetically husky response to my calls to Lemsip the fuck up and come help me.

Over the years I had noticed my male colleagues seemed able to take all manner of physical pain in the line of duty but at the first sign of a sniffle acted like the world was ending. I often thought if our enemies wanted to decimate Eight's resources, forget releasing anthrax through our air supply, just a big dose of flu would be enough to cripple our workforce. They would all head home with blocked sinuses, complaining that it hurt to swallow and how they were cold, so cold.

In Jake's absence, Robin would be in Unicorn's van outside and on standby if I needed back-up. I was nervous. Sandy's warning that I was being closely watched was all the more reason tonight had to go perfectly. It had a been over a year since I had been out on an op. Being not quite back to my fighting weight might simply be an expression for some, but for me it was really quite literal. The extra kilos were not going to help when ducking and diving from aggressive hostiles or leaping across rooftops in a fast escape.

'You need to get approved for active duty.' I looked up to see Sandy in the office doorway. 'You know the drill.'

'I'm busy prepping for a solo break-in tonight. Now's not the time for a shrink appointment and a workout.'

'Tyler, it's non-negotiable. You've been out of Eight for a year. And you've had a bloody baby. You could have post-natal depression and the code to a room full of semi-automatic weapons. Or be so out of shape you collapse right in the middle of a getaway.'

We stared at each other. I broke first.

'Fine. I'm waiting on some Surveillance files so I might as well take a break.'

Doc's office was at the end of a long network of corridors adjoining one of our main tunnels. His door was marked out from the rest by the large red light above it.

It was off. Doc was alone. I knocked and opened the door. A small, slight man with tortoiseshell glasses was sitting at a sturdy old partner's desk with an iPad in front of him. Unlike the rest of Platform Eight, Doc's office was decorated. There was a large Persian rug on the floor and the room was lit by the soft glow of antique lamps. Beautiful landscapes in gilded frames were hung around the room. I had wasted a lot of time in our previous sessions wondering how he had managed to drill holes into the reinforced concrete walls.

Behind his desk hung ornate blue velvet curtains. Sitting there in what felt like the study of a grand house, you could nearly believe drawing back the curtains would flood the room with light from a large, beautiful window, rather than revealing just an empty wall deep underground while the concerto softly playing on his stereo drowned out the rumbling of the tube trains.

'Welcome back, Alexis.' He didn't get up from his leather armchair.

'Thanks, Doc.' We had never been offered his name. None of us knew anything about him or what his actual qualifications were. I wouldn't be surprised if he wasn't even a shrink. Just some low-level data analyst the Platform asked to play the part so it looked like they were ticking all the boxes. I always wondered what kind of qualified psychiatrist would create tests where to 'pass' we needed to be totally okay with killing people.

'You've had a baby since we last saw each other.'

'Yes. A little girl.' I sank down on to the red sofa, its plumped up feather cushions enveloping me in a soft hug.

'So.' He leaned forward. 'How have you found becoming a mother?'

'Great,' I said, in the perkiest voice I could muster.

'You haven't had any feelings that have concerned you?'

'None at all.'

I didn't think telling him I loved my daughter so much that the idea of anyone trying to harm her made me want to tear them limb from limb would be the best way to start my mental assessment.

Or that I had never felt more vulnerable knowing that if anyone ever wanted to hurt me all they had to do was hurt her and I would be done for.

Nor did I want to share with him the dark days where I felt like I was looking down the barrel of a gun, a long tunnel of broken sleep, and days spent being completely responsible for the life of a human being and wanting to howl at the terrifying enormity of it all. The shock of knowing I was forever changed. Assassin to bodyguard. And on a mission that would only end with my last breath.

'I'm glad to hear that.' He leaned forward. 'Did you ever doubt your ability to look after a new baby?'

'I read a lot of books. They helped.'

I was lying. They didn't. I read so many and they all said different things. I thought back to those first few weeks when if Gigi cried I would be hovering over her cot thinking, *Is she tricking me into cuddling her? And if I give in do I become her bitch? Or will leaving her to cry lead to lifelong trouble forming bonds with other people? But if I keep picking her up will she be horribly insecure as an adult unless she's being showered with physical affection? Oh, God, could holding her too much make her a slut? Or is not holding her enough going to make her a slut as she's going to try and make up for it later on? Maybe I could just rock her back to sleep? But then won't that mean she won't ever sleep unless being rocked? Surely someone must have invented a cot that automatically rocks? If not I can build my own. But then what if it malfunctions and it over-rocks and kills her and everyone says she died of shaken-baby syndrome and no one will believe it was my robotic rock cot? Oh, 'rock cot', that's a good name. I should patent that. Maybe I could use a dummy? But don't dummies delay their speech? Or ruin teeth? And aren't they impossible to give up? But then don't they help prevent cot death? So if I give her one she's more likely to live but eventually be a monosyllabic teenager with braces who sometimes still needs a dummy? But then aren't nearly all teenagers monosyllabic and with braces? Is that because they're teenagers or because they all had dummies? Oh, God, maybe I can just feed her again? But then the whole routine will be off for the day. But then maybe I shouldn't follow a routine and just feed her on demand? Didn't one study show babies fed on demand were more intelligent? Or was that the routine-fed babies? Oh, wait, was it the 'tried and failed to get into a routine' ones that were the cleverest? But then if you try and fail, isn't that the same as being fed on demand? Fuck. Can I google that with one hand while I'm holding her?*

I felt like I was tiptoeing through a minefield. One wrong move and everything would blow up. But all I said was, 'I learnt to muddle through.'

'That's good.' He nodded. 'You've got an impressive record here at Eight,' he said looking down at his iPad. 'You've undertaken nearly as many missions abroad as you have on home turf. Venezuela, China, Turkey, Saudi Arabia, Zimbabwe . . . and that was just in your first few years.' He swiped a finger across the screen. 'And so many different adversaries . . . domestic terrorists, drug barons, paedophile rings. I see you got a commendation for that mission.' He took his glasses off and looked up at me. 'After such a busy ten years here you must've really enjoyed having so much time to relax at home.'

'Relax at home? It was hardly bloody relaxing,' I said sharply. 'Work is a hell of a lot easier.' Maybe the comfort of the sofa and the soothing tones of another concerto were taking effect. Perhaps the Platform had encoded a truth serum within each stanza.

'That's interesting. Considering work has a high chance of getting you killed.' He leant back against his armchair.

I needed to explain myself.

'No one ever talks about the boredom of maternity leave. How difficult it can be.'

I didn't share with him how, at the beginning, each morning as Gigi and I stood on the doorstep waving Will off to work I would be suppressing the urge to cry, 'Please don't leave me.'

Doc poured himself a glass of water from the large jug on his desk.

'So tell me, what would you do all day?'

'I did a lot of playing with her on her playmat.' The truth being I would watch TV, or flick through online showbiz gossip and rage at the photos of perky D-listers 'showing off their post-baby bodies', while occasionally flinging toys at Gigi to chew.

'We went shopping together.' I stocked up on things I could easily buy online, but wanted an excuse to get out of the house.

'And we went to baby classes together.' In which I'd determined you could take any activity, stick the word 'baby' in front of it, charge twenty quid and besotted parents wouldn't notice that their offspring's dribbling on a maraca, being dunked in a swimming pool or having their limbs contorted into 'downward dog' was in no way anything like the actual advertised activity. When I had looked around the faces of the ecstatic other mothers enjoying magical bonding time I had felt horribly alone.

As if he could read my mind his next question was, 'Do you think other mothers felt the same as you? That maternity leave was hard work?'

'I don't know. Maybe not.' I had worried that my lack of enthusiasm for the mundane side of parenting was just part of my whole not-normal psyche. The part that helped me find it okay to kill people also meant I didn't cherish every second with my beloved daughter.

Doc started typing into his iPad. He eventually looked up.

'How are things with your husband? Tempers can fray with a new baby.'

In those first couple of months there were days where I wanted to hug Will close. Together we had created the world's most perfect baby and the three of us were now a family.

Other days I wanted to punch him in the face.

Or worse.

Once a full bottle of expressed milk slipped out of my hand. Upon seeing it spill all over the place I'd collapsed to the floor sobbing. Will's jovial, 'There's no use crying over spilt milk,' had me mentally loading an automatic machine gun and spraying him with bullets.

'We're great.'

I may have every now and then thought about killing the father of my child but I never actually did it. Which had to count for something. And now the hormone and exhaustion levels had settled down, so too had my inner rages.

'And how do you feel about your daughter?'

'She's the best thing I've ever done. She's changed my life for the better.'

'So you love having a daughter but you hate being a mother?'

'No. Actually, yes. But no.' This was not going so well. 'I just found maternity leave challenging.' I had missed conversation. Using my brain. Combat. Sleep. My body. Scaring the shit out of people. Being more than just a milk machine.

'So that's why you came back to work. You didn't like being at home?'

I bit my lip and ignored the dig. 'I came back to work because I felt ready to.'

Doc looked as if he expected me to say more. He wasn't going to get it. I wasn't going to confess that I needed my work life down here to balance out my home life up there. To suffocate rather than be suffocated.

The music played on as we stared at each other.

'Look, Doc, I might be a mother now but I can do my job just as well as I did before. Considering how many Rats are parents I'm surprised you're making such an issue of this.' I was daring him to say the unspoken. That it was different because I was a woman.

He remained silent.

'Just sign me off as fit for duty and I promise to not go on a wild violent killing spree.' I smiled. 'Unless it's department sanctioned.'

Safe in the knowledge I had the all-important green light from Doc, I headed to Platform Eight's gym. Adjoining the car park, the gym was a square room, thirty metres wide with mirrored walls and filled with rows of high-tech gym equipment. In the centre was a boxing ring. My latest adversary was perky, blonde and bare-knuckle pounding one of the punch bags along the back wall.

Her ponytail swished as she turned around to face me.

'Holy shit, what happened to you? You look terrible. Your face . . . all the light has drained out of it. You look so much older. And so tired. I know you can't talk about it but whoever held you hostage has really done a number on you.' She circled me and slapped my thighs. 'It's weird to gain so much weight in captivity . . .'

Candy Reardon was Eight's in-house fitness instructor.

I had always hated her.

'Actually, Candy, I just had a baby.'

'Wow.' She clasped a hand to her mouth and giggled. 'Really? That's all?' She gave me another once-over. 'I mean, even your arms have got fatter. How does that happen? It's just so weird – the baby's only in your tummy, right? How does the fat just spread everywhere?'

'Water. Retention,' I said through gritted teeth.

Candy's pink manicured nails were already flicking through her iPad. 'I see your upcoming mission is a residential break-in. Luckily nothing too strenuous but you'll need to pass a fitness test before I can clear you as fit for duty.' She motioned towards the training bike. 'Climb aboard. Then it's the running machine, then the cross-trainer, then weights and then you do it all over again. And again.'

As irritating as I found her there was no denying Candy was good at her job. She had a steely authority that kept even the hardest of Rats in line. We all knew that she had the power to bench us, and as such she needed to be respected.

I got on to the bike and started pedalling.

I knew I should be grateful. Most new mothers hardly have the time to get back in shape, let alone the motivation. When sleep-deprived, getting up off the sofa was tough, never mind doing a few laps round the park.

But here I had no option but to get fit again. As Candy kept screaming at me – my job depended on it. My life depended on it. Since having Gigi I had a newfound respect for my body. It had created, carried and borne life. And now, sporting the after-effects of this monumental act, I needed to remember the bigger picture. I might never fit a pair of jeans the way I used to. But fuck it. I had birthed a human. And I needed to get back in shape not because I really gave a shit about how I looked in a bikini, but because being strong meant being healthy. Being strong meant staying alive.

Who cared about beach body? I needed battle body.

'Okay, Lex, that's it.'

I dropped the handlebar of weights I was holding and sank to the floor. Sweat was pooling into my cleavage.

'You've passed. Just.' Candy shook her head. 'A year ago you were one of my top-performing Rats and now you're barely scraping through. I'm going to up your training sessions to daily. We've got a lot of work to do.'

At 8 p.m., with one hour to go until departure for Isaac Onegin's house, I went over the plans for the break-in. It should be a straightforward job. The easiest break-ins were those when the owners were home and still awake. No alarm system to disman-tle thanks to the sweet belief intruders always waited until eve-ryone was tucked up in bed. Surveillance records showed their cook left every night at 10 p.m. by the basement door. Earlier in the afternoon Robin had succeeded in slotting a small device, which Geraint had named 'the jammer', into its locking mecha-nism by posing as a delivery man.

Tonight, as the door shut behind the departing cook, the jammer, activated remotely by Robin in our van, would stop the lock from working and hold the catch back for a whole four minutes. I needed to be in position to race in as soon as the cook was clear of the basement entrance. Beyond that was a short flight of stairs up to the study on the ground floor. Surveillance had reported that after dinner neither Onegin nor his wife ever ventured back downstairs, preferring to stay on the first floor to continue drinking in the dining room or stumble through to their home cinema.

Nothing shouted wealth more than having a dining room two floors away from the kitchen – who needed them next to each other when you had staff?

I headed to the ladies' toilet. The very few women of the Platform had fought hard for this room. It was a converted broom cupboard with just enough space for a loo and a sink but at least the floor wasn't pee-stained and there wasn't always some guy straining in a stall. No one had gotten round to getting a mirror for above the sink but where one should have been someone had written on the wall in marker pen, 'It's okay, you're beautiful!'

I had yet to work out if it had been done by one of the other women as a shout-out to her fellow sisters, or by one of the guys as a sarcastic piss-take.

The wobbly shelf above the sink was crammed with a bumper pack of Panadol, a large bottle of foundation, a red lipstick (my go-to tool for looking dressed up and made up) and a small bottle of contact-lens solution (Nicola was always complaining how the long days in front of a computer screen hurt her eyes. I had once suggested she should just wear her glasses and she looked at me like I had spat at her). Next to the loo was a small red medical bin marked 'Anatomical Waste: Please Incinerate', borrowed from Interrogation, and used to dispose of sanitary products. All in all, it was nothing much, but it was all-female territory and an important sign that management realised that times were changing, women were capable of working in this world and that we were here to stay. One small room saying so much, all behind a door which had a crudely drawn outline of a woman with massive breasts brandishing a gun.

No confusion over whether it was us or them responsible for that bit of graffiti.

I attempted to manoeuvre myself into my Platform-issue skin-tight breaking-and-entering outfit. All-in-one black cat-suits with temperature-regulating microfiber, and inbuilt holsters for small-calibre pistols were not designed for lactating women with oversized breasts. It was a testament to the quality of the material that despite being severely overstretched it showed no signs of ripping under the strain. I pulled my coat on and headed to the car park.

From: 8teamsexxxy@availablerightnow.uk.com
To: lex.tyler@platform-eight.co.uk
Subject: *HOT*HORNY*READY*TO*GO
MISSION: #80436
UNIT: UNICORN
WEASEL: DIMITRI TUPOLEV
ALERT: ACTION INITIATED: ONEGIN BREAK-IN

Chapter Seven

'YOUR CARRIAGE AWAITS.' ROBIN flung open the passenger door of Unicorn's van.

I clambered in beside him and started to get in the zone. Heading out to a mission was not dissimilar to that feeling you get on the way to a party. You're all hyped up, ready to go, you get in the car, excited, anticipating what lies ahead, then, as the car pulls up outside the venue, the dread hits. What if I have no one to talk to? What if I die?

Tonight, though, the dread hit early. Halfway there I realised I had forgotten to put my breast pads in.

I tried to work out how bad this was.

All our training drilled us to never leave behind any physical sign of our presence. If an op went wrong and the room was swept after we left, there should be no identifiable traces of our DNA that could be kept and filed on a database. We were invisible. We didn't exist. I was in a high-spec specially designed suit, with inbuilt gloves and balaclava, all expertly engineered to limit the risk of leaving behind any remnant of my presence. And I was a ticking timebomb of imminent seepage. Was this going to be a minor inconvenience or a major problem? Did breast milk have DNA in? I outlined the problem to Robin. He looked at me eyes wide, mouth open.

His superior was talking to him about leaking breasts.

'Call Sandy?' Was all he could offer. I looked at my watch. We needed to be in position to operate the jammer in fifteen minutes and were still a few streets away from the house.

I took a deep breath and rang Sandy. From what I could gather, amid the loud expletives, he was not sure if breast milk had DNA in it either.

I tried to placate him. 'It's fine, I'll look it up on my phone.'

This just angered him more.

'Look it up on your *phone*? We have the full resources of the Security Services behind us. We have access to the country's top DNA specialists, experts who have actually undertaken research on this subject. Done studies.'

'Yes but it's nearly 10 p.m. It's going to be a bugger getting hold of anyone. And our window for the break-in ends in under ten minutes.'

There was a long pause.

'Okay, fine.' I could hear the grimace down the phone as he gritted his teeth. 'Fucking google it. Just sort this out.'

My friend Google confirmed yes, breast milk did have DNA in it. Shit. We had seven minutes to go by the time we found an all-night chemist and Robin had raced in shouting, 'Breast pads! Breast pads!' When we finally pulled up outside Isaac's house it was 10.03 p.m.

We could have missed our window.

I stared at the door, willing it to open. Two long minutes later, the cook stepped out.

Robin activated the jammer.

As soon as she was clear of the house I slunk down the stairs and gently pushed open the door.

I was in.

I walked past the industrial-sized kitchen and headed straight to the bottom of the stairs. I stopped and listened. Hearing only the distant noise of a television, I headed up to the ground floor. The large oak-panelled door to the study was halfway down the hallway. Moving fast, I slipped inside and gently closed the door behind me. Along the back wall of the study was domineering mahogany floor-to-ceiling joinery, which, according to the architects' plans concealed a secure fire-proof cupboard within it. I silently opened the large wooden double doors, revealing another door – except this one was made of reinforced metal and had a keypad. Exactly which company had fitted this custom-built cupboard had been easy to track down and thankfully the brand and make of the keypad were exactly what I was expecting. I fixed Geraint's specialist safe-cracker, a small black box the size of a mobile phone, to the keypad. The lights on it flashed red as it started to attempt to break the code. It should only take a few minutes. I stared at the lights willing them to go green.

The silence was broken by the unmistakable click-clack of heels on marble stairs. Shit.

I looked around the study. There was nothing but a large partners' desk, Russian-book-lined shelves, a leather sofa and a flatscreen on the wall. Clearly his territory and not hers. The click-clacks grew louder as she headed down the hallway towards me. I closed the wooden doors as best I could but the bulk of the safe-cracker attached to the keypad stopped me from shutting it completely. I had to hope she wasn't going to come in. I quickly moved across the room and stood behind the door; there were nowhere else to hide. The click-clacks came to a halt. I held my breath and waited for the door to open.

It stayed shut.

Then a whispered, 'When can I see you?' Silence and then low laughter. 'Oh yes, I can definitely help you with that.' A pause. 'I'm going to be thinking of that when I'm alone later.' More laughter. 'You bad, bad boy! That's just the type of cardio I was thinking of. That place next to the gym, then? I'm going to—'

A shout from upstairs echoed down the hallway.

'What's taking so long?'

'I can't find it!' she yelled back.

'Just hurry up.'

'Christ, Isaac . . . Give me a bloody chance.' Her Essex twang came out stronger when she was angry.

I looked over at the mahogany cupboard. The door was ajar and I could just see that the lights on Geraint's device were now amber. I checked my watch; one minute to go.

'Get my iPad while you're down there. It's in the study.'

Shit. I squashed myself up behind the door as it opened and she came in. I bit my lip.

'Do you see what I live with?' she whispered. 'Fucking hell.' My view was blocked by the door but I heard her stalk up to the desk and a rustle of papers as she looked for the iPad. With any luck she might not notice the fact her husband's usually secure cupboards had one door ajar.

'I know, darling. Don't worry, we'll make up for it tomorrow.' A pause and then low giggles. 'I can't. I mean, I want to . . .' She let off a gentle moan. 'Oh yes. That's exactly what I need . . .'

I grimaced. I always knew there would be moments where I would question if coming back to work would be the right thing to do. And now here I was, not at home watching Netflix with my husband as our baby slept upstairs, but hiding behind a door, listening to a stranger about to have extra-marital phone sex.

'What the hell are you doing down there?' Another shout from her oblivious husband.

'For fuck's sake,' she muttered before yelling back, *'I'm coming!'* She lowered her voice again. 'Well now I'm bloody not.' She giggled. 'So tomorrow night, sweetcheeks. We can finish what we started.' She ended the call and walked out the door, letting it slam behind her.

I exhaled slowly and walked quickly over to the cupboard. The green lights were flashing and a four-digit number was displayed on the screen. I entered the numbers into the keypad and heard the welcoming clunk of the locks opening. Pulling open the metal doors I was confronted with rows and rows of drawers, each one neatly labelled with dates. They went back years – Isaac clearly didn't trust any of his many business associates. I flicked through the drawers until I found last Friday's date. There were three tapes for that day but only one of them had the initials 'D.T.' on – I pocketed the tape and returned the empty box.

Now to get out of here.

Isaac and Dimitri had more in common than they realised; they were both powerful, rich men being betrayed by their wives. One was in bed with her personal trainer and the other was in bed with the British security services.

Although only one of these illicit relationships would lead to bloodshed.

'I told you Isaac, I'm not watching another fucking war film,' came the shrill scream from upstairs.

Or maybe not.

I crept out of the study and started to head down the corridor when a faint jangling noise made me stop. What the hell was that? The sound got slightly louder and I looked to the stairs just as a small white Chihuahua wearing a pink diamante colour with a little bell attached to it came into view.

Fuck.

The Onegins' file had clearly stated 'no pets'. There was a pause as the dog observed me. I froze, although I knew it was pointless. The barking began. It flew down the stairs towards me.

I heard Isaac roar, 'Christ. Your sister's bloody dog got out again.'

There was nothing left to do but run.

I raced down the stairs and through the kitchen, the dog yapping at my heels, its barks getting more and more high-pitched. I made it to the basement door, I turned around, picked the dog up and slid it across the polished resin floor, its four legs spreading as it careered back across the kitchen to the bottom of the stairs. The shock of its sudden speedy journey altered its barks into one long low yelp. Better for Isaac to find it shell-shocked there rather than yapping at the door as if someone had just left. I made out a 'What the hell is wrong with you, Sparkles?' just as I quietly closed the basement door and slipped out into the cold and quiet of the night.

I collapsed into our bed, exhausted, and curled up next to a sleeping Will.

Two minutes later, Gigi started crying. And didn't really stop until daybreak.

All night I paced the floors, letting her comfort feed as I counted down the minutes until I could dose her again with Calpol. Bloody teeth. They obviously hurt just as much coming in as they did coming out.

It was a special kind of torture to put in a full day at work and then have to put in a full night at home. I'd had no idea just what I was pulling the pin on when, over a year ago, I had sat staring at a little pee-covered stick bracing myself for impact.

No other inanimate object could give such profound joy or misery to different women, or even the same women just at different times in their life.

Pregnant. BOOM! And everything was changed forever.

As dawn broke, I looked down at Gigi, finally asleep in my arms. Her long eyelashes still damp with tears. Her little chest slowly going up and down. The sound of her soft breathing. It was all worth it.

I crept towards the cot and gently lowered her in. The foghorn screaming started again.

Except maybe on nights like these.

'Lex, get the fuck in here,' shouted Sandy from his open office door.

The next morning I was so sleep deprived I felt like I was seeing stars. There was an ache in the back of my head that wouldn't stop.

'Morning,' I trilled as I walked in. It was a naïve hope that blinding him with perkiness would encourage him to forget the phone call about my breasts being an operational liability. Sandy was sitting with his feet up on his desk chewing on the end of a biro.

'So what the hell happened last night?'

'The operation was successful. Geraint and Nicola are now going through the tape of Dimitri and Isaac's meeting and we should have the names within the hour.' So much for hoping he would focus on the positives.

'Right now I feel like I'm walking into a bathroom and sniffing air-freshener. It may smell of roses but we all know an almighty fucking shit has just happened.' He threw his pen down on to the table. 'Is this what they call postnatal dementia? Total bloody baby brain? There are studies' – he gestured towards the open browser on his laptop – 'that claim mothers shouldn't return to work for at least a year as the hormone imbalance can affect their decision-making.'

'Where the hell did you find such total crackpot information?'

'Consider this a formal warning. You know what's at stake here. If Dimitri and his crew get one hint as to what we're planning the whole mission is at stake and we're one step closer to The President becoming the all-knowing master of the universe.' He shook his head. 'We're meant to be the best of the best. The elite. We don't potentially jeopardise operations by forgetting essential equipment. No matter how bloody weird it is.' He gave a shudder.

'Understood, Sandy.' I stared down at the floor. I knew he was right. Such an oversight was unforgivable. Maybe the last year had taken its toll after all. Made me weaker. A defective weapon. Why hadn't I ever stopped to think that there might be some truth to whispers that I was no longer up to the job?

Sandy sighed. 'Just get out of here.' He dismissed me with a hand wave.

Bennie McGinn was leaning outside the office door.

'Seems someone is in trouble.' I noticed he was wearing a blue shirt with his jeans. His hero worship of Jake had obviously extended to copying his wardrobe.

'Jesus, Bennie, fuck off, please.' I pushed past him, headed in search of a very strong coffee.

'That's no way for a lady to talk.'

'Last I heard ladies shouldn't kill people either.' I stopped. 'Oh, wait, or wasn't that "people shouldn't kill people"?'

'Sounds like Sandy enjoyed his reading material.' I didn't look at Bennie, but I could hear the smile in his voice. He was obviously very pleased with himself.

'That was you? You really don't have anything better to do than look up studies on hormonally deranged mothers?' I shook my head. 'You're a sad little boy. Maybe if you actually used your dick rather than just acting like one you would relax a little.' I turned into the canteen.

'I use my dick all the time!' he exclaimed as he followed me in. His face dropping when he saw that a selection of Rats were sitting at the tables reading the morning newspapers and drinking coffee. There was deep laughter and a few slow hand claps.

'Well done, Bennie, that's great to hear. But I'm still not interested.'

'Fuck you, Lex.' His face twisted as he left to a chorus of heckles and catcalls.

Embarrassing Bennie was not enough retribution for trying to get me in the shit with Sandy but it was a nice start. I poured myself a large coffee, took a pastry and sat down at a table with two Rats who were busy debating an article featuring a German leather-clad dominatrix's affair with a married Brexit-supporting Tory MP.

'I'm telling you that's a bloody Sheep!'

'No chance. It's a Wolf without a doubt.'

We weren't the only under-the-radar branch of the Secret Services.

Another important division, that no one without high-level clearance even knew existed, managed deep undercover agents who were frequently dispatched to unduly influence public opinion. These 'Wolves in Sheep's clothing' would move in for a public-relations kill and then abandon the scene of the crime to continue on with their next takedown.

Joe, the Rat next to me, motioned to another photo of the girl in her underwear, this time draped in the European Union flag.

'What do you reckon, Lex? Wolf or Sheep?'

I leant over and read: *As a prominent MP wanting hard Brexit it was no surprise that when I spanked him he would shout 'harder, harder!'*

'Wolf. Definitely. That line is too good for a Sheep. He can now never say the word "hard" in public without everyone laughing.'

Nothing helped camaraderie more than us Rats enjoying the superiority we felt over everyone else as we reviewed the papers in the canteen. The unsuspecting members of the public thought they were reading news, real-life events. We knew that at least half of what the newspapers were reporting were carefully engineered events and manufactured characters. We may all have been bit players, following the orders of the all-knowing Committee, but at least we knew about it. We had the inside scoop, even if we had as much influence over what was decided as the blissfully oblivious Sheep.

A litre of coffee and two pain au chocolat later I ventured into Unicorn's office. It was a stark room with just five desks, empty except for small laptops. No landlines – we only ever used our mobiles. We didn't need any filing cabinets as we had no paper to file. Although I was sure it was only a matter of time before Health and Safety reached the sanctity of the Platform. I imagined filling out a pre-mission risk assessment form. Hazards: Ten men with automatic machine guns and a few grenades. Potential consequences: Death/ Losing a limb or two. Action required: Shoot them before they shoot us. Secondary action: Keep our bloody fingers crossed.

Nicola was sitting at her desk, wearing a clinging black wool jumpsuit and orange high-top trainers. Thanks to the dodgy air ventilation down here it was always too warm. How could she not be boiling? I bet Nicola didn't ever sweat.

Geraint stood up as I came in.

'Good work on Onegin's tape. We've just got a translated transcript of the recording. It's Isaac and Dimitri talking about everyone who they consider a threat to Rok-Tech and whose business Dimitri wants to either crush or buy out.'

'There are nine men on the list,' added Nicola. 'We've been undertaking some initial research but Russian businessmen who oppose The President and his regime tend to not advertise it. We'll have to dig pretty deep to work out exactly where their loyalties lie.'

I took this in. We needed to narrow down who were going to be the best candidates willing to work with us and help the inexperienced Sergei take over Rok-Tech. We couldn't risk approaching the wrong person and blowing the whole mission.

Doing our own research on each individual would take a lot of time, time we didn't have. We needed a shortcut.

We needed to steal someone else's homework.

'The Russian Embassy. Find out when their next event is and get Jake and me on the list.'

The embassy would have detailed files on every single one of their high-profile high-net-worth citizens. I knew from a previous operation that all the embassy's data was backed up on their main server; which we could gain control of if we were able to insert one of Geraint's 'hack sticks' into it. Something Jake and I could easily do once we had got through the hard part of gaining access into the building under the guise of partygoers.

'You're in luck,' said Nicola. 'There's a "Building Bridges in Business" drinks reception in two days time. You're both now formally attendees.'

Forty-eight hours. Just enough time to familiarise ourselves with the embassy's floorplans, prepare our equipment, and for me to try to find something to wear.

Chapter Eight

'NOT BAD TYLER, NOT bad,' was Jake's assessment of my 'Building Bridges in Business' attire of tailored black dress and killer heels.

Unlike normal heels, mine really were 'killer'. What looked like a standard pair of stilettos had been expertly adapted by our R & D team. With a deft click, each heel slid off and unsheathed blades that were hidden within the sole; a weapon for each hand and shoes I could now easily run in. Fight and flight.

I'd joined him in the street, the embassy entrance in our sights. We watched the numerous black taxis of party guests arriving.

'You just need a little something to complete your outfit.' Jake reached inside his jacket pocket and pulled out a large, sparkly necklace. He looked down at me as he fastened it round my neck. For someone with such big hands he was remarkably nimble at handling fiddly catches. He was so close I could feel his breath on my face. He adjusted it until the largest gem was in the centre. 'Perfect.'

We arrived at the embassy arm in arm and were directed towards two suited embassy security staff. One of them subjected Jake to a pat down while the other opened up my sequinned clutch bag. He pulled out my house keys, which were attached to a large photo keyring of Gigi's chubby, smiling face, before examining each of the make-up items inside. 'That's a tampon,' I added helpfully as he stared at a small brightly coloured wrapped Tampax. He grimaced and quickly dropped it back into my bag before ushering us through to the party.

One token glass of champagne later, we were able to manoeuvre our way out of the bustling main reception room and towards a door opposite it marked 'No Entry'. On the other side of this door, according to the floorplans we'd memorised, were a complicated network of corridors leading towards the server room. All the offices we had to pass to get there belonged to low-level staff who, with any luck, would have already headed home or joined the party next door.

I pressed the large stone on my gaudy necklace, sending a remote signal to Geraint who was outside in Unicorn's van.

Ten seconds passed and my necklace vibrated. A confirmation he had hacked the embassy's camera feed. I took my keys out of my handbag and held the keyring of Gigi up against the scanner next to the door. Her round face grinned out at us as the light above her head went green. We slipped through the door and made a fast series of turns down identical-looking corridors. Halfway to the server room we heard voices coming from the corridor up ahead. Jake checked through the window of the office door we had just passed and pulled me inside. We stood up against the door and listened as the voices and laughter got louder and then passed us by. I opened the door a crack and looked up and down the corridor – everything was quiet; like moths to a flame, any remaining embassy staff had flocked to the free champagne.

Motioning Jake to follow me we continued on to the imposing server room. The large door was made of steel. In place of a handle was a digital entry keypad.

I pulled my Touche Éclat pen out of my handbag. While it was still excellent at concealing dark circles and any unsightly blemishes, this pen was also magnetised. I stuck it on the bottom of the keypad. And excellent at jamming electric frequency. I pressed the stone on my necklace again. The error code flashing on the keypad was replaced with 'Enter'.

The server loomed down from the back wall, dominating the room. It had a small inbuilt screen and a keyboard beneath.

I opened my handbag and pulled out the brightly coloured Tampax. After ripping off the paper I dissected the tampon and took out a small radio earpiece, which I placed in my ear.

'Hello, Lex. This is your tampon talking.' Robin chuckled.

'Very funny, Robin. Get G-Force on, will you?'

'I'm here, Lex,' Geraint crackled in. 'Plug in the stick and we can begin. You've got twelve minutes until the hacked camera loop ends, so this needs to happen fast.' I took out my lipstick and, unscrewing the bottom of it, exposed a USB stick, which I inserted into the server's USB hub. Jake watched from the door as I stared at the hypnotic flashing amber light. The only sound was Geraint's tapping on his keyboard through my earpiece. The screen on the server lit up with a login page.

'Okay Lex. Eleven minutes. You need to follow exactly what I say.' There was a pause and then, 'Shit. Looks like they've added a few security firewalls since our last visit.'

'And that means what?'

'That USB you just put in should link my computer to the server's screen so I can take control of it. But it's not working.

It's asking for a login and password before it will let me get access.'

'How's that a problem? We know the login and password, right?' On our previous break-in, we had succeeded in cloning the embassy's security software, which generated a unique user-name and password every two weeks. 'Just dictate it to me and I can input it directly into the server.'

'Look at the keyboard.'

I looked down.

It was in Russian.

'You only have three attempts to get the login and password right before the whole server shuts down and security storms the room.'

I sighed. To think I had dared to hope this would be an easy in and out.

'What's the problem?' said Jake.

I turned to him. 'I need to log G-Force into the server and the keyboard's in Russian.' I checked my watch. 'We have nine minutes and only three login attempts before we're finished.'

We silently considered what lay ahead of us if we were caught by embassy security in this room. No one would come for us. We didn't officially exist.

Jake spoke first. 'Let's get on with it then.'

I took a deep breath and wished I could forget the images of what the Russians did to a colleague we lost a couple of years ago. They had discovered him somewhere he shouldn't have been. 'G-Man, we'll take it letter by letter. Describe each one to me.'

'Copy that.' I heard the sound of tapping keys. 'Okay, the first letter is a W with a tick on the bottom right.'

Geraint proceeded to reel off a long list of letters that varied from the easy 'It's an R but in reverse. Like it would be in a mirror,' to the more challenging, 'It's like a box on legs, but on a slight angle. Kind of like wiggly legs.' We managed it in less than two minutes.

'Okay let's do this.' I closed my eyes and winced as I hit the Enter button.

The login page remained, but red Russian writing, that I assumed screamed ERROR, appeared across it.

'Shit.'

Jake was at my side in an instant. 'What do you think you got wrong?'

'Not a clue.'

'You must have got the small N wrong,' Geraint said. 'The one you should have pressed has a slight tick at the end like someone lifting their foot up. You probably confused it with the other small N that's all totally straight lines.'

I looked at the keyboard and tried to remember.

'We don't have time to redo all of them. It has to be that one. Try replacing it – it was the second last letter of the password.' Geraint's voice remained level. But then it wasn't his life on the line.

I stared at the line of black dots and moved the cursor to the second last letter and deleted it, replacing it with the tick N. I took another deep breath and pressed Enter.

The screen went blank and then the red writing flashed up again.

'Fuck this,' was Jake's reaction. He started pacing the room.

I checked my watch. Five minutes until the cameras came back online. We might as well go down with a fighting chance of getting the information we came for.

I took a deep breath. 'Is there any other letter you think I could've screwed up?'

'Can you remember if the small B you pressed had a cape or a kind of roof?'

'The B was just before the backward slash, wasn't it? Yes I definitely hit the B with the kind of cape as the backward slash was right below it.'

'The cape was the right one so I've got no idea I . . . Wait, did you say backward slash? It's forward slash. Sorry was that my mistake or yours? I was so focused on the letters maybe I messed up.'

I stared again at the keyboard. I was positive I had hit backward slash. Only one way to know for sure. 'It was third character of the password, right?'

'Yes.'

Four minutes.

I replaced it with a forward slash and pressed Enter. The screen went blank. Jake and I held our breath.

And then a flashing cursor popped up.

A yelp in my ear from Geraint. 'I'm in! Give me two minutes and I'll get everything we need.' The server's screen was now a flurry of numbers and characters as Geraint worked his magic. 'You can go offline – once the screen goes black I'm done.'

I took my earpiece out and looked over at Jake. 'G-Force needs two minutes. Which leaves us just two minutes to get back to the party.'

I opened my handbag and carefully placed my earpiece back inside the tampon.

Jake watched me, smiling. 'Well the good news is you aren't going to have any trouble getting that in now that you've been totally annihilated down there.'

'Stop perving and do your bloody job.' He returned to his post by the door. Once his back was turned I lifted up my dress and tucked the tampon into the inner thigh of my high-rise Spanx shorts. Jake didn't need to know that my sculpted figure was a beautifully crafted illusion created through heavy-duty support underwear. And that trying to pull them down enough to put the tampon where our security protocols dictated it should go, would involve some rather ungraceful vigorous wiggling and ten minutes we didn't have. Besides if we got searched I was sure the Russians would find the Spanx as impossible to get me out of as my husband did.

I watched the server screen – the burst of activity stopped and it went black. I pulled my dress back down and unplugged the USB before screwing it back into my lipstick and dropping it into my handbag. 'Okay. Let's go.'

Jake opened the door a crack and looked outside before motioning me forward. No one in sight.

We ran.

With only a hundred metres to go we heard the sound of heavy footsteps, and the crackle of a headpiece approaching round the corner.

Jake slammed me up against the wall and started kissing me. It wasn't wrong that I kissed him back. It was wrong that I enjoyed it. It felt good to be kissed like that again, with an aggressive passion that was making me forget nearly everything else. Until we were pulled apart with a heavily accented, 'Hey, you can't be here.' A tall, balding Ruski in a badly fitted suit, which was doing a poor job of concealing the two handguns he had holstered, was staring at us.

'Oh my God, I am so, so mortified.' I giggled and shoved Jake. 'Darling, I told you we shouldn't be here. I must look so slutty right now.' I fell on to Jake, prodding his cheek with my finger. 'This is all your fault for getting me so horribly drunk.'

Jake grinned at the security guard and gave him a thumbs up. 'It's a great party right?'

The Ruski ignored him and grabbed my handbag before rifling through it and then throwing it back at me. He turned to Jake and patted him down, feeling inside his pockets.

Jake laughed. 'That tickles.'

He looked between us both.

'Get out of here. The party is back that way.' He motioned to the door behind us.

'We're very sorry, sir.' Jake put an arm round me. 'Don't know what came over us.'

'Yes, sir, we're very, very sorry.' I slouched up against Jake, and made a show of tottering on my heels as we walked away. Out of the corner of my eye I could see him talking furiously into his headpiece. We re-entered the party. Jake kept his hand on my back, as he guided me through the throngs of people.

A hovering waiter passed and we each reached for a glass of champagne and drained it.

Jake turned to the group of people next to us. 'Hi there. Fun party, isn't it? Tell me, what's your connection to the embassy?'

I joined in. 'Oh wow I love your dress, is it LK Bennett?'

The ten minutes of painful small talk with our new insurance-broker friends was by far the most torturous part of the whole evening. But we weren't escorted from the room and Geraint had what he needed. We'd done it.

Chapter Nine

'AND WHAT TIME DO you call this?' Will was sitting up in our bed, his laptop open on top of the duvet. He grinned as I leaned down and gave him a kiss.

'I hate work drinks.' I kicked off my heels and glanced at the baby monitor next to him. The grainy image of Gigi star-fished in her cot lit up the screen. 'Our little girl been behaving?'

'Perfectly. Three stories and a bit of milk and she was passed out by 7 p.m. and not a noise since.'

'How much milk? And did you let her fall asleep on you?'

'Half a bottle, I think. And you ask too many questions.' He tapped me on the nose with his finger. 'Get yourself to bed, sweetheart. I've got a painfully early start tomorrow.'

'That's me every day, *mon cher*,' I called over my shoulder as I walked through to the bathroom, 'especially if you keep breaking the rules.'

I was the routine Hitler. He was the fun-loving cavalier. Nappies, bottles, boobs – me. Songs, tickles, laughter – him. I would watch Will and Gigi together and envy how easy it was for him. Thoughts unclouded by hormones and sleep deprivation, his mind remained untouched and his body remained unchanged. He had taken on the role of father as easily as shrugging on a warm coat. Parenthood had added another layer to him without suffocating or slowing him down.

I was the one trying to catch up. Weighed down by a nappy bag full of fears and insecurities. Wanting to be the best mother I could be but not sure how. Killer instinct? Yes. Maternal instinct? Not so much.

I changed into one of Will's old shirts. In the early days I would pull one on on a lazy Sunday morning and sashay around the kitchen, him knowing I was naked underneath. Now I wore them because they were easy to breastfeed out of. Then sexy, now practical. Just like my breasts.

Will closed his laptop and moved it to the bedside table as I got into bed beside him.

'Remind me where you're flying off to tomorrow? And how long you're abandoning us for?'

It was his third business trip in as many weeks. I was glad I trusted him enough that I had no nagging desire to check in with Special Projects to verify his location. Upon my engagement to Will they had presented me with a two-hundred-page report on his life to date including bank statements, email passwords and social-media logins. I kept it for a week and then handed it back unopened. I knew I needed real life above the ground to be untouched by the dirtiness of the world beneath it.

Besides, if I was ever worried he was cheating I could just go through his phone while he was in the shower, like normal wives.

'It's only three days. I'm seeing a high-maintenance client in Texas.' He yawned. 'So all big guns, big egos and big bullshit.'

Our jobs really weren't so different.

He kissed me and rolled over to turn the light off. I lay staring at the ceiling knowing sleep would take a while. I was still buzzing. Tonight had gone exactly to plan. I needed to feel I could do this. Succeed at both. Rat and mother. Very different roles yet certain similar skillsets; attention to detail, an ability to multitask and an indifference to handling bodily fluids.

I listened as Will's breathing deepened. He was asleep already. I touched my lips. He may not have been my only kiss of the evening but at least he was my last.

Posing as a couple was an invaluable part of how successful Jake and I had been as partners. In response to my post-honeymoon complaint he didn't have to be quite so enthusiastic in our cover story I got a grumbled, 'Surely your husband would prefer my tongue in your mouth to someone else's bullet in your brain?'

It was a fair point.

If that security guard had discovered two men somewhere out of bounds it is highly unlikely they would have been able to talk their way out of it. Long ago I had squared it all away in my ordered mind as totally acceptable cheating but tonight it had felt wrong.

Maybe it was because I couldn't remember the last time Will and I had kissed like that. Tired and grumpy didn't really translate well in the bedroom. My idea of a night of unbridled pleasure was now a deep, deep sleep that would last all night long and end late-morning with a loud, satisfied yawn . . .

Will's hand was lying next to my face, touching my pillow. I kissed it and closed my eyes. I thought of Dasha, in her Notting Hill mansion, and how cold she must be lying next to Dimitri, knowing he would soon be dead.

Unicorn spent the next morning trawling through the data we had stolen from the Russian Embassy. There were huge amounts of background information on each of the names on the list. It was now just going to be a question of narrowing them down to a shortlist and double-checking the intel to determine the best candidates to guide Dimitri's younger brother Sergei in taking over the family business and playing into our hands.

Geraint interrupted the concentrated quiet with a shout.

'Dasha has made contact on the website again.' He clicked a few buttons.

Alexis, you must join us for coffee. We have so much to catch up on. 11 a.m. the Brasserie.

I looked at my watch.

'I don't have much time. I have to go home first.'

At Platform Eight we could wear whatever we wanted, which meant my daily wardrobe involved jeans, old T-shirts, trainers and my hair in a scruffy ponytail usually hidden under a baseball cap.

'What's wrong with what you're wearing?' asked Jake, giving me a once over.

'It's an undercover mission where I'm attempting to infiltrate a group of West London yummy mummies. This' – I motioned towards my outfit – 'will not do.'

'Just head out to the shops and buy something.'

'I could but I can't buy the other thing I need to bring.' I looked round at confused faces. 'My baby?'

Back home, I managed to dig out a few items that might just pass the scrutiny of the discerning eye of Dasha's inevitably designer-clad friends. Smart black trousers with my least scuffed leather boots and a threaded jacket which was trying to look Chanel but was actually Zara. A few chunky necklaces finished the look. I knew what I was up against. I had noticed women like Dasha when on maternity leave. Admired their grooming, their wolf-pack togetherness, united in their perfect appearance and clean-faced, well-behaved children. They would sit enjoying leisurely lunches while I scuttled by with unwashed hair and baby vomit covering the shoulder of my old university hoodie.

I had found such women terrifying.

But this was about playing a role. And this mother was one of 'them'. Strong, confident, rich. I could pull off the first two but the last was going to be a struggle. I wondered if the department budget would stretch to highlights and a new wardrobe.

I packed Gigi into her pram. This time I was prepared. After the initial hurried meet with Dasha, R & D had made amendments to some of the contents of the nappy bag. There was now Snuggles the Bullet-spewing Bunny Rabbit, who had my pistol safely ensconced in his belly. I could slip a hand inside his bum and be firing bullets out of his oversized grinning mouth in no time. Accompanying the bunny was a large purple polkadot baby rattle. The satisfying noise given off with every shake was courtesy of the spare ammo securely stored inside. Importantly, there was also a pram blackout cover, which was now bulletproof. If I sensed a threat I could have the invincible cocoon fastened on in seconds.

The Brasserie was in Notting Hill. I hopped in a black cab – it was important to arrive in character.

I spotted Dasha at the back of the elegant restaurant, holding court to a gaggle of other women. She got up as I approached the table.

'Alexis, hello.' We air-kissed as sickly-sweet vape smoke surrounded us. In all the Surveillance photos, Dasha was clasping her electronic cigarette as tightly as a teenage girl does a mobile phone.

'Lovely to see you, Dasha.'

I clocked her ever-present bodyguards, stony-faced at the next table.

'Let me introduce you to everyone.' She motioned towards two blonde women sat next to her. 'This is Claudia Grimaldi, and this is Cynthia Daudy.'

'Hello.' I found myself looking from one woman to the other, marginally confused by how similar they looked. Similar in that they had clearly used the same plastic surgeon – both had that slightly stretched surprised look and matching plumped-up trout pouts. Surely wrinkles were better than this unnatural mask they were both now sporting? Claudia and Cynthia looked up long enough to give me a short 'hello', and returned to cooing over photos on one of their phones.

'This is Francesca Harvey.' She motioned to the busty brunette on her other side.

'Actually, it's Frankie. Dasha is the only person who insists on using my full name.' Frankie had a soft Scottish lilt and was smiling as she spoke. I was torn as to what to make of her. She looked friendly but was wearing extremely tight leather trousers and a nipple-skimming low-cut top.

'And here is Tamara Smith-Bosanquet.' Dasha took another drag of her vape as she gestured towards a well-coiffed blonde in a shirt dress and suede boots. Tamara gave me a small nod as she fiddled with the string of pearls round her neck.

'And last but not least,' with a look that insinuated perhaps she did not mean this statement, 'Shona Backhouse.' Looking at the group together it was hard to see how Shona fitted in. She was dressed down in workout gear, had her hair up in a messy ponytail, horn-rimmed glasses, no make-up and was simultaneously cutting crusts off a piece of toast for a two-year-old boy and rocking a pram with her foot where another identical one slept. She looked, for lack of a better word, normal.

I looked round at the group renaming them with more memorable monikers for my report to the Platform later. The Plastics were the two Cs. The Glamourpuss was Frankie. The Sloane was Tamara. The Tracksuit was Shona. And the Queen Bee was quite clearly Dasha.

I sat down next to Shona, and parked Gigi's pram just behind me. Dasha continued to stand, as she addressed us all.

'Alexis, you have now met the whole bonfire committee. This year we'll be putting on Chepstow Hall's finest ever Bonfire Night. Everyone, Alexis volunteers for the charity Kids First, which we have nominated to receive the proceeds of this exciting event. As president, I thought it would be nice to have a charity liaison working with us.'

So this was Dasha's play. It was a clever one. I now had an official fake reason for hanging out with her.

Dasha continued, 'Alexis neglected to get her daughter down for Chepstow Hall at birth.' She paused for dramatic effect; the Plastics duly obliged with gasps. 'So she really needs to show the school how serious her commitment is in trying to secure a place.'

I looked over at the bodyguards; this elaborate cover story might be wasted on them, they looked so bored they could barely keep their eyes open.

When Dasha finally finished her monologue there was a long discussion that involved talk of whether toffee apples should be banned as surely we couldn't condone all that sugar (that was Tamara's gem), maybe we could get a celebrity to light the bonfire (Cynthia/Claudia's suggestion) and, 'Who gives a shit about the food – who's sorting the booze?' (Frankie's question). I sensed I was going to like her the most.

Shona had remained disengaged in the whole conversation as her two-year-old had rejected his crustless toast and was now licking each different pastry in the basket on the table.

I listened to them talk. They were all women whose lives were undoubtedly very different to mine. But I could speak the universal language of motherhood and hopefully be accepted into the fold. As Dasha and the two Cs pored over her scale map of the exclusive Notting Hill communal gardens where the Bonfire Night was to be held I turned to Tamara, Frankie and Shona. 'How did you all find weaning?'

'It has to be done properly. I only used bottled water to boil the vegetables. Volvic, of course, as it has the least sodium in,' announced Tamara in a cut-glass public-school accent.

'Oh. Right,' I said trying not to imagine her horror if I confessed how on the days when I was so tired I could barely turn the kettle on, let alone chop up and puree organic vegetables, that I used Ella's Kitchen readymade pouches. Though I still insisted on spoon feeding them to my daughter rather than letting her just suck from the packet. I wasn't a complete animal.

'You just Supermum the shit out of life don't you, Tamara?' cut in Frankie, cackling.

'I just want what's best for my girls,' sniffed Tamara. I imagined her daughters as miniature versions of her.

'Okay, ladies,' Dasha stood up again. 'I have prepared a timeline of what we need to have achieved each week. Study your copy carefully.' She handed out laminated sheets. 'As you know I'm one of those lucky enough to be shortlisted to be next year's head of the Parents' Association.' Knowing looks were exchanged between her and Claudia and Cynthia. 'So Bonfire Night is *very* important to me. I will be upset if anyone lets me down by not giving it their all.' She sat back down and looked pointedly at me. The threat hung in the air.

While the mums at one end of the table were distracted with talk of abnormal smear tests, and those at the other end were debating whether it was better for six-year-olds to be excellent at piano or proficient at both piano and violin, I spoke to Dasha.

'Thanks so much for those recommendations. We really are excited to have some new playmates.'

'You're welcome, Alexis. I had a feeling you would get on.' She sipped the disgusting-looking green smoothie in front of her. 'Bonfire Night is going to be amazing. I'm so glad my husband doesn't have to fly to Russia until the day after. The date was brought forward on some hearing he has to attend, but thankfully he still gets to join in the fun before he goes.' She turned her attention back to the group, 'There is so much we need to do, let's work really hard on killing it.'

Message received, Dasha.

Dimitri's lawyers had been successful in bringing the hearing forward, meaning we had just lost a month of preparation time.

Bonfire Night was six weeks away, and counting.

We needed to isolate and recruit three Russian businessmen to our cause, pinpoint and plan the exact right moment to eliminate Dimitri and make it look like an accident. All while helping organise the grandest fireworks event West London had ever seen.

Thankfully, I knew how to multitask.

Chapter Ten

HER TROOPS NOW BRIEFED and her assassin activated, Dasha had obviously decided her time would be better spent elsewhere. Claudia and Cynthia got to their feet as soon as she did.

'Ladies, I must go. I have another meeting.' We all chorused goodbyes and with a wave of her hand Dasha turned on her heel, followed by two tottering blondes and two lumbering bodyguards.

I had to get back and update the team. But Gigi's grumpy cries reminded me it was feeding time. I pulled her out of the pram and attempted to get her into position without exposing my whole breast to the restaurant. It was not an easy struggle. Breastfeeding in public was something I had managed to avoid. By pretty much never leaving the house. We had been trained to never show weakness and nothing felt more vulnerable than sitting in a crowded restaurant with your tit out.

I was aware that Tamara and Frankie were both unashamedly watching my efforts. Tamara opened her mouth to say something, but her phone rang and her attention was thankfully diverted to berating the person on the other end of the line.

'How have you found breastfeeding?' asked Frankie.

I thought about how to answer this. In those first few weeks I had felt like I was being attacked by a furious, vicious creature, desperate in its need to feast on me. I would try not to weep as she latched on to me and then come away with her little mouth stained red as she wreaked yet more damage. I was convinced I had given birth to a deranged vampire baby. She didn't want milk – just blood. I would sit gritting my teeth as she fed and stare at the box of breast pads, which featured a photo of a smiling mother looking lovingly into her baby's eyes. How dare she be so happy and pain-free? But all I said to Frankie was, 'It wasn't easy at first.'

'That's a fucking understatement. I wanted to grab every woman I'd ever met and scream how had no one told me that this supposedly beautiful natural bonding experience was really more something out of a horror film.'

So it wasn't just me.

'Don't worry, by the time she turns one you might actually feel like you know what you're doing.'

I felt mildly indignant. I had years of expert training at covert operations and had succeeded in many an undercover mission. Yet a civilian had just seen straight through my normal-mother front.

'What do you mean?' I asked, trying to sound nonchalant.

She leaned forward. 'You have that look in your eye I recognise from my early days. The look that says, "Why did nobody tell me how bloody difficult this is?"'

Perhaps the struggles I had were not down to that part of my psyche which meant I was okay with killing people. Perhaps it was normal to have feelings of inadequacy, moments of panic and even flashes of misery.

I should get an official statement from her and take it to Doc.

'As you're new to all this and Dasha has deigned to indoctrinate you into this god-awful committee you're going to need a little help navigating your way through this bloody mosh pit.' Frankie was offering to be my informant, my guide to the piranha tank of West London parenting.

'We're all just mothers,' I offered. 'It can't be that difficult?'

'Darling, you have no idea. Thanks to the dawn of baby classes and exclusive kids' clubs it's a high-pressure cooker of expectation and competition, all broadcast on Instagram. Here child neglect is considered failing to get out of your PJs and take your newborn to the Baby Spa.'

'Very funny.' I laughed to myself at the idea of Gigi having a massage followed by a mani-pedi.

Frankie looked sorry for me. 'You think I'm joking? This is going to be tougher for you than I thought.'

'I never took any of mine to the Baby Spa and they turned out fine,' said Shona through a mouthful of croissant. We looked down at her twins who were now both licking pastry crumbs off the floor.

'Shona, this poor lass has to suck up to all the Super Mamas to try to get her kid a place at school. She needs to know what she's up against.' Frankie looked up as a woman with expensively tousled caramel-coloured hair approached Tamara. 'Perfect timing.'

'Tamara, darling, how are you?' called the woman.

Tamara jumped and rapidly ended her phone call with whatever workman/husband/nanny had upset her. 'Oh, Flossie, hi. What are you doing here?'

Frankie nudged me. 'Just listen. I'll translate.'

'Well I had a little time after Pilates so thought I'd grab a sparkling water before heading back to the office. Things are just so full-on right now. How about you? Having a lovely coffee morning with friends?'

Frankie whispered, *'I'm working hard; you're just pissing around drinking coffee, you stay-at-home loser.'*

'Oh you're still working at that magazine? How wonderful James was able to find a place for you there. How are the kids? I hear poor Seb was having trouble at nursery?'

Frankie continued, *'You only got the job through contacts, you dumb cow. And your son is suffering thanks to you abandoning him all day to go play office.'*

'Seb is doing fine. He just found it tough adjusting to being with children all day. He has this wonderful Norland nanny and she believes he's so advanced he finds his contemporaries boring. We do wish he was as down-to-earth as your girls who play so well with other children; it would make everything so much easier.'

'Your kids are shit.'

Flossie continued, 'Don't you have some very sweet Eastern European nanny? How wonderful to have help round the house as well. The problem with Norlands is that thanks to their degrees in childcare and expertise in child development they just won't even turn the dishwasher on.'

'Your nanny is shit.'

Tamara shook her hair back.

'Olga is an absolute star and she's a brilliant cook; she even does dinner for us. Not that you need to worry about that; it sounds like Tom is getting very well fed eating out at Scott's so often. Ed says he always sees him there as he's rushing home. He's so jealous that you let him eat out so much and with such glamorous companions. It's so heartening to know that banking is no longer a man's world.'

'Your husband is fucking other women.'

'Although Ed did say he just couldn't miss getting back for bath time and tucking the girls in.'

'And he's a crap dad.'

Flossie retaliated through gritted teeth. 'That is sweet. How great Ed doesn't have to work long hours. I do wish Tom also worked for a smaller firm. Although we would then have to give up our place in the South of France.' She let out a high-pitched giggle.

'We have more money than you.'

Flossie did a big show of looking at her watch. 'But, look, I must dash. Lovely seeing you, darling, and I'll be in touch for dates for dinner.'

'That would be great. We could all go to Scott's. See why Tom loves it so much.'

Flossie grimaced. Even as she tried to sashay out with her head held high I could see her heart really wasn't in it. Game, set and match to Tamara. She looked round to see us all staring at her. 'That's Flossie. She's one of my best friends,' she offered as way of explanation and went back to stirring her tea.

'They truly are terrifying,' I breathed to Frankie. I looked around at the women dotted all over the Brasserie. Their body armour may have been designer and their quick-firing weapons simply well-thought-out words, but this was social warfare. And I was now in the front line.

Back at Unicorn's office, Jake was waiting. 'Why don't I get to join you as a hands-on dad looking to pick up parenting tips?'

'Jake, there are many things you can fake, but being a parent would not be one of them.' I didn't add that I actually was one and could barely manage it. 'And, besides, a pretty boy like you sniffing around Dasha would make the bodyguards triple.'

'You think I'm pretty? 8.4 pretty?' Jake fluttered his eyelashes at me. 8.4 was Jake's Hot or Not rating. The fact it was higher than mine was something he often liked to remind me of. He also claimed puffing his cheeks out in his assessment photos was the only reason he rated under an 8.7 and therefore within the threshold for being active for all missions.

'The only thing you are 8.4 in is being bloody annoying. How have you been getting on with the embassy data?'

'G-Man and Nicola have been working on it. I was going over surveillance on Dimitri with Robin, but I got pulled off it to help with Eight's interview backlog. We're fucked without the suitcases.'

Suitcases were vital kit in acquiring individuals for interrogation at the Platform. A Rat would break into the target's home, subdue them with an injection, lock them into a suitcase and wheel them over to the nearest underground station. The tube was faster and more anonymous than driving. I remembered how kind strangers would always help the poor girl with the heavy suitcase up and down the stairs.

Not long ago things had gone bad when one Rat, having got his subject all packed up, heard the unexpected sound of a maintenance man entering, and made a fast exit out of the window only to get hit by a car in a freak hit and run. He woke up in hospital a week later with a bad concussion and headlines about the mystery of a dead man found at home in a padlocked suitcase. The heat that came with that discovery meant suitcases were not authorised until further notice. This had been a logistical nightmare as our new procurement method, the Uber, was not as effective. Precious time was wasted following targets around waiting for them to book a car that, unbeknownst to them, would be driven by a Rat wielding a syringe full of a fast-acting sedative.

The lights flickered. Jake looked up. 'Rude fuckers have started without me.'

I took him by the arm. 'You can play later. It's time for our update briefing.'

Once all of Unicorn were gathered in the meeting room, I took centre stage and announced the development: we now only had just over six weeks until Dimitri flew back to Moscow for the incompetency hearing.

'Jesus,' said Sandy. 'We were tight for time as it was. We need to pop Dimitri before he flies back. As soon as his old man is found incompetent, Dimitri will start the takeover of the company. Geraint and Nicola – you found anything useful in your online sweep?'

Geraint looked up from his laptop. 'Dimitri has many enemies but there's definitely one that stands out from the rest. I hacked a secure chat from last year between a couple of Dimitri's business associates. There's repeated reference to "the Dragon".'

Like all of us, the Russians clearly preferred sticking to a loose code even when supposedly talking privately.

'They seemed scared of him. Talked of how the Dragon wanted Dimitri dead and was looking for someone to do it. They wanted no part in it but were very nervous about displeasing the Dragon.'

'Is the Dragon mentioned anywhere else?' asked Sandy.

'There are several references to the Dragon in other emails and conversations among businessmen in Dimitri's circle – all express fear of him and what he could do. But there's only one other mention of the Dragon specifically targeting Dimitri – this was in a secure phone call we hacked.' Geraint squinted at his screen as he read from the translated transcript. '"Does Dimitri know the Dragon wants him dead?" "Dimitri knows the Dragon is angry but he thinks the power of the three will keep him safe." Then there's laughter. "The Dragon doesn't care about the three –" more laughter – "he doesn't realise how much trouble he's in."'

'"The three"?' Sandy frowned. 'That has to be a reference to Dimitri's three supporters on the Rok-Tech board. They're his closest allies.'

'The Dragon could be the perfect scapegoat to blame Dimitri's death on,' said Jake. 'Do we have any leads on who he is?'

'None,' said Nicola. 'From the way everyone talks about him he sounds like a pretty well-connected bigwig with wide-reaching influence.'

'Do we know why the Dragon wants Dimitri dead?' I asked.

Nicola shook her head. 'The men just make mention of it being for protection, implying the Dragon has some big invest-ments or business deals that are being threatened by Dimitri. I've run reports on all our intelligence databases but no one on file uses "the Dragon" as a pseudonym.'

'Didn't Dimitri screw over a big Chinese company last year?' Sandy tapped his pen against the table. 'I'm sure it was called something like Black Dragon. One of their head honchos could've tried to order a hit on Dimitri as payback. The timing fits.'

'I'll look into it,' said Nicola without looking up from her screen.

'And I'll set up an alert for any other mentions,' added Geraint.

Sandy turned to Jake. 'What have you and Robin learnt about Dimitri?'

'That we need more day-to-day intel on him. Right now he's in the middle of a big property deal in Mayfair. He's trying to buy out half of St. James's as far as we can tell. But he has meetings and appointments all over London and half the time we have no idea where he actually is. He's in and out of cars with darkened windows and going into buildings with numerous exits. Surveillance have been following him for months and we still don't know that much about him – his daily habits, what he likes to eat. We don't even have much on who he likes to fuck. We need his calendar and we need to take our surveillance to the next level. Or we won't be able to work out how best to give him a little "accident".'

'I'll text Dasha to download Dimitri's diary and stick it in the scooter horse head.' I brought out my phone.

Thanks for today. We must compare diaries to plan a play date before Bonfire Night. See you at school pick-up. Alexis.

After witnessing how good these women were at subliminal messages I knew she would have no problem getting what I was trying to say.

The next morning, outside Dasha's daughter's school, I found a USB stick inside the scooter head. I reached down to Gigi and gently squidged her cheek while slipping the stick into the pram's lining. She grinned up at me, showing off the one solitary tooth on her bottom gum. I watched her looking round, taking in the cars driving by, the trees and their leaves moving in the wind. Life felt better when I saw the world through her eyes, where everything was bright and new and exciting. She jigged up and down in her seat and gurgled, brandishing her monkey at passers-by.

I felt lucky. Not many mothers returning from maternity leave would get to spend this much time with their baby in working hours. Playtime on the Platform's dime. With just a small risk of her potentially getting caught in the middle of a violent firefight. I checked down in the pram base to make sure the reinforced blackout cover was still there. Beata had asked about it the other day, enquiring as to why it was so heavy and made of such strange material. I had replied using words like 'organic', 'breathable', 'gluten-free', 'imported fabric' and she had just nodded. There was definitely a benefit to being written off as a paranoid first-time West London mama.

From: 8SEXYMAMA@stillgotit.com
To: lex.tyler@platform-eight.co.uk
Subject: $$$HotMamasGetHorny
MISSION: #80436
UNIT: UNICORN
WEASEL: DIMITRI TUPOLEV
ALERT: 6 WEEKS TO POP DAY

Chapter Eleven

'PERSEPHONE! GET YOUR FINGER out of your nose right now!'
A uniformed nanny was admonishing a three-year-old at the top of a bright red slide that was the crowning glory at the end of an assault course of climbing walls, mini trampolines and large ball pits.

Back in the days of the Cold War, the dead-letter drop was the preferred way to exchange information. Microfilm and documents would be taped to the bottom of benches in grand and commandeering locations like churches and abbeys. Our twenty-first-century update involved USB sticks and the bright, wipe-clean plastic matting of soft play.

Gigi and I were at an exclusive kids' club that Dasha often frequented, admiring its huge-open plan 'Exploration Zone', an enormous labyrinth of toddler-friendly fun. It didn't look too unlike one of our training courses. Except everything was squashy rather than spiked; the cacophony of 'I can't do this' cries a little more high-pitched.

Adjoining this padded play area were a series of tables designed like spaceships, where parents or carers could eat from an Ottolenghi chef's extensive organic menu while admiring their charges' attempts to launch, climb or crawl over various cushioned obstacles. Adorning the walls were murals of rockets, aliens and faraway solar systems. Hanging from the ceiling above the play area was a shimmering silver curtain decorated with cut-out moons and stars. It was very appropriate décor for somewhere that felt like another planet compared to the more low-key activities Gigi and I were used to.

'No, Digby, you cannot have another Babycino. You already had one with your chia porridge.' A mother was rolling her eyes at a five-year-old wearing a check shirt with Burberry written in large black letters on its back – just in case the trademark print was too subtle a nod to its provenance.

Dasha had been at the club an hour before us and left a message through the chatroom that blueprints and a USB stick had been taped underneath one of the trampolines. I could see how she had managed to do so without her bodyguards noticing – the trampolines were in long rows and despite the instruction of close surveillance they clearly drew the line at having to bounce alongside her and Irina. I looked around the club and continued to marvel at its understated space-age luxury. My only previous encounter with soft play had been Gymboree in the town hall; the session had started with us sat in a circle singing the Gymboree song to the tune of Queen's 'We Will Rock You'. The sound of manicured hands slapping down on to thick soft play-mats in time to the rhythm of this bastardised version of a classic song still haunts my dreams. Despite years of training to be a highly skilled assassin, being privy to highly classified security information, there I was wearing a name badge with a picture of a clown on it and forcing my three-month-old to clap her hands like she was my very own living breathing puppet. Having a baby levels the playing field. It didn't matter what your previous life was, what you have achieved, what you haven't achieved, as a parent you were and always would be a slave to your little people.

'Shall we start with the ball pit, Gigi?' She looked up at me, her blue eyes wide at the sensory overload surrounding her. She was wearing a bright purple cardigan, rainbow leggings and a black AC/DC T-shirt Will had got for her in America on his last business trip. I thought she looked adorable but looking around at the little girls here, all dressed in the muted neutral colours of Bonpoint, Gigi stuck out like the class rebel. I wanted to give her a high five. My baby from the wrong side of the tracks.

I took off our shoes and socks and clambered into the moat of multicoloured plastic balls that encircled the rows of trampolines. I gently dropped Gigi in. She wrinkled her brow as she picked up a ball and looked at it, before looking at me. I held my breath and waited for her to decide if this was heaven or hell. Another frown. And then she moved both hands through the balls and giggled. Great. She was happy. Now I could get to work.

I checked the first two trampolines. Nothing. Tucked under the springs of the third was a slightly sodden envelope. I quickly pulled it out – there was no tell-tale USB-stick shape inside. Just a small hole in the corner. I peered between the trampoline's springs but couldn't see anything on the ground below. If it had fallen out any one of the kids here could have got their hands on it. I looked around the multicoloured tableau of well-dressed children and plastic matting, searching for a sign of the USB stick. Five trampolines over and right at the back of the room I saw a one-year-old sitting with it. Putting it in her mouth. There were several large signs along the walls: 'Trampolines are strictly for children only'. Being escorted out of here by security would be both embarrassing and draw unnecessary attention.

The Burberry-clad boy jumped into the ball pit beside us.

'Hello there, Digby'. He looked at me silently. 'You see that little girl over there?' I motioned towards the toddler chewing on the USB stick. 'What she's playing with is mine and not meant for children. Could you go get it for me?'

The boy continued to look at me and then got up. 'Okay.'

That was the joy of well-brought-up, privileged kids. They respected their elders. They had manners. They could follow orders.

I watched my helper jump from trampoline to trampoline until he got to the girl and the USB stick. He leaned down and snatched it out of her hand. The girl started crying and reaching out for it.

I gave him a thumbs-up and mouthed, 'Now come back.' I motioned him towards us. He looked me in the eye and then turned his back on me. The little shit.

'You can't have it, you can't have it!' sing-songed the boy as he waved it above the girl's head. He started bouncing as the girl pulled his leg with one hand and hit him with the other. Jesus. I had started Kiddie Fight Club. I kept trying to get the boy's attention, waving at him, reminding him of his mission. But it seemed he was enjoying antagonizing the smaller child.

And then he screamed. The girl had clamped down and bitten his left calf. With a yelp of rage, amid his tears, he pushed the girl over and as he bounced flung the USB stick up high above his head. I watched as it sailed up into the air and landed on one of the large steel beams criss-crossing the star-covered ceiling.

Bloody brilliant.

I quickly turned my back to the two wailing children as their mothers came racing forward to save them and slumped down into the ball pit. I waited until they had been safely removed from their bouncy arena before trying to determine how I could retrieve the USB stick. While it was now safely out of the reach of any more teething children, it was near impossible to get to. Even if I broke club rules and bounced for my life on the trampoline underneath it I wasn't going to get within grasping distance.

On the other end of the room was a climbing wall. If I got to the top of it ... I went into operation mode and scanned the potential path I could take towards the USB stick. It was doable. Definitely doable. Last time I had tried a move like this was breaking out of a Venezuelan prison. At least here if I fell to the ground padded mats, as opposed to barbed wire, would break my fall. And rather than heavily armed prison guards, the outrage would be from well-to-do parents furious at my putting their precious offspring at risk. Although the wish to see me dead would probably be about the same.

Gigi seemed in total bliss, throwing balls around her in hyperactive spasms and giggles. I whispered, 'Back in a minute, darling.'

The climbing wall had glow-in-the-dark footholds and at the top was a small platform enclosed in safety netting with 'Reach for the Stars!' in giant letters emblazoned above it. The wall was thankfully free of adventurous children and I was able to scale it without anyone noticing a mum appearing to want to recapture her youth. Standing on the platform, I looked across at the nearest beam – it was a leap up of nearly a metre and a half to reach it. At least once I was up there the curtain of moons and stars would hide me from the view of the parents in the spaceships below.

I looked for Gigi and saw she was still happily playing with the balls. The joy of her still being unable to crawl meant I didn't have to worry about her going anywhere. Now I just needed to pick the right moment to climb round the netting and make the jump.

'Mine!'

'No MINE!'

Another fight was breaking out. I could see two toddlers lying on the floor each clinging on to an oversized dinosaur. One was wailing. Their mothers hurried over. The one who got there first was wearing a trouser suit, her hair cut in a neat dark bob. She turned to the other. 'It seems your son just hit mine on the head.'

Would this be enough to draw everyone's attention away from any ceiling acrobatics?

'In our family we don't admonish. We believe in self-regulation.'

Oh yes, this was definitely going to be enough. There was a pause as I could hear everyone at the nearby spaceships stop stirring their coffees and strain to hear the impending showdown.

'Excuse me? You aren't going to tell him off?' Trouser Suit stared at the other mother, who was wearing a long patterned dress, a wide belt cinched at her tiny waist. I was pretty sure I recognized her from a recent shampoo ad. The model gave her long blonde hair a shake.

'We believe children need to learn for themselves what's right and wrong. Not through adults telling them.'

'You've got to be kidding me,' Trouser Suit said. 'I've never heard anything so ridiculous. How is a three-year-old meant to know anything if you don't tell them?'

'Just look at little Finlay's face. He's noticing your son's tears. Absorbing them.' They both looked down at the boy lying on the floor chewing his fingernail.

'He looks like he couldn't give a crap. You can't let your son run wild in a public space and not tell him off.'

The sound from the tables remained muted; children were shushed as everyone continued to listen in.

I quickly climbed round the side of the platform and edged along the outside of the safety netting. I stood on the corner of the barrier, trying to work out how best to fling myself at the beam.

'Are you trying to tell me how to parent?' The model's voice was now rising.

Neither mother had noticed that the two boys had got up off the floor and were now happily playing on a plastic see-saw together.

Trouser Suit continued to talk with big exaggerated hand movements. I made out the words, 'Jesus, I bet you don't believe in vaccination either.' I couldn't hear the model's long response but judging by Trouser Suit raising her hands in despair it seemed her guess had been correct. A couple of staff members dressed as astronauts had noticed the disturbance and seemed to be discussing whether to approach. Now was the time.

I pulled back against the netting hoping it would help act as a spring.

I made the leap, my hands reaching out as I launched myself up towards the nearest beam.

I missed.

Only one hand managed to clasp onto the beam, leaving me hanging precariously. I risked looking down. No one had noticed. Except one little boy in a red T-shirt. He stared up at me, mouth open. I pressed a finger to my lips and propelled myself round, flinging my other hand up on to the beam and pulling myself on to it. I sat straddling the beam as I peered down again at Gigi in her kingdom of balls. From up here she was just a spiky-haired purple blob.

The astronauts had now stepped in and each of the irate mothers was being taken to a separate corner to calm down over one of the club's signature Kombucha green teas. As quietly as I could I jumped between each beam until I reached the other side of the room and the one the USB stick was balanced on. I put it in my pocket and surveyed the best route back to the ball pit without attracting any attention. As long as I kept behind the star-spangled curtain, no one would see the acrobatic mum walking across ceiling beams.

And then Gigi started crying.

Dammit. She was clearly now very aware that she was seemingly abandoned.

Any attempt at a covert re-entry to the ground was forgotten at the sound of my daughter in distress. I leaped back across the beams until I was as close as I could get to Gigi. Her cries grew louder as she looked around the room, searching for me. The guilt at being the cause of her tears stabbed me in the gut. I needed to get down there now. I looked at the figures on the trampolines below, the only witnesses in close proximity would be under the age of five, and who ever believed what they had to say?

I slid across the beam until I was up against the back wall. It was too long a drop to jump. I looked at the wall; the ridges in it had big enough cracks I should be able to hang on. It had been a good couple of years, and I'd been a good couple of kilos lighter since I tried a manoeuvre like this, but the sound of Gigi needing me helped override any apprehension at attempting it. I swung down from the beam, my bare feet grappling against the wall until I found some footing. I slowly climbed down, my arms and legs shaking with the effort of trying to keep me holding on. I was Spider-Mum. I made it far enough down the wall until I was in safe leaping distance of the ball pit. I took a deep breath and jumped in. A flurry of balls bounced out. I swept Gigi into my arms. 'It's okay, Mummy's here.'

She stopped crying and nuzzled into my neck. I clambered out the ball pit and noticed the trouser-suited mother staring at me.

'How did you . . . ?' She trailed off.

I shrugged and flicked my hair. 'Pilates.'

Chapter Twelve

'I THINK A POTTY-TRAINING toddler may have had a little accident.' I was watching Sandy hold the blueprints I had retrieved from the trampoline up against the light. They were a little damp and he was trying to see if he could still decipher them.

'You're telling me this is fucking wee?' He dropped the papers.

'Afraid so. All that jumping . . .'

'Jesus.' He wiped his hands on his combat trousers. 'Any luck with the USB stick, G-Man?'

Geraint shook his head. 'It's too damaged. The files are corrupted.'

'I thought this place was a kids' club, not a bloody zoo. The items were only there for an hour and they ravaged them.'

I didn't bother pointing out toddlers were every bit as destructive as wild animals.

Sandy sighed. 'We need a new strategy on how Dasha can smuggle us the info we need.'

We were now at the planning stage of our mission. Here it was vital we meticulously plotted every detail of the upcoming Pop. One wrong move, a failed attempt, or even a successful one that no one bought as an accident, and we would spark an international incident and violent retaliation. The President couldn't find out that we were on the attack. Nobody could know that Dimitri was a casualty of the silent war raging on the digital battlefield, nor that his elimination was a strike to protect our privacy. Protect our civil liberties. Protect our total reliance on electronic devices for parenting.

This was a mission very close to my heart.

After receiving Dimitri's calendar we had trawled through it looking for areas where he was potentially vulnerable. It wasn't easy. His sexual preferences were too vanilla for 'the S & M Accident'. And he was too high-profile for anyone to believe the randomness of a 'Hit and Run' or 'Mugging Gone Wrong'. 'The Heart Attack' and 'the Laced Cigarette' were both ruled out as a recent Harley Street medical recorded that he was a non-smoker and his heart was in excellent condition. He had no deadly allergies and no risky hobbies. There wasn't a speed-boat, motorbike, shotgun or light aircraft in sight. Dimitri was irritatingly boring.

It was therefore through lack of options that we unanimously settled on 'the Drunk Driver'. This play involved a needle, containing a large quantity of alcohol, in this case, vodka – to adhere to the Russian stereotype – embedded into the driver's car seat. One of the front tyres would have a small explosive fitted to it. Both mechanisms were radio operated and with a press of the button the explosive would go off and the needle inject. The car would veer off the road, crashing through a specially modified section of motorway sidebar before exploding into a fireball in the parkland below. Investigations would determine a tyre burst at a dangerous turn in a fast car driven by a drunk Ruski. Case closed. Weasel popped. Mission accomplished.

The whiteboard in the meeting room now had in scrawled red pen a long shopping list of information from Dasha that we needed to make the Drunk Driver happen. The dead-letter drop at the kids' club had been our first attempt.

Jake looked up from his phone. 'The bodyguards' paranoia has ramped up another notch. Surveillance reported yesterday one actually examined the twenty-pound-note Dasha stopped to put in a charity collection box.'

Sandy looked round the table. 'Anyone got any bright ideas?'

In a more normal set-up we would've gone for a simple briefcase exchange. Put down a briefcase, pick up another identical one. But an exchange is so much harder when the switch item is not a briefcase but a snakeskin Hermès Birkin handbag with a five-figure price tag and a six-month waiting list. And that was only the bag Dasha used for bonfire committee meetings. I remembered from the surveillance photos there were a few Fendi, Chanel and Mulberry masterpieces in there as well. I imagined broaching the subject with Sandy: *Sorry everyone! You'll have to forget those new self-propelling rocket launchers, Lex wants to blow the budget on fucking handbags.*

'What about the baby's nappy?' offered Robin. 'She could stick items in the lining and bin it in a restaurant toilet when she changes her?'

I shook my head. 'She's got two nannies. The bodyguards would be suspicious if they saw her personally handling her daughter's crap.'

Nicola was scanning her computer. 'Ocado deliver to Dasha and Dimitri's house four times a week. Can't she put things in their plastic bags when she returns them to the driver?'

Again her staff were the problem. 'She has a full-time house-keeper and cook. I doubt Dasha ever goes into the kitchen, let alone takes deliveries.'

Sandy turned to me. 'As you're the expert, Lex, what would you suggest?'

'Let's keep it simple. We tell Dasha what we need through the chatroom and if it's too big for the scooter she gets it to me at our weekly committee meeting.'

'How?' Sandy frowned.

'Forget Trojan horses. We'll use Trojan toys.'

'Alexis, my youngest, Irina, has grown out of so many of her toys. Maybe Gigi would like them? It would also give her something to play with, as you insist on bringing her to these meetings.'

'Dasha, that would be wonderful. Thank you.'

Our initial scripted interaction went smoothly and the regular hand over of toys that followed was routinely ignored by the bodyguards, allowing me over the course of the next few weeks to take receipt of everything we needed. At our first meeting I received detailed drawings of their secure garage within a singing bear. There was a nerve-racking moment when Gigi clutched it for the first time and all that could be heard was a loud crackling of the paper inside its tummy before it launched into a high-pitched rendition of 'Twinkle, Twinkle'.

I also got a lesson in the proper terminology for certain parts of the anatomy.

'Walter calls it a fanny?' Tamara had sounded horrified at Shona's recounting of a story involving one of her sons' confusion over exactly what a period was.

'Yes, Tamara, he does. Blame my husband. But, honestly, what else can you call it?'

'Front bottom.'

The others had then all joined in. 'Come on! Really? We call it "foofoo".'

'That doesn't even make sense.'

'We call it "lily".'

'That's Flora's middle name, of course we aren't going to call it that.'

'Veejay.'

'So Essex.'

And on it went. A year ago I never would have imagined my Tuesday morning would involve sitting around heatedly debating what to call a vagina.

At the next meeting I was given a toy xylophone, which Gigi could only get the most tinny and muffled notes out of despite her most vigorous banging with the plastic sticks. Inside it was a sheaf of papers listing the model and make of all Dimitri's cars, notes on which ones were used for what purpose and the chauffeur's schedule and home address.

I also received an important lesson in how appearance was everything from Frankie.

'If you're at soft play and want to kick back and dick around on your phone, just announce, "I'm encouraging independent play," to anyone looking your way.'

Shona had followed up with, 'When I can't face being in the playground another minute and Freddie is screaming his head off, I calmly and loudly say, "Darling, use your words. I know you're frustrated but it's now time to go home," – while secretly handing him Smarties and whispering a promise of more if he just gets in the fucking buggy.'

Next I was able to receive Dimitri's actual fingerprint imprinted into a tub of Play-Doh, while I learnt that Facebook was an essential tool in the daily game of killing time before bath time. Although Shona warned of the pitfalls: 'Last week I discovered a guy I shagged fifteen years ago had just moved in with someone who'd been married to a guy the year before who'd since married another woman who looked look like a less pretty version of his first wife but with bigger boobs and that her sister had a daughter who looked unbelievably similar to my Willow. Does anyone else get so bored looking after their children they end up on the profile of an ex-fling's girlfriend's ex-husband's new wife's sister?'

The end of the month was approaching fast. We had become so confident with the toy exchanges that Dasha even got her driver to deliver me a Fisher-Price Jumperoo. Hidden within each leg of the world's most irritating toy were alarm codes for each entry point to the house. Those codes could have easily fitted in the scooter's horse head. She probably just wanted the bloody thing out of the house.

It was a strange dual life I was leading. Mornings could be spent discussing which symphony was best to set fireworks to and enjoying tasting sessions of mulled wine. Afternoons were more about locating a Lamborghini that was the exact same model as Dimitri's and testing the radio range of a remote detonator. And then there were the daily sessions at the gym that

Candy kept dragging me in for. She was taking getting my pre-baby body back a lot more seriously than I was.

A song from one of Gigi's CDs kept playing in my head on repeat. 'Jelly on a plate, Jelly on a plate, Wibble Wobble, Wibble Wobble, Jelly on a plate.'

I was running in front of a mirrored wall.

'Okay Lex, you can stop.' Candy looked down at her stopwatch. 'Not a totally crap effort but huge room for improvement. Are you not doing any exercise outside of here?'

'I run twice a week before work.' Dragging myself out of bed to jog round the expansive gardens of Chiswick House had started as a chore but seeing as anything outside of work and Gigi could be considered 'me time' I had started to appreciate the solitude of an early-morning run.

'Make it three times and we might see a difference. Now on to the weight machine. I want a hundred reps and no excuses.' Candy motioned me towards the machine and sat down on the floor with her iPad, no doubt to update her spreadsheet with my disappointing lap times.

Candy's weight machine was a slightly terrifying contraption that she had personally modified to combine a workout for the legs with strengthening arm muscles. I got into position on the floormat in the middle of the machine to begin squats while pulling down the large stacked blocks of weights with each hand.

I did one pull; the resistance didn't feel right. The pulley system felt like it was jarring. I let go and went to the back of the machine. Everything looked okay. I leaned forward and gave the handle another pull. The weights went crashing down to the floor.

If I'd been still standing in position half my arm and undoubtedly my right hand would've been crushed.

Candy came bounding over, brow furrowed against her pink headband. 'For fuck's sake, Lex, what have you done?'

'I barely touched it.' I went to the pile of weights on the floor. A short piece of shorn rope was lying among them, while dangling above was the longer piece it had snapped off from. I reached down and picked up the rope.

Candy peered at it. 'So who have you pissed off? This machine has clearly been tampered with. Can't you Rats sort out your differences in the field?' She sighed. 'It's hard enough on the piddling budget I've been given without you idiots sabotaging expensive equipment.' She stomped off, shaking her head.

I fingered the frayed edges of the rope.

Bennie was really starting to become a problem.

It seemed mocking his manhood in the canteen had upset him enough that he'd tried to crush my firing hand. I wasn't surprised, considering what I had learnt about him from the Rats in his current unit.

It seemed Bennie was walking, talking proof that although you couldn't polish a turd, you could polish a vile little psychopath into a government employee his mother could still talk proudly about at dinner parties.

Privilege had always protected Bennie from the repercussions of his actions. Growing up; a neighbour with a missing cat received a new car, the family of a girl with a burnt arm was gifted a new flat. By the time he finished his exclusive private school Bennie had been involved in enough incidents they were able to build a new library. His army career was littered with red flags and after one tour of duty in Afghanistan the duty psychiatrist recommended he never be deployed again. Everyone had breathed a sigh of relief when he left to join the Security Services. The Committee had clearly placed him here to see if he was Rat material or too unhinged to make it.

At Eight there was no understanding Human Resources department we could take grievances to. No one wanted to get stuck in the middle of an argument between a couple of killers. With everything I had going on I didn't have the time to engage with Bennie and his one-man battle to oust me. But if I ignored him, would he go away?

From: 8herpesremedy@riddledwithwarts.com
To: lex.tyler@platform-eight.co.uk
Subject: Herpes Simplex Cure
MISSION: #80436
UNIT: UNICORN
WEASEL: DIMITRI TUPOLEV
ALERT: 2 WEEKS TO POP DAY

Chapter Thirteen

I DIDN'T KNOW IF we were going to make it.

As I went through our mission protocol checklists, nearly every box was still missing the reassuring green tick.

'We need to do better.' I was leading our daily update briefing. All of Unicorn were settled in the meeting room, except Sandy, who was in his office with the door shut. Judging by the raised voice and the shouted threats, he was on the phone to a particularly unshakeable enemy of the state. Or his ex-wife.

I looked round at everyone. 'We need confirmation of what Dimitri's flight plans are, the remote detonator needs testing out in the field and so far we're failing in our trials to disable the garage alarm system. The Drunk Driver is our best chance of success. We have to make this work.'

If we failed we would be deployed to Moscow to undertake another Pop attempt there. Foreign soil, limited intel, increased security, arranging ten days of childcare . . . There were many reasons why I didn't want to have to action the Back-up.

'Nicola, talk us through your trip.' Nicola had just got back from three days in Moscow with Robin. I'd already heard Robin complain that she'd spent the whole trip with her Beats by Dre headphones on and how at least once he'd noticed they hadn't even been connected to her iPhone. I had to confess I didn't blame her.

'We now have a final shortlist of who to recruit to help Sergei take over Rok-Tech. Using the Russian Embassy's files we were able to track down all the known associates of those on Isaac's list and rule out those with business links to The President. These are the ones we have left.' Nicola tapped her keyboard and the photos and biographies of three Russian businessmen projected on to the whiteboard. 'Their joint codename will be the Nyan.'

'That's Russian for what exactly?' asked Jake.

'The Nannies.' Nicola nodded over at a grinning Robin. 'He named them.'

'Did you make any progress with intel for the Back-up?' As much as I hoped it wouldn't come to it, we needed to have a workable plan in place.

'We were able to get the exact time, date and location of the incompetency hearing by hacking Dimitri's lawyers' office but we still don't know where in Moscow he will be staying.'

'And Rok-Tech HQ is a fortress with daily-changing security protocols,' added Robin.

'At this rate we're going to spend our time waiting for him outside in the cold and taking pot shots.' I shivered at the thought. 'Stakeouts in minus twenty.'

'The freezing air sharpens the mind. And the aim.' Jake leaned towards me and said softly, 'Remember that time in Norway? Up in the fjords? How we got trapped in that steam room? Although it wasn't that steamy before we started . . .' He trailed off. 'Remember?'

'I don't.'

I did.

I cleared my throat. 'The incompetency hearing is our best bet. Let's focus on that.'

Geraint's laptop started pinging. He frowned. 'I have an alert set up for any online activity regarding VirtuWorld. It seems a lot of chatter has been coming in. The software has apparently just passed phase one of testing. They're now definitely on track for being fully operational in the New Year.'

We all went quiet as we thought of how we were just months away from the VirtuWorld cars and their scanners being rolled out into the world, mapping our streets and potentially infiltrating our electronic devices. I couldn't imagine a future whereby we had to relinquish technology just to keep our security practices safe.

It would be impossible.

Russia would rule us all.

We continued the rest of the meeting with a renewed vigour and I assigned roles. I'd focus on the logistics and execution of the two different Pop plans with Jake and Robin. Geraint and Nicola needed to work through the multitude of data that needed analysing and monitor online chatter for indications that Dimitri or his associates suspected what we were planning. Sandy's job was to approach and recruit the Nyan. We were going to be stretched thin but I had full trust in our team. We were the best of the best. I had to keep reminding myself of that whenever I felt the added pressure of it being my first mission back since having Gigi.

And the fact I was going to be the one pushing the button.

At 10 p.m. we were all still in the office. I stretched and wondered if seven coffees in one day was too many. Nicola was texting on her mobile. Probably planning some big night out after leaving here. I took in her shiny hair and taut body. She was so free. No rushing to get home to see a baby, no fear of getting woken up by said baby. Just busy planning whatever it was she wanted to do without a care in the world. What did she do with all that free time? I thought back to Will and me on lazy weekends before Gigi was born and wanted to shake us by the shoulders and shout, 'You fucking enjoy this!'

My phone beeped and a photo of a grinning Gigi popped up. She was wearing a tweed flat cap. '*A highlight from today's Daddy Daycare*' was the message from Will. My heart burst a little. I looked back at Nicola, who was still texting. She might get the lie-ins, the constant meals out, the late-night drinks, the fun-filled shopping sessions, the carefree abandonment of doing whatever she wanted, but I was doing okay.

Nicola dropped her phone and stood up. 'I need to go home. My eyes are killing me. This artificial air dries out my lenses something terrible. I don't even want to think about what it's doing to my skin.'

'Why don't you wear your glasses?' Robin asked through a mouth of crisps.

From where I was sitting I couldn't see the look she gave him. But it must have been one of her very best withering ones judging by Robin's face. She left the room without saying goodbye to any of us.

'We could have a big problem.' Geraint looked up from his laptop. 'I've had another alert. This time on the Dragon. I've got a fragment of an email between a couple of Dimitri's associates sent this morning: "The Dragon is coming for Dimitri and Rok-Tech ... The Dragon can tear apart Rok-Tech from the inside ..." That's all I've got.

I squeezed the bridge of my nose. Sandy's theory about the Dragon being a double-crossed Chinese businessman hadn't panned out, and we'd got no further with identifying him. Until we knew exactly who he was or what he was planning, we were at risk of having the whole plan derailed. And the clock was ticking ...

'Do we think any of these men could be the Dragon?' asked Jake, motioning towards the photos of the three Nyan on the whiteboard.

Sandy shook his head. 'None of the Nyan have any current link to Rok-Tech. That email implies the Dragon is already working there.'

'Our mission will only be a success if Sergei takes over Rok-Tech and moves forward with selling the VirtuWorld software internationally. If this Dragon starts causing trouble within Rok-Tech it could all be for nothing.' I looked at Sandy. 'We need to find him.'

'We're stretched enough on resources as it is. We can't afford to lose days trying to track down a shadowy figure we might never locate.' Sandy sucked his teeth as he thought. 'Ask Dasha about the Dragon. She's wired into Dimitri's whole business network and all their wives. She might know something.'

I got out my phone and texted Dasha that I'd see her the next day before the committee meeting in the playground near her house. It was going to be risky talking out in the open with lurking bodyguards but if it got us closer to knowing who the Dragon was it would be worth it.

'Well, well, look who's all grown up.'

Leaving the office and turning down the corridor I had come face to face with Tennant. The years had been kind to him: apart from his dark buzz cut having a few flecks of grey he looked exactly the same. I tried not to wonder if he'd think the same of me.

'Hello, sir. Been a long time.'

Tennant was a no-nonsense Northerner who'd been my lead trainer at the Farm. The nickname for Platform Eight's large training ground, situated in a remote part of West Scotland, was down to the enormous warehouse's rows and rows of tiny cage-like rooms which were our makeshift sleeping quarters and made us feel not dissimilar to battery hens.

'Good to see still you're still here.' This was a much-used line at the Platform. 'How's it all going? Becoming a Rat the right choice?'

'Yes, sir. It was.' And I meant it. I had never looked back.

'You're in Unicorn, aren't you? What's Sandy been like as a unit leader?'

'So far, so good. He's a miserable git but he hasn't got any of us killed yet.'

'I'll need to talk to you and Jake. Chief is retiring next year and Sandy is on the shortlist to replace him – I'm here for an informal interview with him.'

This was big news and something I couldn't get my head around.

'I can't imagine Sandy wearing a suit every day and having to spend time brown-nosing with Pigeons.'

Tennant chuckled. 'I thought the same, but this time when we approached him he did express an interest. Maybe after so long underground he thinks it's time to surface.' He paused. 'Well, that and the alimony payments to the ex-wife. So play your cards right and you could be Unicorn's next unit leader.'

I shook my head. 'I doubt that. For a start, there's Jake. He's got several years' experience on me. And I don't exactly think of myself as management material.'

Tennant shook his head. 'Jake will never leave fieldwork. He needs an outlet. Or there'd be trouble for everyone, particularly him. And don't knock yourself down – you made it here, didn't you?'

'Yes, but I don't think having a baby has done me any favours.'

'It's hard, isn't it? Always having to prove yourself. Us minorities have a tough time of it.'

'Sir?' I took in Tennant's middle-aged white maleness.

'I'm gay.'

'I . . . I didn't know that.'

'I've never hidden it. People just never really think to ask. My Eight profile actually has under special skills "being gay". I thought it was a piss-take at first, but the Platform never joke. I think they worry gaydar is real and can't risk pretend poofs going in undercover.'

I laughed. 'Yes, that sounds about right.'

'I'd better go see Sandy. We've a lot to get through. It was good to see you, Tyler; and remember, you can do anything you put your mind to. Or did surviving the Farm teach you nothing?'

Tennant was right – I shouldn't rule myself out just because I had dared to take a few months off to have a baby. I knew I could do the job.

The glass ceiling was no match for a machine gun.

'Why don't you and Gigi join me in Singapore next week? I just have one day of meetings to get through and then we can stay on and have a proper holiday.'

I had hoped a Chinese takeaway with my husband would be a relaxing end to a long day. But now an argument was coming. 'Just think, me, you, Gigi, out in the sunshine. Five-star hotel. Cocktails by the pool. It'll be great.'

'Of course it would be.' I put some vegetables and the bigger of the two jumbo spring rolls on to his plate. 'But you know I can't. I've only just got back to work and I'm leading a big project right now.'

It was all true, and that was before I factored in the horror of coping with a thirteen-hour flight and jetlag with a young baby.

'I'm sure they can spare you for a week. Most women take a year off for maternity leave.' He put down his chopsticks. 'What are you going to regret more – not doing enough "data analysing", or not spending enough time with your daughter?' He accentuated the words 'data analysing' as if they were swear words.

This was Will, the world's most relaxed man. Except when it came to not getting his way. I took a deep breath and tried not to raise my voice.

'And what about you? Aren't you going to regret doing too much "lawyering" and not enough "daddying"?' He started to interrupt and I cut him off because I knew what was coming. 'We're both her parents. We both have careers. Don't try to make me feel guilty for wanting exactly what you want.' I held his gaze as we waited for him to decide if he was going to fight on or back down.

He sighed. A promising sound of retreat.

'I'm sorry. You're right. We're a team and if your work means that much to you I need to respect that.' I knew he wasn't convinced. The fact was he knew me well enough that it was difficult to understand why I would be so passionate and dedicated to a job that sounded so damn dull. I had never been tempted to tell him the truth about what my job really entailed.

'Honey, I kill people for a living,' would have him grabbing our daughter and running out the door before I could finish with, 'but only baddies.'

We both started eating. Busying our mouths with food and our hands with reaching for more. The Singapore idea may have been shelved but there was the unspoken bright pink elephant in the room. That mothers were judged differently to fathers.

Over the years I had fought hard (literally) to show I was just like the other Rats, just as hardcore, just as ruthless. And it had worked. I had been accepted into the elite assassins' fold and considered an equal.

But now, once again, I was back battling the injustice of inequality. Needing to prove to the office I was just as good at my job even though I was a mother. Needing to prove to even my husband I was just as good a mother even though I was back at my job.

No wonder I felt permanently exhausted.

I went upstairs to check on Gigi. She was fast asleep. I stroked her hair and felt the softness of her cheek. Adjusting to going whole days without seeing her was tough. I wished I'd been there to tuck her in. To see her big blue eyes open and hear her rapturous giggles when I showered her with kisses and tickled her neck.

As I melted into our warm soft bed I thought again of the Farm. I had left it ten years ago. No matter how difficult I was finding life now it didn't even begin to compare to the torment of my time there. It had been nearly a year of being pushed to the limit mentally and physically as instructors like Tennant tested, shouted, prodded and poked at us, weeding out those who were worthy of being a Rat. Every night we would collapse into our tiny rooms, and I would stare up at the wire mesh ceiling and think how we were lined up in what felt like little boxes, training for a job that could lead to us ending in a marginally smaller box all too soon.

It was something that always stayed with me. No matter how grand and beautiful the bedroom was, I would stare at the ceiling and think about how it was just another box. Lying down, looking up, it all felt the same.

I thought of my daughter asleep upstairs. Early death was one of the risks of the job. Before, I only used to hope it would be quick and the pain not too great before I disappeared into the darkness. A shot, a shrug and a goodbye world. A short fast run at life in that fire-engine red I had always wanted.

But now I was starting to feel differently. Leaving Gigi was a sharp fear that kicked me in the stomach. I needed to be there for her.

'I'm sorry about earlier, sweetheart.' Will got into bed beside me. 'I just really wanted us three to get away. I feel like we're hardly spending any time together.' He pulled me over into his chest.

'I'm sorry, too. I guess I'm more stressed than I realised about work.' He kissed my forehead and wrapped himself round me. I always felt safest in his arms. I don't know why. He wasn't the one who could kill an armed attacker without breaking a sweat. And he would be rubbish in a fist fight. But things felt quiet when I was with him. I could take a breath. I knew everything there was to know about this man and nothing about him scared me. Maybe that was why I was so at peace being held by him. He had no secrets.

There were only mine.

Chapter Fourteen

A NOTTING HILL PLAYGROUND on an unseasonably warm and sunny October morning is a perfect location for a covert meeting with an informant. The screams, the shouts, the cries, all perfect for drowning out the noise of conversation as well as any coherent thought.

Dasha was in a long tweed coat and enormous sunglasses, her snakeskin Birkin bag slung over her shoulder. She was pushing a pram with a Missoni print hood; strapped inside was a frowning Irina. Dasha's elder two children, Natalya and Viktor, stood next to her. Her two bodyguards hovered behind them. They looked even less thrilled about being in a playground on a Sunday morning than the several hungover fathers I had already spotted.

'Say hello to Alexis.' Dasha gently pushed Natalya and Viktor towards me.

'Hello,' said Natalya. Her blonde hair was held back in a navy-blue Alice band. She was wearing a tweed coat that matched her mother's.

Viktor had his father's dark eyes. He nodded at me and walked off towards the picnic tables clasping a book.

'He's very advanced for seven. Loves reading,' Dasha offered as way of explanation.

'Gigi loves the swings. Shall we go there first?'

'Wonderful.'

One of the bodyguards went to sit next to Viktor. The other followed us.

'Mama, look, it's Leonora and Iona!' Natalya had spotted two friends in the sandpit.

'Go on then, darling, we'll be right here.' Natalya skipped off towards them. Dasha watched her go. The two little girls looked up when Natalya joined them, but didn't smile. Dasha stiffened. One of the girls then held out her hand and pulled Natalya down next to her. The three of them leaned in together and started giggling. Dasha's shoulders slackened and she leant down to unclip Irina from her pram.

I got Gigi out from her embarrassingly stained Maclaren and plonked her in a swing. Dasha put Irina in the one next to her.

I kept staring down at Irina's empty pram. How was it so immaculate? Was there a drive-through pram wash I didn't know about?

I moved to the front of the swings so my back was to the bodyguard. I started pushing and Gigi squealed with delight. I looked down at her little chubby face, Mohawk hair blowing in the wind as she went back and forth. Irina was now swinging alongside her, her hands clapping. 'High! Want high. HIGH!' Dasha laughed and pushed her harder.

'What do you know about the Dragon?'

Dasha kept pushing the swing as Irina giggled.

'What is it? A new restaurant?'

'It's a codename. The Dragon is an associate of your husband's who wants him dead. He tried and failed to get someone to do the job for him last year. Yesterday we intercepted an email about how the Dragon is coming after Dimitri and Rok-Tech. We can't risk him interfering in our operation.'

'I've never heard of anyone called Dragon. I know this Mayfair property deal Dimitri's been working on has upset a lot of people so he could be one of the sellers he's . . . disagreed with.'

A wine merchant on St. James's had been burnt to the ground and the high-profile landlord of the property next door to it had been stabbed to death in a supposed mugging gone wrong. It was fair to say Dimitri's disagreements were a little more violent than usual London property negotiations.

Dasha adjusted her sunglasses. 'If you know about this Dragon, Dimitri will too and that means he won't be around for long. When it comes to his enemies my husband usually strikes before they do.' She chewed her lip as she looked over at Natalya, now running around the playground with her friends. She knew Dimitri better than all of us. No wonder she was nervous.

'What about "the three"? There was a mention of how Dimitri thought "the three" would protect him.'

Dasha kept pushing Irina as she thought. 'Three of the men on the Rok-Tech board are very close to Dimitri. They're all well connected, useful allies to have.'

'Could one of them be double-crossing him?'

'It's definitely possible. Last time I saw one of their wives she implied all was not well. There was talk of a management buyout at one point. But they're all based in Moscow – if they had plans for Dimitri or Rok-Tech they would only strike on Russian soil. If you British succeed it will be too late for them.' She shook her head. 'And if you fail, it will be too late for all of us.'

'You don't need to worry, Dasha. We're professionals. We won't fail.'

Dasha pushed her sunglasses back on to her head and looked me in the eye.

'You'd better not. We all have a lot to lose. No one more than me.'

'Mama! Come, please!' Viktor was standing in front of the picnic table, pointing to something in his book.

'I'll drop my children home and see you at the committee meeting.' Dasha plucked Irina out of the swing and carried her over to Viktor. The bodyguard who had been behind me came round and collected the Missoni pram. He stared at me unsmiling as he pushed the pram round the swings. I took Gigi out of the swing and strapped her into her pram. If Dasha was right and the Dragon was one of 'the three' they would not be a threat to the Pop – we could eliminate Dimitri without fear of interference. It would be back in Moscow, when Sergei and the Nyan were taking over Rok-Tech, that we needed to be on the alert.

As I was leaving the playground, I heard Dasha call for Natalya. The little girl was by the hopscotch court. She shook her head and motioned for Dasha to come to her. Dasha, with one arm around Viktor and the other pushing Irina in the pram, headed towards Natalya, who was now hop-skipping over the numbers all the way to the end.

'You try, Mama, you try!'

I stopped and watched, wondering how Natalya would take her mother's refusal. She must have got used to understanding that four-inch Louboutin heels, although fabulous, were movement-restricting. But Dasha touched her daughter's cheek, threw her snakeskin handbag to the ground, kicked off her shoes and hopped and skipped her way over the numbers on the ground. Natalya cheered her on, jumping up and down while clapping her hands. Viktor stood by Irina's pram laughing. At the end Dasha threw her arms in the air in triumph. The two of them hugged as Dasha swirled Natalya round. Her happiness made her beauty shine.

Dasha and Natalya walked hand in hand back towards Viktor and Irina. Dasha picked up her handbag and gave it a little shake; sand sprinkled off the sides. She slipped into her shoes just as one of the bodyguards came towards her pointing at his watch. The face I knew returned and she gave him a curt nod. Back to business for the Queen Bee.

An hour later I watched, silent, as a high-stakes negotiation played out in front of me.

'You do it.'

'No, you do it.'

Sitting in the Brasserie I was distracted from Dasha's to-do list monologue by a long-drawn-out argument at the next table. A mother had been asking her three-year-old daughter to put her coat on for the last fifteen minutes; over the course of which the little girl had been told there would be no television for the day (obviously something that the mother could not face withholding for longer), had been banned from play dates for a week and had lost pudding for a fortnight. It was excruciating to listen to. I stared at the little pig-tailed girl with her arms crossed and mouth set in a stubborn frown and was marvelling at her mother's ability to not scream, 'Just put your fucking coat on!'

Why didn't the girl do it? What did she have to gain by not doing it? Didn't she realise all the pain she was causing herself? Why upset the person who was quite obviously in charge? It was not dissimilar to the frustration we had with uncooperative interviewees. They had that same insistence to not comply despite the pain that was coming their way. At least they had reasons for trying to resist our persuasions. Here there was nothing other than, 'I just don't want to,' which was what the child was shouting now. Kids were a different entity entirely. How could you negotiate with individuals who lacked all rationality? It was a terrifying insight into what lay ahead. I made a mental note to sign up for the upcoming training talk that we'd had a memo about the week before: 'Mind Over Brain Matter: Why Talking Can Be More Effective Than Torture'.

'Alexis? Isn't that right?' Dasha drew my attention back to our table where everyone was staring at me.

'Yes, exactly.' I had no idea what I had confirmed but decided agreeing was by far the safest option.

'Great.' She looked down at her clipboard. 'Alexis will supply one hundred home-made cupcakes,' and made a small tick.

Fuck.

With the bonfire business finished, Claudia immediately launched into a hushed monologue to Cynthia and Dasha about her doctor's advice on her Valium dependency. Cynthia cut her off by turning to Dasha. 'What are you going to do about Natalya's party next month?'

Dasha eyes narrowed. 'What do you mean?'

'The church fundraiser is the same day. You must've seen the email?'

'You can always change the date?' offered Claudia.

Dasha was already scrolling through her phone. She looked up. 'It's Natalya's actual birthday. I have members from the Cirque du Soleil booked to do a private show and they are back on tour the day after.'

'Don't worry, I'm sure you won't lose too many guests to it. Only those in the school choir, as they're performing,' said Cynthia.

'Natalya's two best friends are in the choir.' Dasha took a long drag on her vape. 'I need to go.' She shrugged on her fur coat and got to her feet. Claudia and Cynthia practically tripped over themselves in their rush to accompany her out the door.

As Frankie ordered us another round of coffees I assured myself that staying here was an important part of my cover, a way to glean useful information about Dasha and Dimitri.

The truth was, I actually enjoyed these little snapshots of what life as a normal mother would be like. Drinking coffee, comparing notes, asking questions; it wasn't unlike the group therapy us Rats were occasionally forced to sit through. There was a lot of over-sharing, commiserating and getting to walk away cleansed of all 'counting down the minutes until bedtime' sins. Worries that had consumed me when home alone at 3 a.m. were laughed about here out in the open.

I listened as Shona regaled us with the lowdown of what her day out at Kew Gardens had been like.

'It was a good day, actually. Had an Insta:Shit ratio of 2:1.'

'What the hell's an Insta:Shit ratio?' Having spent years learning all the Platform's lingo it seemed I now had to get to grips with a whole other terminology.

Frankie laughed. 'It's the calculation of how many insta-grammable moments there are to how many hours of shit you had to put up to get them. A ratio of 2:1 is great – it means for the one hour of shit Shona had to get through; the rush-ing around packing the car, the backseat fighting, the whines about being hungry and tired legs, she got two instagrammable moments where everyone was smiling. You should always be aiming for a 1:1. But more often than not it's a 1:4.'

I thought back to last weekend's trip to the park. A painful hour of packing supplies into the nappy bag, two random crying fits, a poonami up the back requiring a full outfit change on a park bench but then . . . Gigi's elated face as she fed the ducks. Click. A total 1:1. They really did have it all figured out.

'Hallelujah!' Frankie was looking at her phone. 'The church fundraiser next month has been cancelled as they've already exceeded their fundraising target. I no longer have to give up a Saturday manning a hook-the-duck stall. Prayers really do work.'

But I knew better.

'I'd better go, I need to drop Gigi home before heading into the office.' I had mentioned I was back working part-time as a 'civil servant'. Years of experience had taught me those two words sounded so dull they made sure no one asked any further questions.

'Does your work not have a crèche?' asked Frankie.

I imagined Gigi lying on a colourful playmat in my grey stark office, while in the background the only noise interspersing the rumbling of the tube trains was the screams of reticent inter-viewees. I involuntarily shuddered.

'No, they don't have any facilities like that.'

Tamara watched me gather Gigi's things into the nappy bag.

'I used to be a stockbroker,' she said, 'but I genuinely believe raising my family is the most important job in the world. The high I got when Flora crapped in the potty for the first time was every bit as exhilarating as closing a deal that netted my firm millions. Walking through my kitchen admiring my daughter's faeces was my high point of 2013.'

'Right.' I didn't know what to say to that.

In the last few weeks, having infiltrated a group like this, I was starting to see the all-encompassing, life-changing truth of what being a mother really was.

No one ever talks about the strength you need to have. Not just the day-to-day muscles to cope with picking up a contorting tantrumming kid, or lugging a toddler-filled buggy up a steep flight of stairs, but the actual mental strength to realise it's not about you anymore. No matter what's going on in your life you have tiny humans relying on you to get out of bed each morning, to feed them, to dress them, to act like the world isn't sometimes a shitty place where shitty things happen.

Tamara took her youngest to her first day of school while still bleeding and cramping from the miscarriage she had just had.

'She needed me, I wasn't going to miss it,' was all she said.

'It was the same when my father died,' offered Shona quietly. 'I wanted to just curl up in a little ball and sob for days on end. But I still had to come out of my room every now and then, look happy for the kids, and listen about how their day was and try to field questions about death and heaven without wailing so much it would frighten them.' I pictured Shona holding back the tears as she sat listening to her chattering and oblivious children.

As much as what we did at the Platform involved the frequent casual throwing around of words like 'courage' and 'hero', this bravery was more raw. These were real-life, day-to-day traumas and these mothers just picked themselves up and got on with things. That was what was expected of them. Christ, give me a gun and a room full of men to take down any day over having to tell a three-year-old that they weren't ever going to see Granddad again. Being a mother was such an under-valued job.

I looked round at all the women in the restaurant. All deep in conversation, all drinking heavily caffeinated drinks.

We were all warriors. Pounding the pavements as we pushed our prams. Locked and loaded with enough supplies to make sure we were prepared for combat at every corner; a tantrum here, a spit-up there.

Parenting was a war that left marks on us: physically, through the scars and stitches from the battlefield of labour; and, for some, mentally, in the big black dog of depression. It wasn't easy for any of us and the losses could be great: sleep, bikini bodies, social lives. But the victories were so very sweet. A smile, a hug, a kiss, a step, a word, every milestone a cause for celebration, a time to rejoice in the little miracles we had made. Our legacies. Living and breathing and growing all because of us.

And we would never raise the white flag of surrender.

Not even when they drove us fucking nuts.

I finally felt like I was getting it. Understanding what being a parent was all about. For the first time since we drove Gigi home from the hospital, at a steady 5 mph scared every little bump could hurt our precious cargo, I was starting to feel more relaxed. That maybe it was all going to be okay.

And then my phone beeped.

Please come to dinner on Saturday. Bring your husband. Dimitri wants to meet you.

'It could be a trap,' was Jake's immediate reaction to my admission that my playground date had spooked the bodyguards. Clearly they'd decided I warranted a report to their boss. 'I should come with you.'

I shook my head as I swallowed another mouthful of canteen cereal.

'It'll be okay. He just wants to put a face to a name and make sure I'm not a threat. Taking you would be too risky. We don't know how much he actually knows about me.' I sat back in my chair. 'The only person who could play my husband better than you is my actual husband.'

He took a long drag of his cigarette. 'I don't like it. You've no idea what you're walking into.'

'You know we aren't meant to smoke in here.'

Jake looked around the room bustling with Rats, caffeine, fry-ups and newspapers. 'Let's see who has the balls to report me.' It was not by chance Jake was sitting alone when I found him this morning, his reputation was such that people tended not to approach him unless invited. 'And what's the point in forcing rules on a bunch of people they hired to break them?' He ashed into his half-empty coffee cup. 'So what's your big plan, Tyler? You and Mr Lawyer walk into the Weasel's lair and bore him to death with how normal you are?' Jake had met Will several times but still refused to ever use his name.

'It's going to be easy. No tricky cover story to remember. I'll just be myself.' I paused. 'But perkier. More into babies, less into guns.' I continued eating my cereal.

Jake leaned forward. 'Dimitri's file is full of reports on his talent for making anyone who's pissed him off disappear. He's ruthless, violent and suspicious of exactly who you are.'

I put my spoon down. 'I can do this. Don't worry so much. If I say no to the invite he's going to find some other way to get to me. Saying yes means I have nothing to hide and I get a golden opportunity to plant a tracking device.'

I pulled out my phone and typed back a message to Dasha.

We would love to. You must show me Dimitri's favourite watch, I really need inspiration for what to buy Will for Christmas.

I looked at it for a second and then added an exclamation mark after 'Christmas'. I pressed send. Me but perkier.

I could do this.

On my way to Sandy's office to update him, my mobile rang.

Gillian. I braced myself for another conversation about what else the *Daily Mail* had informed her was a potential hidden danger to her granddaughter. Last week it had been baby wipes. The week before, limescale in the kettle.

'All okay?'

'Yes, everything's fine, Alexis. We've been having a lovely morning at home.' GigiCam had shown that Gillian's mornings at home usually involved Gigi wriggling on her playmat while Gillian snoozed in front of *Loose Women*. 'I just can't find Monkey and I know Gigi likes sleeping with him.'

I tried to think back to where I had last seen him. The nappy bag.

'Monkey is in the bag.'

'Oh, yes, why didn't I think of that? I'll just check. It's right here on the table.' There was a pause as she rummaged through it. 'Ah, yes, found him.'

I looked up to see Bennie standing next to me. I stared at him. 'I have to go,' I told Gillian, and ended the call. 'Looking for another chance to try to crush my firing hand?'

'I don't know what you're talking about.' He smirked. 'Sounds like all that sleep deprivation is making you very clumsy. Better quit now before you really injure yourself.'

'I'm never going to quit, Bennie. So stop with the attacks. I'm too much of a professional to engage in this playground bullshit.'

'I wouldn't say personal calls on work time were very professional.' He tutted.

I wrinkled my brow. 'What are you talking about? I just came off a high-level call of the utmost importance. Why would you . . .?' I stopped. 'Oh, of course. You wouldn't know about Monkeys.'

I walked off, leaving him frowning that there was an animal codename in our glossary he was not yet privileged enough to know about.

Sandy had none of Jake's reservations about the dinner.

'Excellent. This is just the break we need.'

'What about back-up?'

Sandy shook his head. 'Too risky. Signs of our people watching the house could be what he'll be looking for. Besides if he's on to you then back-up won't help. The mission is blown.'

Eight had no interest in saving me if it looked like Dimitri and his team were going to take me out. It was better for the Platform to let me die than show their involvement. Rats were there to make problems disappear. Not create them.

'And if your husband makes any fuss about going with you remind him of all the things he's dragged you to.'

I didn't bother pointing out that as tedious as the numerous partner events and work drinks Will had insisted I attend were, they had not at any point endangered my life.

Sandy opened up his laptop. 'What's the update on the Drunk Driver?'

'We've confirmed Dimitri is flying to Moscow by private jet from Farnborough airport. R & D are about to start work on embedding a needle into the Lamborghini driver's seat we sourced and we're slowly making progress on ways to neutralise the complicated alarm system in Dimitri's garage.'

'We're on the final countdown now.' Sandy looked up at me. 'We can't afford any setbacks. This dinner party had better end with Dimitri thinking you're just a boring mum friend or we're fucked.'

From: 8inchesatleast@sizedoesmatter.com
To: lex.tyler@platform-eight.co.uk
Subject: GirlsLikeBigD**ks
MISSION: #80436
UNIT: UNICORN
WEASEL: DIMITRI TUPOLEV
ALERT: 8 DAYS TO POP DAY

Chapter Fifteen

D-DAY.

Tonight Will and I would be dining with Dasha and Dimitri. I stared at myself in the mirror. I was preparing for social warfare and my husband was my wingman. It had taken a while to find a dress that would help me do my best 'rich and thin' impression. I'd settled on a burgundy Whistles number with a gold trim and inbuilt support.

'Wowzers,' was Will's reaction as I came downstairs. 'Now remind me who these people are again?'

'Remember I told you about that kids' charity I had got involved with? Dasha works with them too. And her children are at a school we might send Gigi to.'

'She's not even seven months old and we're talking schools?' He laughed.

'Actually, we're already late to the waiting list. You're meant to put them down for it at birth.' For some reason I wasn't laughing with him.

'That's just crazy.'

'Well, it's the way things are done.' I was very aware I was sounding like Tamara. I tried to shake it off and adjusted his tie for him. 'And, darling, don't mention GCDSB. If anyone asks about my work let's just stick with "civil servant". Her husband is one of those paranoid Russian types and I can't face an evening of being interrogated over what British security practices involve.'

'You don't need to worry. Even after all these years you do realise I have no idea what "Government Data Co." is actually called. GC . . SDBG . . . GC . . I give up.' He gave me a long kiss then stroked my cheek. 'Let's go before I decide to keep you here instead.' He took my hand.

I really hoped I wouldn't regret walking into this exclusive Notting Hill dinner party unarmed.

Having observed Dasha and Dimitri's house several times from outside in all its detached glory I had to admit I had more than a professional interest in seeing what it was like inside. I rang the doorbell and looked up and down the street while we waited. In the large communal gardens opposite, lit up by the overhead street light, was a man wearing a baseball cap with his back to us sitting on a bench smoking. I watched the way he took a drag.

Jake.

Ignoring orders as usual. I smiled.

The front door opened and we were welcomed inside the marble hallway by a uniformed maid. In front of the grand sweeping staircase was a gilt table supporting an enormous white floral centrepiece that wouldn't have looked out of place at a royal wedding. We followed her through to the drawing room where there were lavish armchairs and plump sofas in grey velvet, and in the corner a large grand piano self-playing Mozart.

Dasha was standing alone in the impressive room, dwarfed by its ridiculous proportions. Her blonde hair was piled high on her head and she wore a pale blue silk jumpsuit and sky-high strappy heels. Round her neck was a diamond necklace that was so enormous it looked as though it had to be fake. Yet the way it beautifully caught the light from the oversized chandelier told me otherwise.

'Alexis, Will, welcome.' She held out her arms in greeting. One hand gripped her ever-present vape.

I had brought lilies. Beautiful white lilies. A funeral flower. I think she got the joke as she looked surprisingly happy at receiving them before handing them over to the maid.

She motioned for the waiter to come forward with his tray of champagne glasses.

'Dimitri is coming shortly. It's so nice having a relaxed dinner at home.'

'Yes. Quite.' I nodded in agreement although my idea of a relaxed dinner didn't involve Spanx, catering, or fake friends.

There were some noises at the front door and Frankie and her husband Boris were led in.

'Darling, this place is looking incredible.' Air kisses were exchanged.

A door slammed from somewhere in the house and a minute later Dimitri entered the room. He was larger and more imposing than the many photos we had of him would suggest. His thickset eyebrows gave him such a dark gravitas I could not imagine how he would look smiling. He gave a brief kiss to Frankie, a friendly back slap to Boris and said something obviously very witty in Russian as it made the smaller man laugh out loud. He approached Will and me.

'Good evening. Welcome to my home.' He stared at me, unsmiling, as we shook hands.

'Thanks for having us. Beautiful place you have here.' Will seemed totally unintimidated by the grand surroundings, the distractingly beautiful wife and the sinister-looking husband. I had underestimated just how used he was to forced socialising from his years as a high-flying lawyer. Or maybe I had just underestimated him.

Dimitri took a glass and sat himself down on one of the sofas. We all followed his lead.

'Papa! Papa!' Natalya came running into the room, having left her hiding place at the top of the stairs at the sound of his voice. She raced on to his lap, jolting his hand holding the glass, spilling champagne over him. He spoke shortly to her in low Russian. I couldn't understand what he said but I saw the girl's face fall and her eyes fill with tears. She bit her lip, nodded her head, and ran out of the room. Dasha's face darkened as she got up and followed her daughter. Natalya threw herself into her arms at the bottom of the stairs. Dasha held her for a few moments and stroked her hair before gently taking her hand and walking her up the stairs.

Tamara and her husband Ed walked in.

'Hello everyone!'

Happy to have an excuse to not focus on the awkwardness of our host's foul mood we all got up to greet them with an enthusiasm that I think surprised them. Dasha returned to the room, her hostess smile once again in place. As soon as greetings and air kisses had been undertaken we all sat back down again. Tamara was the first to break the silence.

'So, how are you Alexis? How's little Gigi?'

'Good, thank you. Gigi could do with sleeping more but she's going through such a sweet stage. I must have about a million photos of her on my phone. I—'

'Show me.' Dimitri interrupted. There was a pause as we all looked at him. 'I love babies. Don't I, darling?' He turned to me and said again more insistently, 'Show me.'

Dasha drained her champagne glass.

'You don't need to tell a new mother twice.' I reached into my bag and pulled out my phone. I clicked on to photos and straight away a grinning Gigi popped up. I looked down at her beautiful face and felt nauseous. It felt as if somehow this man's darkness could sully her very innocence just by his glancing at her image. I cleared my throat.

'So this was today. Look how pretty that dress is. And here,' I flicked to the next one where Gigi was covered in puree, frowning. 'She wasn't so sure about the new flavour we tried at dinner.'

Dimitri took the phone out of my hand and started to flick through the photos himself.

A sign that he was suspicious of exactly who I was, or he was so lacking in social etiquette he didn't realise that going through someone's camera roll uninvited was the equivalent to rifling through their underwear drawer.

'Okay, you just go ahead. As you can see, she loves the swing, and . . . yes, there she is in the bath with Daddy. You can't see anything can you? Lucky for bubbles!' I took another gulp of champagne.

'Now, yes, there's a nice one of me and her; a selfie, of course. Husbands never take photos. There are hardly any nice ones of me with her and hundreds of them together.' There were murmurs of, 'That's so true' from all the wives except Dasha; she was now drinking her second glass of champagne as she stared straight at Dimitri, who was continuing to flick through the two thousand four hundred and fifty-six photos I had on my phone.

Suddenly the sound of Gigi gurgling came into the room, along with my embarrassing baby voice saying, 'That's it! Come on, roll over! Come on, you can do it! Who's a clever baby?'

Somewhere around the halfway mark Dimitri stopped and tried to hand my phone back to me but by now I was actually quite enjoying my Gigi slideshow.

'Actually, if you go a little further back there's a great one where she's holding a rattle in each hand. It's quite amazing – at this point she was only four months old and Google told me that it was very advanced to be dual holding so young.' I leaned over and flicked through until I reached the photo I was looking for.

'See?' I showed him Gigi's triumph.

'Yes, I see. Very nice. Lovely daughter.' He directed this at Will.

A golden Labrador came into the room. As Dasha desperately wanted to reinvent herself as a member of English high society it wasn't surprising she'd selected a breed of dog in keeping with the social class she was trying to break into.

'He's not allowed in here.' Dimitri grabbed the dog by his collar and took him through to the next-door room.

Frankie moved into the space on the sofa he had vacated.

'Darling, I have to ask. Your interior designer, was it Sergio?'

Dasha leaned back and folded her arms. 'Yes.'

Frankie clasped her hands to her chest. 'Sergio only takes on two projects a year. I cannot believe you got him.'

'Would you like to look round?'

The Queen Bee was offering up the keys to her kingdom. Of course we weren't going to say no.

The house was, as expected, perfect. But too perfect. It had been interior designed to death. In the elaborate drawing room every coffee-table book on the velvet ottoman had been precisely positioned and quite obviously never opened. The modern kitchen, all clean lines and smooth countertops, was so stark it was hard to believe there was real food in the cupboards.

I thought of our small terraced home, how it was positively straining at the seams to contain all the life within it. Cupboards that couldn't quite completely shut because of all the toys inside. Bookshelves heaved with battered paperbacks and the odd loose photo – ones that had made us smile but we hadn't quite got round to finding a frame for. Laundry haphazardly hung to dry round the house. A pile of shoes by the door. It was a home that was well worn but real. And, sleep deprivation and secret job aside, pretty happy.

Dasha's home felt cold, devoid of love, a monument to the unhappiness of the family that lived there. Or maybe I was being dramatic. Maybe it said nothing at all except that they were rich with good taste and I just knew the lady of the house wanted her husband dead.

Chapter Sixteen

'ALL YOU NEED IS LOVE' was the somewhat hopeful senti-ment in red curly script above a four-foot black-and-white close-up wedding photo of Dasha and Dimitri. Staring into each other's eyes, hands clasped, proudly showing off their bling wedding rings. This testament to their love was hung on the wall opposite their bed.

'That song was our first dance.' Clearly the irony of that choice when marrying a man worth billions was lost on Dasha. 'The rings are a Cartier special commission. Russian wedding rings in gold, platinum and black diamond to com-memorate his mother. She had very simple and traditional taste.'

I looked at the three interlocking rings on each of their fingers. There was nothing simple or traditional about those rings – even the gold and platinum ones were glinting with extra diamonds.

Dasha had already led Frankie and Tamara through to her dressing room. I took a quick glance around and followed them.

'Oh my fucking God, woman, this place is insane.' Frankie slumped down on to the ornate chaise longue in the centre of the room. 'I never want to leave.'

'We're really happy with how it turned out.' Dasha ran a finger along the corner of one of the shelves. She looked at it and rubbed it against her thumb. 'We carefully planned everything. Even a hidden safe for my jewellery and Dimitri's watches.'

'Does he have many watches? I'm thinking of getting Will a new one for Christmas.'

'Dimitri has quite a collection and wears a different one every evening, although he always wears the same one during the day. A gold Rolex. It was made especially for him. He takes terrible care of it though. Never puts it back in the safe like he should. I even found Natalya playing with it in the bathroom this evening.'

'Jesus! Lucky he didn't see her, can't imagine he would've taken it calmly,' said Frankie, half laughing. There was a pause as we remembered his flash of temper earlier.

I cleared my throat. 'Dasha, please could I use your loo?'

'Of course, it's right through there.' She gestured to a small door at the back of the dressing room.

Inside the expansive marble bathroom I saw Dimitri's Rolex next to the sink. I reached into my dress and pulled the small bespoke metal picks out of my underwired bra. I turned the watch over and, using the delicate tools, unscrewed the back of the watch. I took off my right earring and used the other end of the picks to dislodge one of the tiny gems from its setting. I placed the gem inside the watch and carefully replaced the back. The whole operation took just under a minute.

You've still got it, I thought, as I watched myself in the mirror putting my earring back in. I flushed the loo, ran the taps for a moment and opened the door to find myself face to face with Dimitri. He filled the whole doorframe.

'Sorry, I didn't realise you were waiting.' I kept my voice level as I looked him in the eye, small grin fixed to my face. Normal. Boring. Harmless. This was what I needed him to think of me.

He made no move to get out of my way.

'Such a beautiful home you have, it really is impressive. Love everything you've done with it. You must be so used to compliments about it, but it really is wonderful.' I paused for breath. 'So are the others back downstairs?' I tried to peer behind him. The dressing room was quiet.

His eyes ran slowly up and down my body. I couldn't tell if he wanted to seduce or frisk me.

'I'd better go, give you your privacy.' I took a step towards him. He didn't break eye contact as he moved back and crossed his arms. On his right hand the skin on his knuckles was broken. I stared at the Cartier wedding ring and wondered how often he had to wipe blood off it.

'Panadol,' he said as I passed him.

I stopped and turned round. 'I'm sorry?'

'I needed some Panadol. I have a headache.'

'Oh, right. Hope you feel better.'

'The ladies are downstairs.'

'Okay, thank you.' I turned and walked through the dressing room, feeling his eyes boring into my back.

Everyone was sitting back down on the sofas in the drawing room, except Dasha, who was standing in a corner of the room clutching a champagne glass so tightly her knuckles were white. She looked up as I walked in. I gave her a brief nod and her shoulders slackened.

I sat down next to Will. He put an arm around me and handed me my glass. 'I'd better check in with Beata.' I reached for my handbag on the floor and pulled my phone out. Clicking on to my Geraint-modified Google Maps I saw a new blue dot on our exact location. The Rolex's tracking device was up and running.

As soon as Dimitri rejoined us, Dasha interrupted the somewhat strained small talk.

'Excuse me, everyone.' She paused until we were all quiet. 'Dinner is served.'

We were escorted through to an impressively laid dining table. Enormous floral arrangements were interspersed with tall solid silver candlesticks. We took our seats, aided by beautifully calligraphed place names. I looked around the room. In any social situation there can be an undercurrent of something else, an alternate dialogue, a secret whisper. And tonight was no different. Except rather than the inappropriate lingering looks between a man and someone else's wife, instead of a bitchy whisper about the hollandaise being bought not made, there was a woman who wanted her husband dead, and a dinner guest who had been tasked with doing it. And all without arousing the suspicions of a foreign superpower wanting to take over the world with a weapon of mass intrusion.

Thank goodness there was Tamara hissing that she couldn't believe Dasha had copied her monogrammed linen napkins down to the exact font and Pantone colour, otherwise it wouldn't have been a proper West London dinner party at all.

Frankie and I were sitting on either side of Dimitri. Before I could even take a mouthful of the smoked salmon and caviar starter he was firing questions at me:

'Where did you meet your husband?'

'How long have you been together?'

'Where did you meet my wife?'

'How long have you known each other?'

'What's that writing on your necklace?'

I hadn't realised that over the course of his questioning I had been fingering my pendant. Will intervened from the other side of the table.

'It was her push present. Although I always said it was a bit of a cheat as she didn't actually push.'

'I think what I went through still warranted a present, though?' Will would be getting an elbow in the ribs for that later.

'Of course, my darling. Absolutely.' He grinned at me, as if he could read my mind.

'Was it a difficult birth?' asked Frankie. She took another glug of wine.

'It was a shock. I didn't expect it to hurt so much.'

With all my years of training, and not to mention work out in the field, I believed I had a pretty good pain threshold. I'd been captured and, tortured three times. Once I was shot in the thigh and, in our makeshift tent in the middle of the Sahara, Jake had to get the bullet out with a heated spoon. I'd therefore considered childbirth a slightly irritating formality that needed to be undertaken before I got to meet my daughter. After all I had been through, pushing out a baby, a wholly natural act that women all over the world did every minute of every day, I thought would be, well . . . a bit easy.

I was wrong. So fucking wrong. Each contraction released guttural barely human cries and a searing agony I had never felt before.

'Lex isn't great with pain are you, sweetheart?' Will grinned. 'She actually threatened the midwife with violence. Can you believe it? This delicate little flower screamed at the poor woman that she would rip her apart limb from limb unless she got some drugs.'

I laughed, hoping it wasn't unheard of for women to get a little aggressive when in the throes of labour.

'Will does like to exaggerate. But she was very annoying.' I bristled, remembering how the perky midwife's fanny-side repertoire had only seemed to consist of 'Oh dear.'

'So Gigi was whipped out via the sunroof?' asked Frankie.

'Yes. She got herself into the wrong position.' I took another mouthful of my starter.

'Next time, you must use my doctor at the Portland. The man is an artist. Barely leaves a mark,' said Tamara.

I thought of the starting line Gigi had burst through upon her arrival. Of all the scars I had got over the years, all mementos of bravery, lucky escapes and war wounds for my country, this was the scar that would always mean the most. A permanent reminder of the life I brought into this world and so much more meaningful than reminders of the lives I took out.

'So now I understand,' intervened Dimitri. 'This necklace you are wearing was your reward.' His mouth curled. 'For the hardship.' He was mocking me. I gritted my teeth, remembering I was in polite company, and that now was not the time to end his life.

'Yes. Exactly. The G on it is for Gigi.'

'What's on the other side?' He had caught a glimpse of the engraving on the back. I turned it over so he could read it. '*Mes filles sont mon monde*. You're French?' He looked between Will and me.

We caught each other's eye and laughed.

'No. Not at all. It's well, it's a bit funny really . . .' I trailed off.

Will continued for me. 'We were in a café one morning, and this couple next to us started arguing. Even though they were so angry with each other because it was in French, to us it still sounded beautiful. So it's kind of became our thing. Any big insult. Or any big compliment. We do it in French. Don't we, *ma chérie*?'

'You two are just too sweet for words,' said Frankie. 'But my French is awful. What does the engraving mean?'

'My girls are my world,' I said quietly.

'And you really are, my beautiful.' Will toasted me with his glass. '*Mais vous ne pouvez pas faire cuire du tout* . . . But you can't cook for shit. See which sounds better?'

We all laughed; even Dasha. Only Dimitri remained stony-faced. This bringing-your-husband-to-work thing was turning out quite nicely.

My interrogation from Dimitri over with, we thankfully reverted to more talking as a table. We may have all been very different but being parents gave us common ground that brought us together in a way no other subject could.

First of all, schools were debated. It was agreed that if a school wasn't featured in the Tatler Schools Guide, it didn't matter how well it did in the league tables, there was obviously something wrong with it.

Next, sleepless nights got a lot of airtime. Tamara told us about sleep consultants who could sleep train your baby, or you could call them for pay-by-the-minute advice. They may have had the same extortionate rates as high-class hookers and dodgy phone lines but they were selling sleep rather than sex. Two lucrative industries; one for bored husbands and another for exhausted wives. I wondered if they did package deals for couples where the women had got so used to outsourcing their duties to staff they wouldn't see it as cheating, just as another inconvenient task ticked off the list.

Then we moved on to the joys of dressing toddlers. Frankie was despairing about her son's refusal to wear anything that didn't have Spider-Man on.

'Do you have any idea how difficult it is to try to dress a convulsing hysterical octopus? One day I'd love to see Prince George turn up for a photo call not perfectly dressed in Edwardian Sunday best but his Thomas the Tank Engine PJs and Kate shrugging her shoulders saying, "The little fucker insisted." That right there would help people relate more to the monarchy.'

The way Dimitri was staring at her, I couldn't work out what offended him more, her language or how she was gulping the Château Lafite faster than the waiter could pour it.

As we were all enjoying the most delectable pear tart I had ever eaten, the waiter stepped forward to fill up glasses, Dimitri caught his eye and shook his head. He stood up.

'Apologies. I have a conference call to make. Good to see you all. No need to get up. Please, as you were.' Dasha continued her conversation with Tamara's husband, Ed, without openly acknowledging her husband's departure, a slight clenching of her jaw the only outward sign she had noticed his early exit. Dimitri disappeared into the kitchen, no doubt to recover the rest of the wine to drink alone. As the door was swinging shut I saw him give the Labrador a good kick as it begged for leftovers.

'Sorry for Dimitri.' Dasha directed at this at Ed and Boris who were sitting either side of her. 'He's been having a bad day.

His big property deal is taking longer than he hoped to come together and he just found out his beloved Lamborghini will be under repair for the next couple of weeks. He will have to make do with his Ferrari. This is what you call first-world problems? Yes?' She looked over at me as Ed and Boris laughed. Great. All the prep we had done for the Lamborghini was now wasted and we had only a week to source and steal a limited edition Ferrari.

With the host and the wine's departure it was clear our presence was no longer expected. We were all fast to make our excuses and leave in a flurry of compliments and promises to do it again soon. As we were walking out I looked at the family portrait by the front door. I stared up at Dmitri's likeness.

He had proven to be a poor host; he'd made his daughter cry, cut off the wine supply, and assaulted his dog.

I really was going to have no problem killing him.

'Dasha and Dimitri are a funny couple, aren't they?' was Will's analysis as soon as we were in the safety of a (genuine) Uber and assessing the evening and the other guests.

'What do you mean?'

'They didn't exchange a word all evening.'

'I don't think they're very happy.' Understatement was everything.

'They're not even playing for the same side.'

I got exactly what he was saying. Will and me were a team; we prepared together, applying war paint and armour, ventured out into the field together and fought alongside each other. And now here we would get to do a post-action evaluation. Notice weaknesses that were exposed. Forms of attack that were successful. Areas where our defences needed to be higher. It was us against the world. Dasha and Dimitri were fighting tooth and nail on opposite sides and if it was evident to even Will who had just met them, her supposed friends must know more about it than they were letting on.

Chapter Seventeen

Halloween was always a busy time of year at the Platform. The season's traditions were used to finally clear through our interview backlog. With fancy dress and excessive alcohol intake expected, a line of masked Rats could walk the streets propping up unconscious 'friends' and no one would look twice. In addition, Big Man Bert, our resident little person Rat, was dispatched to the homes of unsuspecting targets who would open the door proffering candy to the small silent Batman on their doorstep. They got easily tricked and then badly treated.

While other units were tasked with the Halloween offensive and responsible for very real screams in the night, Unicorn were focused on finalising the Pop plans. It was a whirlwind couple of days. Sandy had been called into Head Office for reasons he didn't divulge but were undoubtedly related to him being shortlisted for Chief. I had to field constant calls from him demanding updates, as well as calls from Will asking why I was working so much, all as we frantically searched for a Ferrari identical to Dimitri's. Yet somehow, I still managed to find the time to chuckle at photos of Gigi dressed as a pumpkin. It was good to remember the other side to Halloween; the one where the only danger in sweets were E-numbers and the biggest threat from small caped-crusaders skipping down the street was sugar-induced meltdowns.

'Are you absolutely certain Dimitri doesn't suspect you?' Sandy was back in the office and using our update briefing to grill me further on the dinner party.

'I'm positive.' I relayed the stand-off outside the bathroom. 'If Dimitri had any doubts about me he would've made a move—'

Jake cut me off. 'And what if his move had been, you know, a seduction move?' He smirked. 'Would you've been as willing as you once were to lie back and think of England?'

I winced at the memory. On my very first operation as a Rat in a joint briefing with a couple of the other units Sandy had assigned us our roles. Mine was to distract the target, swipe his phone and then safely return it to him after our Tech team had worked on it. The discussion that followed had led to some confusion over exactly what 'distract' meant. I'm still not sure if it was an enthusiasm to prove to my new colleagues I would do whatever it took to get the job done, or the Italian target's razor-sharp cheekbones and piercing blue eyes staring out at me from the glossy Surveillance photos. But I had made a fast analysis and decided this was something I would have no problem doing. For my country. Another look at the photos had helped. Yet my bravado-filled response of, 'Fifteen minutes? You aren't giving a girl long to get things going,' was met with a silence eventually broken by Sandy saying, 'Lex, when I say "distract" I mean spill a drink, ask him about the weather. Not anything else.' It was a credit to my colleagues' professionalism that they had remained straight-faced. Well, all except one, who drawled, 'I think for what you had in mind we'd need an 8.7, not a 7.2,' before collapsing into laughter. And that was my first introduction to Jake.

I ignored him and turned back to Sandy. 'We all know that Dimitri is both ruthless and violent with a small army of security to undertake his every whim. If Dimitri thought I could be a threat we would know by now. I haven't had anyone following me and Surveillance report Dasha is going about her usual routine. I'm positive Dimitri has written me off as "just a mother".'

'Let's hope you're right. I don't need to remind you how important it is that this Pop doesn't fail.' Sandy drummed his fingers on the table. 'How are we doing with the car?'

I outlined the issue we'd been having. 'Dimitri's limited-edition orange Ferrari has custom-made grey leather seats with black piping. There are only seven like it in the world. It's been difficult locating one, let alone working out how to steal it.'

Sandy ran his tongue over his teeth making a loud sucking noise. I tried not to grimace at hearing him trying to remove some remnant of his breakfast. 'Jake, how long will you have to fix the car once you're in Dimitri's garage?'

'Thirteen minutes,' said Jake. 'His team do frequent security sweeps. I can fix the explosive in that time but embedding the needle is not easy. Just one tell-tale rip in that Italian leather will give us away. I need to have an identical pre-prepared seat to swap over.'

Sandy stood up. 'Well you all need to work a fuck of a lot harder at sourcing one then. The whole Pop is reliant on Dimitri's Ferrari being fitted with a needle seat before Bonfire

Night.' He stared at me, 'You have three days to rig that car, Lex. No screw-ups. No excuses.'

We resumed our search for the six other Ferraris with a renewed vigour. Although hacking Ferrari's customer database had given us the owners' details it was difficult tracking down the exact location of the cars. All of those who owned this very exclusive model of Ferrari had houses all over the world, and their toys would be shipped over to whichever country they were currently in, or driven across a border for a particularly good party.

'There's one in London right now!' shouted Geraint, his fist punching the air.

Jake moved over to Geraint's desk, checked his computer screen and looked up at me.

'Okay, so the good news is: there is one currently sitting in a garage in the East End.'

'Thank fuck for that.'

'The bad news is it's owned by Ray Ray Campbell.'

'Shit.' Ray Ray was a bona fide East End gangster. A throwback from the good old days when people broke legs, shot off toes and asked questions later. All the Security Services knew of him. He was on every watchlist going. Thanks to his well-oiled drug-dealing enterprise he had so far managed to stay out of jail but we all knew that if anyone with any ties to that world turned up dead in his patch it was down to him. He had a killer temper and enough muscle to form his own army.

And we needed to steal his favourite car.

'What the hell's going on?' Sandy threw on to his desk a pack of photos that captured various moments from our last few committee meetings. 'I don't see Dasha in any of these. What the fuck are you playing at?' When he had called me into his office I had assumed it was for an update, not an ambush.

I flicked through the photos. In one I had my head back, laughing, Gigi clutched in my arms, a large croissant on the plate in front of me. It was actually quite a nice photo.

'Where did you get these? Who would waste time doing surveillance when I'm actually there?' As soon as I asked the question out loud I knew the answer. Bennie. That little prick. 'Sandy, these are bonfire committee meetings. Dasha usually leaves first and I leave ten minutes or so after. I can't go racing out after her every week. Don't you think that would look a little suspicious? And these are Dasha's friends I'm spending time with; who better than to give me the inside track on Dasha and Dimitri?'

'What have you learnt?'

I didn't want to say the only information relevant to work I had learnt in my bonus coffee after Dasha had left was Tamara's special stain-removal formula, which would work a treat on stubborn bloodstains.

'Nothing specifically operationally useful but it's all background. Although the Dasha I'm getting to know is nothing like the Dasha in the intelligence reports. She strikes me as someone who couldn't give two shits about politics or Russia.' It may have started as an excuse but I did believe what I was saying. I'd seen no indication Dasha was anything other than a West London yummy mummy who only cared about life in her privileged bubble.

'Right, Lex, so a few coffees later you think you know better than five months' background research. Dasha is a fucking pro. That posh mummy mask is just a front. She's happy to be written off as a rich bitch obsessing about her manicures but behind all that you have a calculating activist who hates The President and what he's doing to her beloved country. Feel free to go through any of the many gigabytes of data' – he motioned towards his laptop – 'we have confirming this,' his voice was rising, 'including numerous magazine interviews she gave back when she lived in Moscow. Just think about that – she was willing to risk her personal safety by going on the record to criticise that man.' Spittle flew out of his mouth. 'While you're out there on the front line flicking your hair and planning a party, some of us are doing the hard graft back here.'

'I know what I'm bloody doing, Sandy. You need to trust me and not little upstarts like Bennie who are after my job.'

He stared me down.

'It's not just Bennie who's questioning your commitment. You're the one with something to prove. So fucking act like it.'

I headed back into the meeting room, letting the door slam behind me. Jake was going through the blueprints of Ray Ray's garage.

'Will you please get that little shit Bennie off my back?'

Jake looked up at me, 'The Lex I know would never get someone else to fight her battles.' He picked up the sheaf of papers from the table. 'Maybe all that mummying has made you soft.' He headed out of the room. 'Don't lose your balls, Lex. They're what got you here in the first place.'

I slumped down into the chair. He was right. A year ago I would never have asked him for help. I was just tired. Tired and angry and fed up. I shouldn't be having to prove myself to Sandy or anyone else.

My angry solitude was interrupted by Joe Copeman, one of the Platform's more senior Rats, walking in brandishing a complex-looking device.

'Just been in your office and I see we have some new interrogation kit. I've never seen one of these before – how does it work?'

'Joe, that's mine.'

'Well talk me through it then. Let me guess. These clamp on to a guy's bollocks.' He turned it on. A loud vibration noise started up. 'Or do we have to cut them open first and use it to electrocute their kidneys. Or—'

'Joe, it's my breast pump.'

'Your what?'

'I clamp it to my breasts, it stimulates my nipples and then with a gentle suction motion it expresses milk out my breasts and into these bottles. It basically milks me. Like a cow.'

The breast pump went clattering to the floor. Joe looked pained.

'Lex, come on, don't leave shit like this lying around. It's making me feel all queasy.'

I looked at him. This was a man who had answered the phone to his mother as he rummaged around the insides of a gutted drug mule. A man who had carried on eating his egg mayonnaise sandwich as he hosed blood and brain matter off the inside of a storage container. Yet a breast pump was too much for him to handle.

'I need to get some air.' He left the room only to poke his head round the door a minute later. 'You' – he pointed at me with a sharp stabbing motion – 'have fucking ruined breasts for me.' He disappeared again.

I was really bonding with my colleagues today.

By early evening the plan to steal Ray Ray's car had been finalised and I released the team from the Platform. I just wanted to get home, gulp down a large amount of alcohol and vent to my husband. I had learnt how to 'Willify' events so I could still discuss work without risking national security. One time Sandy pissed me off by neglecting to mention the supposedly docile informant I was meeting was schizophrenic – and I ended up pinned against a wall with an eight-inch hunting knife in my face – I had told Will how Sandy really let me down by sending me into a meeting with an important supplier unprepared. Although the level of drama and risk of me being quite literally scarred for life were different, the advice he was able to offer ('tell him you're disappointed he didn't have the respect to give you the information you needed to do your job properly') was the same.

But Will, although home, was locked away in our spare bedroom on a conference call to America. I sat in our kitchen drinking a large glass of wine. Even a Willifyed version of the jibes about motherhood affecting my work ethic would spark talk of civil lawsuits with him not understanding that I'd signed away such rights the minute I'd signed up.

I had to deal with this myself.

He smiled the first time he felt something tickling up his leg under the duvet.

Perhaps dreaming it was a lover's gentle fingernail. The second time he twitched a little. The pressure was getting a little harder and it seemed to linger a little longer just at the top of his thigh. The third time his hand came down and he tried to brush away the cause of his discomfort. I'm not sure if it was feeling the cold metal of my revolver or hearing the click of the safety coming off which finally woke him. But with a start he sat up and was grasping at the side of the bed for his gun. Which wasn't there.

'I wouldn't move, Bennie.' My gun was now no longer lingering, no longer teasing, it was firmly ensconced right up against his crotch. 'You move and I fire and you get a new nickname. One-ball Bennie. Or maybe No-balls Bennie. Who knows how much of a mess a 30 calibre bullet will make down there.'

'What the fuck are you doing here? How did you get in?' Bennie's hair was ruffled, his eyes bleary as he tried to adjust to the dark.

'This is my job. Getting into places I shouldn't.' I tutted. 'Maybe you thought up here in your tenth-floor fancy gated apartment building with a twenty-four-hour security guard and two secure Banham locks, you'd be safe. But lookie here, in I waltz without so much as breaking a sweat. You know, I only came tonight as there was nothing on the telly. There was no reconnaissance, no planning, no nothing. Jesus, it was just so easy.' I laughed. 'It just goes to show you really should never underestimate a woman. It's sad how everyone does. The couple who let me drive into your secure garage behind them as I had been such a ditz and lost my car-park card. The security guard who kindly gave me your spare key so I could totally like surprise my boyfriend with like the most amazing birthday treat ever. And you. Let's not forget you, Bennie.' I jammed the gun against him a little harder. 'Did you not ever stop to think that to make it in a man's world a woman needs to be not just as good as a man but better?'

'You're not better than me,' he hissed.

'Really? Look at yourself. In bed, unarmed, with a gun against your balls. You need to leave me alone. Or you'll lose more than a ball or two.'

I slammed the door on my way out.

Chapter Eighteen

'WHERE THE HELL HAVE you been?' I got home to find Will pacing around the kitchen, Gigi crying in his arms. 'I heard you come home but when I finished my conference call you'd gone.'

I took Gigi from him and she quietened.

'I was an idiot. Realised I'd forgotten to lock my filing cabinet so had to race back in. Breaking security protocols is a fireable offence.'

He looked at Gigi in my arms, a podgy hand holding on to a strand of my hair.

'I've tried a bottle, singing to her, nothing worked. She clearly just wanted you.'

'Go to bed, I'll put her down.'

Will yawned as he walked up the stairs. 'God, look at the time. See, this is why we need a holiday.'

I had tried telling him that rather than embracing lie-ins babies tended to sleep worse when away. Will had restarted his campaign for me to book some time off. But I knew there was no time for a holiday any time soon, not with an upcoming Pop and the inevitable fallout from it. All of the Security Services were going to be on high alert, braced for retaliation in case our adversary suspected it wasn't an accident. And Eight needed to make sure that The President wouldn't try to interfere in Sergei and the Nyan taking over Rok-Tech. Until we owned our own copy of the VirtuWorld software it was still a looming threat.

As we got to her room, Gigi looked up at me, her hair even more skew-whiff than usual, her little chest still heaving from the effort of tears that were still glistening on her cheeks. Did she really only want me? I was the chosen one. Picked not because of any special skills, no particular talent, simply selected just for being me. Purely wanted for who I was and not what I could do. I was her mother and she knew it. And that gave me a warmth I didn't think possible.

I kissed her soft flushed cheeks and sat rocking her until she fell asleep. I stared down at her eyelashes and held her foot, marvelling at how snugly it fitted in the palm of my hand. I held my breath as I transferred her from my arms into her cot, crept out of her room and back downstairs into the blessed warmth of our bed. Will was already snoring. I lay awake listening to him and struggled to sleep. My mind, rather than shutting down, kept running over everything at work. Something was niggling. I didn't understand what. I had undoubtedly solved the Bennie problem, we had two tentative Pop plans in place, Sandy had said we were moments away from confirming the Nyan, and we even had a decent idea of how we were going to steal a violent gangster's car. With just days to go – this was pretty good. I should've been feeling confident; settling into that adrenalin-pumping excitement of being in the final stages of a mission. Everything we had been working towards was about to come to fruition. We were all set.

But clearly, lying here in the dark and quiet of the night, I didn't think so.

Dasha.

She kept coming into my head. She was what was bothering me. I had spent enough time with her to know something wasn't ringing true. I was finding it very hard to reconcile the living, breathing Technicolor Dasha with the black-and-white reports of a passionate activist wanting to sacrifice her husband, the father of her children, to take a strike against The President. Sandy seemed convinced that the intel we had was right – but I wasn't buying it. My training had taught me to always do a full, objective analysis of a mission. To look at all the different variables and isolate points of weakness, anticipate problems before they arose. And right now all my instincts were telling me she was the weak link. That she was going to be a problem. And we couldn't afford to fail. Not when what was at stake was life as we knew it.

By the time morning came I knew I was going to have to act. I listened to the strains of the radio coming from downstairs. Will was singing along as he made Gigi her breakfast. 'You gotta leave this place, you gotta get right out.' I recognised the song despite Will murdering it in the wrong key. It was another Platform Eight classic. Our busker in the Underground tactic was often rolled out on a worldwide scale through malleable young stars and lyrics containing important code words. Or in this case, broadcasting a pretty clear message. This song, released by a twenty-year-old Bromley boy with spiky hair and tight jeans, had been a massive hit. And led to the safe evacuation of every single asset we had in a country that was otherwise notoriously impossible to get communications into. Music that saved lives and royalties that boosted department budgets. We always had it all figured out.

But right now it didn't feel like that. In the shower I thought over my options. I needed something solid to take to Sandy. Dasha had been at the very heart of this operation from the beginning. If I was questioning her I was questioning the whole validity of the mission.

And in four days' time, I needed to push the button.

I needed to be sure. When I got out of the shower I texted Frankie. She pinged back straight away, inviting me to come join her for a kiddie swimming class and breakfast smoothie afterwards. Great. Squeezing into a swimming costume. The things I had to do for my country.

Lycra was undoubtedly a new enemy. Having shoehorned myself into my costume I got Gigi into the all-in-one swimsuit Gillian, her sun-fearing grandmother, had bought for her. Her arms and legs were fully covered and there was a non-detachable hood with cap and ear flaps that swamped her tiny head. Totally inappropriate wear for a leisurely splash around an indoor eighty-degree heated Kensington pool. But I hadn't had a chance to get her anything else, so burka baby it was.

As we came out the changing rooms and into the pool area, I was greeted with, 'Morning, Lex.' There was a well-built six-foot-five man, with a distractingly hairy chest, in a pair of ill-fitting red swimming trunks holding a baby who looked a few months older than Gigi. I stared at him.

It couldn't be.

'Tank?' I managed to get out.

'Actually it's just Tommy here. And this is Sophia.' He proudly held up his gurgling daughter, who was wearing a bright pink swimsuit with 'Daddy's Little Princess' on.

Tank was a highly respected Rat with a long track record of both bravery and brutality. He was a solitary, silent figure, who was always put forward for jobs that needed his particular level of brute force. Until now I had been pretty sure he was part animal. It was strange enough seeing him in swimming shorts, but him clasping an adorable pink-cheeked baby was too surreal to even comprehend.

'Good to see you, Lex. She looks a sweet one,' he said, pointing at what little he could see of Gigi peering out from her hood. With that, he deftly clambered into the water with Sophia tucked under his arm. I averted my eyes as he began singing 'Ring a Ring a Roses' while swinging Sophia. From mean machine down to cuddly, doting dad. It was heartening to know that even the strongest, most masculine of Rats could be reduced to a gibbering wreck who worshipped his child.

'Morning, Lex! You ready?' Frankie joined me by the side of the pool. I guessed if Tank could do it, so could I.

After a strained thirty minutes of wondering how dunking and near-drowning my baby was meant to be fun for either of us, I sat in the juice bar as Frankie ordered us both what she claimed was the best smoothie in London. I was debating how to bring up Dasha and Dimitri in a way that didn't appear too much like I was digging for information when she brought our drinks to the table and opened with:

'So let's talk about Dasha's fucking car crash of a marriage. He's a right miserable git, isn't he?'

If only all informants could be this easy to get talking.

'Slightly terrifying, right? Do you see them together a lot?'

'We go to a lot of the same godawful social functions as them. My husband has always been slightly in awe of Dimitri as his family are a big deal back in Russia.' She started vigorously stirring her smoothie. 'Dimitri likes strutting around like he's some god to be obeyed and not just a dodgy-dealing bastard who can't keep it in his pants.'

'He cheats on Dasha?' I looked suitably horrified even though Surveillance had numerous photos of him leaving smart hotels with women that were clearly not his wife. 'Do you think she knows?'

'I'm sure she has an idea but turns a blind eye.'

I tried not to wince as I took a sip of my smoothie. I was pretty sure it had kale in it. Jesus, it got everywhere.

'So if his family are a big deal out in Russia does that mean they're heavily involved in politics?'

'Dimitri's family business is some multibillion-dollar corporation so I'm sure he can't avoid it.'

'And Dasha?'

'Dasha?' Frankie laughed. 'The only loyalty she has is to the holy trinity of Chanel, Gucci and Prada. I don't think she gives a crap about Russia. She's a fully indoctrinated West London yummy mummy. Pretty amazing, considering how she was a total outsider when her eldest first started at Chepstow Hall.'

I thought of Dasha and her furs, confidence and disdainful looks.

'Really? I find that hard to imagine.'

'If you think Dasha is stuck-up you should meet some of the other Super Mamas at that school. They tore her apart when she first arrived.' Frankie put on a hoity-toity high-pitched voice. 'Too much make-up, horrible skin-tight clothes, trying to buy everyone's friendship with extravagant gifts.' She shook her head and laughed. 'But credit to Dasha, the whispers, the bitchy looks; they didn't break her. She kept pushing her way in, learnt all about what was considered socially acceptable and transformed herself. She started as the trashy Russian who'd wear a Hervé Léger bandage dress to a parents' evening and everyone avoided, yet by the end of the year she was the one holding court at the school gates head to toe in understated Stella McCartney.'

I was impressed. Dasha had clearly made it her mission to break into the school's elite and she had more than succeeded.

Frankie took a long gulp of her smoothie. 'I know Dimitri talks about moving back. He has to when he takes over the whole family business, but he's going to have a real fight on his hands getting Dasha out of here. Right now all she cares about is becoming head of the Parents' Association and bragging to everyone about how the school have recommended her eldest should try for a scholarship at St Paul's.'

Everything Frankie was saying seemed to ring true. The sensible conclusion was that Dasha had aligned herself to Eight because we both had the same motive, which was wanting Dimitri eliminated. The more I got to know her the more I realised it was most likely less about wanting to take a stand against The President, more about getting to stay in London. An informant having their own agenda shouldn't have worried me, but it did – if she was lying about her true motivation for cooperating with us, what else could she be lying about?

'Does Dasha ever confide in you?'

'God, no. We did have one moment last year where she seemed to warm to me. It was after I told her my son had mentioned one of the boys had been giving Viktor a hard time.'

'He was being bullied? That's terrible.'

'No, I don't think it was anything like that. You know what boys are like. Anyway Dasha clearly didn't think anything of it. She actually became quite good friends with the boy's mother and the father is now working for Dimitri's company in Moscow.'

I took this in. 'So the boy and his mum are still here in London?'

'No, they all moved out with him. Whole family got a rather nice relocation package.' Frankie took another sip of smoothie. 'It clearly pays to be friends with Dasha. Although Claudia and Cynthia, Tweedledumb and Tweedledumber, seem to be the only ones in the inner circle. Not that you'd get any gossip out of them. They only talk to people who they think can give them something.' She drained her glass. 'Wow, I feel so much better already. I can literally feel my body absorbing all those nutrients and goodness.' She stood up. 'Now I need a cigarette.'

Frankie's words stayed in my mind. Later that afternoon, at our final bonfire committee meeting, we sat listening as Dasha went over everything from confirming the location of the rotisseries for the pigs ('We need them displayed so people can be impressed by them but not so prominent those who are vegan might find it distasteful') to whether there was enough fuel for the bonfire ('We want huge roaring flames that the *Tatler* photographer can capture but we must also abide by the Gardens' Health and Safety recommendations').

'Don't forget people need a drink in hand within four minutes of their arrival . . .' Dasha looked down at her notes before checking her watch. It was the third time she had done so since she sat down in her usual flurry of fur and vape smoke. Today she was rattled. It was impossible to determine whether this was down to nerves over the upcoming social event going perfectly, or last-minute fears about being complicit in her husband's murder.

'Don't worry, Dasha, there's no harm in repeating things,' said Claudia, putting a hand on her arm.

'Exactly. We want everything to be perfect as much as you do,' added Cynthia.

I knew Frankie was right – if I wanted to get into Claudia and Cynthia's good graces I was going to need help. They had written me off as a boring, slum mum with nothing to offer. If I wanted them on side I was going to have to make myself a lot more interesting.

I excused myself from the table and headed outside to put in a call to Demon Communications, a press relations agency that, although it had no formal link to the darker underground world of the Security Services, unofficially handled Wolves. And what I needed to ingratiate myself with Claudia and Cynthia was a metal Wolf.

Metal Wolves were celebrities. They were classed gold, silver and bronze according to their level of fame and therefore operational effectiveness. They did the same jobs as Wolves, getting the headlines we wanted, except a hundred times more successfully. Metal Wolves could install bugs in restricted locations that would take us months to break into and even get up close and personal, sometimes very personal, with people we couldn't get within ten feet of.

Metal Wolves were usually recruited but often created. A few years ago the Committee were concerned that the candidate they wanted to be prime minister was not bonding enough with the blue-collar public. A Wolf was dispatched on to *Big Brother*. With his academic background in sociology, UN experience in tactical negotiations and agency training in psychological profiling (all backed up by a brief stint at drama school) he became a lovable dim-witted character who entertained the public with his innocent, eyebrow-raising stupidity and memorable catchphrases. He walked out the winner and the week after that did a cover shoot for *Heat* magazine with his favourite politician, 'a guy who really seemed to care about people like him'. The candidate's ratings went through the roof.

That poor Wolf was then, however, trapped in character, occasionally having to turn up to D-list celebrity parties and do glossy magazine shoots with his adorable sidekick Giggles the pug ('You can't have a life without Giggles!' was a much-repeated house favourite). He was desperate for his alter-ego to be killed off in a glitter-laden funeral so he could stop fake tanning, continue with his PhD and, most importantly, get away from the bloody dog he was allergic to. It may have taken a year but his request was finally granted. It was a suitably ostentatious affair with inappropriately dressed sobbing mourners and an affectionate eulogy from the politician. The whole sombre event was broadcast in an ITV special while the image of the politician paying his respects to the chief mourner, a black-tied Giggles the pug, was the most retweeted photo of the year. His party won the election by a landslide.

Our metal Wolves were a huge operational asset and therefore worth protecting. Stories we didn't want coming out were quashed by trading up for a much bigger scoop. To save a gold, a silver or bronze would be sacrificed. This was the risk they took when they made a deal with the devil. Demon could build careers and just as easily crush them.

Ten minutes on the phone with Demon and I secured a bronze Wolf to turn up and light the bonfire. I had tried for higher but the hard-talking publicist I had spoken to had torn me down. ('Look darling, we're all for helping the Rats but we just can't let one of our silvers turn up to such a shit event.')

When I returned to the table it was to triumphantly announce that I had secured a celebrity to do the honours of lighting our enormous bonfire. The Committee were suitably impressed. Well, all except Dasha, who barely glanced up at me as she was staring at her phone. It pinged and she looked down at it frowning before getting up with such force the table rattled, shaking all our drinks.

'I have to get home. I have a big meeting to prepare for.' She looked at Claudia and Cynthia.

'Actually we're going to stay for another,' said one.

'Yes, we have a bit of time before Pilates,' offered the other.

They turned back to me, poised, ready to fire celeb-related questions. People this shallow were so easy to get to.

An hour later I had learnt bugger all else from Claudia and Cynthia. I had made progress – they now seemed to view me as someone worthy of actually exchanging conversation with – but I had a long way to go until they spilled any dirt on their beloved Dasha. As we exchanged goodbyes and air kisses a text came in:

Royal Mail will attempt to deliver your item 'Queen-BeeOnFoot' today. For tracking please click here.

Dasha was on the move and I was going to be right behind her. She was clearly on edge and I needed to know why.

Chapter Nineteen

'TWINKLE, TWINKLE, LITTLE STAR, how I wonder what you are.' I kept singing in a low voice as I rocked a sleeping Gigi in her buggy. The bulletproof cover was safely secured on. It was a bonus that the reinforced material worked excellently as a blackout blind.

I checked my phone – Dasha should be coming around the corner up ahead any minute. I spotted her straight away. She was now wearing sunglasses and a long black coat with a fur collar. Her bodyguards were following a few steps behind.

I kept back as they made their way down the pavement and entered Holland Park. Dasha had to be meeting someone here, and considering the direction she took, it was most likely at the park café – which was not a location I could imagine Dasha choosing to meet her fellow well-heeled mothers.

I slowed my pace but kept them in sight. The park was busy for a cold November day but the tall, smartly dressed blonde and her two suited, burly companions were easy to spot amid the joggers, cyclists, mothers and children. As the café came into view I moved off the pathway and on to the grass, parking the buggy next to a large oak tree. I watched Dasha and her bodyguards enter the café and then lost sight of them in the bustle of people arriving and leaving.

I needed to see who she was meeting.

The café had large windows. How could I get close enough without being spotted?

And then I saw them.

Steaming down the pathway next to the river, the glorious sight of around fifteen women in workout gear. All pushing prams. Leading them was a woman wearing a bright purple hoody with 'BuggyFit' emblazoned on the front. They were walking in lunges. And heading towards the café. I took off my coat and stuffed it under Gigi's pram and pulled on my baseball cap. Seeing as I was wearing what Shona liked to call the 'mum uniform' of baggy black top, leggings and trainers, I should fit right in. I waited until they drew parallel to me before I jogged up to them, pushing Gigi, and started lunging alongside them.

'Hiya!' I said to the rosy-cheeked brunette nearest to me. 'Glad I caught up with you.'

'Yeah, we're easy to spot, aren't we? This is the best class. Cazza is such a great trainer.'

'Okay, ladies,' shouted the purple-hoodied woman at the front. 'Let's up the pace. A full lap round the park and then a grand finish back at the café, where we get to ruin all our good work with cake.'

The brunette grinned at me. 'See what I mean? She really gets us.' We lunged on together to the soundtrack of the odd cries and gurgles of our charges. I listened to everyone talk breathlessly in amid the panting and exclamations of 'God this hurts'. I was just another one of the pack; comparing notes on sleepless nights, complaining at ruined bodies and cooing at our cubs. We powered along the pathway and were soon right next to the café. I looked across at the tables outside. No sign of Dasha. I scanned inside and caught a glimpse of her next to a window. She was sitting down at a table with a balding man. I kept on moving with the BuggyFitters until the café was behind us. I glanced back. I couldn't see the bodyguards. I slowed down until I was at the back of my new lunging buddies, and peeled off to the side towards the bicycle racks round the back of the café.

I now just needed to get inside without being seen by Dasha. There were two different entrances; Dasha was sitting facing the door nearest me, which ruled out using that one. If I walked the whole way around the back and used the door on the other side I should be able to slip inside while staying out of sight of Dasha and her companion. I set off, pulling my cap down low in case her bodyguards were lurking outside.

Halfway there I knew something was wrong.

Someone was following me. My instincts weren't so rusty I didn't know when I was being watched. The dread was rising in my stomach. They had picked the right moment to approach me; this part of the park was quiet, with only a few people even in view. I silently cursed. Not here. Not now. Not when I had Gigi with me. I took a deep breath and knew one thing for certain. It didn't matter how many of them there were. And how many weapons they had. I wasn't going to let anything happen to her.

My nappy bag was attached to the pram, gently swinging as we walked. I unzipped it and put my hand inside it just as two arms reached around and grabbed me from behind.

'Supri— Arghhhh, Jesus!' I elbowed my would-be attacker in the stomach before flinging them up against the café wall with my left hand, my right grasping the pistol inside the nappy bag ready to pull out and fire into him or any other incoming hostiles. I took one look at the man crouched over holding his stomach and let my gun fall back into the bottom of the bag.

'Will! Oh, God, I'm so sorry! You scared me!'

My husband looked up at me and shook his head, smiling. 'If I wasn't so bloody winded right now I would be laughing. How the hell did you do that?'

'I just . . . I did that self-defence course at the town hall last year, remember?' I put my arm round him. 'Funny, really – I didn't think I'd learnt anything, but guess I must have.'

He straightened himself up. 'Well, there I was thinking I would surprise you, but you surprised me.' He rubbed his stomach. 'How are you so bloody strong?'

'I have no idea. Must be maternal instinct or something. I'm sure I read somewhere that fear of incoming danger to her baby can give a mother unnatural strength.' I attempted a laugh. 'Just call me Supermum. But what are you doing here?'

'I came to find you, of course. I'm flying to Singapore tonight, remember? All the way to the other side of the world for an action-packed twenty hours trying to stop our biggest client from leaving us. Everyone in the office is stressing out about it.' He loosened his tie. 'Seeing my girls is all I need to be reminded of how there's more to life than work.' He tapped my nose with his finger. 'I feel better already.'

'How did you know where I was?'

He pulled his phone out of his pocket and waved it at me. 'Find My Friends, remember? We downloaded it together last month. I just clicked on, saw where you were and hopped into an Uber.'

'Oh right. Of course. What a nice surprise.'

Wow. How embarrassing. Rat extraordinaire. Secret agent. Trained assassin. Tracked down by a free iPhone app.

'I've just finished a fitness class so let's go ruin it with an ice cream.' I motioned towards the café.

'Sounds good to me.' He slung an arm round me as we walked towards the café entrance. Before a waitress could show us to a table I marched right up to one that was a few tables behind Dasha.

'Let's go here.' I parked Gigi next to me and motioned for Will to sit opposite. I was now facing the man Dasha was sitting with. I surveyed the room. I couldn't see her bodyguards. How had she escaped them? And, more importantly, why? Whoever this man was, he was clearly important enough she had somehow given them the slip. He didn't look handsome enough or rich enough to be a lover. The blue suit he was wearing was clearly off the peg.

The man reached down to his briefcase and took out a folder. Dasha leaned forward, hands clasped. He opened it and spread out the several sheets of paper within. Dasha picked up a couple of them and started shaking her head.

'Why don't we try that?' Will was looking at me.

'Sorry, what were you saying?'

'You get the Choc Surprise and I get the Strawberry Cream Sundae so we get to try both?'

'Yes, great.'

He held up a finger. 'But I mean it, we have to share. No pulling the breastfeeding mama card on me and inhaling both.'

He grinned and called over a waitress. As he placed our order I watched the man Dasha was with vigorously motioning towards one of the pieces of paper. He was frowning. Dasha put her head in her hands. For the ice-cold Queen Bee to be betraying such emotion he must have something pretty devastating on her. I needed to identify him. I kept staring at him. Was he in one of the many files we had on Dimitri's business associates?

'Agggggg, purrrrrrr, goooooo.' The half-cat half-vacuum cleaner noise Gigi had been perfecting in the last month was coming out of the now shaking pram.

'Great, the bubba is awake.' Will unzipped the blackout cover and pulled our daughter out of the pram on to his lap. She looked between us, frowning as her eyes adjusted to the light. She blinked several times and then clapped her hands together. Will gave her a big cuddle. 'I've missed you, little lady.' He gazed at her as she poked a finger into his mouth.

'Ahh, you look so sweet together.'

'Really?' asked Will. She now had her finger up his nose.

'Totally adorable. Just wait, let me take a photo.' I picked up my phone and aimed it at my husband and daughter. I clicked a couple of times, capturing Gigi exploring the contents of her father's nose. 'Hang on, haven't got it yet.' I zoomed in on the man with Dasha in the background. It was just about clear enough. I clicked a few times. 'Perfect.'

'You mothers really do go overkill with the need to photograph every moment.'

I was already flicking through the photos and sending the clearest one of the man with Dasha to Geraint with a message to urgently ID him.

'Well, we just want to remember everything.'

Gigi was now sucking on Will's chin.

'Don't tell me she's mistaken this for a nipple?'

I reached into the nappy bag and pulled out Sophie the giraffe.

'She's just teething. Try this.' Will gently unattached her from his chin and handed her the giraffe. She crammed its head into her mouth.

'Look at you now. Officially a parenting expert.' Will reached over and cupped my cheek.

'It's not so hard.' I shrugged, but it made me glow a little. I don't know at what point it had happened but I did now feel as though as I knew what I was doing. That Gigi and I understood each other.

I looked over at Dasha and the man; they were now both talking heatedly. He reached over and put a hand on her shoulder. Her head dropped. Dasha was clearly in trouble. Could this man be working for Dimitri? Or an enemy who had discovered she was involved with us and was now blackmailing her? My head buzzed with all the different and dangerous scenarios we could be facing. Dasha compromised was a disaster. If she betrayed us or backed out of helping us the whole plan would crumble. VirtuWorld would be unleashed on the world and we would be powerless to stop it.

'Can you even remember what life was like before her?'

It was hard to draw myself back into my husband's conversation when I was contemplating whether or not I was now in the firing line from a mob of pissed-off Russians.

I shook my head. 'What on earth did we do with all that free time?'

The waitress came over and put our heavily laden sundaes down between us. Will moved Gigi back into her pram.

'I wouldn't change it for anything, though. Just look at her.' Gigi was pulling on her pram book, wrinkling the pages as she gurgled. Will was transfixed by his daughter. His hair was ruffled, his suit rumpled and his eyes, so like Gigi's, framed with faint laughter lines.

I couldn't have imagined doing this with anyone but him. He had bounded into my life like an overenthusiastic puppy, filling a part of my life I didn't realise was missing. Making me see a bigger picture than just living day to day, fling to fling. He had been my anchor. Holding me down, stopping me getting swept away in a flurry of big guns, bloodshed and baddies. And look at us now. We were a family.

I reached across the table and held his hand. 'I do love you, you know.'

'I love you too, sweetheart.' He creased his brow and tilted his head. 'You're not just trying to get my sundae, are you?'

'If I was I'd just fight you for it. I'd clearly win.' I took a spoonful of mine followed by a spoonful of his.

'You absolutely bloody would. I'm still sore. Sometimes I worry who exactly I've married.' He grinned. I stared at him as he tucked his napkin into the top of his shirt. I needed to be more careful.

Our spoons clashed as we attacked each other's sundae, seeing who could get the most the fastest. He looked over at Gigi. 'So when does she get to eat fun stuff like this? Surely there's only so much mashed-up banana a girl can take?'

'Not until she turns one. If you give them anything like this' – I motioned towards my double choc chip brownie with caramel ice cream and chocolate sauce – 'you can apparently risk ruining their tastebuds by getting them hooked on sugar. Which, of course, can lead to childhood obesity, hyperactivity, all kinds of problems.' I parroted back the highlights of a lecture Tamara had given us last week on the perils of sweet treats.

'Really? From one mouthful?'

I nodded solemnly. 'Oh yes, definitely.' Gigi wriggled in her pram and held her arms out to me. 'You want Mama? Come here, then, baby girl.' I plucked her out the pram and sat back down. I gave her a clean teaspoon to bang on the table as I continued to watch Dasha and the mystery man. Dasha seemed calmer now, the man was leaning towards her, talking fast. Whatever he was saying was comforting her. I looked down at my phone. Still nothing from Geraint. I needed that ID.

'Do you need to get back now? I've got enough time for a nice walk round the park.'

'That sounds good.' I glanced again over his shoulder. The man was gathering together the papers on the table. He was getting ready to leave. I couldn't let him out of my sight until I knew who he was.

'Gigi just ate some of your sundae.' Will interrupted my thoughts about how I was going to rush after the man without arousing anyone's suspicions.

'No she didn't.'

'Look at her.'

Her face had chocolate smeared round it. The clean teaspoon was no longer clean.

'I'm guessing this is something we aren't going to be adding to the First Tastes section of her baby book?' Will was laughing as he leaned forward and wiped Gigi's face. She bounced on my lap, eyes wide, arms flapping, clearing loving her new flavour sensation.

Ping. The email from Geraint came in. He had found him. I scanned over the man's name and biography.

Shit. I had just potentially ruined my daughter's tastebuds, and put her at risk of a myriad of future health problems, because I was distracted watching Dasha have a strategy meeting with Andrew Nunneley – a tutor from Elite Educators who specialised in seven-plus entrance exams. Dasha's distress was clearly down to her son scoring an unpleasing grade in a mock exam. I shook my head as I threw my spoon into the empty sundae glass. I should have known that in Dasha's world a threat to her social status was every bit as terrifying as a threat to her life.

'The Nyan are confirmed,' Sandy announced.

After a quick walk round the park with Will and Gigi, I had returned to the Platform in time for Sandy's update briefing in the meeting room. 'The Nyan are fierce opponents of The President, and have agreed to discreetly assist us in exchange for a place each on the Rok-Tech board along with a small percentage of company stock.'

'A small percentage that translates to tens of millions,' added Jake, shaking his head.

'The Pigeons agree to the deal?' I asked.

'I met with Dugdale yesterday and he confirms we have the unofficial support of Five and Six.'

Good old Duggers. I didn't like how someone from my past, my above-ground life, tied to all my old university friends, knew the truth about what I did for a living. At least our paths had never crossed socially over the years, and I suppose if I ever did spot him at a university reunion, my friends would just assume I was avoiding him because I had once slept with him. And not because he knew I was a killer.

'The Nyan have stipulated that they need to meet you, Lex. You're the one pushing the button on Dimitri. They want to be reassured you're up to the job and are flying over from Moscow especially. The meeting is set for tomorrow morning.'

I understood why the success of the hit was of the utmost importance to these men. If Dimitri was able to walk away unscathed but with suspicions that an attempt had been made there would be frenzied investigations from his highly trained security team into exactly who was involved. The Nyan were on Dimitri's list of enemies – they would immediately be suspects. Considering Dimitri's violent reputation it was very much their lives that would be on the line if we failed.

'Don't worry, Sandy. I've got this.'

'You better have. If you leave that meeting without convincing them, the whole hit is off. There is no point Popping the Weasel if we don't have an ironclad takeover plan to set in motion. And without the Nyan there's no way that halfwit playboy Sergei can take control of the company and set up the black market sale of the VirtuWorld software. So, Lex, no fuck-ups. Everything we've all been working towards comes down to you proving yourself to these men.'

No change there, then.

I ran home.

Gangsta rap on full blast on my iPod as I went over everything I needed to say to the Nyan as I raced across London. There was a tube strike. Traffic was gridlocked. And I wanted to see my baby before she fell asleep.

Beata stood up as I collapsed through the door.

'Sorry. I just couldn't keep her awake.'

'S'okay.' I went to the kitchen and drank a long glass of water. And poured myself a large glass of wine.

'I go now,' called Beata from the hallway. She popped her head round the door, her coat already on. 'You know, Gigi nearly crawled today.'

'Great!'

I didn't mean it.

I wanted to be there when she crawled for the first time. To will her on and clap excitedly at her triumph. Then get to show off like that smug-but-pretending-not-to-be-smug mother I overheard at Gymboree: *'It's so exhausting now Isabella can move. I just can't take my eyes off her for a second. You're so lucky Wilfie still just sits there. Doing nothing.'* Okay, well, maybe I wouldn't be totally like her.

I could get Bryan in R & D to work on adding a crawl-notification alert to my phone. We would probably need to update the camera systems to a more sophisticated motion sensor, and add a zoom and record function but it was definitely possible. At least then I could witness the big moment. Even if it was only on a screen.

Perhaps I could talk to Beata and Gillian. Tell them to keep Gigi strapped into a buggy during the week. To make sure the big event happened on my watch.

Or maybe I just had to accept that there were going to be some things I was going to miss. That by making the decision to work I wouldn't always be there for every milestone.

That I couldn't have it all.

I sat still for a minute and finished my glass of wine.

Bugger that.

I would get Bryan on the case tomorrow.

From: 8thelifelottery@ifyouliveyouwin.org.uk
To: lex.tyler@platform-eight.com
Subject: Congrats! You're a £££winner!
MISSION: #80436
UNIT: UNICORN
WEASEL: DIMITRI TUPOLEV
ALERT: 3 DAYS TO POP DAY

Chapter Twenty

I STOOD ALONE IN the bathroom staring at myself in the mirror.

'I can bloody do this, I can do this.' I kept chanting it over and over again.

This morning's meeting was everything. Failure was not an option. I tried out differing serious-yet-intense faces. I needed to come across as professional, ruthless, organised, poised and remarkably astute.

All on three hours' sleep.

It was quite amazing how on the nights when I needed my sleep the most, Gigi would choose to play up. All night she had screamed and screamed. Teething, reflux, growth spurt, satanic possession, who knew? I would half fall asleep in the nursing chair by her cot, one hand touching her leg, and wait until her breathing became heavier. Then I would dare to move. Every creak of the chair, of a floorboard, made me wince as I slowly crawled across the nursery on my hands and knees. And just when I thought I had made it, was in touching distance of the doorknob to freedom and my warm, comfortable bed she would wake, notice I wasn't there and start screaming again. I would rush back to her and repeat the whole cycle another hour later, the whole time cursing Will for being in Singapore when he should be here doing a shift with the demon baby.

It amazed me that I had excelled in all the stealth training we had undergone at the Farm, exercises designed by experts in their field to test our ability to covertly enter and leave a room without setting off any alarm. But this little baby had a better sensor than the most high-tech of surveillance equipment. More than once in a sleep-deranged moment I imagined returning to the Farm to announce a new training exercise: filling the warehouse with babies and challenging anyone to leave the room without setting one of the fuckers off. I had smiled to myself as I dozed off imagining all the big hard men trying to daintily tiptoe round them.

Watching her now at breakfast I could see Gigi was still miserable. Even smearing her favourite yoghurt over her face couldn't cheer her up. I tried to make her laugh, balancing a cup on my head – nothing but a stare; putting her disgusting bright pink pretty bow hairclips all over my hair – a slight smirk; stubbing my toe and swearing my head off as I got up to let Gillian in – hysterical laughter. As I rushed around the house locating shoes, coat, bag and motorbike helmet I wondered if this was a sign she had my propensity for violence or just that babies had very slapstick humour. The meeting was at Chelsea Harbour; the Nyan had decreed the safest place to meet was on a boat. Considering I was going to be battling rush hour I had settled on my bike as the best way to get there. I also hoped arriving on a 200 horsepower Ducati would add a certain edge to my appearance. Killer biker chick reporting for duty definitely felt better than killer-girl-just-got-the-tube-and-then-a-number-170-bus.

When I arrived at the harbour with five minutes to spare I identified the correct vessel by the burly Russian standing outside it. He motioned me and my bike on board the rundown container boat. I rode up on to the large loading bay and, as I got off the bike, the boat's engine roared into life. I steadied myself as we lurched forward. The guard nodded his head towards the cabin. Inside, I found the three Nyan sitting round an immaculately laid table that looked as though it belonged in the dining room of a five-star hotel rather than on a dilapidated boat speeding down the Thames. There were scrambled eggs, a plate piled high with bacon, dozens of pancakes and a basket of enormous croissants. I could feel my stomach rumbling and my eyes were drawn to the tall pot of freshly brewed coffee.

'Alexis, hello,' said the largest of the men. He was busy helping himself to a bit of everything from the table.

The shock on their faces as I removed my helmet was painfully obvious. I think a couple of jaws may have even dropped.

'I'm guessing Sandy neglected to mention I was a woman.' I put my helmet and jacket down on the table next to me. 'Well, let me assure you gentlemen my sex is irrelevant.' I pulled a chair up to their table. I sensed they weren't about to invite me to sit and it was important to let them know I had enough balls to both kill Dimitri and gatecrash their breakfast. It was a vital tactical move to assert myself as a level partner, an equal player.

Well, all that and I was bloody hungry.

They all continued to stare at me, seemingly unable to move past my gender. I reached for a croissant and started wolfing it down as I lounged back in my chair.

'I have been in this game a long time, I have done things, I have seen things . . .' I paused – 'that would turn your stomachs. I've never failed in a mission. When I set my mind to do something I get it done.' I stopped, aware that I was starting to sound like an interviewee trying to show they were management material.

The largest man clicked his fingers. 'Vasily!'

Vasily, the brute from outside the door, entered. The largest man spoke to him briefly in Russian. Vasily turned to me, then stopped and stared, tilting his head. These Russians were clearly more used to women wearing tight dresses and purring about what big men they were, not arriving in biker gear to discuss an assassination. Irritated at the delay, the large man called his name again and Vasily snapped back into action, pulling my bag off my shoulder and emptying it on to the table. Motorcycle gloves, a gun, ammunition, and a small cloud of white powder landed in front of me. Shit. I had used this bag when rushing out the door with Gigi last week. That bloody formula container had obviously leaked again. I reached towards the powder, dabbed a finger in it and rubbed it into my gums.

'Sometimes we need a little pick-me-up.' I brushed the powder on to the floor just in case any of them wanted a taste. They might not be coke connoisseurs but anyone would be able to tell the milky foam now filling my mouth was not quite right. 'But don't worry, it only makes me shoot sharper.' I tried what I hoped was a bit of a manic grin.

The three men began talking quietly among themselves in Russian. There was a lot of hand gesticulating before the largest asked, 'Why should we trust you to get the job done?'

They took it in turn to fire questions at me. They asked me everything from my operational experience down to exactly what we thought we were doing meddling in the succession of a private Russian company. I was surprised they weren't crass enough to ask my kill number. I always thought putting a number to how many people you've killed is just like a list of how many people you've slept with – you don't really know the number off the top of your head and you adjust the figure to whoever is asking. It's not like anyone will ever find out the truth.

Our little chat lasted nearly an hour. By the time the coffee had gone cold and all the platters of food in front of us were empty they seemed satisfied. They spoke quietly in Russian before the lead one spoke.

'Tell Sandy we're in. But we want no trail. We can't be seen to have any part in this.' He waved a dismissive hand towards me. 'You British messing in our business.'

'That is understood.' I leaned forward. 'But before I leave, you need to tell me what you know about the Dragon.' Dasha was most likely right in that the Dragon would not be a problem until Moscow, but I wanted further reassurance he wasn't an imminent threat.

'The Dragon?' The big man looked confused. They talked among themselves quickly and then all laughed.

'We will not talk to you about the Dragon. Move on.'

'You need to give us his name. We have to know he's not going to interfere in our plan.'

He shook his head. 'No one will ever give you the name of the Dragon. Remember that you're still outsiders. We know who to betray and who not to.' He stirred his coffee. 'Rest assured, the Dragon will not be a problem.'

I got up to leave.

'Alexis. That is a Russian name. Do you have any Russian blood?'

'Only on my hands.'

I stared at him in what I hoped was a suitably sinister way as I exited the cabin.

I got home in record time. I had done it. I had convinced them I was up to the job. That I wasn't someone to fuck with. I glanced up at the mirror. And I did it all wearing my daughter's pretty pink bow hairclips.

'The Nyan are in.' Sandy was sitting alone at Nicola's desk in Unicorn's office eating a bacon butty. I had been dreading coming into the Platform. I could only imagine the ribbing I was going to get for having turned up to such an important meeting looking like a deranged two-year-old girl. I braced myself for the onslaught.

Sandy shook his head and laughed. 'I don't know what you did, but their main worry is that you're so unhinged you might flip out before it's done. He kept saying –' he put on a bad Russian accent – '"How can you control someone so crazy?" He took a large bite and through his mouthful I made out, 'What the hell did you do?'

I was thankful they had obviously not mentioned my questionable hair attire but just written me off as a bit of a cokehead nut job that enjoyed killing people while dressed like a preschooler. I was not about to let slip all this to Sandy.

'I just told them what they needed to hear.'

'Well congratulations, Tyler. We're finally ready to Pop the Weasel.' He took another bite of his sandwich. Ketchup squelched out of the middle and dripped on to his T-shirt. 'With the Nyan happy we have the green light. That means the Ferrari seat needs to be swapped over in two days' time – everything has to be in place before Bonfire Night. Brief the team. And you and Jake had better not screw up stealing Ray Ray's car. We're cutting it fine.' He looked down at his stained top. 'Oh, bloody hell.'

I reached into my bag. 'Here you go.' I handed him a baby wipe. 'Jake and I will have the car by the end of the day.'

Cleaning him up and giving him reassurance. All men needed mothering.

An hour later I was pushing a pram past Ray Ray's expansive garage. It had enough space to house five cars and took over most of the redbrick East London side street it was situated on. I walked round the block a few times, now and again adjusting the blanket on top of the pram. A very realistic plastic baby was trussed up inside an enormous sleepsuit with only a little of its sleeping face visible. A mechanism inside released breathing noises and the odd gurgled murmur. R & D had proudly informed me a foul stench could also be emitted at a press of a button if it looked like any admiring bystander was about to get too close.

'The Mother' was a new persona I was going to roll out whenever it was deemed appropriate for an operation. I was inspired by Norm. Norm was one of Eight's most successful Rats. His unique talent was being Mr Forgettable. He looked so normal and insignificant people didn't really notice him let alone assess him as a threat. He was in his early fifties, slightly balding and with large glasses that looked like they were NHS-issued in the eighties. Wearing an anorak, he'd shuffle around in scuffed shoes holding a Tesco plastic bag containing his mobile phone, keys and a bottle of water. The bag added to his overall look and was also for practical purposes as his pockets were full with the tools of his trade. I don't even know if his name was really Norman or if Norm was just a nickname for Normal. All I could think about on maternity leave was how when I was out pushing a pram I felt like Mrs Norm. Mama Norm. No one really saw me. I was invisible. A non-threat. And now I knew how I could use that to my advantage. A pram full of weapons and ammo hidden under a stunt baby. They wouldn't see me until it was too late.

But today I was just doing surveillance and a little mission for Geraint. Tucked inside the pram was a large black box designed to record the electronic signal of Ray Ray's garage-door buzzer. I just needed to be close to the garage when it opened so the box could do its work. On my fourth round of the block the door finally screeched into action and rolled back; I got a glimpse of the make of the alarm keypad on the wall as a Bentley drove out with Ray Ray in the back. He was wearing sunglasses and looking at a broadsheet but I could just make out his distinctive bald head and the tweed cuff of a tailor-made suit. There was some shindig he was due at tonight in the country meaning the Ferrari would be left back here locked up and without the usual roster of security that went wherever Ray Ray did. I watched as a black Range Rover with a selection of well-built men inside followed the Bentley. With satisfaction I noticed not a single one of them gave a second glance to the mother hovering right next to their boss's garage door.

The black box inside the pram beeped twice. It was done. Time to head back to the Platform and let Geraint work his magic.

Chapter Twenty-One

'Oh, this is going to be fun. Isn't that Johnnie Mac?' Jake had found me outside Unicorn's office debating whether to hide just as a group of men walked out of the meeting room. They were all wearing suits except one, who had on weathered jeans and a jacket that looked equally battered except the cut betrayed the fact it was probably extremely expensive.

Johnnie Mac was a rockstar. When nineteen-year-old Jonathan Macaulay had first started out, his boy band Daylight had found fame quickly by winning a TV talent show. Platform Eight had taken control of them pretty much as soon as they left the stage in a sea of sparkly confetti. Young, manufactured bands were ideal vehicles for coded songs; as it was their first foray in the business they were safe bets for doing exactly as they were told. With their talent and our management, Daylight had immediately become an enormous international success. Five years ago, Jake and I had been assigned to them for one of their early world tours; being a part of their entourage had given us the perfect cover for undertaking dark ops abroad without raising any suspicions. We were just another PR manager and record-label executive that were part of the Daylight circus.

'How do you think he's going to take the news you're married?' asked Jake as we watched him talking animatedly with the suits.

'Don't be ridiculous. He won't give a shit.'

'Who are you kidding, "Lady"?' smirked Jake. 'Lady' was Johnnie's breakout single. He had eventually left the band to go solo, reinvented his sound as more edgy rock than fresh-faced pop and that was the first track he released. It had been a massive hit, going platinum worldwide. I think it may have even won a Grammy. It was a song about a man who had his heart trampled by an older woman, a lady who 'didn't act like no lady I had ever met, but on her my foolish heart was set'. Other lyrics included 'her green eyes flashed, she had scars to see, I had been afraid for her, but I should've been afraid for me'. I had naively hoped Jake had never heard it.

'Don't forget I've been down that "pathway" more than a few times myself,' he continued. In case I had had any doubt the song had been about me the line 'those three freckles were my pathway to heaven, a heaven that'd torment me to hell' had made it impossible to ignore. I had three freckles beneath my hip bone, that someone with a flair for poetry could interpret as leading the way towards my foofoo, lily, front bottom, whatever you wanted to call it. I know most would have found it flattering to have inspired such a famous song but I just found it slightly uncomfortable.

'Come on, let's go the long way round.'

'Now why would I do that?'

'Jake, don't be a—' But it was too late.

'Johnnie!'

Johnnie turned around. Although it was Jake who had shouted his name it was me he zeroed in on.

'Lex!' He came up and hugged me hard. 'Jesus, it's been so long.' He was studying me so intensely I was starting to squirm.

Jake cleared his throat. 'Good to see you, Johnnie.'

Johnnie turned to Jake. 'Oh, hi, mate. How are you?'

'You know, same old. Actually I just remembered I forgot a file I need. I'll be right back.' He walked back into our office merrily humming 'Lady' to himself.

Straight away Johnnie's arms were round my waist.

'Jesus, I've missed you. It's been, what? Over three years?'

'Come on, Johnnie, I'm at work.'

'I'm here, you're here, let's have some fun before you bugger off into the sunset on some "data analysing" assignment.' He grinned at me. He had always known more than he should.

It had only been the second stop of Daylight's world tour when an encounter with one of our informants hadn't gone as planned and I had taken a hard beating. I had got back to the hotel at 4 a.m. and, having noticed that the bar was still open, went for a sharp stiffener to ease the pain in my ribs. It was only once I had ordered my drink I noticed why the weary bartender was still serving. Johnnie was sitting alone in the corner smoking.

'Busy night, PR lady?' he had offered upon seeing my dishevelled state. Unlike the rest of the band, who were from nice middle-class backgrounds and pushy stage-show mums, Johnnie had grown up on a rough London estate. The extensive background checks we'd run had flagged up gang-related activity for which he had never been arrested. The Platform had been uneasy about him, although the genuine music executives insisted he was essential as he brought the band some much-needed raw sex appeal. He was a cocky twenty-year-old whose swagger hid an intelligence that was easy to underestimate. I certainly had. His pertinent questions about exactly what I did for a living made it clear he knew I was more than just entourage fodder.

In response to my 'crazzyyy night with some old journalist pals' explanation he handed me a napkin.

'You're bleeding from that cut on your head.'

'Oh, drunken tumble. Man, I should know better at my age.' I was only eight years older than him but it felt a lot more seeing as when he was a teenager learning how to sing, I'd been learning how to kill.

'You're not drunk, Lex.' He took another long drag on his cigarette. 'And you know fuck-all about music.' He blew the smoke in my face. 'And you have the worst press relations skills I have ever seen.' (He may have been referring to the fact I had told a journalist, 'I don't know, fucking google it,' when cornered about when the next album was being released.) I took the fag out of his hand as he continued, 'So exactly what are you doing touring with a band whose names you haven't even bothered learning?'

My earlier 'Hey, In-the-closet-guy, pass me that bottle' – directed at his gay bandmate – had obviously not escaped his attention. I took a drag of his cigarette.

'Well, Johnnie,' I said slowly to show I had bothered learning *his* name, 'you have lots of interesting questions, which I could either give long boring answers to' – I looked up at him – 'or we could get out of here and I could just do long interesting things to you instead.'

Seducing him was the quickest and easiest way out of the situation.

And there was the fact I had really wanted to.

Those record-label execs had known what they were talking about when they said he had sex appeal. He could make rolling a cigarette look like an obscene act. We had enjoyed late-night 'press strategizing sessions' for the rest of the tour. As to my suspicious behaviour, I had fobbed him off with a story that implied I hated my job but was still doing it as I was moonlighting in some shady sideline in drugs. I got away with being so vague as all the sex was a good distraction. A genius selfless move on my part.

When we were nearing the end of the tour the Platform agreed it was worth risking coming clean, to a certain extent, to recruit Johnnie as a golden Wolf. The band's access as bona fide superstars was unlimited. I knew on that tour alone they had dinner booked at at least two presidents' homes; even the most powerful men were still slaves to their teenage daughters. Johnnie had been unfazed by my revelations to the point where he pushed for a solo deal before he would agree. It was with a knowing look he accepted my explanation that I was officially a data analyst but unofficially a data gatherer, code for spy.

The tour finished and what I thought would be an easy goodbye turned into a messy one.

'What the fuck do you mean, that's it?' he had demanded, as I got ready to leave our Istanbul hotel.

'Johnnie, you're insanely famous and could be with a different girl each night. You don't want to be lumbered with an old lady like me.'

I thought I was doing him a favour; he thought I was a cold bitch who had used him to advance her career. The irony being I advanced his; with a solo record deal and by providing worthy inspiration for a hit single.

Yet time heals all wounds, although it didn't dampen any desires, and over the years whenever we had bumped into each other at the Platform, we had ended up in bed together.

Which explained why he now thought we could just pick up where we had left off.

'Johnnie, it's different now.'

'Babe, it's never different. Let's skip the bit where you play hard to get and we just cut straight to going to the nearest hotel.' He grabbed my hand.

'I'm married.'

He stared at me. 'The fuck you are. You said you'd never settle down. What was all that other bullshit you spun me? That you could never be one of those dull people who lived the same life every day?'

I paused. That did sound like something I would have said back then.

'People change?' was the best cliché I could come up with.

Thankfully Jake had obviously decided I had been tortured long enough and was back at my side. 'We need to leave,' he said.

Johnnie's eyes did not move from my face despite Jake's reappearance. 'It's not this prick, is it?'

'Johnnie! I thought we were mates?' Jake feigned hurt.

'God, no! Of course it's not this prick.'

'Lex, come on! *Et tu, Brute?*' We both ignored him.

'I'm sorry, Johnnie. We have to go. It was good to see you.' I gently touched his arm. He shook it off.

'You're a fucking liar. A professional liar. Everything you say is toxic bullshit.' He spun on his heel and stalked off.

'Boo fucking hoo, go write a song about it,' Jake called after him. He turned to me. 'Good work, Tyler. You've just seriously pissed off one of our top assets.'

No one had ever suspected our country's biggest superstar of planting bugs or tracking devices and Johnnie had helped us gain valuable intelligence in every territory he had ever toured in. He was, without a doubt, our most prized golden Wolf.

'Johnnie knows we made him and that we can break him. He's not going to throw his dream life away because he's not getting the occasional shag from me. I'm good but not that good.'

'Fair point. Come on, we need to go.'

I comforted myself with the idea Jake was still smarting from being called a prick and that was why he hadn't challenged my modest assessment of my bedroom performance.

Johnnie's surprise at my marital status was understandable. Back then 'buzz kill, sex-drive kill, fun killer' were all terms I used to describe marriage.

It was only when I met Will that I started to look at it another way. The big buzz of marriage, of any long-term relationship, was the whole fact someone wanted to do 'boring' with you. It was you they wanted to wake up to every single day, to stare at a wall painted five different shades of white and argue heatedly about which you prefer. It was you they wanted to debate with in the supermarket aisle about what to eat for dinner, and it was you they wanted to go to bed with and not have sex with when something good was on the telly. Marriage itself was mundane, but the fact someone wanted to be married to you was pretty fucking amazing.

Chapter Twenty-Two

IT WAS TIME TO steal a car.

I was sitting with Robin and Jake in a van opposite Ray Ray's garage.

There was silence except for the tapping of Robin's fingers on the laptop keys as Geraint talked him through his hacking programme for the security cameras.

Jake and I were both wearing jeans and dirty hoodies. We needed to look like down-and-out druggies hoping for an easy score, far less of a threat than professionals with questionable motives. Jake put his hood up and locked and loaded his gun. I did the same.

He looked at me. 'Remember, no deadly force.'

'Of course. Just hugs and high fives for anyone trying to kill us.'

This no-kill directive made the operation higher risk but even with the mighty Demon behind us, if anyone was badly injured or worse in a car robbery gone wrong it could make headlines. Someone as paranoid as Dimitri would be immediately on edge if he discovered the only car in London identical to his had just been stolen in a violent crime.

'Okay, it's confirmed.' Robin looked up at us. 'Cameras are down and the jammer is blocking the alarm signal.'

We walked across the street. Jake took Geraint's remote out of his pocket and pressed it as he aimed it at the garage. There was a pause and then we heard the reassuring screech of the door rising. We slipped under and Jake went to disarm the alarm keypad. Two beeps and the light went green.

We looked at the line of cars facing us. The orange Ferrari was at the far end of the garage alongside a tarpaulin-covered large car, a yellow Porsche and a lime-green Bugatti. A fruit bowl of cars that proved money couldn't buy taste. Next to us was the space where the Bentley had been and a vintage Land Rover, behind which was a flight of metal stairs leading up to a mezzanine-level workspace of filing cabinets and tool chests that arced round the whole expanse of the garage.

We walked down towards the Ferrari.

'Okay, Tyler, let's get to work.' Jake took a small pouch of tools from his hoodie pocket. 'You can be on top.' He winked as he slid under the car to disable the security system. I sat in the driving seat and got to work on the ignition.

I checked my watch. If we got this done fast enough I could be home in time for bath time. I had missed tucking Gigi in all week.

Robin's voice crackled into our earpieces. 'Two hostiles approaching. Two minutes from the garage door.'

'Dammit. I was nearly done.' Jake slid out from under the car.

We both looked round the garage.

'Under there.' He motioned towards the indistinguishable covered car next to us.

I got out of the Ferrari and lifted up the bottom of the tarpaulin. Jake rolled up against the side of the car and I lay down next to him. The tarpaulin fell short – part of my midriff and legs were not covered.

'I'm still visible.'

'Lean in more,' said Jake. His arm snaked round my waist and he pulled me further up against him. His legs entwined mine. His head just above me. We breathed in unison. I could feel his heart beating up against my back. His arms were crisscrossed in front of me, one holding me close, the other holding his gun.

I'd forgotten how well we fitted together.

The tarpaulin now just brushed the floor. We were covered.

The garage door opened and two sets of footsteps entered. I heard the tail end of a bad joke, chuckling, then one of them said, 'The bloody alarm's not set.'

'Maybe Keeno forgot to do it again?'

'He'll be out on his fucking ear if he has. Let's do a check. You go upstairs, I'll do down here.'

There were loud clanks as one of them ascended the metal steps to the mezzanine level. We heard steps as the other man came towards us. He was undoubtedly armed. I focused on staying completely still. One movement and the tarpaulin crinkling would echo round the garage. At least Jake had his gun in hand. And he was a fast draw. I knew he could down the man the second he lifted the tarpaulin.

Unless the man fired without warning. Our files on Ray Ray Campbell and his mob detailed their trigger-happy nature. I tried to block out images of their enemies' bullet-ridden torsos in shallow graves. Jake must have felt my body tense. His grip tightened round me, he felt for my hand, his index finger brushed mine and he started gently stroking it. He was trying to calm me. And setting the rhythm to which I needed to breathe to. I slowly exhaled and then adjusted my breathing to his timing.

The footsteps drew closer. The man was now walking past us. I could see the shadow of his feet. He stopped halfway down the car.

Jake's heartbeat remained steady. Mine was hammering.

'You got anything up there, Steve?' the man in front of us shouted up to his partner.

Loud clanks as Steve walked across the metal platform. 'Not a thing, mate.'

'We'll call Keeno later and tell him he's a fucking muppet. Let's finish adding the armour plating to that Landy and we can get out of here.'

The sound of a drill starting up blocked out the rest of what the men were saying to each other.

'Fuck,' said Jake. 'They'll be here for hours. I only needed five more minutes with the Ferrari. I just need to reconnect the two outside wires. If we miss this window the security system won't let me in for another twenty-four hours.'

'I can distract them. You finish with the car.'

'It's too risky.'

'It's our only option.'

His grip on me didn't loosen.

'Come on, Jake. I know what I'm doing.'

He held on to me for another second and then let go.

I left him my gun and earpiece and crept round the side of the car to the back of the garage, where there was a second set of steps leading up to the mezzanine. I got to the top of them and picked up a spanner. I took a deep breath and hoped that this evening would end in me being back home in time to put my baby to bed, and not in a Campbell gang body dumpsite. I waited for a pause in their drilling and then dropped the spanner.

'What the hell . . .?'

The two men came racing up the metal staircase next to the Landy, the whole floor shaking at their weight. They thudded round to the back wall and then stopped. I was clearly cornered with nowhere to go.

They both looked at me and started to grin.

'Bit out of your depth here, darling,' said the one nearest to me. He was bald with bad teeth.

The second, the larger of the two and wearing an ill-fitting leather jacket, wasn't so polite. 'You stupid bitch! Do you have any idea who you're trying to rob?'

They may have been big men but were more flab than fit; both were breathing heavily from their short run up the stairs. I knew I could take them. But that would take time. And I really wanted to see my baby. I needed to neutralise them fast and without harming them enough to create headlines.

'I'm sorry, okay,' I held my hands up. 'Please, let me go. I haven't got anything.' I did a little circle to show I was unarmed.

'Not a hope, love, our boss is going to want to talk to you.' The baldy moved towards me to grab me but the leather-jacketed one held his arm back.

'Take off that top.' He stared at me as he tucked his gun into his waistband.

'What, this?' I motioned towards my hoodie.

'Yes. Do it.' He licked his thin lips.

I unzipped it and threw it on the floor. I was wearing a fitted black vest underneath and three long chunky silver necklaces. Very street. I did another circle. 'See? No weapons.'

He nudged his friend. 'No harm in having a little fun with her first.'

The other man gave me a slow once over. 'Guess not. All part of teaching her a lesson.'

The two of them laughed.

Now I really wanted to hurt them. Enough to blow the mission by causing headlines about a stolen car and castrated security guards. But all I said was, 'Oh God, oh, please no.'

Leather Jacket roughly grabbed me under the arm. I pulled his hand off me and twisted one finger back until he screamed. I pulled on the bottom of one of my necklaces, and plunged the needle now protruding from it into his side. He collapsed to the ground, the fast-acting knock-out sedative doing its job. I saw the bald man fumbling with the safety on his weapon. I launched one well-placed kick at his hand and the gun went flying. He charged at me, I dodged out the way and, jumping up, put all my weight into my elbows and crashed on to his back. He fell to the floor. I flicked the cap off my second necklace and needled him in the neck.

Platform Eight certainly knew how to make statement jewellery.

The unmistakable roar of a Ferrari engine filled the garage, I ran down the steps and slid into the passenger seat. The garage door was already opening.

'You took your time.'

'They liked to talk. Could you give me a lift home?'

'You want me to be a taxi service in a fucking stolen orange Ferrari?

'Yes.'

He revved the accelerator. 'Why the hell not? The tracker's disabled. And I always wanted to see if these things were worth the hype. Seatbelt on.'

We sped through the streets of London, turning people's heads as we roared past. In record time we screeched to a halt outside my house. I shouted a goodbye to Jake and skipped up the steps to my front door.

I got to the bathroom just in time to see Gigi splashing water everywhere as she smacked both hands against the water. After thanking a now sodden Beata and wishing her a good evening, Gigi, soft and pink, was out the bath and wrapped in a towel in my arms. I walked into her nursery making funny faces at her. A good day at work, men twice my size knocked to the ground, a car successfully stolen, a mission on track and back in time to feel the soft squidge of my daughter's cheeks before bedtime. I sat back in the nursing chair smelling her hair, and holding her little hand in mine. Forget Johnnie Mac. I was the real rockstar.

From: 8johnniemacsuperfan@getmearockstar.tv.uk
To: lex.tyler@platform-eight.com
Subject: FreeJohnnieMacTickets
MISSION: #80436
UNIT: UNICORN
WEASEL: DIMITRI TUPOLEV
ALERT: 2 DAYS TO POP DAY

Chapter Twenty-Three

'**D**UHDELDEL DELEDA DUH DUH duh.' I couldn't get the music from Gigi's bloody Jumperoo out of my head. I was walking down the tunnel to see R & D humming it to myself. Of all the toys Dasha had handed over, what we called 'the circle of neglect' had been without a doubt her favourite.

Bryan and two other men in white lab coats stood around a sweet-looking old-fashioned bicycle which had a wicker basket at the front filled with roses. Jane Thornton, the only other active female agent currently serving in Eight, was in the seat, dressed in all black. She was in her late forties, half-Japanese and half-German and everything you would expect from such heritage.

There were a series of targets lined up on the far wall.

'I'm ready,' Jane said.

The men stepped back and Jane set off bicycling across the vast empty lot alongside the row of targets. *Pfft, pfft, pfft, pfft.* They went down one by one. Jane's hands never left the handlebars and she never slowed her pace.

'Amazing,' I said to Bryan. 'How did she do it?'

'Each target has a tracker on it giving out a radio signal. The gun in the flower basket is programmed to find that signal. Trigger is on the handlebars.'

Jane got off the bicycle and put it on its stand. It didn't look quite so picturesque anymore.

'Nice work, boys. I'll come back for it later.'

She nodded at me as she walked towards the tunnel. I could see the large burn on her forearm creeping out from under her cardigan. Everyone had a different dramatic story of how she got it. No one knew the truth as no one had ever dared ask; she had a demeanour that did not invite personal questions. Being scarred in the line of duty definitely gave her a certain gravitas, which was something I sometimes worried I was lacking as I bounced around in my jeans and dimples.

One of the men wheeled a fur-lined pram over to Bryan and me.

'It looks good.' I was impressed. I never would have guessed it was anything other than a luxury stroller.

'We're pretty much there, Lex. We embedded the needle into the Ferrari seat with no problems. The seat is now safely enclosed within this sheepskin cover and we have added these clasps here, which is what is holding it into place on the pram base. It's actually a pretty nifty design. Thinking we could patent it and make a killing.'

'Is it easy to take apart and put back together? Jake won't have long to make the swap.' The plan was to deliver this stroller to Dasha today with instructions that it needed to be stored in the garage. That would mean when Jake broke in tonight he could swap the Ferrari seats over so that the needled one was in Dimitri's car and the normal one was back atop the stroller.

'It shouldn't take more than three minutes.' I thought back to the painful two hours and forty minutes it had taken me to construct Gigi's obscenely expensive pram and thought Bryan definitely had a point about setting up their own sideline.

'Let's get it delivered.'

I headed straight to the meeting room to update Jake.

'R & D are getting the pram to Dasha in the next hour. We need to . . .' I stopped.

He was not alone.

Bennie was sitting opposite him with his feet up on the table. They each had a mug of coffee in front of them.

I stared at Jake unsmiling. He knew how much trouble Bennie had been giving me. Where was the partner loyalty?

I felt like I'd walked in on a boyfriend with another woman.

'Good to catch up, Jake.' Bennie got up. He brushed past me on his way out the door. 'Looking tired, Lex. Hope you're not overdoing it.'

Jake was quick to defend himself.

'It's not what it looks like. I was busy working on this.' He motioned towards the replica of Dimitri's garage alarm panel next to him. 'Bennie brought me a coffee and asked for my advice on a current op.'

Bennie clearly knew how to ingratiate himself with Jake – caffeine and hero worship.

'Are you coming to Bonfire Night tomorrow? Going to be quite a show.'

'Did Sandy not tell you? I'm out of here in the morning. He said if I don't take a blower now Eight says I can't take the lead on our next mission, which is starting right after this one. Bloody department guidelines.'

After months of working straight on an intense mission that could have been abroad, could have led to taking numerous lives, could have led to us nearly dying, could have been all of the above, the Platform decreed Rats needed time off to recuperate. There was genuine concern that too long spent doing what we do could lead to a psychotic breakdown. That was why these little sabbaticals were affectionately called 'blowers', because they were to blow off steam and to stop us blowing our own heads off.

'You're buggering off before the mission is even finished?'

Jake looked up at me from the many multicoloured wirings of the alarm keypad's interior.

'Don't worry, Tyler, you'll be fine. No one, not even the ever-cautious Sandy, thinks we'll need to action the Back-up.' He tweaked a few wires and the alarm keypad beeped twice and the light went green. 'Nailed it. This is going to be easy.'

I wasn't happy about Jake not being in the country when I undertook the Pop in two days' time but I didn't want to further strengthen any idea that I had changed since becoming a mother by weeping and begging him to stay.

'Of course I'll be fine. Be safe tonight.'

'Will do. And you be careful. It's good having you back.' He left the office with the keypad tucked under his arm.

'I bet you say that to all the girls,' I shouted after him.

'There's only you, Tyler. There's only you,' came his voice echoing down the corridor.

I left the Platform telling Sandy I had important work to do preparing for Bonfire Night. Thankfully he didn't ask for details so I didn't have to volunteer the information that I needed to get home to make a hundred cupcakes. Dasha had commanded they be delivered by 6 p.m. today.

By the time Beata came back from the park with Gigi I had been baking for over an hour. She walked in and looked round the chaos in the kitchen. There was flour all over the worktops and up the side of one wall. I had not realised the white puff explosion that would happen from attempting to whisk flour. I had overestimated my level of skill. Just because I could disarm a bomb, assemble an assault rifle blindfolded and hack a fortified alarm system did not apparently mean I could just whip up some cupcakes.

'Why you just not buy?'

'They need to be red and white in the school colours and have a CH on each one.'

'Do you know someone who can cook? Maybe ask help? You have buttered the wrong side.' She held up the cupcake tray which I had slathered in butter thinking that at least I could get the easy part out of the way.

'Right. Yes. There must be someone who can get this done in' – I looked at my watch – 'two hours.' I needed to play to my strengths. I picked up my mobile and rang Demon. 'It's Lex. Who do I need to intimidate into doing a small baking favour for me?'

It was with great satisfaction I was able to text Dasha that the cupcakes were being couriered over to her in the next hour. I didn't add that the school logo, in the correct Pantone colours as taken from their website, had been hand drawn in edible food dye on each one's rich fondant icing. Or that the cupcakes themselves were made with the finest Belgian chocolate and mixed with a popping candy that meant every bite was an explosion of crunchy sweetness. She would know what she was dealing with when she saw the signature boxes of the Michelin-starred restaurant they were arriving from. I sat back in my armchair. I was so fucking Super Mama right now.

Well except for the part where I had to threaten a celebrity chef with the loss of his flambéing hand unless he helped me out.

The text came in as I was sitting drinking a glass of wine in front of the television.

Ocado: Dear Ms Tyler, Your 9–10 p.m. order was delivered by Jake in Rat van LEG3ND. You have no missing items.

It had all gone to plan and finally everything was in place. Jake had fixed the Ferrari and now he was off. His blowers usually involved him disappearing for a month and coming back thin and hollow-eyed, and everyone knew better than to ask what he'd been up to.

Before Will, my blowers would be trips to faraway places that I'd always wanted to visit. One of the many benefits of being a trained killer was that I never felt nervous about being a woman travelling solo. Yet, although I always booked the trips alone, more often than not a man would enter the frame.

Planned solitude at a remote cabin in the Rocky Mountains was interrupted by a French artist I met at the local grocery store. I would pose naked for him as he made strong purposeful brush strokes on his canvas while smoking a roll-up, only breaking for hot frantic sex in amid the paint and empty wine bottles.

Then there was the idea of a solo motorbike trip through the Himalayas. Yet while picking up an old Royal Enfield from a rundown shop in Delhi I also picked up a stupidly handsome Israeli biker. The first day I had my guard up, convinced he could be a member of the Aman, the supreme military intelligence branch of the Israeli Defence Forces. By the second day, I still had doubts. By the third, the sex was so good I didn't really care. A month later we parted and I was still no closer to knowing if he really was just a chance encounter. But seeing as I only ever travelled with an old Nokia with no email and no contacts there was no data to steal. And unless during my slightly out-of-body orgasming he was able to do some kind of hypnotic mind-hacking (which if he did, all I could say was well played, sir, very well played) then he didn't get any information out of me.

Blowers all over the world were the chance for me to see if there was another kind of life out there that would make me happy. Happy enough to give up the life I was currently living. Hippy Lex, Arty Lex, Daredevil Lex, Biker Lex, I kept on trying. But in all my searching, nothing seemed to be more satisfying than Killer Lex. After each trip I found by the time the tan had faded so, too, had the memories, and I was back into the hard grind of the Platform planning my next getaway, my next trial life.

Blowers now would be a little different. Big suitcases of essential kit, noisy family-friendly hotels, plastic water slides, bad food, and a probable Insta:Shit ratio of 1:3. Mummy Lex with a baby and husband in tow. Would I come back happy with my new life or missing my old one?

From: 8arrangedmarriage@oldandrich-youngandhot.ru
To: lex.tyler@platform-eight.com
Subject: $HotRussianBrides$
MISSION: #80436
UNIT: UNICORN
WEASEL: DIMITRI TUPOLEV
ALERT: 24 HOURS TO POP DAY

Chapter Twenty-Four

BONFIRE NIGHT.
One final day of prep before the big social event tonight, and the final Pop tomorrow morning. Two important missions each headed up by domineering, aggressive micro-managers – both of whom seemed likely to resort to violence if their every demand was not met. I had no idea who was more terrifying – Sandy or Dasha – and I had the joy of working for both of them.

It was 7.30 a.m. and Dasha had already sent eighteen WhatsApp messages to the 'Bonfire Committee' group she had created, all varying in hysteria on subjects from ticketing issues to rain concerns.

Apart from the frequent pings from my phone as Claudia and Cynthia kept replying to the group chat with reassuring words and contradictory weather reports it was oddly peaceful throughout Platform Eight. Just the low hum of the air vents and the electricity powering the lights.

I walked through to the meeting room and looked at the whiteboard where the whole plan was tacked all over it. I didn't have that excitement that usually came on the cusp of mission completion. The anticipation that all the weeks of work were about to come to fruition in one bloody conclusion was not, for once, doing anything for me. I still had doubts and today was my last chance to quash them. I needed to believe that everything was as it should be and that tomorrow after a push of a button the mission would be finished.

Eight in the morning. Geraint, Nicola and Robin had joined me in the meeting room. All with large receptacles filled with varying types of caffeine. Geraint had also brought a large box of Krispy Kreme donuts. I tried resisting but then thought I was gearing up to a big day and a big kill so deserved some extra calories.

Dammit, there was always an excuse.

I was on my second by the time Sandy arrived and took his position in front of the whiteboard.

'Tomorrow is Pop Day. This is it.' He brandished his iPad with the mission checklist. 'Lex – the car?'

'Dimitri's Ferrari now has a driver's seat with imbedded needle and a tyre fitted with a quick-firing explosive.'

With a flourish Sandy ticked the relevant box on the checklist.

'G-Man and Nicola, Dimitri definitely still flying to Moscow tomorrow?'

Geraint looked at his laptop. 'Dimitri's pilot just submitted a flight plan confirming their departure from Farnborough Airport to Moscow International early tomorrow morning.'

Sandy continued to flick through the checklist.

'Robin – today you're on Dimitri. Report back on anything he does that isn't on his calendar. G-Force and Nicola – keep on the Nyan. Monitor their emails and any online chatter. Lex, I want you going over the route to the airport; test all the variables. When are you checking in with Dasha?'

'Tonight at the big Bonfire Night.'

'And you and Robin are set for tomorrow?'

We both nodded.

'Talk it through.'

'Robin will be in position outside the house to confirm as soon as Dimitri has left the garage. I follow the Ferrari along the early-morning empty motorway. At the designated spot I will push the button, activating the charge and the needle, and speed off into the distance.' I used a tissue to try to wipe away the stickiness of the donuts on my fingers. 'Robin will be on standby in a Platform Eight ambulance ready to swoop in once the first 999 call is made and to confirm the Weasel is popped. I've also briefed Demon to be on standby with a good think-piece about drink driving and Russians believing they are above the law. If that gets published a few days later it will help make sure every-one's singing from the same hymn sheet.'

'Nice touch. By lunchtime tomorrow the Weasel will be popped and we'll be popping the champagne on another suc-cessful mission. No one fucks with the security of this country. This is us taking a stand against The President and stopping the damage an army of VirtuWorld cars being released across the world could do. The stakes don't get higher than this.' This was Sandy's attempt at a pep talk. 'Anyone have any concerns?'

I had to try one last time. 'We're definitely secure on the intel we have on Dimitri?'

'One hundred per cent. We've gone over every statement and every hacked email from intelligence dating back over a year. And it's all backed up by Dasha. Everything fits. Don't ask again as it's only going to piss me off.'

Robin and Geraint both reached for another donut.

Sandy looked round at us. 'What the fuck are you all doing still sitting here? You all have jobs to do, now get out there and bloody do them.'

As the bonfire celebrations approached I spent four hours riding my motorbike between Junctions 13 and 14 of the M25 – the designated 'kill zone', chosen as a result of R & D's numerous reconnaissance missions determining a crash at this location would have the highest chance of fatality. Along this stretch of motorway was a fifteen-foot section of side barrier that last night had been replaced with Eight's special modified version. It may have looked as solid as the rest of the barrier it was linked to, but one small bump would be enough to make it crumble. The start of this faulty section was marked with a yellow painted arrow. I slowed down as I biked past it. I needed to push the button just as Dimitri was level with the arrow to guarantee the blown tyre would send him straight through Eight's specially made barrier. With the speed he would be going and the steep drop down to the parkland and the river below R & D's simulations had calculated a 99.97% chance of fatality. If the force of impact didn't kill him, the car catching fire as it crashed into the parkland or filling with water if it landed in the river were useful back-ups. If all went to plan it would not just be the end for a dark man who had led a dark life, but the end of Russia's plans for a worldwide intelligence monopoly.

I went back and forth along the route, checking the surroundings for markers to look out for in my lead up to the arrow. I factored in everything from unscheduled pouring rain, to an unusually busy early-morning rush. R & D had informed me that pressing the button after the arrow meant with every second that passed the chance of a successful outright kill would drop by twenty per cent.

After finishing my practice runs in the kill zone I went down to what would be the crash site. It was deserted with no sign that anyone had been down there in the last few months. The perfect location for a fireball car to hit. I checked my watch. Two hours to go until the first trickles of parents and their well-educated offspring were due to arrive at the school for Bonfire Night. After weeks of preparation, Chepstow Hall was going to bear witness to a night of unforgettable excess lovingly organised by a committee formed with social climbing, intimidation and murder at the heart of it, yet all working together in the name of charity.

I needed to get home, pull my just-back-from-Singapore jet-lagged husband off the sofa, pack my baby into her pram and prepare for one final soiree as a wannabe Super Mama.

Chapter Twenty-Five

THE SMELL OF BURNING. It was in the air.

Walking through the streets of Notting Hill bonfires were already alight. Other people's celebrations had already started. Above the rooftops the crackle and fizz of the odd solitary firework permeated the dark night sky.

'There's a bloody programme?' was Will's reaction at being handed a colourful booklet as we arrived at the entrance to Dasha's private communal gardens.

'This is no ordinary Bonfire Night,' I said. An understatement. The event was going to shortly kick off with a fifteen-minute fireworks display set to Mozart's Symphony No. 6 in F Major, watched by parents and children enjoying organic marshmallows on sticks, non-toffeed toffee apples and a Châteauneuf-du-Pape mulled wine. Then, once a small fortune had been set off into the sky, there would be spit-roast pork in gluten-free buns, freshly procured from the line of five pigs that were turning on rotisseries, champagne from a straw in mini bottles and a large selection of themed cupcakes. In case that didn't warm us up enough a twenty-foot bonfire would be lit by the low-level celebrity Demon had thrown me, any disappointment at his level of fame as a travel-show presenter buoyed by the fact he was good-looking and went to a minor public school – making him socially acceptable enough for all the yummies to fawn over him. I could see him now surrounded by a circle of fur-lined parkas and tinkling laughter.

Will bit into a toffee apple. 'Jesus, what the hell is this?'

'It's a Noffee apple. A non-toffeed toffee apple. I think it involves liquidised dates.'

'So it's totally biodegradable.' Will dropped it on the ground as we walked round the gardens pushing Gigi in her pram. My gun was snugly fitted in the right hand of the Mummy Mitts attached to the handlebar. If faced with an oncoming threat I could fire while still keeping my hands toasty warm.

Dasha approached. She was wearing a white mink coat with an enormous matching fur hat. This was her big night and she was going to make sure she stood out.

'Alexis, Will, how lovely to see you. Isn't everything just wonderful?'

'Yes, Dasha, it really is. Quite an event you ladies have put on,' said Will, putting an arm around me.

'And aren't we lucky? No rain,' I added. 'What's the forecast for tomorrow?'

'Clear. Totally clear.' She said over her shoulder as she moved back towards her family.

The music started up and the sky became alight with blues and greens and reds exploding in time to every beat. I looked around the gardens at all the families staring up smiling in wonder. Only five heads were not tilted up: Dasha and Dimitri's bodyguards circled them, well positioned to take on any incoming threat. Dasha and Dimitri stood side by side behind their children, who were exclaiming as they pointed at the different colours, now and again turning around to check their parents were really seeing what they were seeing. Her children's joy broke through Dasha's usual refined demeanour and she couldn't stop smiling at their big eyes and frequent cries of, 'Wow, Mama, did you see? Did you see?' She bent down to kiss their cheeks and straighten their woolly hats. Dimitri's face remained impassive.

I looked over at Dasha's flawless profile as she stared up at the sky. I still didn't trust her. I didn't care what Sandy and his wealth of intelligence was saying. It just didn't add up. I didn't see her as a political activist devoted to her country. More a socialite devoted to her social standing. A mother who loved her children. A wife who hated her husband – a man who, tomorrow, I had to eliminate. Something wasn't right and I needed to try, one last time, to find out more. I saw Claudia and Cynthia over on the other side of the gardens. Since our bonding session over celebrities and coffee I was confident they might actually be a little friendlier now. It was time to stir things up a little.

I left Will talking to Tamara and Ed and pushed Gigi over to the two Cs.

'Evening, ladies.'

'Oh, Alexis, hi.'

'I think we've done a wonderful job.' I took a sip of my wine as we all looked up at the sky. 'Who cares what Dasha says? We all know we were a big part of this and that's all that matters.'

There was a pause as they digested the dig.

'What do you mean? What has Dasha been saying?' They were both now looking at me rather than the bright colours showering over us.

'Well, I heard those mothers over there' – I pointed towards a well-heeled group wearing Canada Goose jackets and holding large handbags – 'tell her that she had done an amazing job and she said something about it being tough not having enough support. Can you believe that? After all those meetings we sat through? She was really complimentary about you two, though.' They made no comment but started to look back towards the sky. 'She said it was amazing how you didn't miss a single meeting despite being so busy with surgery appointments and meetings at the Priory.' Their heads swivelled back to me.

'She said fucking what?'

'She was being really nice about how much you contributed despite all that was going on in your lives.'

'That bitch.' Claudia spat.

Cynthia stared at me. 'Alexis, if you're going to try to infiltrate this world, you need to recognise when people are fucking you over.'

'What? I thought . . .' I stopped and put a hand to my mouth. 'Oh no! People didn't know you were going to the Priory? Or having surgery? I'm so stupid. I thought she was being a good friend.'

'After all we've done for that Russian whore.' Cynthia shook her head and looked down at her chest. 'It's only a bloody boob lift. Barely counts as surgery.'

'And so what if I needed a little help with that Valium dependency? Who doesn't have therapy these days?' Claudia folded her arms. 'She should bloody try it. Rather than ranting to us about how much she hates her husband.'

'So things aren't good between them? I could've guessed that.' I leaned towards them. 'I heard rumours she was going to leave him.'

Claudia and Cynthia burst out laughing. They took it in turns to talk.

'Oh no, she would never do that,' Claudia started.

'Ironclad pre-nup. She'd end up with nothing. No money, perhaps even no children. His team of lawyers would make sure he could whisk them off back to Russia.'

'She is totally stuck with him. And worse than that, his father is on his last legs and he's getting them ready to move back to Moscow to take over the family business.'

'He told her to give Chepstow Hall their one term's notice.'

'But she hasn't. I checked. No one has any idea they're out of here after Christmas.'

'Serves the bitch right. Bye bye, St Paul's. Bye bye, Parents' Association. It's going to break her heart,' Cynthia finished, and the two of them sniggered together as they looked over at Dasha and drank their wine.

'Surely Dasha would be happy back in Russia? They'll be even richer if Dimitri takes over the company. And wouldn't it be nice for her to be back home?'

Cynthia wrinkled her brow. The Botox did its job and only one tiny line could be seen. 'She doesn't need any more money and she couldn't give a shit about Russia.'

'She has no family over there, no friends,' added Claudia. 'I just can't believe that rather than be gracious about her departure she's trying to ruin our chances with the Association.'

'She must be jealous. She obviously considers you two a threat.' They murmured agreement to this idea. 'I'd better get back to my husband.' I looked over at Will, who was being attacked with marshmallow sticks by Shona's twins. They offered a distracted goodbye and continued talking between themselves about how best to damage-control Dasha's supposed exposing of their vulnerabilities.

The fireworks display was coming to an end. The sky exploded in a crescendo of flashes, bangs and colourful confetti as the letters 'C' and 'H' were spelt out in a flicker of falling stars and met with gasps and applause from the crowd. Chepstow Hall was certainly having an unforgettable Bonfire Night. I looked back towards the dark scheming faces of Claudia and Cynthia. Another fireworks display could be coming our way.

'I'm so glad we have a daughter,' was all Will said when I rescued him from the clutches of Shona's hyperactive calf-kicking sons.

'Girls come with their own problems.' It was with regret I knew that only women would be so easy to manipulate with a simple 'she said'.

'Note for Nigel? Note for Nigel?' Two CH prefects were wheeling round a life-size Guy for the Bonfire.

Will looked confused. 'Shouldn't it be Penny for the Guy?'

I opened up the Bonfire Night programme and drew his attention to the 'Negativity Nigel' section, which outlined how all the CH children had written down their biggest fear and stuffed it inside Nigel. The piece ended with, 'And parents are invited to do the same. Let's all set fire to that negative energy!'

'You aren't actually seriously thinking of sending Gigi here?'

'Come on, let's get into the spirit of things.' Like many of the parents around us I took one of the notes and pens proffered by a prefect. I scrawled a sentence down and stuffed the paper under Nigel's shirt. Nigel was wheeled off round the groups of parents, getting fatter and fatter. I watched as he was lifted out of the wheelbarrow and dragged up a ladder by two fathers. With a great heave they threw him on to the top of the bonfire. The wind rattled against Nigel, his shirt billowed, yet he held steadfast, keeping close his precious cargo of Negativity. I watched thinking how one large gust of wind could tear him open, blow his contents all round the gardens and how in among the no doubt identical notes saying, 'My child not getting into their first-choice school,' 'Never getting back to my pre-pregnancy weight,' 'My husband having an affair,' 'Losing all our money,' one original note would flutter down: 'Not seeing my daughter grow up.'

A gong sounded, announcing the bonfire's imminent lighting. We each took a pork bun and bottle of mini champagne from one of the waitresses and watched as the travel-show presenter approached with a lighted baton. He got a high-pitched cheer from the crowd. The fathers clearly did not share their wives' enthusiasm for his presence. The baton touched the bonfire, there was a roar and whoosh and it was alight. I watched the flames crackle and dance and started to feel the heat.

While Will was talking to Shona, Dasha came storming up to me. 'This is my life,' she hissed. 'These people are my friends. What are you trying to gain by turning them against me?'

'I was just having a gossip with my new buddies.'

'Causing a scene now could get us killed. What are you playing at?'

'I'm just showing you a little glimpse of what trouble I can make if you haven't been straight with us.'

We stared at each other. Our steely eyes and straight faces at odds with the cheery socialising and small talk surrounding us.

Dasha took another step towards me. 'I have done everything you've asked of me. If tomorrow fails it will be down to you, not me.' Her lips curled. A perfect face ruined by vitriol. A couple of mothers tapped her on the shoulder.

'Darling, this is all so amazing.' The sound of their voices turned her sneer to a smile and she turned towards them to soak up the compliments.

I was pushing Gigi towards a waitress holding a tray of Irish coffees and whipped cream when Claudia and Cynthia blocked my way. Their mouths were set in thin lines. Round Two.

'We should've known you weren't to be trusted.'

'You're a nobody and you think you can turn up to a few meetings and be one of us?' They continued to tag team with: 'You can forget your daughter ever getting a place at this school.'

'We're going to make it impossible for you.'

'We should've known better than to think Dasha would betray us like that.'

'Who do you think you are?'

Click. I cocked the safety of the gun nuzzled in my pram mitt. It was tempting. So very tempting.

'There you are.' Will was back at my side. 'Oh, hello, we haven't met. I'm Will.'

'Darling, let's go. Gigi needs to get to bed.' I turned round and took him by the arm.

He looked back over his shoulder at the two Cs. 'Aren't you going to say goodbye to your friends?'

'They aren't my friends. I never have to see them again.' The mission was nearly over. No more fucking wannabe Super Mama. Just back to being a regular mum with a gun.

From: 8itallcomesdowntothis@gobigorgohome.com
To: lex.tyler@platform-eight.co.uk
Subject: **High Stakes Poker***
MISSION: #80436
UNIT: UNICORN
WEASEL: DIMITRI TUPOLEV
ALERT: POP DAY!!!!!

Chapter Twenty-Six

DIMITRI TUPOLEV WOULD DIE today. I stood next to my bike in a small side street in Notting Hill, rubbing my gloved hands together and jiggling my legs in a futile attempt to keep the cold out of my limbs as Robin sang Aerosmith through my earpiece.

I winced.

'Robin. It's 5.30 a.m. Please shut the fuck up.'

'Sorry. Just trying to kill time.'

'Well you're killing my eardrums.' My motorbike helmet meant my earpiece was crammed into my ear.

I'd had a bad night's sleep. I always do just before a Pop; my mind races with details that we might have forgotten, a threat we haven't yet anticipated. But this time it was different. I had doubts. This was a first. The intel I got from Dasha's friends was going against everything the Platform was reporting. Not that there was any point bringing this up with Sandy. He was convinced Dasha was playing the part expected of her.

Robin crackled in.

'Weaselmobile is leaving the garage.' There was a pause. 'Confirmed sighting. Weasel behind the wheel.'

I got on my bike and started the engine. The sun had yet to rise and the streets were dark and empty. The Ferrari should pass me in three minutes. After two I saw a flash of orange go past, the street lights reflecting off its shiny exterior. I waited until he turned a corner and was out of sight and then followed him.

I heard Geraint in my ear.

'Weasel on correct route to airport.' Back in the warmth of Unicorn's office he was following Dimitri's progress from the tracker inside his watch.

The streets were empty. London was still sleeping.

I caught sight of the Ferrari as I reached Kensington High Street.

I kept him in my sights as I followed him down through Hammersmith. He weaved in and out of the few other cars on the road. The remote detonator was fitted on my right handlebar. I kept glancing down at it. This was what it came down to. Me pushing the button. Finishing the mission. Popping the Weasel.

Coming up to the Hogarth roundabout I looked up at the signs to Chiswick and thought of my husband and daughter tucked up at home, thankfully oblivious to what I was doing as they slept.

Robin crackled into my ear. 'I've switched vehicles. Paramedic Robin reporting for duty.' Robin would now head straight to the crash site with Geraint and Nicola on standby to intercept any 999 calls from concerned motorists, ensuring ours was the only emergency vehicle dispatched.

'Roger that. Weasel in sight. Fifteen minutes from kill zone.'

Dimitri zoomed past Chiswick and accelerated as he entered a near-empty M4. I kept my distance and checking my speedometer worked out he must be doing at least 95 mph. Good to know our prediction he wouldn't be able to resist the empty roads and the Ferrari's 500 horsepower engine was correct. The higher the speed the better the odds of a fatal crash. Although the tighter the window I had for hitting the button.

'G-Force, check in with traffic report please.'

There was a pause before he replied. 'Looking totally clear. Checking live camera feeds at junctions 13 and 14 and road is practically empty. And . . .' I heard the tapping of keys – 'no upcoming incidents.'

Everything was on track. So why was I gripping the handle-bars so tightly?

I could no longer see the orange of Dimitri's Ferrari. He must be going over 100 mph by now. 'Weasel out of sight. Confirm location?'

'He's about to turn off on to the M25, he should be—' Geraint broke off with a yelp. 'Fuck!'

'G? Come in? Come in?' I knew things had been going too smoothly.

'Shit, sorry. Burnt my tongue on my coffee.'

I sighed. 'I'm chasing down Weasel now.' Once on the M25 we would be within five minutes of the kill zone so I could now risk following him closely.

I accelerated, feeling the vibrations between my legs as the Ducati roared down the motorway. This type of speed felt good. I was flying. With the dark motorway lit only by the overhead lights and the streak of the few other cars on the road it felt more like a computer game than real life. Just another simulation.

As I approached the turning for the M25 I caught sight of the Ferrari. Dimitri had slowed down to make the junction, giving me time to catch up. I now couldn't let him out of my sight.

There was one car between us as he passed a sign warning of a speed camera. He didn't slow down, and a second later there was the inevitable flash. I reduced my speed as did the car in front. I may've been able to expense it but I didn't need attention drawn to my proximity to Dimitri in the run up to his death. Even with the anonymity of my helmet and an Eight-registered number plate.

Entering the M25, Dimitri was a little further ahead but still in view. I overtook the car in front and was soon parallel with the Ferrari. I looked over and saw Dimitri behind the wheel. A dark hulk of a man hunched over the steering wheel. His wedding ring glinted in the early-morning light. If only he knew the wife who had commissioned that ornate symbol of their marriage was in on this plot to end his life.

My motorbike's presence alongside the Ferrari made Dimitri accelerate further. Needing to prove he was the fastest on the road. I let him take the lead but stayed close. The radio range of the detonator was nearly ten metres.

We were now in the final stretch, nearing the tell-tale yellow arrow. But where was my buzz? My satisfaction in knowing it was all about to be over? Nothing but a nagging feeling in my stomach and a head full of doubts. Were they well founded? Or was this just from being out of the game for a year? Had becoming a mother changed me? Lessened my ability to do the nitty-gritty of what this job entailed? I clenched my jaw. I was starting to sound like Sandy or Bennie now. I shook it off. I knew myself. I was just as good at my job as I always had been. And if my instincts were telling me things were off there had to be a reason.

We were three minutes from approaching the mark. Conditions were ideal. There were only two other cars in the distance, far enough away they would be at no risk from any impending crash. My finger hovered over the button. I needed to push it as soon as he was level with the tell-tale streak of yellow paint. Timing was everything.

Two minutes to go . . .

Something had given me a jolt.

What was it?

Dimitri's ring.

Why was that sticking?

Dimitri's Cartier-commissioned Russian wedding ring. Three interlocking rings, bound together in a symbol of marriage.

Three.

The power of the three.

Does Dimitri know the Dragon wants him dead? . . . Dimitri knows the Dragon is angry but he thinks the power of the three will keep him safe . . . The Dragon doesn't care about the three.

Could it be?

That 'the three' weren't three men but three rings.

Dimitri thought his wedding ring would protect him from the Dragon.

But why would he think that?

My blood ran cold.

Because he was married to her.

Because Dasha was the Dragon.

The Dragon.

Not a ruthless man with investments to protect but a ruthless woman with children to protect.

Dimitri's many enemies would be much more proactive at finding ways to hurt him when he was back on home turf. Our sources had picked up chatter on how the kids would be at high risk of kidnapping.

The Dragon was a menacing presence circling Dimitri. A fire-breathing, fearsome enemy. Ruthless ... Intimidating ... Calculating ...

My mind was racing. Images flooded my mind.

Dasha at the head of the table at bonfire meetings.

Dasha sucking on her vape, swathes of smoke surrounding her.

The Dragon.

Dasha holding her children close. The steely glint in her eye.

The Dragon Lady.

Dasha had the connections. The money. The knowledge. Everything that could intimidate Dimitri's business associates.

Sixty seconds to go ...

Dasha was the Dragon. And she had been wanting Dimitri dead long before Platform Eight and VirtuWorld came on the scene. Her helping us had nothing to do with making a strike against The President. She had wanted anyone to do the job.

She had tried to recruit Dimitri's business associates to arrange his assassination and failed. And then along came the Platform. Asking for her help.

But who was helping who?

Was she working for us or were we working for her?

Did it really matter? We had the same objective. Dimitri needed to die. She had her motives, and we had ours – his desire to keep the VirtuWorld software private meant he was a threat to our country, a threat to the wider world. He was a die-hard supporter of The President who was putting patriotism above profit.

30 seconds ...

But what if he wasn't?

What if Dasha, the wife who wanted him dead, had set him up? Set all of this up? Everything we had heard about the Dragon was how far-reaching their influence was. All the intel we had received over the course of the last few months could have been tainted.

Surely someone who could manipulate and cajole her way from Russian outsider to shortlisted head of the Parents Association would have no problem using the underground branch of Her Majesty's Secret Service to do her dirty work? What no one at the Platform seemed to realise was that Dasha was a formidable force to be reckoned with. A whirlwind of diamonds, fur and unnerving social ambition.

She was capable of anything. Especially when it came to protecting her children. She had bought a church a new roof just to make sure her daughter's best friends would be at her birthday party. She'd had a boy who was thought to be bullying her son relocated to another country. If this was how she reacted to the small stuff, how would she react if she thought their actual physical safety was being threatened?

The Ferrari was seconds away from the yellow mark.

This was it. Time to press the button.

My hand hovered over it.

And then I put it back on the handlebar.

I was going to get hell for this. It could even be the end of my career, but I couldn't do it. I slowed my speed and watched Dimitri roar off into the distance.

I had better be right. These nagging doubts had better not be down to baby-brain. Otherwise I had just potentially fucked my whole career because of hormones and a hunch.

Part Two

Crawling

crawl, *v.*
Gerund or present participle: **crawling**.
Move slowly on the hands and knees or with the body close to the ground.

Chapter Twenty-Seven

'WHAT THE FUCKING HELL happened, Lex? What the fuck? We're totally fucked now.' Sandy raised a fist to punch Unicorn's office wall, then remembered it was solid concrete and thought better of it.

'I told you. The button didn't work.'

'Are you kidding me?'

'I pressed it four times and nothing.'

Sandy walked up to me until he was inches from my face. 'I don't believe you.'

'It's the truth, Sandy.' My eyes didn't waver from his. 'Run tests if you want. The button didn't *work*. Technology sometimes fails. Shit happens.'

He broke eye contact and stormed up to the whiteboard, still covered in all our notes for the Drunk Driver plan.

'Shit shouldn't happen to *us*.' He turned back to look at me. 'Not on a mission we've been prepping this bloody hard for.'

'We just need to move to the Back-up. Everything is in place.'

'You mean the plan that at the last projection gave us a success rate of thirty-four per cent? Do I need to remind you again exactly what's at stake here? Fuck!' He picked up his mug of coffee and threw it against the wall. Broken china clinked to the floor as dark liquid streaked down the wall. 'I'll be in my office trying to convince the Nyan that we're still up to the fucking job.'

I lay on my back under the dining table in the meeting room. The bottom of the table was covered in carvings. Every time we lost a Rat, someone from their unit would come under here and engrave their name and dates of service into the table. Within London there were many memorials marking the names of those who had given their lives to serving this country. But we didn't exist. We were never to have our name up on a board anywhere. This was as good as it got. It was our way of honouring our fallen comrades. A small reminder that even if no one else knew, we did. I came here every now and then to think, to clear my mind, and to try not to dwell on how long it would be before my name was up there. As I traced out the names of departed Rats with my finger I thought of whether I had made the right call.

'The greater good.' That's what we repeat to ourselves when faced with an order that makes us pause to question whether we can be the ones to do it – to push the button, pull the trigger, inject the syringe. Just like the soldier in face-to-face combat who spots the wedding ring of the man he's about to shoot, or the fighter pilot who thinks he sees a school next to the target's location, you may stop, then take a breath and think, 'If I didn't, someone else would.' The order has been made. The Committee decrees who lives, who dies and what is an acceptable sacrifice. Our job is just to do their bidding. And not to fucking think about it.

I hadn't saved Dimitri. He was still a dead man walking. I had just delayed his execution by a few days. If I stalled again Sandy would be on to me and all hell would break loose.

I needed to look over all the intelligence myself and set up a few meetings. Dimitri either wanted VirtuWorld kept private just for Russia or available for international sale on the black market. He was either a President-supporting patriot or a money-loving capitalist. I needed to know a hundred per cent for sure which it was. My phone beeped. A text from Dasha.

Alexis. You missed that big meeting this morning. Can you see me urgently so we can talk about what happened?

I imagined her attempting to control her rage as she wrote that message knowing her communications were being monitored. I had no intention of seeing Dasha until I had done my own investigating. If she was the Dragon there would be a trail. I just needed to find it. I couldn't go to Sandy until I had proof.

'What the fuck are you doing under there?' I looked up at Sandy's upside-down face. He didn't give me time to reply. 'Get up. To save this mission you need to head out on an op. You leave in four hours.'

I got up from under the table and faced him.

'What is it?'

'A simple break-in. The Nyan are furious about the failed Pop and getting nervous. They've said if we want to keep them on side we need to do them a favour.'

I grimaced. 'So we're their bitches now? They can use Rats to run errands for them?'

'Don't give me shit, Lex.' Sandy smacked his hand against the wall and pointed at me. 'You were the one who failed to make the Pop. You have some making up to do. If I were you I would do everything your boss fucking says without questioning him. All they want you to do is break into some restaurant, crack a safe, and steal a brown envelope inside it.'

'And we have no idea what's in this envelope?'

'Right now this op is the only chance we have of saving us all from Russian world domination. The contents of the envelope are confidential and way beyond your security clearance. You do this, we're good with them, and there's still a chance to salvage this fucking disaster.'

He had a point. Chances were the Nyan were now spooked. We needed them on side. This little job should only take a few hours and I could come back to the Platform afterwards and do some research of my own in peace when the office was empty.

'Fine. Give me the details.'

I hated going into an op unprepared. The envelope I needed to obtain was apparently time sensitive and the Nyan were not budging on it being undertaken today. To make up for going in blind I was going to wear a head camera linked back to the Platform so that Geraint and Sandy could see what I was seeing. We didn't even know what model the safe was so I was going to need all the help I could get. The only upside was that the restaurant, a basement dive in Kensington famous for its Russian dumplings, was closed today so at least I didn't have to worry about the inconvenience of other people.

By the time daylight had disappeared we were ready to go. Rats were probably the only people who actually liked the clocks going back and darkness enshrouding London by teatime. The quicker nightfall came, the quicker we could get to work and the quicker we could get home.

Robin and I pulled up outside the restaurant in a Platform-issue white van. I'm pretty sure the aggressive and erratic way Rats drove their vans were how 'white van man' got his terrible reputation.

I checked my gun and zipped it into my suit. Sandy crackled into my earpiece.

'Green light. Cameras down.'

The restaurant was on a quiet side street and I was able to slip out of the van and up to the front door without spotting anyone else.

'Blowing the door.' I affixed a small charge to the lock, stepped back and pressed the button. A small *pfffttttt* emitted as the lock was blown. The alarm keypad by the door was counting down. I fixed another Geraint gadget to it. The beeps from the keypad started counting down and then sped up until they went silent and the lights turned green. 'Thanks, G-Man. I'm in.'

Sandy cut in. 'Safe is likely to be in the back room. I'll guide you through.'

'You ever been here before?'

'A fucking Russian restaurant? Are you kidding me? Don't worry, I can read a blueprint as if I was right there with you holding your fucking hand.'

I descended the stairs leading into the main restaurant.

'Door up ahead. Turn right once through. It's the last door at the end.'

I crossed through the tables and chairs and opened the double doors at the back with a 'Private' sign on. I turned right and passed the kitchen and a couple of other doors before I reached the end of the corridor and a grey door that was slightly ajar.

I listened outside it and then pushed it open. The office was a small room with only a large desk and chair, a rickety wooden bookshelf and a hideous abstract painting on the back wall.

'Who wants to bet it's behind here?' I took down the painting and uncovered a small safe built into the wall.

'Jackpot.' Geraint came in through my earpiece. 'That is one shit safe. Standard model from a hardware store. Forget wasting time cracking the code, the charge you used to blow the door will work easily.' He was right. In seconds I was looking inside the safe with the broken keypad on the floor. There was nothing inside except a brown envelope and what looked like a few Russian passports.

'Envelope secure.'

I put the envelope down the front of my suit, shut the safe door and replaced the painting.

I was making the mistake of thinking things were going like clockwork when Robin crackled through.

'Four men approaching. Shit. They've seen the door, and are entering the building now. They're armed. One's on the phone.'

Fucking brilliant. I was trapped in the back office of a basement restaurant. Badly outnumbered. And that was before the reinforcements they had called for arrived. My heart rate sped up and the adrenaline kicked in. I had to get out of here. This wasn't going to be the end for me. A Russian dumpling dive was not where I was going to expel my last breath and leave Gigi without a mother.

'Back exit – where is it?'

'There's a fire exit leading into the next-door alleyway. Looks like you passed it on your way to the office. Robin, get the van over there now.' If Sandy was remotely worried for me his voice didn't betray it. I agreed with his assessment I needed a fast exit and a fast getaway. Robin was going to be little help to me down here.

'Keep the engine running. I'll be there in two.'

My odds were not good. The men were likely to split up once they had searched the main restaurant. It would only be a matter of time before they found me and I didn't back my chances of taking out all four solo.

I looked around the small office. *Hide in plain sight.* I reached inside my suit and took out my small penknife. I opened it and slit it across the palm of my hand. The blood came fast. I smeared it all over the side of my face. I looked around the room. On the desk was a large package wrapped in brown paper and string. Inside the desk drawers I found nothing but pens, paperclips, papers and a small roll of masking tape. I took out the masking tape and placed my head cam and earpiece inside the drawer. I heard the slam of the double doors as the men entered the corridor. I figured I had less than ten seconds. Picking up the safe keypad and its broken wires off the floor I placed them on top of the package and pulled the desk chair to the centre of the room. I sat down and stuck the package on top of my lap along with the small charge I had used to blow the door. I set the timer and pulled off a small piece of masking tape.

When two of the men entered the office guns drawn, they were confronted with a terrified bleeding woman, hands tied behind her back, a strip of tape across her mouth while on her lap was a large package with a lot of flashing lights and wires.

They stopped and looked at each other, unsure what to do. The first man came towards to me slowly, still with his gun drawn, and ripped the tape off my mouth.

'Oh thank God, help me please help me! You have to call the police. It's a bomb. A fucking bomb. I'm so scared, oh Jesus, I'm so scared.'

He looked back to the other man and started talking in fast Russian, then reached out a hand to the 'bomb'.

I screamed. 'Oh God, don't touch it, don't touch it!' The timer lit up and started beeping. 'Oh God, it's about to go!' The numbers started counting down from three minutes. 'Please help! Please!' The men looked at the timer and then at each other again and, without speaking, started running. I could hear them down the corridor shouting to their colleagues, who, from the clattering and banging sounds, were searching the kitchen.

I quickly pushed my little invention off my lap and replaced my head cam and earpiece.

'Coming out now.'

I stood by the office entrance until I heard the sound of the double doors swinging as the men raced into the main part of the restaurant.

It was amazing how the threat of an imminent explosion would wipe any coherent thought. The questions of who was I? What was I doing there? Who did this to me? All forgotten about in favour of running before the force of an explosion pulled them apart limb from limb.

I could hear the faint sounds of the men as they stumbled past tables and chairs.

I started down the corridor.

'You seeing this? Which way?' Sandy's answer was blocked out by the sound of the double doors smashing open. Fuck, they were back. I ran down the corridor away from them and heard the burst of gunfire behind me. As I was turning the corner I could hear Sandy saying, 'Try the blue door.'

It was right up ahead. I raced towards it. I had my hand on the handle when by my feet I felt a gust of cold air coming out from under the door. A cold room. I bypassed it for the kitchen. The fire exit had to lead out from there. The voices were getting nearer. I heard the cold-room door open and slam.

At the back of the kitchen was a large door. I charged through it, tripping over three crates on the way. I was down, but only for a minute. Concrete steps ahead of me led up to two large fire exit doors. I had nearly made it. I ran up them three a time and felt bullets missing me as they hit the wall. I burst through the doors and straight into the passenger side of the van. We screeched out of there without a backwards glance as bullets pinged off the back of the reinforced van doors.

Back at the Platform I went straight to Sandy's office and dropped the brown envelope on to his desk. He was on his laptop and barely looked up, not surprisingly as, considering he still used two fingers to type, he couldn't afford to lose his concentration.

'Here it is. Hope that shuts the Nyan up.'

'Good work, Lex. See you tomorrow. Have a lie-in.' He was still staring at the screen.

'I have a baby. Those words don't exist anymore.'

He looked up. 'I don't give a crap. I'm attempting to be fucking nice. Things got pretty hairy back there. Come in late.'

'All heart, you are.'

'Don't you forget it. Now fuck off.'

I obliged and went straight to the showers. I peeled off my suit and got into the cubicle and turned the water on and stood underneath breathing slowly as I let the hot water rush over me. The showers were adjoining the locker room and the cubicle I was in was the only one which had a small shower door made from a crude piece of MDF fixed to it. A token attempt to offer a modicum of privacy to those who desired it – it barely hid much but at least those of us who chose to use it felt a little less exposed.

I used the shampoo to wash my hair with my good hand and scrub at the dried blood on my face. That was fucking close. I stood back against the cold tiles and shut my eyes.

What made them come back?

One minute they were hightailing it out of there and the next they were back, guns blazing. What happened? I thought back over everything as steam filled the cubicle. I remembered something. Amid the clatter of chairs as they brushed past them, a mobile had rung. A stupid ringtone just before the bullets started coming.

Someone told them to get back in there.

Someone who knew there was no bomb.

'Lex?'

I opened my eyes to see Jake looking at me over the shower door, through the steam. I walked up to the shower door and rested my arms on it.

'Back already?'

'Sandy rang screaming about a fucked Pop and you having a near miss. I'm sorry. I should've been there.' He reached out to my face and with his finger rubbed a spot of blood off the side of my cheek.

'It was an easy break-in that went bad. Nearly had to unleash a Movie Star Run.'

This was what we called that movie favourite of the hero charging towards baddies with all guns firing, cutting them down while not getting hit by a single bullet. Over the years many a Rat had been cornered enough to have no choice but to attempt the Run.

But it was real life. The bullets would hit, they would bleed, and never get to walk away from it. Much less with a shrug and a smart line.

'Sorry you had to cut your blower short. Was it a good twenty-four hours away?'

'I was in Italy.' He adjusted his shirt cuff. 'Managed to get a couple of bowls of pasta in before Sandy rang.'

'But you're back for good now?'

'Yes. My blower is officially on hold until after we've completed the Back-up. We'll sort through this fucking mess together.'

I smiled. 'Good.'

He smiled back.

'See you in the morning.' I stepped away from the door and back under the shower head and closed my eyes as I rinsed out the rest of the shampoo. It felt like he was still watching me but when I turned back round the space above the door was empty.

I slept badly. Gigi slept well. The wind rattled the windows and whistled down the fireplace. Perhaps the howling gales outside worked as a form of white noise keeping her asleep.

I was infuriated. Cheated of what could have been a blissful unbroken night's sleep by my own mind, which would not shut down. How did an easy break-in escalate so quickly to a firefight I was lucky to walk away from? It was a rushed op that we didn't have enough time to prepare for – did we miss something? The more I thought about it the more I knew that a mobile had definitely rung and whatever was said on that call was what made those men come back for me. And the only words that could have been said to make them want to return to a potential bomb site was the knowledge there was no bomb.

Who had made the call?

Chapter Twenty-Eight

'ALEXIS TYLER. WE NEED to talk to you.'

It was nearly lunchtime when I made it into the Platform. I was getting out of the lift when the short woman wearing a dark skirt suit with pristine white blouse and patent black heels spoke to me. Her greying hair was in a smart, tight bun. Anne Agius was from Eight's head office – she reported directly to our section chief.

Head office was far away from the dark and grime of Platform Eight itself, within Thames House. All missions that were thrown our way by Five or Six were agreed with our section chief in that nice smart above-board office. Orders that were then filtered through and actioned by us in our underground lair. Anne and her associates never visited the Platform unless there was a serious external problem or internal disciplinary matter to handle. Her presence was always bad news.

'Do I have something to worry about?'

'Just come with me, please.'

I followed Anne through the network of corridors thinking how out of place this smartly dressed woman looked click-clacking her way across the uneven linoleum flooring. We arrived at a small meeting room far removed from the busier unit offices. Inside the room were two suited men I didn't recognise. One was thin and in his fifties with a receding hairline. The other was round-faced and bearded. Neither was smiling. I was offered no introduction to their names or positions but motioned to sit. Anne sat down next to the men and I took my place in the solitary chair facing them. The room was set up for an interview and I was clearly the one in the hot seat.

The thin man cleared his throat. 'Alexis, we asked you here because your log of items taken from last night's op doesn't mention the money.'

This I did not expect.

'There wasn't any money. I retrieved the brown envelope as instructed and I was lucky to get out alive.' I looked between each of them. Their faces remained expressionless.

The thin man continued, 'The video footage clearly showed money in the safe. On estimation from the size of the pile, around five hundred thousand pounds. Five hundred thousand pounds the Nyan are now complaining is missing, which they say they're getting heat for.'

I was silent. The dread I had been feeling since the realisation someone had tipped off the Russians about the absence of a bomb was mounting. I was pretty sure this was what the beginning of the end felt like.

'There must be some mistake. The safe only contained the brown envelope and a few passports. That was it. My head camera footage should show that. It will also show that at no point am I handling any money.'

The thin man leaned forward. 'There are a good four minutes when you removed your camera so we have no idea what you were doing.'

'I removed the camera as I was busy trying to save my life.'

'Convenient. You just had to remove the camera. While alone in a room with five hundred grand.' He sat back and folded his arms.

'You can see why we're finding it hard to believe,' the other man cut in. 'Especially considering your personal circumstances. Children are expensive, aren't they? Particularly when you start looking at private schools like Chepstow Hall.'

They couldn't be serious.

'Being interested in Chepstow Hall has been part of my cover. Do you really think I would throw my whole career away because I want my daughter to go to a fancy school in a few years' time?'

The second man rubbed his beard. 'You can't deny that priorities change once you become a mother. And there's been talk. Concerns that your head's not really back in the game. We have here a transcript of your session with Doc. Sounds like motherhood did not come easily to you. It's an upheaval that can bring on a lot of change.' He looked at me unblinking as he pushed his hands together to form a little pyramid. 'Having an agent like you, a Rat, with responsibilities at home is a first for us.'

I stared at the three people facing me.

'Responsibilities at home? The majority of Rats are married. At least a third have children. Let's be clear here and say what you're really thinking, which is just because this Rat actually gave birth to their kid it means they're more likely to become a total fucking loon?' I bunched my hands into fists. 'So please tell me what it is about my vagina that makes me so damn crazy?'

The two men looked at Anne. They obviously felt whatever they had to say would come better from someone with their own crazy-inducing vagina.

'It's not that at all,' Anne replied. 'Any new parent feels a certain level of newfound responsibility and normally women are the ones more affected by the child.'

The way she stumbled over the words 'the child' made me realise she had no children of her own, was in no way inclined to be on my side, and that the men were likely to be more understanding.

I took a deep breath.

'And what part of what I do, for you, for this country, makes you think I am anything like normal women? How many people do I need to kill, torture or maim before you get that? I've had to work ten times as hard as any of the men here just to prove I'm capable of doing what we do. And now you're saying I have to work even harder to prove I can still do this job because I took a few months off to have a baby?' I was clenching my fists so hard now I could feel my nails digging into the palms of my hands. 'When's it going to stop? What do I have to do to get treated like everyone else?'

Anne pursed her lips. 'Look, Ms Tyler, we're very grateful for all you have done for your country, for your service, but you have to understand we would not be doing our jobs if we weren't carefully monitoring you and your change in circumstance. There are discrepancies and we need to be thorough.'

'This is bullshit.'

'This is protocol. You need to take the day.' She stood up. 'Go home. Spend some nice time with your daughter.'

I knew the drill. I was being sent home because I was being investigated. My clearance would be frozen and they would right now be running over everything that happened yesterday with a fine-tooth comb. I could forget going into the office;

Unicorn would be banned from speaking to me. And I could forget using Eight's resources to double-check the intel on Dimitri, as I would be barred from our internal network.

Anne and the two men escorted me back to the lift. We passed Jake standing outside Unicorn's office. His eyes never left mine and I blinked twice.

The lift reached the ground floor. Anne walked me out into the street.

'Your access card, please, Alexis.'

I took my specially modified Oyster card out of my pocket and handed it to her. 'We'll be in touch.' With me safely dispatched to the outside world, she disappeared back inside.

I stood amid the hustle and bustle of the street as people rushed around me, all on their way somewhere, all with things to do. I watched the faces of strangers coming past me, talking, laughing, life carrying on for them as normal. For the very first time I felt envious of the Sheep and their sweet oblivion.

This was my own doing. I didn't want normal and now I didn't have it. I may have felt sick to my stomach. Furious at what they were accusing me of. Terrified as to what could come next. But I couldn't complain. I chose to not have the desk job and the nine-to-five. I wanted this. And with that came risks, that one day I could be out in the cold, investigated, and made redundant. By people whose interpretation of the word was a little more final. More Colt 45 than P45.

I got home and had a long cuddle with Gigi. I smelt her hair, I kissed her cheeks and I told her she was the very best girl in the whole world.

'How come you're back so soon?' Gillian was hovering next to us watching.

'My afternoon of meetings got cancelled.'

'That's lucky, isn't it? I've just made lunch so I'll eat and then be off. Do you want any?' I looked over at the indistinguishable white stuff on the table. It may have been macaroni cheese.

'I'm fine, thanks. You go ahead. I just need to sort out some laundry.' I headed out of the kitchen as Gillian began attempting to get Gigi to eat her lunch. I felt guilty for how grateful I was that Gillian planned to leave – after a day where I had been disgraced at work and now feared my whole career, maybe even my life, were on the line, having to spend an afternoon making small talk with my mother-in-law could be what pushed me over the edge.

I went straight to our bathroom. Behind the panel under the sink, alongside my gun, was the old Nokia phone that I used to take with me on blowers. Eight didn't know I had it so I knew they couldn't be monitoring it. I switched it on and waited. I paced up and down the bathroom trying to remain calm. I couldn't let the anger take over. I needed a clear mind.

Ten minutes later the Nokia finally rang.

'What the hell is happening?' was what Jake greeted me with. Jake was the only one with the number. Back in the day, so far back I can't even remember when, we had devised a simple one blink for email, two blinks for phone.

'I have no idea. They've accused me of stealing cash from the op last night.'

'That's ridiculous.'

'They claim my head cam shows the safe was full of money and now the Nyan are complaining it's all gone. It's bullshit.

There was nothing in there except the envelope and a couple of passports.' I bit my lip. 'You need to get hold of that footage. It'll be on our main server by now.'

'I'll call back as soon as I can. Relax, Tyler. We'll sort this out.' The line went dead.

There was nothing I could do until he rang back. I headed back down into the kitchen where Gillian was eating her lunch and trying to persuade her granddaughter to do the same. Gigi's mouth was clamped shut in a stubborn line.

'Don't worry, Gillian, some days she's just not hungry.' I plucked Gigi out of the highchair and put her down on the play-mat. 'Can I get you anything else? A cup of tea?'

'No I'm fine, thanks, love.' She scraped her plate and checked her watch. 'If I leave now I can get back in time for my programme.'

Will and I had given up trying to explain to Gillian that she could record everything she wanted or watch it on catch-up. One afternoon spent trying to teach her how to use BBC iPlayer had caused more head-banging frustration than we would ever choose to put ourselves through again.

'Now remember what I said about the Facebook. You mustn't put any photos of Gigi up there or strangers can see them and find out where you live.' Gillian frowned. She clearly couldn't quite remember the article she'd read. 'Or something else bad.' She put her plate in the dishwasher and went over to Gigi. 'Bye bye, my angel.' She turned to me. 'Let me know when you need me.'

'I will do. Thanks so much, Gillian.' I meant it. As infuriating as she could be with her constant safety lectures, I was grate-ful. Without her stepping in I couldn't have gone back to work.

With both Will and me often working late, Beata's hourly rate would have eaten away any financial gain to me returning to the Platform. And it would have been unbearable confessing to Will that even running at a loss I still wanted to do it. Gillian fussed around looking for coat, handbag and car keys and then the door closed and we were alone.

I lay down next to Gigi on the playmat.

'It's just you and me, bubba.' She gurgled back and reached for Sophie the giraffe, sticking it straight in her mouth. I tickled her feet as she squealed. I passed her a squashy ball, she dropped the giraffe and tried to cram that in her mouth instead.

I kept running over everything, trying to work out why this was happening. It was all linked to Dimitri, it had to be. I hadn't Popped the Weasel and now it seemed I was the target. It must be the Nyan. I was on an op for them when I nearly got killed. They were the ones claiming money was missing. But how did that explain the video footage? It had to be a lie. A bluff to see if I would crumble and confess.

Gigi threw the ball at my head. *Boing.* A tinny noise sounded which made her laugh. It was the best sound in the world. Even now, under investigation, cut off from my colleagues, potentially about to see my whole career tanked, seeing her happy filled me with joy. I watched as she concentrated on trying to get the ball to make a noise again. Maybe this was the wake-up call I needed.

I could leave the whole underground world behind and embrace the daylight and the safety of my suburban bubble. This was a neighbourhood where the only violence making headline news was the murder of an aged oak tree with a preservation order protecting it. A rusty nail had been hammered into its trunk; the tree equivalent to slitting a person's throat.

Except without all that inconvenient blood spurt. Tree-assassin could be a nice job for my retirement. Housewives frustrated at pesky branches ruining the light into their fancy drawing rooms would covertly hire me to prowl the streets armed with a head torch and tool belt. In Chiswick I could be a more wholesome killer.

My Nokia rang. I got up and went to the kitchen window. I was sure I had read somewhere that babies could pick up on stress levels. And this phone call was going to cause a lot of it.

'I got the footage. It shows what looks like about five hundred grand in cash sitting in that safe next to a large brown envelope.'

'You're kidding me.' I stared out at the garden. A squirrel was burrowing into our immaculately laid lawn.

'If it's an edit job it's a pretty professional one, and whoever did it would've had to take the time beforehand to set it up.' I gently tapped my forehead against the window. 'I spoke to Sandy and he's effing and blinding and in a complete piss that you've been sent home when we should be getting ready to fly out to Moscow for the Back-up. We're trying to get Robin up to speed to take your place. It's a mess.'

'How do they know the money didn't go missing after we left? Anyone could have gone in afterwards.'

'The Ruskis left straight after you and no one else entered the building until the police stormed it three minutes after your departure. They catalogued everything they found and the reports are saying there was no cash.'

'What about—'

'Before you ask there were at least four officers from two different units in that room when they discovered the safe. Not a chance all of them were dirty.'

I took a deep breath. 'So the case against me is the Nyan's word there was money there and that video cam footage?'

'Yes exactly. That's— Gotta go.' The line went dead.

The situation was worse than I thought. Doctored video footage on our server meant a Snake. Someone inside Eight was dirty. Slithering through the underground tunnels alongside us. An unidentified threat poised to suffocate us in a vice-like grip when we least expected it. A Snake was a danger to us all. But right now that Snake was targeting me.

Bennie.

He wanted my job. And more than once I had hurt that most precious intangible essence: male pride. That was more than enough to make him take the leap. Pigeon to Rat to Snake. A busy few months.

It had to be him.

But who was he working with? And was there a bigger plan than just disgracing me?

I looked at the playmat and watched Gigi trying to move. Lying on her front, her arms and legs flailing as she tried to propel herself forward. That was how I felt. On my hands and knees, barely making tracks, trying to work out what the hell was going on. She was so determined, though, pulling herself across the floor, in a half crawl, half roll, doing the best she could. And still smiling.

She could do it and so could I.

I had a fitful night.

Even before Gigi woke in the early hours.

She fed from me sleepily, her eyes closed. One little hand resting on my breast, giving it the odd appreciative pat. By the time I put her back in her cot my mind was whirring.

I couldn't see a way out. If Bennie was a Snake what else could he have fixed against me?

As light started to creep in through the curtains I gave up on sleep. I changed into my running kit, pulled on a baseball cap and turned the monitor up to full volume – Will could sleep through a foghorn – and left the house. I followed my usual route to Chiswick House – I knew it so well by now I went on autopilot, my music on full blast. I kept a fast pace, shaking the remnants of tiredness off.

I passed down Duke's Avenue and kept going. It would've been easy for Bennie to access the server and edit the video footage. But how did he make the phone call in the restaurant at exactly the right moment? He would've had to have been monitoring our office remotely. Or actually working with someone in Unicorn.

I could barely bring myself to think it – could someone in my own unit really betray me?

Apart from the odd car passing down the High Road I had yet to see anyone. I came to the start of the underpass that would take me under the main road, to Chiswick House and paused my iPod. It was one of those habits I could never remember if it had been drilled into us or if it was now just instinct. As I entered the passage I saw a man wearing a hi-vis jacket, jeans and a hard hat on a small step ladder using a screwdriver on one of the overhead light casings. Every internal sensor I had started ringing. Workmen never started this early.

There was a large piece of tarpaulin laid out beneath him. But no toolbox. He also hadn't turned to the sound of my footsteps echoing down the underpass. He was trying a little too hard to pretend he was focused on the task in hand. I had three seconds to make a decision. I was unarmed in a tunnel, each end of which could by now be blocked by further hostiles, and this guy was big. He would not be an easy takedown. The only advantage I had was surprise. He wouldn't expect an attack. Right now he was waiting for me to get close enough that he couldn't miss. I started thinking back over my route here. My baseball cap would have mostly hidden my face from any prying CCTV cameras. If he did turn out to be just a poorly equipped, early-rising workman who got attacked out the blue by a deranged female jogger it would be hard for them to track me down. I made my decision.

I sped up to a fast sprint and launched myself at him – with a fast stomach punch followed by a knee ball-crush he went toppling to the floor. The clatter of his gun, with silencer attached, falling to the floor confirmed that I had made the right call. I jumped on his back and put him in a chokehold until I felt the reassuring slump of his body going slack as he passed out. One down. But how many were out there? I gave him a quick pat-down. He had an earpiece. Not a good sign.

I took his gun and packed it into the waistband of my leggings. Now, which way to go? They could be at either exit or both. I looked from one end to the other and ran back up the underpass the way I had come, my hand resting on the gun in my waistband. I got to the top, and saw no one except a dog walker coming towards me down Duke's Avenue, followed by a couple of cyclists. Exactly what I needed. Witnesses. An engine started. Turning towards the noise, I saw a van heading straight for me. I dived to the right but not fast enough. I felt a sharp pain as the van clipped me in the ribs. Lying there winded, looking up at the sky, I reached for the gun. If they were coming I would be ready. But I heard loud shouts and then the screech of tyres as the van reversed back and tore away down the road. It took two tries, but I got to my feet.

'Christ, are you okay? What the hell was wrong with that maniac?' The dog walker had run up to me, his panting spaniel alongside him. 'Shall I call an ambulance?'

'No, I'm fine. Thank you. Just a little shaken. Just want to get home.' I attempted a slow jog, trying to ignore the searing pain in my ribs. I gritted my teeth. Every step was a further jolt of agony.

'What about the police? I got a bit of his licence plate!' he shouted after me. I kept on going. I knew the van's plates would lead nowhere. Once the dog walker headed through the underpass he would discover a poor workman who had knocked himself out falling off his ladder. An eventful morning to report back to the wife.

I ran as fast as my bruised and battered body would allow.

Gigi.

Will.

If they wanted me dead, if they were coming for me, they could be after them. I kept having to stop to draw breath. My mind screamed at me to get home, but my body was letting me down. Like a bad dream where you need to run, but your legs won't move. Where you need to shout for help but no sound comes out. It felt like running through treacle.

I was shaking by the time I saw our front door. With one last burst of energy I raced up to Gigi's nursery, flinging open the door. Her cot was empty.

Jesus.

They had her.

I went charging back down the stairs to our bedroom and stopped.

There she was, propped up in our bed surrounded by about five pillows, a sleeping Will's arm around her and *Peppa Pig* on the television, with no volume. And the subtitles on. In his half-asleep daze Will had been thoughtful enough to consider that if there was no sound our baby needed another way to follow the plot. I picked up Gigi and held her close, covering her head in kisses.

The gun tucked into my waistband was digging into the small of my back. A reminder of what I had just been facing, outside of this room that still smelt of musty sleep. I tucked Gigi back into her pillow nest and went through to the bathroom. I hid the gun behind the panel at the back of the cupboard and stripped off and got in the shower. The warm water helped soothe the aches all over my body. I dried quickly, changed and got back into bed and snuggled up to Gigi. Will started to stir and felt for my hand. This was my family. My world. I wasn't going to leave them anytime soon. I was going to do whatever it took to get to the bottom of this. Whoever the fuck was trying to take me away from them was going to pay.

Chapter Twenty-Nine

MY FAMILY WOULD SOON be safe. That was all I kept reminding myself of as I got breakfast ready. As soon as Will had woken up I had convinced him that Gillian seemed very down he hadn't spent any quality time with her recently. I suggested that as I was on a big deadline and working horribly long hours for the next few days he and Gigi should go stay with her and he could cheer up her lonely evenings. The guilt of being an only son to a widowed mother meant he was notifying his office he'd be working from home as I was still talking. I had already briefed an old colleague who had moved to the private sector to keep watch on them at Gillian's house. Before I could get to work I needed to feel completely confident Will and Gigi were not at risk.

I stared down at the saucepan of porridge and kept stirring it. Next to the cooker lay Gigi's bright pink plastic Peppa Pig bowl and matching spoon. Cheery Tupperware and cold metal guns existing in the same world. My world.

I poured another splash of milk into the pan. Things were far from over. For my would-be killer to be waiting for me in the underpass they would've had to know my running route and to head to the underpass as soon as they saw me leave the house. They must have been watching me for who knew how many weeks, maybe even months. Long-term surveillance and an attempted assassination couldn't just be about Bennie and some petty office rivalry.

There had to be a bigger picture.

And it must be linked to Dimitri and the failed Pop. Everything had started to fall apart as soon as I failed to push the button.

Whoever was after me would strike again when the moment was right. I knew the drill. They needed to make me disappear but couldn't afford a scene. Take me out early morning in an underpass and wrap my body in tarpaulin and into a van: that worked. Taking potshots at me in the street: that wouldn't.

The next hitman might not be as amateur as the one this morning or as easy to spot. In Eight the hi-vis jacket was the king of props for making you invisible to members of the public. Commuters seeing us walking through Underground tunnels, or stepping over a barrier marked 'no entry' would think we were maintenance and not bother with a second glance. The man in the underpass, just like us Rats, had chosen not to wear the matching hi-vis trousers. Real highway maintenance wore both, whereas those in covert ops wanting a token disguise, to easily shrug on and off, just wore the jacket.

As for his partner in the van, who knew what he was trying to achieve? Trying to slow me down so the gunman could finish me off? Poor planning and poor execution by idiots who should've known who they were dealing with.

I needed to go off the grid. But I had an important appointment this morning that I couldn't miss.

'I think that's done now.' I hadn't noticed Will come up behind me. I looked down at the pan. The porridge was drying out, the bottom stuck to the pan. I took it off the heat and spooned some into Gigi's bowl.

'Sorry, I was miles away.' I dolloped two portions into our bowls and sat down at the table.

'When do you have to be at work?' Will poured milk over his rather congealed offering, followed by a gallon of honey.

I glanced up at the clock. 'I've just enough time to take Gigi to music class as soon as she's finished eating.' We both watched her smearing porridge into her hair.

'Okay, *ma chérie*, you girls enjoy banging your tambourines together and I'll pack up the car so we can leave as soon as you get back.' Will stretched and poured himself another coffee.

I gave him a kiss as I cleared the table and baby-wiped down my daughter, her highchair, the table, and parts of the floor.

I winced as I picked up Gigi and strapped her into her pram. I quickly popped several Panadol from my pocket. 'Period pain,' I announced to Will's questioning gaze.

Once I'd checked that the bulletproof cover was securely fixed on to the pram, I picked up the nappy bag and stepped out into the crisp November air.

I walked fast. We were halfway down the High Road when Gigi started crying.

'What is it, bubba? Please be good, we're nearly there.' I peeked at her through the cover and recoiled at the smell. Great. I sighed and checked my watch. Babies never gave any warning. Just like in life. You think everything is going fine. Right up until the moment you're surprised by a gigantic amount of shit.

I detoured into Starbucks' disabled toilet and after changing Gigi checked the bruises the van had given me. I looked from the angry purple marks on my stomach down to the soft pink cheeks of my daughter. I was going to get through this. Those wanting to take me down were going to suffer for daring to try to end my life and leave my little girl motherless. A capital punishment for a capital crime.

With a clean and once again sweet-smelling Gigi, I powered on towards the meet.

When I had spoken to Jake again last night I had made one simple request: for him to get his Platform-issue login calculator to me. It allowed us to log on to our secure network from any computer outside of the office. I needed to get online to use Eight's innumerable resources to try to work out what was happening. A face-to-face in daylight was out of the question. Eight would be watching Jake, maybe even investigating him as well. It was too big a risk to be seen together. I had named the 10 a.m. Monkey Music class at the town hall as the exchange point. Right now, safety was being out in public, not hiding away at home.

'Leave it to me,' was all he said before he clicked off.

I hadn't heard anything from him since. I had to trust that he had found a way.

Once settled with Gigi in my lap and the room slowly filling up with mothers and babies I scanned the room, trying to determine where Jake could have dropped it. I checked my phone again. No text or voicemail to give me a clue. This wasn't good. I had seen a decorator in the hallway when I arrived. Could he soon hover by the door and give me a nod?

I was distracted by a beautiful young Brazilian walking in. The white-haired baby she carried on her hip was quite obviously not hers. Who on earth would be crazy enough to have a nanny that hot? She was dressed down in jeans and a cashmere jumper but she had the type of body where everything clung in the right place. A gay couple. She must work for a gay couple. I was so busy staring at her body that I didn't notice she was waving at me.

'Lex? Hi, I'm a friend of Jake's.' She had the good grace to look a little embarrassed. Obviously she'd realised 'friend' might be a push for someone she had clearly met the night before, but then also 'friend' was not quite descriptive enough for the more-than-friends activity that had been undertaken.

'Oh, hi, nice to meet you.'

She pulled what looked like a furry toy rat out her bag. 'He said you would be here and to give this to you.'

'Thank you so much. We were desperate to get good old Mr Rattykins back.' I took the rat from her. It had goggly pink eyes, white whiskers and yellowing teeth. It looked more Halloween prop than cuddly soft toy. Giving it a squeeze I felt something reassuringly solid within its belly. 'It's my daughter's favourite.' I stuffed it into my nappy bag before Gigi could catch sight of it and give the game away by crying.

She sat down next to me as the class began. I had to suffer through an hour of music making which mostly involved Gigi sucking every instrument she was handed and listening to Hot Nanny ask me questions about Jake and tell me how she'd never met anyone like him before. It turned out she worked for a recently divorced father. I was cross I hadn't worked this out myself. When the class finished I bid my new friend goodbye and dissected the rat as soon as she was out of sight.

'Don't say I never do anything for you,' said the note wrapped around Jake's login calculator. I was impressed. He had had twelve hours to find a way to infiltrate a baby class and deliver

303

me the calculator. Not only had he managed it but he had succeeded in ensuring it wasn't exactly a chore.

Outside our house Will was slamming shut the boot of the car. He stretched out his arms at the sight of us.

'It's time to go, sweetheart.' He plucked Gigi out of the pram.

I hugged them both tight as we said goodbye.

'I love you so much, little girl.' I stroked Gigi's cheek and adjusted her pink hat. '*Je t'aime, mon cher.*' I kissed Will hard.

'*Je t'aime*, beautiful. I'll call when we get there. Don't work too hard. Try to escape and come join us.'

'I'll do my best.' I always noticed how literal the phrases everyone used in everyday conversation were to us Rats. '*Work is killing me.*' '*I nearly died.*' '*Try to escape.*'

Will carefully strapped Gigi into her car seat, dropped a small mountain of toys on her lap, and with another kiss for me got into the driver's seat.

I waved until they were out of sight, my other hand gripping the empty pram, the seat still warm. I wanted to collapse in a heap on the ground and cry and cry in fear that it could be the last time I ever saw them. But I didn't. I bit my lip until it bled, took three long, deep breaths and went back inside. Crying wasn't going to do us any good. Fighting back was.

'Good morning,' I greeted the uniformed concierge at the reception desk. 'I'm using Apartment 31.'

'Yes, of course. I have a key waiting for you, Mrs Chang.' He turned to the cupboard behind him.

Logging on to Airbnb, I had booked a flat in a luxury apartment building on the Strand. I'd used a Chinese pseudonym as, having been on the searching end of a hunt before, I knew we were all too quick to write off ethnic names if looking for a white subject. But while a white man called Chang might lead to identity-theft questions from suspicious cashiers, people were so used to women taking their husband's surname they wouldn't think twice.

'I see you're here for three nights.'

'It may be longer. Depends when I need to return to Hong Kong.'

'No problem, Mrs Chang. You're on the tenth floor and the lift is just through there.'

The flat was costing me a small fortune but it was a necessary expense to get the level of security I wanted. With cameras in the reception, lifts and corridors on every floor I could hack into their feed and keep an eye on exactly who was headed my way. I also wanted to be close to the office. My hideout had been carefully chosen for practical reasons yet, as I let myself into the flat, I couldn't deny the luxury part was an added bonus.

I looked at the beautifully decorated bedroom with plump pillows and a cashmere blanket draped over the thick duvet. It was my first night away from Gigi. Yet I wouldn't be enjoying the extra rest but sleeping with one eye open, bracing myself for any incoming threats.

I turned on the large flatscreen television in the living area and connected it to the small black box I had brought with me. With a few tweaks, the DVD channel was now broadcasting the building's security feed.

I unpacked the rest of my small case, including a large bag of food I had thrown together from our kitchen. Needing enough energy to find out who was trying to kill me was definitely a valid reason to break my diet. I made myself a large chicken and avocado sandwich and opened a bag of crisps. I fired up my laptop and got to work.

Using Jake's login calculator I got on to Eight's network and hacked the CCTV records of the day of the restaurant op. Whoever was setting me up would have needed to make a visit just before I arrived. If it was Bennie I just needed one shot of him on camera to take to Anne to prove his involvement.

The only cameras for that street were right above the restaurant and the way it was angled meant I could only see people who were walking on the edge of the pavement. No one seemed to be going anywhere near the restaurant. I fast-forwarded until I saw someone approach. Someone who seemed to know exactly where the cameras were as they knew how to make sure they weren't in shot; all I got was a glimpse of an arm. The restaurant door then opened as they walked in. Half an hour later the restaurant door opened again and the man headed back the way he came. Again a flash of dark jacket as he walked back down the road was all I could see. I watched it three times. I stared at the screen thinking about my next move now this was a dead end as I watched it for a fourth time. A small flash of movement along the car doors caught my eye. The cars lined down the road reflected the man's progress down the street. All I could see were legs walking away. No visual on the face.

But I didn't need one.

I could recognise that walk a mile away.

Ten years together.

Working side by side.

And now he wanted me dead.

I replayed it again, watching the lopsided gait of his left leg dragging behind his right.

Sandy, you piece of shit.

Chapter Thirty

'*TRY THE BLUE DOOR.*'

When the bullets were flying and all hell had broken lose Sandy had shouted this down my comms. Running back over the whole restaurant operation, this was the one phrase that kept sticking. It wasn't right. But why? I kept replaying the scene over and over in my mind.

And then it all clicked. He had visuals from my head camera but he was shouting before even I had seen it was blue. He claimed he'd never been there yet knew the colour of a door. A door he wanted me to go through that led into a cold room with no means of escape. If I'd listened to him I would've been shot to death in an icy walk-in coffin. Cut down amid the cuts of meat. How could I have missed that?

I was fucked. Sandy being a Snake meant I didn't have a chance. Right now Anne and her colleagues would be asking him for all the intel he had on the op. I could go to them myself but with what evidence? Some grainy CCTV footage and my word that he had said 'blue door' over a hail of gunfire. I thought for a moment. Sandy could barely work an iPhone, let alone edit together faked footage of a safe full of money. He had to be working with somebody. While Sandy was running point, supposedly helping save my life, they would have been the one to ring the Russians and tell them there was no bomb and to get back in there and finish me off.

It had to be Bennie. Sandy could have been working with him from the beginning and brought him in as my maternity cover to set all this up.

I closed my eyes. I needed to think this through.

Bennie being involved didn't rule out someone else in Unicorn. Geraint and Nicola would have been running comms together in our office. Robin was in the van outside. And Jake. Where was Jake in all this? Where was he when I was running for my life? Conveniently out of the country. He'd been partnered with Bennie throughout my maternity leave. Could Jake right now be sitting with him and Sandy laughing that I'd asked for his help when Anne cast me out? After everything we had been through together over the years I couldn't believe that he would be in on this.

But things weren't adding up.

And he had lied to me.

When I had spoken to him in the shower after the restaurant op he had lied about where he had been. He had fiddled with his shirt cuff. He always did that when he was lying. I had noticed it years ago and had always meant to tell him. Although chances were no hostile would ever notice such a tiny detail, there was always a chance they might. And that was why I knew it was important for me to let him know.

But I hadn't. Maybe because I knew one day it might be useful. Maybe always in the back of my mind I thought this could happen. That I would need to know when he wasn't telling me the truth.

We had worked side by side together for ten years but what did I really know about him? He gave away nothing about himself. Judging from his accent he seemed, like me, to come from the Home Counties, and despite him giving off an air of ex-public-school entitlement I don't think he had actually gone to one – this was only judging from a rant about the smug elitist schooling system when we had come out of a meeting with Six run by a couple of particularly obnoxious Hooray Henrys. I only knew he had been in the armed forces because of the small nod of recognition he would exchange with other ex-army agents, and the tattoo he had on the back of his shoulder. I had assumed it was military as it had that look – swords, fists, Latin – yet I hadn't been able to find it on any of the databases I had scoured when I was bored in the office one afternoon.

All I really knew about him was that he was a perfect Rat. A formidable enemy.

He excelled not just in hand-to-hand combat but also in the more difficult missions that required expert planning. Forget thinking outside the box. He would think outside the warehouse the stupid box was sitting in. The crazy shit he had come up with over the years was in equal measures terrifying and awe-inspiring to behold.

A few years ago we were tasked with taking out an African dictator who was even madder and more brutal than what usually came to mind when you heard the words 'African dictator'. Paranoid about his safety, the dictator had retreated to a fortified bunker in the middle of the jungle guarded by what seemed like a third of his poverty-stricken country's population. It was an impenetrable fortress he had no intention of ever leaving.

Jake studied his file for days and got hold of his hotel bills from all the trips he had taken before he decided to run his empire from a bunker. He determined that this terrifying mass murderer had a major thing for a certain C-list actress. Without fail, in every hotel he had stayed in he had viewed one of her films. Jake contacted this actress, posing as a big hotshot agent and convinced her to do a stunning calendar shoot that would be both tasteful and tantalising and remind Hollywood producers she was a force to be reckoned with. Thanks to a top photographer and a team of the best hair, make-up and lighting people, in a few weeks he had a calendar which was definitely more tantalising than tasteful.

Geraint then hacked the Wi-Fi of the bunker with pop-ups detailing the 'exclusive' calendar and where to buy it. Within thirteen minutes of the first pop-up we had our first order. The next day a very special edition of the calendar was delivered to the actress's number-one fan, wrapped in a cellophane packet. Three days later the dictator was dead. Every page had been laced with arsenic and days of continuous leafing through the pages meant he'd absorbed enough to kill him. His inner circle were in uproar; it looked like an inside job. A mess of in-fighting and accusations meant his whole military junta fell apart in a mass of paranoia and executions and the key players barely noticed when a legitimate government was formed amid all the chaos. It was genius. Even more so as we easily made back the budget we had blown on the expensive calendar shoot by the thousands of (non-arsenic-laced) copies we sold online. Turned out the dictator wasn't her only fan, although she never did hit the big time. Her body may have done the world a big service but she couldn't act for shit.

Jake was not someone I would ever want as an adversary. Although I still couldn't imagine he would do me any harm. But then, was that not naïve? We'd been long-term partners, occasional lovers, frequent co-fighters but never friends. He was a borderline psychopath who I suspected enjoyed killing and torture. Did he even know what loyalty was? Upon being confronted he could just say, 'Well, Tyler, you must understand it was too much money to say no to,' and not even comprehend my sense of betrayal. My despair. A thought that turned my stomach.

I had to talk to him. But before I did I needed to work out where he had been.

Ten minutes later I had my answer.

After accessing CCTV of him departing his flat, the cameras at Heathrow airport parking picking up his licence plate and the flight manifests for the eight flights departing in that timeframe I knew where he had gone. On the morning of the much-lauded Bonfire Night party Jake had boarded a 10.10 a.m. BA flight to Marseille.

My enforced pregnancy leave at Five had not been a total waste of time as I had used the months stuck in the office to brush up on my IT skills. Skills that helped me hack Avis's rental database until I found the exact make, model and registration of the car Jake had hired and its mileage upon his departure and return. That, combined with the French toll booth records, meant I had an idea of his route from the airport. Seeing where he turned off the main A7 road helped me narrow it down to four different towns.

Thankfully I knew him well. I felt not unlike a cuckolded wife; using my knowledge of him and his habits to help track him down. Countless times the Platform had informed us we were due to head out the next day and we needed to plan our trip accordingly. Upon being given the name of the town we were being dropped into Jake had always followed the same routine:

1. Narrow hotels down to those with Trip Advisor 4.5 or 5 star rating. (*'Luxury hotels are the best, security wise we can hack their feeds, no one is likely to try to storm us, and fucking hell, don't you think we deserve somewhere nice to rest our weary heads after having the shit kicked out of us for Queen and country?'*)
2. Check they had a restaurant with outdoor dining. (*'All I want is to have a cigarette with my morning coffee. Why does that have to involve being made to feel like a second-class citizen drinking out of a Styrofoam cup hunched in a doorway?'*)
3. Confirm if there was an indoor pool. (*'I run everywhere, mostly across rooftops, in a hail of gunfire. Why the hell would I run for fun? Swimming is exercise. And I get to see women in a state of undress I normally don't get to see unless I at least talk to them first.'*)

It could be a dead end considering that I had no idea what he was doing. He might not even be staying in a hotel. But I had no other leads. I felt vindicated when the first hotel in the second town I rang confirmed that Jake had stayed there last week, but no, they had not discovered the scarf he'd left behind.

Jake had spent three days in a town called L'Isle-sur-la-Sorgue. Why would he lie about being in France? If it was for work and confidential he could just say so. If it was for play, why hide what country he had been to? Knowing Jake, a blower was more likely to involve hard partying in Ibiza with a flurry of drugs and bronzed, long-limbed women, not antiquing in a quaint little town in Provence.

I scanned Platform Eight's database of ongoing missions. Nothing came up on L'Isle-sur-la-Sorgue. Whatever he was doing there was something he felt he had to lie about to me. And right now, with my life on the line, I couldn't take any chances.

Chapter Thirty-One

I RANG JAKE AND SAID we needed a face-to-face that evening. I named a storage unit that Mrs Chang had been renting a container at since I started at the Platform. All us Rats had an escape box in place, a container somewhere, with a crate filled with guns, money and passports. We all knew a time could come when we needed to disappear.

It was a risk to leave the apartment. I could have asked him to meet me there. But I didn't know how things would pan out, and if I was going to be on the run for a while I didn't want my Airbnb rating ruined through this landlord complaining about bloodstains not coming out of his expensive polished wooden floor.

I met Jake outside the storage unit. I unlocked the roller door and together we pulled it up. The light came on automatically as we walked in.

The room was empty except for a large metal box in one corner and a metal chair in the centre. Jake walked up to it and, pulling at it, saw it was bolted to the ground. I moved fast and kicked his legs out from under him, the chair catching his fall as I handcuffed his right hand to it.

'What the hell, Tyler? Motherhood is definitely making you kinkier.' He pulled at the handcuff as he looked up at me.

'Sandy's a Snake. I've got CCTV footage of him going into the restaurant the day of the op.' I stared at him, seeing what he would give away. I saw a flicker of confusion but nothing more as he processed what I was telling him and what it meant that I had handcuffed him to a chair.

'And you think I'm in on it?' He clenched his jaw and shook his head. 'I don't see any machines anywhere. No instruments of torture. Is there someone outside to come in and do your bidding?'

'It's just you and me, Jake. No props. I'm going old school.' I straddled him, our faces only inches apart. I put my finger on his neck.

'Do we really have to go through this charade?'

I dropped my hand and stared him straight in the eye.

'Jake, think about it. I'm being set up. By Sandy. Right now, Anne and her cronies are no doubt listening to him as he talks about how the Pop went wrong and next thing we know money is missing. Who do you think everyone is going to listen to? The hormonally deranged new mother? Or good old boy Sandy, twenty-five years in the service, few medals in there somewhere, and everyone's favourite bet to be our next section chief? They think I am a traitor. A Snake who's been bought off. Do you really think they're going to give me the benefit of the doubt? Call me in for an interrogation, allow me to hire a lawyer, let me voice my concerns to HR? Or will they take me out and leave my daughter without a mother?'

Despite my best efforts my voice caught a little when I said this – saying it all out loud made me focus on how terrible the situation was and how there was a very real chance that I might not see Gigi again. I took a moment until I was sure my voice wasn't going to crack again and said calmly, 'So can you under-stand why I'm being more than just a little cautious?'

Jake sighed and closed his eyes. 'I get it. Okay, I get it. Just get this over with.'

I put my fingers back on his neck and my other hand on his heart. I locked eyes with him again.

'Are you betraying me?'

'No.' No flicker in the eye, no twitch, no change of pulse.

'Do you know why Sandy is trying to set me up?'

'Tyler, I have no fucking idea.' No change.

'Can I trust you to help me?'

'Always.' Said more softly, but nothing faltered.

'Have you been keeping anything from me to do with this Dimitri mission?'

'I've told you everything I know.'

'Where were you last weekend?'

'Italy.' His pupils dilated.

'Lying.'

'Okay, fine. But I can't tell you. It's confidential. Came direct from Chief.'

'Still lying.'

'It's not relevant to this, trust me.'

'Everything could be relevant. Tell me.'

We were both silent as we sat staring at each other. I leant my forehead against his and whispered, 'Please, Jake.'

We sat like that for a minute before Jake turned his head.

'Fucking hell, Lex,' he said hoarsely. 'Fuck this.' He tugged roughly at his hand cuffed to the chair. The clink echoed round the small room.

I leant back, waiting.

'I was seeing Glenapp.'

'Glenapp?' I was confused. Glenapp had been Jake's unit leader when he first joined the agency. I had only met him briefly a few times as he had taken early retirement just after I started. All I remembered was that Jake seemed to respect him and treated him with a deference I had not seen him show any other authority figure. 'What were you doing seeing him? He's out of the service, isn't he?'

'It was a personal matter. I was checking on him.'

'Why? Is he considered a threat? What's it to you?'

'What's it to me?' Jake's voise rose. 'He was a friend. A mentor. I check on him every now and then. He has no one else. Look, as we seem to be all about making sure we trust each other, let me trust you with this: he has dementia. He left the service when he was diagnosed, didn't tell anyone except me. He's living in a small town in the South of France. He has a little shop, selling antiques. Mostly just sits there all day, drinking wine, telling stories. He's doing no harm but just occasionally he has a bad turn and needs to be checked on.'

'He has dementia. He's drinking and telling stories. And he was previously level-five clearance? You don't think that's a cause for concern?'

'Of course it fucking is. That's why I check on him. I've also got a local woman I trust, she keeps an eye on him, reports back to me. It's not ideal but do you really think after a lifetime of service to this country he deserves to be packed off to some secure hospital where he sits in a room alone all day? Or is conveniently wiped out in an accident? This is his retirement; he gets to enjoy the weather, enjoy the food, enjoy the wine and everyone he meets thinks he's a kook. Tourists might get sold a total piece of crap he found in a junkyard or a genuine piece of Gulf War memorabilia. He's just written off as a drunk with a good imagination. He gave his best years to the service, never married, never had children, never had much of a life outside of this grotty world we live in and now after all he's been through I think we can at least let him have his retirement.'

His heart rate had sped up, but I knew it was more because he passionately believed in what he was saying rather than because he was attempting to deceive me. I'd never realised Jake was so loyal. What he was doing was a big risk. He was putting his whole career on the line to try to allow an old colleague to have some kind of life.

'So can I trust you to keep this between us?'

'Of course. Anyway, you're in luck. No one upstairs is listening much to what I have to say anyway.'

We smiled at each other. It brought us back to the reality of the situation. Him cuffed to a chair, and me sitting on top of him.

'Now can you take these stupid things off and let me help you get on with clearing your name?'

I got up and uncuffed him. He stood up, rubbing his wrist.

'Let's not do this again. Next time you don't trust me, just kill me. It's far preferable to all this oversharing. What do you need me to do?'

'Get to Moscow. Meet with any of the informants that were listed in the intelligence reports. We need to know if what they say in person matches their statements in Eight's database. Then try to get to anyone in Rok-Tech's inner circle. They must be getting ready for Dimitri to take over. They will know what he's planning. Get them talking.' I looked down. 'Whatever it takes.'

'Won't you need me back here?'

I shook my head. 'It's more important you find out exactly what Dimitri is going to do with the VirtuWorld software. We can't trust any of the intel we've had to date – Sandy's been all over it, he could've altered it at any point.'

'And what are you going to do?'

'Sandy can't have done all this alone. I'm going to figure out who else is working with him.'

'I'll fly out tonight.' Jake headed for the door. I touched his arm and he stopped.

'As soon as you don't turn up at the Platform tomorrow they're going to know you're working with me. You realise what that means?'

He turned to face me. 'I get it, Lex, but I'm not doing this just for you. If they're up for taking you out, it could be me next. And with you gone who the hell is going to come save me?' He pulled his blower phone out of his pocket. Like mine, it was an old Nokia. 'Presuming we're still using just these for comms?'

'Exactly. But take a camera – you need to film all your meetings and send the footage to me. We need a new email address.'

Us using email involved setting up an email account to which we both knew the password and saving messages in the drafts folder. It was the only way to make sure no one could track any emails being sent.

'How about youmessedwiththewrongmum@gmail.com. Usual password.'

'Very funny.' We walked to the roller door and pulled it up together. We stepped into the corridor and I turned back to him.

'What you're doing for Glenapp is good. He must be so grateful.'

He reached behind me and pulled the roller door down. It crashed to the floor with a loud bang, the sound echoing around us. Neither of us flinched.

'He doesn't have a clue, would be furious if he did. Before it got bad he told me if he ever showed any signs of being a threat to take him out myself rather than let him get carted off to what he called a "hospital prison". Said he'd avoided being locked up his whole career and wasn't about to end his life that way; would rather it be done properly and quickly by a friend.'

'But you couldn't do it.'

'Of course I couldn't. That could be me one day. Alone, washed up with nothing to show for it. Makes me think maybe you got it right with this whole settling down thing.'

He started down the corridor. I followed him.

'It's not too late for you, Jake. Having a little normality in our lives is a good thing. There could be someone out there who might just be brave enough to take you on.'

He stopped and turned to me. 'Maybe it's you that I want.' He cupped my face with his hands. 'Maybe you're the one person who knows everything there is to know about me and it doesn't scare the fuck out of you.' He stared at me unblinking. 'Maybe you're my one reason to think there might be something worthy about me.' He pinched my cheek. 'Or maybe I really can't feel anything and you're just someone I liked fucking. And now I need you to stay alive.'

He laughed and walked off. I exhaled slowly. Until then I hadn't realised I had been holding my breath. I shook my head. Not the time to be drawn into Jake's bullshit.

I got back to the flat and sank into the bed; it was as comfortable as it looked. Not that it helped me sleep. The room was dark except for the glow from the television broadcasting shots of the empty corridors and reception. I thought of Jake and how right now he was up in the sky heading out to Russia to do what he could to help save my life. I always loved that view of London. Flying at night and looking down on the bright lights of the darkened city below. All the people in it oblivious to the work we were doing around and underneath them to keep them safe.

I used to pity them for not knowing the real truth. The real London. Now I envied them; right now I would give anything to be one of the Sheep tucked up in bed, oblivious to the real darkness of the place they called home.

I let myself fall asleep in the early hours, just as light was beginning to seep through the curtains. I dreamt Gigi was in a snake pit, the largest one slithering up to her, ready to wrap itself round her and start squeezing, while I was chained to a chair, screaming.

I woke with a start, drenched, my heart beating fast. Gigi in danger unleashed a primal roar, a knowledge I would do anything to protect her. Lock and load every weapon in my arsenal and charge towards anyone threatening us in an almighty Movie Star Run. Forgetting my own life in my quest to save her.

I wiped my brow. Waking up covered in sweat reminded me of the first few weeks after Gigi was born. Hormones flooding out and soaking the sheets. Now it was just fear.

I went through to the kitchen and took a long drink of water. I fired up my laptop and tried Jake's login for the Platform. 'Unauthorised' was the red message that flashed up. Jake's absence had already been noticed and he was now joining me as persona non grata.

Without access to any of Eight's online resources, I had no leads to follow other than to head to Sandy's flat. It was unlikely that someone who had made a career of life in the Secret Services would have a big folder with 'My Cunning Plan' written on it with a full breakdown of exactly what he was up to and who with, but a girl could hope.

Sandy lived in a small flat in Westminster. He had moved in only recently, after his messy divorce. It was surprisingly easy to break in. Not a good sign for what was going to be within if he hadn't even bothered reinforcing the locks. Inside, everything was as ordered as I would expect it to be from a man with a military background. It was sparsely furnished and very tidy. The open-plan kitchen and living room offered no clues as to anything other than the fact the person who lived there was a neat freak. I went through to the bedroom and opened all the cupboards, nothing but rows of folded jumpers and well-ironed T-shirts. Hanging on the side of the bed was a pair of handcuffs. Gross. I cringed at the thought of Sandy and some girlfriend using them to spice up their sex life.

This was turning out to be a total dead end.

Inside the small bathroom was a large mirrored cupboard, I opened it and was confronted with about five different bottles of pills. All prescribed to Sandy and all differing levels of pain medication. There was another bottle that was a strong sedative. The agony in his leg obviously didn't let up enough to give him a good night's sleep. I shut the cupboard. And then stopped. Something in there had looked familiar yet out of place. I opened it again. Aside from the medication there was a razor, shaving foam and a small bottle of contact lens solution.

That was it.

I saw a bottle just like it every time I went to the toilet at work.

Sitting on the shelf above the sink.

Nicola.

Sandy had 20:20 vision. He'd bragged about it numerous times when boring us with stories of his years as a fast jet pilot. Yet here inside his bathroom cupboard was a bottle of contact lens solution. Of the exact same brand as the one Nicola used.

The cliché of newly divorced man with much younger woman was only outdone by the cliché of younger woman sleeping with her older boss. I felt nauseous imagining Nicola in handcuffs looking bored as Sandy sweated and pounded away at her. I couldn't believe it. I had always pictured Nicola with a good-looking twenty-something hipster with a man bun. Not our middle-aged boss whose idea of being well-dressed was a T-shirt he hadn't managed to spill his breakfast down the front of.

Nicola would've been the one to edit in the money in the safe footage, she would've been the one to call the Russian heavies saying there was no bomb. This was bad. With Nicola's computing expertise and Sandy's level-five security clearance, between them every single bit of intel we had could have been altered or deleted.

My blower phone beeped. '*Met with two Rok-Tech employees. Both separately stated Dimitri is planning great things for the company – starting with arranging the sale of the VirtuWorld software. Meeting with three more Rok-Tech contacts in an hour. Will update when can.*'

Nicola was obviously the one switching and falsifying intelligence reports to turn Dimitri into a deep-rooted President supporter putting national interests above his own capitalist ones. Sandy was the one pulling the strings and preparing the way for me to be the obvious fall guy. Fall gal.

I texted Jake back informing him Nicola was Sandy's partner. In more ways than one.

My phone beeped again. '*I never liked that grumpy bitch.*'

Things were starting to make sense now. But there were gaps. I needed someone to fill them in. Someone who had been at the very heart of this mission from the beginning, and if I was right, the very reason it had been initiated in the first place.

Chapter Thirty-Two

I LOVED BEAUTY SPAS. Little havens away from the dirt and grime of the streets. The air was always scented, the décor tasteful, the uniformed technicians brimming with the promise of transformation. Leaving spas everyone always had a spring in their step; life was that little bit better now they were new and improved.

I remembered Dasha's schedule with ease. Today was waxing day at her favourite exclusive Knightsbridge salon. I approached the tall woman flicking through a glossy magazine behind the reception desk. She was wearing a crisp white tunic with the salon's name embroidered on it.

'Hello! I'm Dasha Tupolev's PA. Please could you tell her technician to not come into her room until quarter-past? We have a few things to go over that I need her urgent attention on.'

'Right.' She didn't look up from her magazine.

'Please can I wait for her in her treatment room?'

She looked up at that. 'You're her PA?' I was wearing a black jacket and carrying a folder. She paused. 'Then that's fine. And I will, of course, let her know you're waiting for her.'

'Actually, it would be better if you didn't.'

'Really?' she cocked her head. 'That would be very unprofessional of me.'

'Here.' I handed her a fifty-pound note. And then another. It was hard to tell if her heavily pencilled eyebrows were raised in disgust at my first offering or if they were just drawn that high.

She pocketed the notes into her tunic. 'Mrs Tupolev is booked into the Zen room. It's the third door on your left.'

I barely had time to appreciate the mood lighting, soft chanting music and scented candles before I heard the door opening.

The Zen room was about to get not so Zen.

Dasha walked in wearing a white dressing gown and holding her Hermès Birkin bag. I could understand why she didn't want to leave an item worth twice the price of your average car in a changing room.

'You.' Her eyes narrowed. 'Why haven't you been answering my texts?'

'It's time we had a little chat, Dasha. Your bodyguards think you're having a bikini wax, so bear in mind they aren't going to come rushing in if they hear pained screams.'

She dropped her bag on the treatment table and folded her arms. 'What do you want?'

'I know you're the Dragon.'

She shook her head. 'So that's why Dimitri is still alive? You think I'm this Dragon?'

'Drop the act, Dasha. If I were you I would start talking. We know about Sandy.' At the mention of Sandy's name Dasha's eyes closed and her jaw clenched. 'Whoever makes a deal first is the one we go easy on. Eight is a Secret Service that doesn't exist and we have prisons that don't exist. Places where people will never find you. Places where you don't get visitors.' I took a step towards her. 'Places where you don't even get to say goodbye to your children before we take you away. Maybe we'll tell them you left because you didn't love them enough.' I knew what I needed to say to get her to talk. I knew because it would work on me. I spoke softly. 'Sorry, Natalya. Sorry, Viktor. Sorry, baby Irina. Mummy just doesn't care.'

Dasha let out a stifled roar and slammed her hands down on the bed. She stared at me with such rage I tensed, ready for an attack. But she took a deep breath and started pacing around the room muttering to herself in Russian. She stopped, calmed herself and said, 'What do you want to know?'

'Let's start with the Dragon.'

She grimaced. 'I always hated that nickname. Dimitri's friends and business associates started calling me the Dragon once they realised I was not the pretty little pushover they all thought I'd be.'

'The Dragon had everyone in Dimitri's business circles so scared we assumed it was some bigwig with contacts and muscle behind him. Not a bored housewife.' The more she lost her temper the more she might let slip.

'This bored housewife has more power than half those men.' Dasha hissed. 'Of course Dimitri's business associates are scared of me. I'm friends with their wives. We lunch, we drink, we talk. I know all their secrets. Who's trying to hide their homosexuality from their colleagues. Who's double-crossing who on an upcoming business deal. Whose taste in young women is far too young . . . Some women just enjoy the gossip. I enjoy the leverage.'

'But you didn't have enough of it to convince them to murder Dimitri for you.'

'Sadly not.' Dasha adjusted one of her gold bracelets. 'So I had to think of another plan.'

'And that's how you decided to work with Sandy.' I had to keep her talking.

Dasha stared at me. 'Why have you snuck in here?' She motioned round the Zen room. 'If Eight really knew everything we would be at your headquarters.' Her lip curled. 'You're here on your own, aren't you?'

'My partner is outside our chief's office with proof of Sandy's betrayal. He just needs to hear from me as to whether to add you as an ally or an enemy. What do you see in your future, Dasha? Parties or prison?'

'You don't know anything.'

'I know that you, the Dragon, are the one who created this whole mess just because you wanted your husband permanently out of the picture. Dimitri should not be a target for Eight – just like his father he wants to sell the VirtuWorld software; intel that says otherwise has been tampered with.' I spoke with confidence, although everything was still theory.

'Let's not forget if you don't help me, I can fucking destroy the nice little life you have here.' I leaned closer to her. 'Don't underestimate the power of Her Majesty's Secret Service. One whisper of the word "terrorist" from us and you won't even be able to get your son into the local underperforming comp, let alone St Paul's.' She chewed her lip as she took it in. 'And I can set a few home fires blazing with your Super Mama crew too. A few whispers about an old soliciting charge back in Mother Russia. Rumours about your husband's business being investigated. Claims of an affair with the gardener. Or does plumber sound more unseemly? Might suddenly find yourself with no little charitable committees to sit on, no friends to have long lunches with and no black-tie events to show off at. And all this before we freeze all your assets and you're left with not even enough money to buy food for your kids. Let alone the organic crap they're no doubt used to.'

I saw the panic in her eyes as she digested each threat. She was going to crumble.

'Start talking, Dasha. How did this begin? Who did you approach first?'

She took a deep breath, flicked her hair back and looked at me levelly.

'The men you call the Nyan have been circling Rok-Tech for years. Desperate to buy into it and get it under state control. The more they can offer The President, the more power they will get in the running of the country. I contacted them after I knew none of Dimitri's associates had the balls to kill him. I made them a deal – if they made sure Dimitri was eliminated I would help them take control of Rok-Tech. Sergei is easily manipulated. Especially when you know the things about him that I know.'

I wasn't surprised. I was sure Dasha had files on everyone. Information was power – that's what we kept repeating to ourselves in our battle to try to limit the damage VirtuWorld could do. It was clearly a mantra Dasha fully embraced.

'How did Sandy fit in?'

'The Nyan knew Sandy from a previous mission. They brokered the deal and we worked on everything together. Falsifying intel. Covering our tracks. Framing you. It was going to solve all my problems.' Her head dropped and she pulled the dressing gown tighter around herself.

'And what are your problems, Dasha? Why did you do this?'

'My children.' She brought her hands to chest. 'My beautiful children.' Her voice broke and she paused to compose herself.

'Dimitri wanted to move us back to Moscow. He'd make an enemy of The President and all his supporters by selling the VirtuWorld technology to countries Russia consider enemies. Do you have any idea how much danger we would be in?' She bit her lip. 'Did you know Dimitri has been receiving anonymous letters for months, saying how they can't wait to welcome him back to the mother-land and asking which child he wants to die first? It was a choice between him and our children and of course I chose them. If he dies then my children are safe. I am safe. We can live in London in peace. Enjoying his money without him. No one could've ever linked me to his death. I could be the grieving widow with no cloud hovering over my family. And I would never need worry about The President and his henchmen as I would've helped them gain control of Rok-Tech.'

'You didn't have to try to get him killed, Dasha. You could've handled it differently.'

'You tell me how.' She raised her voice and then adjusted it back to a strong whisper, remembering the bodyguards outside. 'Last year, as soon as Dimitri's father began talking about retir-ing and the potential of VirtuWorld, Dimitri started building a house in Moscow and told me we would be moving back there. I begged him for a divorce. He refused, said he would sue for sole custody, cut me off without a penny. He said if I tried to leave him he'd take his children from me and I'd never see them again. You don't think he could do that with his billions and his private jet and his team of people who do whatever he says?' The anger in her voice was at odds with the calming twangs of undistinguishable chords playing over the speaker system. 'Why wouldn't I want him dead? I owe him no loyalty. He didn't think of me or my feelings when he had my cousin killed. And now he's trying to take my children away too.'

'So you started working with The President. You went against everything you believed in to help empower that man further.'

'All I believe in now is my children. I pledge my allegiance to them. When I was younger I could afford to have morals, I could afford to have beliefs. Now I don't care about anything except keeping them safe.' She put her hands to her head.

I understood Dasha now. All this time she had put on a front of being in control, exuding ice-cold calm from a perfect exterior. But inside she was screaming. Rage at Dimitri. Rage at her situation. Marrying him was meant to be a clever move. A safe move. His money was meant to guarantee she had everything she wanted. A good life. An easy life. But then she was faced with moving back to Russia and Dimitri making an enemy of The President and his associates. It would be a lifetime of being constantly afraid for her children. Dasha had felt forced into action.

She looked up at me.

'After all this, after everything I've done, I'm back where I started. Stuck with a husband who doesn't seem to care his children could get dismembered the minute we set foot in that godforsaken place. And now I have you British on my back, too.'

'Help us and then we'll help you. We want Sandy. Set up a meet with him tonight and tomorrow you can come into Eight and go on record with our chief.' I handed her the folder I had been carrying. 'Evidence of Dimitri's various extra-marital affairs. This combined with copies of the death threats you mentioned will help. If you work with us, giving us everything you have on Sandy, we can get you a hotshot lawyer, a sympathetic judge and you should get your divorce and your children.'

She opened the folder.

'Thank you. All I want is to protect my children. It's all I've ever wanted.' She tilted her head. 'You British are better than I thought you'd be. You were convincing. I don't know how they even found a baby who actually looks like you.'

'I can't promise it won't get very public and very ugly. But you might be looking for some new friends anyway.'

She started leafing through the photos.

'That fucking two-faced bitch Claudia!' She flicked through some more. 'And that whore Cynthia!' She was flushed with rage. 'At least I can take them down with me,' she spat. 'See what their husbands think of this.' She shoved the whole folder into her handbag. I had a feeling she was going to enjoy destroying them.

Chapter Thirty-Three

Five for five. All confirm Dimitri is a staunch capital-ist wanting to cash in on VirtuWorld so he can expand Rok-Tech globally. Check email for statements and video interviews. Flying back now.

When I got back to the flat I re-read the text Jake had sent while I was at the spa. We were getting there. I realised now why Sandy had been so clever in the way he had set up the whole mission. I had been solo on nearly everything. He had played upon my new-mother insecurities and implied it was all part of testing I was still up to the job. I was the only one who had had face-to-face contact with all the major players. I had been Dasha's handler. I was the one who met with the Nyan on the boat. Eight would have eventually realised killing Dimitri had killed all our chances of getting our hands on VirtuWorld's software and that we were responsible for one major fuckup. And all the evidence would point to me being the mastermind behind it.

But I'd ruined things for him by not making the hit. When I didn't push the button Sandy must have known I was acting on my own doubts and that I was now a threat.

At least things were looking more hopeful now. With Dasha on side and the statements Jake had procured at least I now had something to bring to Anne. Although it would not be enough. Sandy could come back with his dozens of intelligence reports that Nicola had no doubt been busy doctoring to say exactly what they wanted to say. If I tried going to them now, with just Dasha, an unreliable witness at best, it wouldn't be enough. They still had the upper hand.

I needed to do more.

I rang a few old contacts until I got the address I wanted.

The man walked up his front door steps and paused as he reached inside his coat for his keys.

'Hello, Duggers.'

He froze for a split second, I heard the jangle of the keys as they fell back into his pocket. He turned around.

'Lex. Heard you were in a bit of trouble.'

'I need your help. For old times' sake.'

'I shouldn't be talking to you.' He looked sideways up and down the street.

I spoke softly. It was unnervingly quiet in this empty Pimlico mews. I was taking a big risk but I needed his help.

'I'm being set up. You need to know that Sandy is a Snake. He's working with Nicola, our unit's tech support, and the Nyan – who are all close allies of The President. The target should not be a target. Dimitri wants to sell the VirtuWorld software.' I spoke fast; I didn't know how much time he would give me.

'Sandy dirty?' Even in his loud whisper his surprise was evident. He frowned. 'His life is the Service. You have any proof?'

'Yes. But I need more. Make a list of any of your sources who said Dimitri was an ambitious capitalist and not some President-obsessed patriot. Send it to Eight's section chief.'

'I guess I can do that.' He paused. 'We had trouble determining from our sources exactly what Dimitri planned to do when he took over Rok-Tech – he kept his cards very close to his chest, as you can imagine. Some definitely said he was eyeing up global expansion but Sandy steamrolled in saying his assets were in the inner circle and they said he was all for The President and protecting the motherland.' He shrugged. 'We didn't have any reason to doubt him.'

'That's how he's been able to pull this off. Everyone trusts him.'

'What are you going to do?' Duggers walked down the steps to the pavement so we were facing each other.

'Try to take down Sandy, of course. I can't go back to Eight until I have enough proof or Sandy's head on a platter.'

He shook his head. 'That won't end well for you, Lex.'

'I know that. That's why I wanted you to know the truth. If Jake and I don't survive this, I need to know someone will try to make sure Sandy can't get away with what he's done. Just do what you can.' I made to leave.

'Lex?' He reached a hand out to my arm. 'Do you regret joining?'

I thought back on my life as a Rat. I had never felt more alive. I had seen how the world worked. My life had purpose. I had that glint in my eye I had been searching for. And if I hadn't been a Rat I might never have had Gigi. I might never have had that near-death experience I needed to realise how, no matter what I thought I wanted, deep down a baby was important to me. It had given me everything I wanted and if it was going to take it all away I couldn't complain.

'No. Not for a minute.'

'I . . . How . . . ?' He was struggling to get the words out.

'How do I do it?'

'Yes. How?'

'Just how you do what *you* do. It's a job. I'm good at it.'

'But I, well, I never would have guessed. Never would have thought you could.'

'That's what makes me so good at it. And the Committee knew. That's what the testing is for. They saw I could. And they were right.'

His front door opened.

'Darling, what are you doing out . . . Oh hi.' We both looked up at the blonde woman staring at us. 'Lex?'

'Yes?' I struggled to place her. Another university face. 'Annabel?'

We had moved in different circles. I would see her in our college bar, wrapped in a pashmina sipping on a G and T with other nice-looking girls with receding chins. I was sure more than once I had seen her, out of the corner of my eye, shaking her head at me as I would swig from a bottle of beer while loudly playing pool with the boys, pausing only to whoop when a favourite song came on. I had always thought she never quite fitted in with the plastic cups and sticky floors of an under-graduate bar. She was much more in her element now. On the polished stone steps of a nice house in Pimlico. Christ, she was even wearing an apron.

'Lovely to see you. I had no idea you two were married.'

'Hello, sweetheart. We just bumped into each other here on the street, isn't that funny?'

'How nice. It's been a long time, Lex. How are you?' She barely waited a beat before she asked, 'Married? Children?'

Even at university she struck me as one of those girls to whom those two things were the only real measure of success. I remembered thinking it strange that someone so bright was only there to find a bright male to mate with. She looked between me and Duggers, obviously uncomfortable her husband had been talking unaccompanied with someone she had never really liked.

'Yes, both. I have a baby daughter.'

Annabel didn't respond. Perhaps she'd hoped that having seen me last winning at being the fun student, she would be winning at being a better grown-up.

'Really? I had no idea.' Duggers shook his head and closed his eyes. He knew it was touch and go whether or not I'd live out the week.

Annabel clearly mistook this reaction as an indication he still held a torch for me. Her face darkened. 'Darling, come in now, please. Dinner is getting cold and the children want to say goodnight.'

'Right. Goodbye, Lex, nice to see you. Good luck with everything.' He walked up the steps to his wife who had already gone inside. 'And I'll pass on that message to our mutual friend.'

'Thank you.'

I stood in the street as their front door closed behind them. The lights from inside the house glowing, I could picture the scene inside, good smells wafting out of the kitchen. Kids tucked up in bed waiting for a story from Daddy. A fire burning in the living room and the table set for two. Legoland didn't seem such a bad place to work now. I was the one out in the cold, my family sent away, and about to fight to the death.

My phone beeped. A text from Dasha.

You must go to the Opera tonight at Syon House. I'm meant to be meeting Sandy there at 10 p.m. at the door but may not make it. She will be so surprised to see you.

I checked my watch. Nearly three hours to go. We had Dasha. And now we had Duggers. With him backing up the statements Jake had got from Moscow we had enough of a paper trail to show that the intel Sandy had been presenting as solid was not. But I knew it still wasn't enough. Whatever Jake and I were doing now to clear our names, Sandy and Nicola would be working hard to further condemn them. And they had the full resources of Eight behind them. It wasn't going to be over until we brought Sandy in or took him out. Everything rested on tonight.

I got back to the flat and sat down at the dining table. I opened my laptop. There was a high probability I would die tonight and I needed to say goodbye to my daughter. To write down thoughts and sentiments that one day, when she was old enough, she would cherish. A way for her to know me and what was important to me. My last words to her.

I sat staring at the blank page and flashing cursor.

So I needed to make them good.

I tried to picture Gigi the teenager. On her bed reading a printout her father had given her on her sixteenth birthday. Perhaps it had been something he had always said would happen and she had looked forward to it. Counting down the years, months, days until she got to hear from the elusive figure that was her mother. Or maybe it had been a surprise. Left at the end of her bed after a long day of loud music and party guests. And now she was reading and rereading every word. She loved me even though she never knew me. Her fingers would stroke the page. Read it over and over long into the night.

Or would she hate me for not being there? Leave it unopened for days until one evening she would tear apart the envelope, read it once and crush it up into a ball, dropping it on to the floor for Will to unfold later and put back on her bedside table. *What good is a dead mother? Where was she when I needed her?*

I closed my eyes. I wanted to be there, picking up her clothes, complaining that she was wearing too much make-up, arguing about where she was going that night and what time her curfew was. Sitting up with Will, laughing as we drank wine and glancing at the clock whenever the other wasn't looking.

I needed to be there.

Because if I wasn't, Will might marry again. Marry the type of woman I'd always hated. The sad lonely widower could have his head turned by some grabby blonde who liked the fact he was a high-flying lawyer and would muscle in on this ready-made family. No need to ruin her nubile body with a baby, he already had one. And she, this gold digger, would be the faux mum to my beautiful daughter. What if Gigi grew up thinking high-heeled shoes and skin-tight clothing were expected of her? And, worst of all, what if she grew up wanting to marry well rather than do well?

Gigi's imaginary evil, vapid stepmother was an excellent muse.

An hour later I had a rambling ten pages that went from random ('please don't be a goth; no one understands them and with your colouring you just couldn't pull off all that black'), to rousing ('you can be anything you want to be, boys are your equals, always remember that'), then through to preachy ('work hard in school; don't do drugs, they make you stupid'). And finished with sentimental: 'Be good to your dad, he's a very nice man. I love you very much. I'm so sorry I'm not there.'

I looked at her spiky hair and big blue eyes staring out at me from my screensaver. I touched the screen.

At least she was still so young. At first she would miss me, look around the room wondering where I was. Check the face of each person that walked in hoping for me. But then, slowly, she would forget. Forget what I looked like. Forget I was ever even there.

I clenched my fists and squeezed my eyes shut.

I wouldn't get to ever hear her call me 'Mama'. To see her take her first steps. To see her try to run. To catch her when she fell. She would never know me and I would never know her. If she was a tomboy or a little princess. If she was loud or quiet. I would never get to know what she was going to be when she grew up. Or what kind of life she was going to lead. I wanted to know everything about her. Everything that was going to happen to her. But I wasn't going to get the chance to. And that thought was breaking my heart.

A family was bittersweet. Having people to love, who loved you back made life so much better when you were living it, yet so much worse when faced with leaving it.

I took one last look at what I had written and closed my laptop.

This wouldn't be the first time I walked into an op I didn't think I would survive. But this was the first time I was truly scared. I had never had more to live for.

Chapter Thirty-Four

'IT'S TIME TO GO, TYLER.'

Jake had arrived at the flat an hour ago straight from the airport. An assortment of guns were laid out on the sitting-room floor. Having checked them all he was now packing them back into his duffel bag.

I went into the bathroom and fitted my bulletproof vest under my clothes. I tied my hair back in a tight bun and stared at myself in the mirror. This was it.

I thought again of Gigi.

She had done nothing to deserve this.

I wanted to fight angry. I wanted to channel the rage I felt. I didn't want to walk in there drained, resigned to my fate. I was going to go in guns blazing and fight for my life. The Snake had to be stopped. Cut off his head and his decapitated body would slither around blindly trying to find its way before it too would stop thrashing and come to a silent halt. With Sandy neutralised the Nyan would no longer be a threat to me. With no inside man in Eight they would no longer be able to use our resources to covertly eliminate Dimitri and walk away with full deniability. They would have no need to kill me.

One way or another after tonight it would all be over.

I came out of the bathroom. 'I'm ready.'

'I took the liberty of procuring a car for us. It's waiting in the underground car park.'

'We can finalise the plan on the drive there.'

'What plan? All we have is a vague idea that needs a small miracle to actually succeed.'

Jake was right. There was no real plan. Our mission objective was to secure Sandy for interrogation. We needed answers. But if extracting him alive proved to be too difficult we had to kill him. Take him in or take him out. Both would put the Snake out of play.

Sandy would turn up with muscle, undoubtedly handpicked from his bulging contact list of Ghosts. These private guns for hire didn't officially exist – they lived off the grid, never carried ID and would happily kill on command and ask no questions. At the end of a job they'd take their fee and disappear. He would know that there was a risk Dasha had been compromised. And that he and his gammy leg were no match for Jake and me. His agents. His protégés. He had trained us to be the best of the best, never expecting that one day he would be up against us.

Carmen would be the soundtrack to our showdown tonight. We passed the front of Syon Park where a fleet of black cabs and chauffeur-driven Mercedes were waiting for men in black tie and women in long dresses to finish their night of champagne, canapés and opera. I could already hear strains of music floating through the cold November air. Ear-shattering, beautiful and wonderfully dramatic. Good music to fight to. Good music to die to.

The evening had started a few hours earlier when the well-dressed pack would have made their way through the large imposing gates and down the sweeping driveway towards Syon

House. Lacking an invitation, we would be forced to make a somewhat less graceful arrival.

Round the back, after a few hoists and a little swearing, we were over the wall and within the grounds of Syon Park. I reached for the duffel bag we had thrown over the wall ahead of us. I stripped down to my bulletproof vest, strapped a gun-filled holster to each thigh, and pulled on a long black dress.

Next from the bag came a blonde wig and large fur coat. The coats Dasha favoured were made of the softest fur of a thousand dead animals; mine was the best Oxfam had to offer. But it should do the job of making me memorable. And it managed to conceal the strange outline of my dress. I tugged on the wig.

'How do I look?' I tried to smooth the blonde hair down as I snuggled into the coat and pouted at Jake.

'More cheap hooker than rich Russian, but let's hope it does the trick.'

The sound of an engine and headlights made us slip into a stone alcove hidden behind a tree. It was a small cramped space. We watched as a groundsman got out from his truck and emptied the bin a few feet from us.

We were squashed up against each other. Legs entangled. Jake brushed a strand of blonde hair out of my face.

The man got back in his truck and drove off. We slipped out of the alcove.

'Right,' said Jake. 'Let's go get fucking murdered.'

'Where's your fighting spirit? We know what we're doing. Remember, we're the best of the best.'

'Yes, and Sandy is our boss so that makes him the best of the best of the best.'

'You're not being helpful.'

He turned to me and held my shoulders. 'Don't worry, Tyler. If anyone can do this, it's us. We've got each other.'

He was right. Out in the field Jake and I were a perfect pairing. We didn't need to talk. We'd move with all the grace of ballroom dancers, totally in sync. A step here, a slice there, in perfect unison; cutting our way across a bloody dance floor. And we'd always come out the other side. Together. Still standing. So far.

'That's better. Fighting talk.' I squeezed his hand.

We waited until the truck was out of sight and set off across the manicured lawn.

The opera evening was being held inside the Great Hall. From across the grounds we could see the ground floor alive with lights and people passing the windows. As we approached the front lawn there was a scattering of party guests standing outside, taking advantage of the intermission to have a quick cigarette.

'I'm getting into position.' Jake disappeared into the darkness. I kept on walking until I reached the side of the house and slipped in the service entrance that the catering staff were using to ferry their equipment to and from their truck outside. I hoped I wouldn't have long to wait. I paced up and down the echoing corridor trying to smoke the vape I had brought with me. It was disgusting. How could Dasha love them so much? Finally a white jacketed waiter came walking towards the door.

'You there, hello! Helloooo!' I did my best fake Russian accent.

'Yes, madam?' He quickly detoured to my side. 'If you're looking for the party, it's back this way.'

I took a long drag before blowing sweet-flavoured smoke in his direction.

'You can help me.' I handed him a fifty-pound note. 'You find this man.' I pointed to a photo of Sandy on my newly procured iPhone. 'He will be at the entrance. And tell him to meet me in the Conservatory immediately.' He took the note and looked at the photo. 'You get this message to him and there'll be another few notes like this.'

'Of course, madam. That's not a problem.' He scuttled off in the direction of the party, whatever task he was meant to be doing at the truck forgotten in favour of a little extra spending money.

With any luck, if Sandy asked him for details of the woman who had summoned him, a vague description of a blonde Russian in a fur coat smoking a vape and brandishing fifty-pound notes would be enough to convince him that Dasha was out there.

I headed outside past the genuine smokers and towards the Conservatory. It was separate to the main house, and with the ear shattering opera about to start up again, the sound of the inevitable gunfire was hopefully likely to be drowned out.

Jake crackled into my ear, 'In position. No sign of hostiles.'

'Roger that. Five minutes out.'

I entered the Conservatory and walked to the back of the silent building. It was one long glass corridor. I came to the end and positioned myself by a large floral display. On my left was a view out towards the back wall of the Visitor Centre. It was a reassuring blank canvas. No one could be out there without their face being pressed up against the glass. On my right I could see out into Syon Park, where hidden from view, behind one of the trees was Jake and his long-aim rifle. Picking the location was the one advantage we had. Anyone looking through a night lens would see a blurry visual of a lone blonde in a fur coat in a cold, darkened, empty glasshouse. We were banking on that being enough to convince Sandy to venture in.

I started my best impression of an impatient Russian pacing the floor as the clouds of vape smoke surrounded me. I took another drag. I had now got used to it. It was oddly comforting. Shit, it would be really annoying to survive this only to become addicted to the stuff.

I was the bait. Out and exposed, calling the predators towards me. Jake was the hunter who could pop them off one by one, and make sure he left the one we wanted, the prize Snake, alive.

It was a terrible plan. But we had no choice.

The building was quiet except for the distant strains of music coming from the Great Hall. Jake crackled into my ear again.

'Male approaching. Can't get a full visual but it seems to be Sandy.'

Sure enough, I could make out a limping figure coming towards the Conservatory door.

'Confirmed visual. Neutralise him as soon as you get the shot.' It didn't matter if Sandy looked as if he was alone. He wouldn't be. Our only chance was to knock him out with a sedative and attempt to extract him without falling foul of his henchmen.

The slamming of the door announced Sandy was now in the Conservatory. I had my back to him, my phone against my ear. He needed to get at least ten steps closer before Jake could take the shot. I made to look like I was far too busy angrily muttering to notice his arrival. I heard the sound of his footsteps echoing through the hollow hall as he headed towards me.

Just a few more steps, that was all we needed. My heart was racing now. Come on. Keep on walking.

And then I heard it. A *pffffttt* through the glass as Jake took the shot and the thud of Sandy's body hitting the ground.

We had him. Things were looking up. I felt stirrings of hope that I really could make it back safely to Gigi and Will. And then I heard the noise of an engine. A large engine.

Headlights lit up the ground on my right. A large truck pulled into view.

I took both my guns out. They were coming for him.

'Jake? Come in.' Nothing but silence. Our comms were blocked.

I raced towards the unconscious body ahead of me. They couldn't risk firing at me when I had their boss as a shield. I just needed to hold our position until Jake got here and we could carry the fucker out together.

I looked down at the man on the floor. A great plan. Except it wasn't Sandy.

We should have known better. Rat on Rat. We were always going to be thinking the same way. Misdirection. The eye sees what the eye want to see. Just as we relied on a fur coat and a blonde blinding him, so he had relied on a heavy build and a bad limp blinding us.

And now I was trapped in a glass box. With Jake's visual blocked by the truck parked in front of us. I heard the sounds of multiple feet hitting gravel.

No longer bait. Just dead meat. Waiting to be scooped up and devoured by the fast-approaching pack who knew I had nowhere to run.

I patted down the fake Sandy. Whoever this man was, he was clearly so disposable Sandy hadn't even given him a weapon. I looked around. There was only one door. The Conservatory was empty except for fifty or so gilt-coloured dining chairs and not so much as a side table I could upturn and use for cover. It was why we had chosen it. It was all out in the open with nowhere to hide.

Chapter Thirty-Five

TWO GUNS WITH FULL chambers, and words. That was all I had to save my life. Five men walked into the Conservatory. I stood with my hands up and watched as they approached me down the long glass corridor. I had to try words first. Opening fire would be certain death.

'You look shit, Lex. You don't suit blonde.' I could barely see Sandy as he spoke from within his circle of Ghosts. Even with the truck blocking the glass wall, he wasn't taking any chances. 'I wouldn't be relying on Jake coming to save you. I have men out there chasing him down. Did you really think you could out-smart me? I fucking trained you. Just not well enough to ever get the better of me. Any final words before I end this?'

'You end me and you're ending your career. If I die, Chief, and Five and Six, all get a nice little folder of proof on all the dif-ferent ways you've betrayed your country.'

Sandy laughed. 'Don't you think I have enough resources to get to grips with any little pack of lies a couple of disgraced agents concocted?'

'Don't underestimate the evidence we have. We know every-thing. Everything except why you were so easy to buy off.'

'Nice stalling attempt, Lex. But I'm going to kill you without letting you know a fucking thing.' He raised his gun. I heard the click of the safety come off. Then he pressed his ear and frowned. 'Jake is proving evasive. And I don't like loose ends. We need to get him here.'

'Forget it. He's gone. Following procedure. On his way to Chief.'

'No.' He shook his head. 'Not when he thinks he might be able to save you.'

He shot me three times.

The force flung me on to my back and I hit the ground hard, my head taking the brunt of the fall. Sandy leaned over me and spoke into my mic. 'You hear that, Jake? Lex is down. She's bleeding out fast. Better hurry.'

I lay there staring up at the beautiful glass ceiling. It really was magnificent. My head was throbbing and my chest was agony. I could barely breathe. Two of the shots had hit me straight in the bulletproof vest, rendering my chest bruised and battered but were otherwise no great concern. The third was going to be a problem. It was at the base of my neck. I could only guess by the agonising pain that I was feeling from that area and the large pool of blood that was now covering the floor. I focused on my breathing.

Sandy was now ordering his Ghosts into position.

'Check her for weapons,' he directed to the Ghost nearest to me. I recognised him from the underpass. I should have killed him when I had the chance. He roughly patted me down. He found one gun in my coat pocket and pulled it out. He stood up to hand it to Sandy, just as I fired the other one.

I don't like to make the same mistake twice.

Underpass Ghost went crashing to the ground.

'What the fuck!' Sandy came up to me, gun drawn, and kicked me hard. A strangled scream echoed round the Great Conservatory. I guessed it was me. Sandy booted my second gun across the room.

He pressed his ear. 'Any sign of him?' He paused to listen. 'Fuck!' Sandy motioned the Ghosts over to him. 'Sounds like he made a run for it. Finish her.' He dismissed them with a wave.

The blood was flowing faster now. I could feel it. With each pulse from my neck more seeped away. All the fur was matted with red. A wounded animal, down in the dirt, and now they were circling. I looked up at the Ghosts approaching me with guns drawn.

'Gigi.' I whispered it quietly. I wanted my last word on this earth to be her name.

A shot rang out.

The Ghost on my left went down, and then so did the one on my right. I turned my head.

Jake.

Doing a Movie Star Run.

He was charging towards us, gun in each hand firing. Sandy and his two remaining Ghosts were firing back. Jesus. This was about to get bloody.

Another one of the Ghosts went down. Sandy was running out of human shields to hide behind. I watched him throw his gun to the ground. Empty. He had wasted too many bullets on me. He picked up a chair and threw it through the conservatory glass and stumbled through the opening, the jagged shards tearing into his clothes. It was a short few steps to the safety of the truck.

Gigi.

Gigi.

Gigi.

She was all I thought of as I slid over towards my gun that Sandy had kicked across the room. My blood, coating the floor, helped propel me forward. My hands were shaking. I knew it wouldn't be long before I blacked out. I just had to hope I would wake up again.

Jake and the one remaining Ghost were now both out of ammo and fighting hard on the ground. There was blood on them both.

I reached the gun and gripped it.

I lined up the sight of my gun and aimed for Sandy's head. He had one hand on the truck's door. This man had wanted me dead. I had worked alongside him for years. But the first sniff of some cash and he had sold me out, sold the whole unit out, sold the whole Platform out. He deserved to die. He would leave behind a legacy of betrayal and I, Jake, all of us at Eight would be tainted by the fact he had been dirty. But what made me hate him more than anything was that his plan, if successful, would have left Gigi without a mother. Without me in her life. And that was unforgivable.

For that he deserved something worse than death.

I changed my aim to his good hip. A lifetime of agonising pain and whatever punishment the Committee deemed fit. I fired. Twice. The scream as he went down made me smile.

I heard a roar from behind me and looked back to see the crumpled body of the last of Sandy's Ghosts fall to the floor.

Jake. Bleeding, but somehow still standing. I slumped back to the floor.

I saw him head over to the writhing, howling figure of Sandy on the ground and put him in a sleeper hold. There was a thud and no more sound. Jake pulled out his phone, tapped a number out and rushed back to me.

'It's okay, Lex. I've called it in. Help is on the way.' He slid down next to me. 'I thought I nearly lost you there.'

I managed a chuckle. 'No such luck. How long?'

'Eleven minutes. So I just need you to keep warm.' He pulled his coat off and put it over me. 'And put some pressure on this little scratch.' He put his arm round me so he could press down on the bullet wound on my neck.

'What you just did was fucking crazy. It was practically suicide.'

'It worked, though, didn't it? I pulled off a Movie Star Run. I'm going to be a fucking legend. And you're still here to give me shit.'

My throat was tickling and I wanted to cough but knew that would make the pain worse. I tried to clear my throat instead.

'Well, it was nuts.' He had taken a crazy risk and nearly gotten himself killed and I knew why. 'You went against all your training, all our procedures, and were a reckless maniac.' I winced in pain as I tried to move slightly. 'Because at the end of the day, don't all women need saving? Even armed ones.'

Sexism had clearly saved my life. I should be more grateful. But there I was, near death, berating my partner for how he hadn't treated me the same as one of our colleagues. Principled to the bitter end. A feminist martyr. Or just a fucking idiot who was bleeding out and delirious.

'Lex, saving you had nothing to do with you being a woman.'

'Come on, you—'

He cut me off with a gentle hand across my mouth as I continued to mumble about what a bloody fool he had been. He talked over me.

'I saved you because you have been my partner for the last ten years. I saved you because you have a child, and the world would miss you more than me. I saved you because, in my own little screwed-up way, I love you.'

He saw my eyes widen as I finally went quiet. He took his hand away.

'All that would be the same if you were a man.' He paused. 'Okay, well, maybe except the last one.'

I blinked several times. 'You don't have to overdo it, Jake. I'm not going to die.'

'Sweetheart, it's the absolute truth. I know it because it's what I thought when we were kneeling there together, in the dirt in Tianjin, fucking holding hands. All I could think was, I'm going to die but it's okay, I'm with Lex. I'm dying with someone I love.' He shook his head. 'It scared the shit out of me, and I've tried to ignore it. Ignore you. But I guess it must be true as nothing else could've made me do something that stupid. And right now we're not hiding and no one is going to find us, so I can't pretend it's going to save your life, there is simply no reason to kiss you other than because I really, really fucking want to.' He leant down and gently brushed my lips with his, then pulled back and held my face with his hands. 'Just don't die, okay?'

I stared up at this crazy, damaged, beautiful and brave man. This man, who in so many ways knew me better than my own husband. This man who had risked his life to save mine. This man who I had fought alongside for so many years and had never taken the time to notice that he had a heart too. That he wasn't the psychopathic machine I had written him off as. This man, broken in so many ways, opening himself up to someone for the very first time in his strange, dark life. And I knew what I had to do. What I needed to say to him.

But then everything went black.

Chapter Thirty-Six

I WAS AWAKE BUT I felt like I was floating. I blinked a few times until everything came into focus. I was lying in a bed with crisp white sheets. Looking around, I recognised the room. I had been in an identical one to this many times before. There was an en-suite bathroom, a large wardrobe, a mini fridge and a good-sized flatscreen television fixed to the wall. The only give-away that this was a hospital room and not a hotel room was the intravenous drip attached to my arm and an array of switches and buttons behind the bed. The exclusive private Kensington Wing of Chelsea and Westminster Hospital was where all injured Rats ended up. We all had comprehensive health insurance which covered our frequent stays here, where we were cared for by a fleet of security-cleared doctors and nurses who knew not to ask any questions and write reports to fit in with designated cover stories.

I took a deep breath in and out. I was alive. I had made it. And I was, judging by the lack of pain and tell-tale light-headedness, flying high on morphine. I felt the bandages covering the place the bullet had entered. Physical proof it hadn't all been a drug-induced bad dream. Another scar to add to the collection.

How long had I been here?

Gigi. Will. My heart started racing. Were they safe? I tried to fully sit up and failed. I reached to the side of the bed, grappling for the call button.

The door opened and Jane Thornton walked in.

'Hi, Lex. Glad to see you're awake.' She sat down in the chair next to the bed. 'You've been out for just under twelve hours. The operation to get the bullet out went well. Don't worry, I've spoken to Will. I told him you'd been in a bad hit and run. He's on his way.'

The fog in my mind started to lift and I looked down at my hands.

'I'm taking it as a good sign that I'm being treated here and not in handcuffs in the Box?' High-level interrogations took place in a remote building next to the Farm which had numerous soundproofed rooms that housed an array of very special toys. Its nickname was both on account of the large square concrete building's box-like appearance, and a reference to what a great deal of interviewees would leave in.

'You're in the clear.' Jane frowned. 'Sandy's attack on you and Jake was completely unauthorised. If that wasn't enough to make us question his motives Dasha has come in and Dugdale delivered a large number of intelligence reports that back up Jake's evidence from Russia.'

'I need to see Jake. Is he okay? He was also hit.' I remembered the blood staining his white shirt.

'Jake's already been treated for his injuries and released. He's now back at the Platform being debriefed.'

'And what about Sandy? Where is that piece of shit?'

'He's the one at the Box. I hear they're withholding pain medication until they get the answers they want.' We both took a moment to enjoy the image of Sandy writhing in agony.

I lay back on to the pillow. It really was all over.

'How long do the doctors say I need to be in here?'

'A few weeks. You've lost a great deal of blood and they need to keep an eye on how the wound heals.'

I stared up at the ceiling.

'I can't believe it came to this. Sandy set me up brilliantly.'

'When everything kicked off he told everyone at the Platform that having a baby had made you go crazy, sell out your unit and betray us all.'

'Did you buy it?'

'Not for a minute. No woman who makes it to becoming a Rat would throw it all away for one big payday.'

I slowly nodded my head. 'You're right. Before all this, my job was everything to me. But now . . .' I kept staring at the ceiling, thinking about how close I had come to dying, to leaving Gigi behind. 'Maybe this isn't for me anymore.'

Jane's brow furrowed. 'Really? After all you've been through to get here you would give it up? Being a trailblazer is never an easy path. But by proving to Eight we belong, we're making it easier for the women who'll come after us. Look at Tennant. When he started out he was one of the first openly gay agents – no one knew what to make of him. Now no one bats an eyelid at a Rat's sexuality. Breaking down barriers – that's how the world changes.' She leaned forward in her chair and stared at me. 'By people like you and me, taking the first steps.'

Thanks, Jane. No pressure, then.

'Things were easier before I had my daughter.' I didn't know how to explain to Jane that now I had Gigi in my life, death was a more terrifying prospect. 'You've never been tempted? To settle down? Have a family?'

Jane wrinkled her nose. 'Never even occurred to me. Being a Rat is all I need to feel complete. Doesn't make me any less of a woman not wanting to procreate. Just as it doesn't make you any less of a Rat for wanting to.'

I knew what she meant. If I hadn't had Gigi, if I had gone down a different path, I don't doubt that I would have been happy. I would have had a different, definitely less complicated, but just as full life. Having spent all this time fighting to be taken as seriously now I was a mother, I hadn't ever stopped to think how someone like Jane would have to sometimes deal with questioning looks for not being a mother. We were judged if we did, judged if we didn't.

'Besides, I don't do so well at homemaking. You see this?' She rolled up her sleeve to show the famous burn. 'I know what everyone says. But no one knows the truth.' She paused. 'I burnt it while trying to make a casserole.'

'Come on. Really?'

'I speak five languages, I can kill a man twice my size with my bare hands without breaking a sweat.' Her eyes glistened as she said this. 'I have an IQ of 164. I've lasted at Eight nearly fifteen years without ever failing in a mission. I can do pretty much anything I put my mind to . . . but I can't cook. Domesticity is not a part of life I enjoy.' She pulled her sleeve back down. 'Wife and mother wouldn't work for me. Doesn't mean it can't for you. And surely if anyone can have it all, it's someone who's made it to being the best of the best?'

'I know. I just . . .' I trailed off. I didn't know what I wanted anymore.

'Don't let this little hiccup put you off. Take an extended blower. After what you've been through the Platform aren't going to deny you taking a few months off. Assess your situation again when you're back. I don't want you to leave. I need to know there's at least one other Rat who isn't going to fall apart the next time it's flu season.'

My room door burst open and a dishevelled Will came rushing in.

'Oh, Jesus, there you are. Thank God.' He rushed past Jane and came straight to my bedside, picking up my hand. 'How are you?'

'I'm fine. Bruised and battered but fine.' I looked up at his worried face and chewed the inside of my cheek to stop the tears I felt prickling. He never needed to know how close he had come to losing me. I cleared my throat. 'Where's Gigi?'

'I left her with Mum and drove straight here as soon as I got the call from your colleague.'

I motioned towards Jane. 'This is Jane. The one who rang.'

Will whipped around, seeing her for the first time. 'Jane, sorry, I was so worried. Thank you for calling and staying with her. I got here as fast as I could. I just bloody hope they catch the maniac who did this.'

'Yes, he deserves to be punished.' Thankfully Will had turned back to me so missed Jane's smirk and her eyes brightening at this thought. 'I'll leave you two alone.' She got up. 'Goodbye, Lex. Get well soon and think about everything I said.' She closed the door gently behind her.

I reached up and stroked Will's cheek. I had defied the odds and made it back to him and Gigi. Our family was still intact.

'You know what, *mon cher*? It's time to start planning that holiday you keep going on about.'

Three months later

Epilogue

Cruising

cruise, *v.*

Gerund or present participle: **cruising**.

1. To proceed speedily, smoothly or sail about, especially for pleasure.
2. (of a young child) Walk while holding on to furniture or other objects for support, while learning how to walk.

Chapter Thirty-Seven

A LARGE BUNCH OF flowers was on my desk with a note.

Every time you fuck with Johnnie Mac's head he writes a
hit song – keep up the good work! Your friends at Demon.

Johnnie had just released another song that looked destined to be an even bigger hit than 'Lady'. It was called 'Killer'. Thanks Johnnie, real subtle, that one. It seemed our last encounter had provided worthy inspiration for a song.

'The lady was a killer, armed with a poisoned dart, she stomped all over my dreams, she slayed my foolish heart. Why did I have to fall for a killer, killleerrr, killer.'

The riff was irritatingly catchy.

It was my first day back at the Platform since the events that nearly cost me my life. After several long bedside debriefs I was discharged from hospital and granted an extended blower. It meant I got to enjoy the run-up to Christmas without any of the usual overtime at the Platform. Walking around town with Gigi, I saw another side to the season of sparkly tinsel and brightly coloured lights. One where jolly bearded men in red weren't packing secret weapons in their oversized tummies, and their little elves weren't brandishing beautifully wrapped explosive devices. After a quiet Christmas Day spent with Gillian and my parents the three of us waved them goodbye and headed to Thailand. I had been nervous about going too far away; getting through a long flight and jetlag seemed too much to do with a young baby. But then people kept trying to kill me and it didn't seem such a big deal.

Our time away was every bit as exhausting, magical and unforgettable as I knew it would be. We took on the role of proud parents with vigour. There were photos of the first time Gigi's podgy little feet felt sand, photos of her drinking a fruit punch wearing Mummy's sunglasses (I could nearly hear Tamara's horrified reaction of 'Don't you know juice rots their teeth?'), photos of her first salty dip in the sea. Will and I rushed around after her all day achieving a healthy Insta:Shit ratio of 2:1. And when she was finally asleep we enjoyed the balmy nights, sitting outside our beachfront villa, drinking cocktails and talking about her. Our first blower as a family and I returned happy. Wife-and-Mother Lex was a role that seemed to fit.

And now here I was back down in the darkness of Platform Eight. It was Sunday and all the offices were empty, the hallways quiet except for the distant rumble of the trains. I was here to meet with the section chief. One final debrief with the big man himself before supposedly starting back at work tomorrow.

I wasn't expecting to learn anything new from this meeting. Geraint had filled me in on most of the news when he came to visit me in hospital. He was crushed by Nicola's betrayal and felt guilty he hadn't spotted it.

The Rok-Tech hearing had gone ahead as planned and Dimitri's father had been declared incompetent, an inevitable result of the stroke that Sandy and the Nyan had inflicted upon him to put their plans in motion. Dimitri was now living in Moscow running the company as chairman. The black market sale of the VirtuWorld software to numerous international intelligence agencies fell apart when due diligence discovered a glitch was wiping the data off the electronic devices soon after the user took control. VirtuWorld would still be launched next month and looked likely to overtake Facebook, Snapchat and Instagram as the world's most downloaded app. It means whenever they fixed that glitch, the superspy software would be all the more terrifying. Rok-Tech was still being closely monitored, although we at least had a little security in knowing that the man in charge loved cold hard cash more than his country.

Dasha and her children were still in London. She started divorce proceedings against Dimitri the minute he left the country, and although it was going to be a long, messy battle, with our help things would undoubtedly work out in her favour. In exchange for Eight not punishing Dasha for her leading role in the doomed mission to kill Dimitri, she had handed over to us her files on everyone in Dimitri's business circles. They were right to fear the Dragon. Her records were meticulous and most illuminating.

To anyone watching her, including us, she was just a lady who lunched and enjoyed frivolous gossip in between beauty treatments. But every whispered rumour, each confided secret, she would work out how to use to her advantage. A mention of someone's husband being seen more than once in a hotel with a woman of questionable repute would end with Dasha in possession of photos of them in the act. Dasha would hold the hand of a woman crying over her husband's terminal cancer diagnosis and then threaten him into doing her bidding if he didn't want his company's board of directors to find out. She was ruthless.

With the information she held close, blackmail came as easily to her as bloodshed did to her husband.

Dasha's deal with Eight also included her agreement that we could call on her whenever her assistance was needed. The battle with Russia was ongoing and we knew having Dasha as a secret weapon would be a huge asset. I had no idea if she'd managed to become head of the Parents' Association. I just hadn't cared enough to find out.

I knocked on the door of the meeting room.

'Come in.'

I walked in to see Anne and Chief at the table.

'Good morning, Lex. Please do take a seat.' I did not know our section chief's name. People who did know it were encouraged to forget. For security, it was better if he was never referred to by name, so he just went by Chief. 'I'm sure you've heard that Sandy told us everything.'

I wasn't surprised. Even without the added incentive of receiving much-needed pain relief for what were now two messed up legs, Sandy knew we had Dasha, that Nicola would be easy to turn and that the Nyan were in Moscow pretending they had nothing to do with anything that had transpired. The brown envelope Sandy had instructed me to steal from the restaurant was found in his office safe and contained nothing more than a recipe for Russian meatballs.

Sandy's grand plan had been to use the failure of the mission and my treachery as evidence that Eight had been compromised by Russia. And that, in retaliation, we needed more action, more violence and less regulation. With him at the helm as section chief he would lead a blood-thirstier, more merciless Eight. And one that, thanks to the dawn of VirtuWorld, would not be reliant on technology. With Russia winning the digital war the only solution would be to surrender our electronic devices and carry on without. He wanted to lead Eight into a future where technology was obsolete and violence was absolute.

For all Sandy's grandstanding about honourable intentions we knew he had a demanding ex-wife and two kids to support. His actions were clearly more motivated by the eye-wateringly large amounts of money the Nyan were offering. I had wondered, as someone who worked with a fleet of assassins, why he didn't get one of us to just take the ex out. That would have definitely helped with his cash-flow problems. Maybe, as a father, he couldn't do that to his children. Or maybe, as a father who didn't seem to like his children, he didn't want to end up stuck with custody.

Sandy recruited Nicola to his cause as he needed her IT expertise to help doctor all the intelligence Eight was receiving. He figured her loyalty could be bought with the vast amount of money on the table. He didn't realise Nicola had her own agenda. She was a member of an underground hacking organisation that believed all software should be free. Open and available to the worldwide web community so everyone could learn from it and improve it. She was a digital communist looking for a way into Rok-Tech to cause mayhem.

It turned out her relationship with Sandy was never sexual.

Handcuffs plus her contact lens solution. I'd put two and two together and got sixty-nine. Nicola had spent a lot of time at Sandy's flat as they worked together on their intricate plan. Long days at the Platform followed by long nights at his flat as they worked hard on covering their tracks and planning their next move. They had both looked somewhat horrified at the suggestion there had been anything more to their relationship than traitorous intentions.

'Where are Sandy and Nicola now?'

'Nicola is at the Sweat Shop. She'll be there for a good decade or so.'

The Sweat Shop was a prison that didn't officially exist and therefore was not held back by the need to respect any pesky human rights. Its prisoners were high-level assets or Security Services employees who due to their skills or knowledge were considered too important to be placed within the mainstream prison system. At the Sweat Shop prisoners were put to work, divided up according to ability, and given allocated assignments to complete. It was just like any large corporation. Except longer hours, no pay and serious micro-management. Everything they did was monitored. Not so much Golden Handcuffs, just hand-cuffs. Those who did their time and managed to not burn out were released back into the world, some even to the same job they'd had before. Most went on to be model citizens, suddenly appreciating a place of work that gave such civil liberties as days off and lunch breaks. Those who ended up back in the Sweat Shop for a second time didn't get out again.

I wondered if Nicola's hair was still shiny and if she had cus-tomised her prison jumpsuit in some way. Asymmetrical hems. A turned-up collar.

'Sandy is up in maximum security at the Box. We still have more questions for him. He'll either end up at the Sweat Shop for an indefinite stay, or just be sent straight to Medical Research.'

'Considering his health they surely won't get much use out of him?'

'They'll try their best. It's what the programme is for, after all. Using those we deem disposable as trial patients for new treatments. A way to use his life to save others.'

Rat to Snake to Guinea Pig. It was a fitting end for Sandy.

'Either way, you don't need to worry; you won't see him again. We know he put you through a trying time.' I nodded and thought that yes, that was exactly how I would've described nearly dying three times in a week.

'We owe you an apology.' This was Anne's contribution. 'That's what this meeting is for. We wanted to welcome you back personally and try to make things right.'

'And how do you plan on doing that?'

'We'd like to offer you the role of unit leader of Unicorn,' said Chief.

My face remained expressionless. I stared him in the eye as I spoke.

'Having these last few months off gave me time to think. To go over everything that happened and think about what I want. And to be honest, right now I'm not even sure I want to come back. You' – I nodded towards Anne – 'were all too quick to believe I was some crazed mother willing to betray my country to get my kid a private education.' I leaned forward. 'Do you have any idea how hard I worked to get here? A spotless record, years of hard graft and still I get penalised for being a woman. That attitude is clearly never going to change.' Months may have passed, but my anger hadn't.

Anne and Chief turned to each other. Chief cleared his throat.

'You don't know my name, do you?'

'No, sir. I don't.'

'How do you know I'm your section chief?'

I paused. It was a good point. Over the years I had seen him at a couple of joint-unit briefings. He had never introduced himself but he had stood at the front of the room and acted like a big boss and the whispers of other Rats had told me he was. His appearances down at the Platform were rare but for big missions he was always there rallying the troops.

'I don't have the energy for mind games. Are you Chief or not?'

'I use the name but no. I'm not the decision maker. I'm not for all intents and purposes the one who runs Eight.'

'But then who does?'

'I do,' said Anne.

I looked from one to the other.

'Why are you telling me this?'

'Because after what you've been through you deserve to know,' said Anne. 'Don't think this is just one big old-boys network looking after its own kind. Eight is a place where being a woman will not hold you back. Although I'll be the first to admit it was unfair to question your ability to be both a Rat and a mother, and for that I apologise.'

'Why use a Chief imposter?'

'It's how it's always been done. There's always been a Chief in name and a Chief in action. We need a figurehead to draw everyone's attention to. If he' – she motioned towards the nameless man – 'is compromised, blackmailed or eliminated, it will have no bearing on anything we do. And don't think it doesn't give me a certain satisfaction watching everyone write me off as just a secretary. Hide in plain sight. That's what we teach you all.'

'And knowing this is supposed to make me want to stay? Forget everything that's happened and just report for duty?'

'Eight has been home for you for a long time. Don't turn your back on us just because we were a little short-sighted in how we handled your situation. We've learnt from our mistakes. We don't want to lose you. You're a fine agent and we need you here.'

'I appreciate what you're saying and I'll think about it. But I need to do what's right for me.' I gave a nod to them both and left the room.

I walked down the corridor running my hand against the rough wall. Could I really walk out of this underground world of mine and never look back?

I headed to the canteen. A package should be waiting for me there. I checked my watch. If it wasn't, all hell was going to break loose.

Chapter Thirty-Eight

'HAPPY BIRTHDAY, GIGI!' CAME the frequent chorus from guests arriving. Gigi was turning one. The house was full of the noises of a kids' party – laughter, tears, screams and corks popping as the adults tried to self-medicate. I remembered what everyone said about the first year being the toughest and internally toasted myself for quite literally surviving it. Will came up behind me and wrapped his arms around me.

'Look at her. Isn't she perfect?' Gigi was sitting on the floor, playing with wrapping paper, grinning. Chocolate was smeared all over her face and the hideously pink frilly dress my mother had bought her. We gazed at her together, feeling pretty proud of ourselves.

We had succeeded in keeping Gigi alive to make it to her first birthday – none of those things that had so terrified me in the early days had happened; she didn't choke on a grape, she didn't get strangled by a blind cord, she didn't overheat from being put in too many layers and she didn't get kidnapped and held to ransom by a pack of pissed-off Russians. We were totally winning at parenting.

The radio was on and there was a pause from the fast-talking DJ before the unmistakable strains of 'Killer' entered the living room.

'I love this song.' Will reached over and turned it up. Gigi started nodding her head along to it and gurgled as she clapped her hands.

'Do you think this is really appropriate?' sniffed Gillian from the large sofa she hadn't moved from all afternoon. I couldn't help but laugh. If she thought it was inappropriate now she would choke on her finger sandwich if she knew just how inappropriate it really was. I was saved from answering her 'What on earth is so amusing, Alexis?' by the doorbell going.

'I'd better get that.'

I opened the door to Jake. He was holding a large present and a pink balloon.

Jake. I had him so wrong.

After the big shootout I had passed out just before I was able to do what I wanted.

Which was to ask him to be Gigi's godfather.

He had been somewhat floored by my proposition of being the significant other father figure in Gigi's life. He thought of as many reasons as he could to turn it down ('I have never met a baby I liked,' 'Wouldn't it be incest then if I made her my third wife?' 'What if she senses evil and cries every time she sees me?'), but I wasn't having any of it. It may have seemed a crazy idea to bring him into our lives officially, but it was the only solution I had for working through whatever messed-up feelings I had for him. I knew myself well enough to admit that whatever I felt for him went far beyond what it should. And the only way to simplify things was to confront it.

I was not going to go through my marriage wondering 'what if?' So I invited him into our lives and most importantly that of our daughter. Will was a little surprised when I pressed him to ignore his university best friend in favour of Jake, my somewhat mysterious and mostly grumpy colleague. But a Willifyed version of exactly how Jake had saved my life (bravery in the face of an oncoming car, as opposed to oncoming guns) helped him understand why making him godfather was so important to me.

Jake has been coming round for Sunday lunch for the last couple of months. He mocks my cooking, has a few beers with Will while discussing whatever game is on, and even does a little babbling at Gigi on her playmat. He may never admit it but I think he enjoys it. I keep telling him it's trial family time – dipping in and out to see if it's a lifestyle he thinks he can one day adopt. I know now above all that Jake values loyalty and getting to know Gigi and Will was the key to getting him to abandon any thoughts of wanting to tear me away from them. As godfather to our child keeping her parents together is part of his job.

I could already feel the way he looked at me changing.

My crazy ploy had worked. Obviously I was delighted, although my ego was a little miffed that he was so easy to convert.

'Darling, your glass is empty. Here, let me top you up.' Frankie bounded up to me with another bottle of Prosecco.

I had kept in touch with Frankie, Tamara and Shona. I needed some fellow mums to hang out with, and without Dasha lording it over us in the strained setting of committee meetings they were becoming more like friends. They weren't really so different to me. It all came down to the fact we were all mothers wanting the best for our children. They were normal, really.

'So are these made with cocoa or cacao?' asked Tamara, brandishing some chocolate biscuits at me.

Well, nearly.

I looked around our living room, bursting at the seams with friends, family and children in party hats. I tried to imagine the years ahead. What would I be like when Gigi started school? Forever using my Platform-learnt skills to help me navigate the world of competitive parenting? Relying on my hostile negotiation experience to stage a coup at the PTA? Breaking into school to get advance copies of exams? Taking out a teacher that was giving Gigi a hard time?

And that was just at school. How would I be at home? Sewing state-of-the-art GPS trackers into her coat? Running full background checks and surveillance on anyone she showed an interest in? Making the boy who broke her heart disappear for good?

It was going to be very difficult to not be a heavily armed helicopter mum, always hovering over Gigi, unable to let her make her own mistakes. It was a natural parental urge to want to protect your child, especially when you knew the things I knew. But not everyone had access to the resources I had, not everyone had the skills I had.

It had been months since Sandy was imprisoned, the Nyan were still in Russia, there was no existing threat against me, and certainly not Will or Gigi, but the blackout cover was still in the pram base. I liked the security of knowing it was there. Just in case. I knew that was how it was going to be for the rest of her life. Wanting to keep her secure in a bulletproof cocoon so no harm could come to her.

'Thank God you're back at work tomorrow. I've been stuck with a dumb Pigeon who can't shoot straight.' Jake came up to me eating a pink frosted cupcake.

'It might not be tomorrow.' I looked over at Gigi. 'I haven't decided yet.'

'But you are coming back?'

I ignored the question.

'Better get over there, she's opening your present.'

Jake turned and saw my daughter ripping at his brightly coloured wrapping paper and went to help her. Together they pulled it apart until a huge cuddly sheep came into view. Jake wiggled its head at me. 'Thought I would help encourage her on to the right path.'

I shook my head, smiling.

'Get ready, everyone, the cake is coming out!' shouted Will from the kitchen. I sat down next to Gigi as we all began a rather off-key rendition of 'Happy Birthday'.

Out came Will brandishing an enormous cake in the shape of the number one. It was covered in hand-made ornate marzipan butterflies and dainty winged fairies in differing shades of yellow, pink and purple. One solitary lit candle was at the top, looking a little underdressed in such magnificent company.

The crowd oohed and ahhed as it passed them.

'Jesus, where the hell did you get that from?' said Shona through a mouthful of biscuits.

'I picked it up from my office this morning. A friend owed me a little favour.' The cake box bearing the logo of a Michelin-starred restaurant lay crushed in the bottom of our recycling bin. That celebrity chef would be ruing the day he made a deal with the devil now that I had decided he was my go-to man for all things catering-related.

Gigi's eyes were transfixed on her father coming towards her with the masterpiece cake. He presented it to her as the song finished. 'Blow it out, Gigi.'

She gave it her best try, and with a little help from us, the flame went out.

Everyone clapped and cheered. I looked around at all the smiling faces, and my daughter already munching the head off a purple fairy.

It had been a long, crazy year since she burst through the starting line, beginning her life and forever changing mine. I had learnt a lot, cried a lot and nearly died a few times. And only now did I feel I was getting to grips with what it was all about.

A baby's natural instinct on seeing a tower is to smash it down. When seeing a box of toys to empty it. Destroy. Bash, smash, crash. Revel in the chaos. The mess. And every noise, every bit of destruction makes them squeal with happiness. This is what comes naturally to them. Then they grow, and they learn and they find fun in building up the blocks. The satisfaction in creating. They see the praise they get for tidying toys away. Nurtured, loved and taught. They take slow, faltering steps into a more grown-up world, but always knowing, always relying on there being someone there to catch them when they fall.

Before Will, before Gigi, I was just a Rat. Running around in my underground world, causing chaos and destruction without retribution. Because it was expected. That was what Rats do.

But I grew up. My eyes were opened to what life could be like if I didn't just break, bash, smash and run away. If I stopped to see the joy in making something. And I did. I made a life with another person, and I made a baby. And now we're a family.

I had at first struggled to understand why I was finding the juggling of the two worlds so much harder than my male counterparts. Everyone seemed to openly discuss how mothers were more bonded to their children. I had been outraged when Anne had first accused me of such but I had to confess to myself she was right. I looked at the other Rats and somehow knew they were not lying in bed at night worrying if their child was eating enough vegetables, if they should switch to cow's milk or the next stage up of formula, or even notice that it had been eleven days since they were the one who'd tucked them in at night. It had fallen to Frankie to explain it all to me.

'Mother's guilt,' she announced after I'd ranted about why it was so unfair that I seemed unable to be as relaxed as the men I knew. 'It's different for them. For men. They don't have the inbuilt natural guilt we do. We care more, mostly about stupid shit that makes no real difference, but it's just part of being a mother.'

'Here you go, *ma chérie*.' Will handed me a piece of cake. 'Cheers to us.' I gave him a kiss and then took a big bite of the rainbow sponge with buttercream filling. It really was spectacular.

It may have taken me some time but I finally worked out what 'having it all' really was. It was simply being happy. And ignoring what everyone else thought.

I had to stop comparing myself to my colleagues. I wasn't a man. And I didn't need to be a man. My whole career at Eight had been a success not in spite of being a woman, but because I was a woman. I used what I had to be the best I could be. And now I just needed to keep doing that as a mother. I would find my own way. My own path. Work out what made me happy and find a balance. I needed to feel I was doing enough as a mother and enough to feel more than a mother. Gigi was important but I was important too. And I was a role model now. With a bit of editing I could be an inspiration; I had triumphed in a field no one thought I could, I had seen down colleagues out to get me. I had proven a woman could do anything she put her mind to. And that a mother should never be written off. But put on a fucking pedestal.

I thought about Jake's question. Was I going to go back? I didn't like the message I would be sending if I didn't. Now more than ever I was fighting for equality. It wasn't just for me, but also for my daughter. And I could do that by continuing to fly the flag for women at the Platform.

Yet I couldn't ignore the fact that a fear of dying was a major obstacle in my line of work. If my objective started being how best to keep me alive rather than how best to make someone else dead my success rate was going to dramatically drop. Before Gigi the idea of not being a Rat would have horrified me. But now she was my priority. Was a job that could increase my chances of being permanently separated from her really worth it?

Perhaps the answer was somewhere in the middle. Give up on the dream job and move to one that fitted in more with my familial responsibilities. I could go into the private sector and as a gun for hire pick and choose jobs that were low risk. More flexible hours. Much better pay.

I could always switch to Five or Six. Try being one of the Pigeons we so looked down on.

Maybe I could even have another baby.

This was me, back to where I should be, back to believing the world was mine for the bloody taking. I watched Gigi cruising around the sitting room, cake in hand, smug smile in place as she wobbled between conveniently placed furniture. Here we were together, learning how to walk in our strange new worlds, and both doing it with our heads held high.

My mobile rang. I looked down at the 0845 number and stepped into the hallway to answer it.

'Have you ever been mis-sold PPI insurance?' was the automated message that greeted me.

I waited for the beep and spoke. 'Alexis Tyler.' There was a pause as the voice-recognition software listened.

Another message played.

'You are needed on an urgent operation. Please confirm attendance.'

From the doorway I watched Gigi giggling as she took another faltering step forward.

The beep sounded and I took a deep breath.

Acknowledgements

A very big thank you to Katherine Armstrong and Eleanor Dryden and everyone at Bonnier Zaffre for believing in this book and being so passionate about it. You have been a joy to work with and made this whole experience all the more special.

To my brilliant agent, Alice Lutyens at Curtis Brown, I am thrilled and so lucky to have you in my corner.

I am forever grateful to the Faber Academy for helping me transform my late-night ramblings into a workable first draft. A massive thank you to my tutor, Tom Bromley, whose teaching and mentoring were invaluable.

To the very talented author Rebecca Thornton. When I told you I had an idea for a book you could've laughed, gently pointed out I hadn't written more than a shopping list since school and I would've forgotten about it. But you told me you loved the premise, hassled me to pursue it and cackled your head off when I finally had the courage to show you my first few pages. So for all that and for being my best friend for as many years as we've been alive, thank you.

There are many other amazing women in my life but I owe particular thanks to Caroline Barrow, Lara Smith-Bosanquet and Georgia Tennant. This book has been in your lives as long as it has been in mine and your constant reading and re-reading, encouragement and support has meant the world to me.

Tavie, Arlo, Gus and Silva – my totally wonderful, utterly perfect and completely exhausting children. It turns out boredom at soft play can make for excellent inspiration – so when I say without you this book would never have happened, I truly mean it.

To Andrew Trotter. I don't know where to begin or where to end. Thank you for it all. Nothing in my life would be as much fun without you.

Finally, to my dear Dad – as a man in his eighties you were hardly my target audience but as the very first person to read my very first draft it meant everything when you said you loved it (even if you were a little biased). Thank you to you and Mum for always being there and always telling me I could do anything I put my mind to. Pep talks work – look I wrote a book!

In Conversation with Asia Mackay

***Killing It* is your debut novel, how did you come to write it?**

One night I was crawling across my kids' bedroom floor trying not to wake the baby and I thought; *if only I had some kind of special ops training, maybe I'd manage to get out of here without him waking.* It sparked the idea of a hard-core secret agent busy on important missions for the good of the country, but still having to rush home for bath time. I found myself jotting down notes on my phone when feeding – 'Gun in nappy bag, pretend formula is cocaine, does breast milk have DNA in it?' – the mad ramblings of a sleep-deprived mother. After a few months of this I realised I needed to either make a go of it or just forget about it. I sat down one evening and started writing. The very first paragraph I ever wrote is still the opening to *Killing It.*

As this is your first book, how did it feel when people first read it?

Exciting. And terrifying. I would alternate between wanting to sit next to them as they read it (what do you think about that bit? Is that funny? Why aren't you laughing? Do you think that's clever? Do you get it? I don't think you get it. Are you enjoying it? ARE YOU?) to hiding under a duvet cringing at the thought they were all hating it.

Having never written before how did you approach the writing process?

Although I'd loved writing at school I had never tried to pursue it. Even when I came up with the idea of a secret agent Mum, the thought of actually sitting down and writing a book seemed too intimidating to even try. Then I read an article about National Novel Writing Month – the idea quite simply is to write a whole novel in a month. Although it was something I knew I wouldn't be able to do amid work and the kids I really took their philosophies of 'no plot, no problem' and 'just write' to heart. I started writing as Lex and just went from there. The more I wrote the more I realised how much I wanted it to be a book. I did a seven month online Writing a Novel course at the amazing Faber Academy and by the end of it I had a very rough first draft. My writing process throughout has been write first, structure later. I jot down ideas for potentially amusing spy/mum crossovers before having a go at writing them into a scene. If the scene works I then fit it into the plot.

You have four children and a busy life, how do you juggle this with writing?

Support. No mother is an island. If she was it'd be more like a sinking ship.

Our children are aged one, three, five and six. To make writing deadlines, fulfil my other work responsibilities and still feel present in my children's lives is something I couldn't do without my husband and our nanny. It's chaos. Even before you add two leg-humping, yapping dogs to the mix. What helps me manage is starting the day early (a choice the kids make for me, really) and forgoing the post-children-in-bed celebratory Netflix sofa slump for writing on my laptop at the kitchen table. Every now and then I might sit back and smugly toast myself with a green juice for my awesomeness at fitting it all in, and that's normally when it all falls apart. I forget to pick up one of the kids from somewhere. A dog vomits on our bedroom floor. Microsoft Word crashes losing the edits that were finally perfect. A daughter says 'b . . . b . . but Mama I've hardly seen you'. And all that can be done is bed with a box of Maltesers and a hope tomorrow will be better.

2018 is The Year of the Woman, was creating a feminist hero part of your inspiration?

I wrote the only book I knew how to – one with a woman at the centre of it. I was influenced by my own experiences as a first-time mother and a belief women deserved their own secret agent heroine. Lex is just as well-trained and ruthless as James Bond but while his private life is merely about juggling romantic liaisons, Lex is trying to persuade her daughter to eat her vegetables and wondering if she'll ever get a full night's sleep again. Whereas Bond might need the flashy car with the machine gun headlights, Lex can get the job done just as well in a Volvo with a rear-facing car seat. She's a capable, relatable hero who has to battle sexism at work and Mum guilt in among life or death operations. In my opinion that makes her more hard-core than Bond!

I can't wait until the time comes when we don't have to identify as feminist but that those who really do believe women shouldn't have equal rights to men are simply written off as sexist. 'Feminist' can still bring up negative connotations of angry women who want to burn their bras, which is ridiculous – I've had four kids – my bra belongs on a pedestal. Back in Neanderthal times men may have been considered superior because their height and strength made them better hunters. With food came power. Nowadays women can Ocado just as well as men. It's about time the world shook off prehistoric notions that women are in any way inferior – we need to be regarded as equals – whether that be at parenting, working or fighting bad guys.

Can you give us any hints about what to expect next for Lex?

Lex's story is far from over. As Gigi gets older she will have new parenting problems to battle and new enemies to takedown. Coping with the terrible twos when facing her latest mission of global significance might be more than even she can handle . . .

Who are your five favourite female fictional characters, and why?

Scarlett O'Hara (*Gone With The Wind*) – a calculating bitch who messed up numerous times but would pick herself back up again and come up with a new plan. She was as determined as hell and I couldn't wait to read on to see what she'd do next.

Buffy Summers (*Buffy the Vampire Slayer*) and Sydney Bristow (*Alias*) – these were my favourite TV shows when I was at school.

They were bright, fearless and in charge – everything awkward, teenage me wanted to be.

Elizabeth Bennett (*Pride and Prejudice*) – a woman with principles. I loved her slow-burn relationship with Mr Darcy and her refusal to accept him (and his vast wealth and palatial mansion) until he had proved himself and his good character.

Bridget Jones (*Bridget Jones' Diary*) – one of the most relatable and funny characters I've ever read. In a world that too often only celebrates the perfect and aspirational it's good to remember Bridget who smoked too much, drank too much, wore big pants and made us all laugh.

Who are the women that have inspired you the most?

I have to say my mother or she'd kill me. You don't upset a Chinese matriarch. The women I find inspiring are the ones in my life I see going through utter hell and somehow come out the other side. They're people you know everything about and seeing how they cope with their traumas makes me realise there's strength in all of us. They inspire me to think I too might just be able to cope with anything life throws at me. So yes, all the amazing women in my life. And Beyoncé.

What are you currently reading?

I just finished *The Power* by Naomi Alderman which I loved as much as everyone said I would. Next is *Little Fires Everywhere* by Celeste Ng.

If you were stuck on a desert island, which three books would you take with you and why?

War and Peace by Leo Tolstoy – a book I know I should read yet haven't managed to so far.

Rivals by Jilly Cooper – when I need some relief from *War and Peace* I can revisit my old friends Rupert and Taggie Campbell-Black.

Teach Yourself Mandarin – with all that peaceful, kid-free time I might finally succeed in a life-time goal to be fluent in Mandarin.

All the best intentions but I have a feeling I'd just work on my tan and read *Rivals* every day.